MW00791461

RESISTANCE

RESISTANCE

BOOK THREE OF NOMAD
THE NEW EARTH SERIES

MATTHEW MATHER

© 2017 Matthew Mather ULC

RESISTANCE

MATTHEW MATHER ULC.

Copyright © 2016, 2017
Matthew Mather ULC
978-1-987942-12-5
Cover image by Momir

This is a work of fiction, apart from the parts
that aren't.

All rights reserved.
No part of this work may be reproduced or
transmitted in any form or by any means
without written permission of the author.
All the characters in this book are fictitious
and any resemblance to actual persons living
or dead is purely coincidental.

For free Advance Reading Copies of my next
book and more, join my community at
MatthewMather.com

Find me on Facebook and YouTube
search for
Author Matthew Mather

**OTHER BOOKS BY
MATTHEW MATHER**

Standalone Titles
Darknet
CyberStorm
Polar Vortex

The Atopia Series
Atopia Chronicles
Dystopia Chronicles
Utopia Chronicles

The New Earth Series
Nomad
Sanctuary
Resistance
Destiny

The Delta Devlin Series
The Dreaming Tree
Meet Your Maker
Out of Time

RESISTANCE

Prologue

Mars First Mission
Deep Interplanetary Space
November 29th

A keening siren bled into the hibernation chamber.

At first it echoed only in the distant void of his subconscious, but when Commander Rankin's mind focused on it, when its urgency came to him, it brought a terrifying understanding. No gentle drift from slumber. No soft halo of growing light. No whisper from systems that seeped away cold before they fed in comforting heat.

Instead…

A heavy hiss as the last vestiges of the chamber's gases shot away. The front of the compartment lifted, and Rankin stumbled forward and fell. Dropped to the floor and retched something cold and opaque that congealed with the viscous fluids discharged with him.

Pain lanced through his knees and elbows on impact with the metal deck. Cold stinging bites as intravenous lines tore away from his arms and neck. Eyes shut tight against blinding light. The screech of the siren, louder now, drilled through his temples. His stomach muscles tightened and he dry-heaved, his neck tendons flaring.

"Mars First, this is Rankin," the Commander croaked between stomach spasms, his voice hoarse. "What's going on?'

The only reply was the shrieking alarm.

He spat out a mouthful of yellow phlegm, fought back a gag reflex, and gasped: "Mars First, report!"

No answer.

The pain in his knees faded, replaced with an ache that shot into his feet and fingertips. He opened his eyes a crack. The emergency floodlights seared through his optic nerves and dove deep into his brain. More blazing pain. His heart pounded high in his throat, his mouth pasted together around a swollen tongue that tasted metal. The urge to retch competed with the need to breathe.

Rankin's mind raced. Decompression? Why were the cabin lights on full?

Hair prickled on his arms. Teeth clenched. Hard to breathe. His skin was clammy and cold, even though he knew the temperature and humidity were probably regulated high and dry. He dragged himself to his feet and lurched for the nearest terminal. Rankin had awoken from chemically-induced hibernation enough times to know the effects of Rapid Emergency Animation Procedure. The grim REAP'er was an exercise every new recruit had to go through. Years of drill training took over and he pushed down the fear.

The blaze of light subsided. The echoing pain eased.

Commander Rankin blinked and wiped away the sticky residue on his face. Steadied himself and stood up straight. On the other side of the twenty-foot circular hibernation suite, Elin Cuijpers, the team's Dutch communication specialist, had been regurgitated onto the metal floor from her hibernation pod. Her face was slick with sweat, her short-cropped blond hair matted, her blue eyes unfocused as she gasped for air. The three other hibernation pods were still closed; their occupants still blissfully unconscious.

"Mars First, report," Rankin repeated, his voice calmer.

Still nothing.

The computer terminal before him remained stubbornly dormant, its screen blank, but the LED mission clock above it glowed bright: seventy-eight days, sixteen hours and twelve minutes since launch. He was supposed to be revived on Day One Hundred for his physical and some exercise, but not REAP'ed like this. Something had set off an alarm, something urgent enough to risk the bright lights and alarms and violent awakening he'd just endured.

Seventy-eight days.

Rankin attempted a quick mental calculation. His neurons were like molasses inside his skull.

Mars First was on a ballistic capture orbit, forgoing the usual Hohman trajectory of Mars missions. Their total transit time was three hundred and two days. At seventy-eight sols, they should be about thirteen million kilometers radially outward from Earth's orbit, but their solar-orbital velocity had been matched for Mars's for the ballistic capture, a slow burn deceleration resulting in a differential of about twenty thousand kilometers an hour. So in the past seventy-plus days, Earth had sped ahead of them by maybe thirty-five million kilometers. He'd been the last crewmember to go into hibernation sleep on Mission Day Four, just after they'd passed the moon's orbit and celebrated being the first humans to venture beyond it.

So Earth had to be more than forty million kilometers away.

The Dutchwoman had pulled herself to her feet, her body shaking, but her eyes were on Rankin now.

"Cuijpers, are you okay? Can you understand me?"

"What in the world is going on?"

"Don't know yet. Mars First is down. Can you get a system diagnostic up?"

The Dutchwoman stared into space for a moment, her mind still fighting its way out of the hibernation fog. She physically shook herself awake, walked over to Rankin and pulled open a wall panel. She clicked switches and a second later, lights flickered across the terminal.

Rankin backed up to give her space. "Anything?"

"One section of the hull lost pressure and was closed off automatically." Her fingers scrolled across the screen. "Some physical damage. Guidance is down, but communications are still up."

"What about power?" Rankin said.

3

"Rerouting now. Hydrogen cells are offline." Cuijpers studied the display. "Electronics fried all across the ship. Maybe a solar flare? Explains why Mars First is offline. The main power grid—" Her eyes widened. *"Ben je helemaal besodemieterd!"*

"English please?"

"The radiation readings are...I've never..." Cuijpers' voice trailed off.

"Just your best guess."

"Thirty-thousand nanoTeslas. That was the field induced by a radiation blast."

Rankin blinked as his sluggish mind tried to absorb and find context. "That can't be right. Must be a sensor malfunction."

Cuijpers' fingers swept across the control surface, checking and re-checking. "Sensors are fine." A frown erupted between her fine blond eyebrows. "We were sheltered from the worst of the radiation storm by the hab shielding. Telemetry and guidance are offline."

Rankin rubbed his throbbing head with one hand. A massive solar flare might explain the electronics, but not the loss of pressure. Or maybe it could? Mars First was heavily shielded—well beyond specifications even—but no amount of preparation could have anticipated that degree of exposure.

The Dutch communications specialist held Rankin's gaze.

"What?" he asked.

"Do you know what a radiation blast like that would do down there...?" Cuijpers pointed at her feet, but Rankin knew what she meant.

"You mean Earth?"

"The biggest geomagnetic superstorms induce maybe three hundred nanoTeslas, and those can knock out national power grids. This was two orders of magnitude higher..."

She hesitated again.

"And?"

"It would send everything back to the Stone Age."

"But flares are directional, right? Earth must be forty million kilometers away. If it hit us, then I doubt it hit them." It was hopeful rather than analytical, but probably true. Rankin strode around the room to look at the other hibernation pods. "You said comms were up. Orally relay me all the messages from Command."

"Nothing in a month."

"Pardon?"

"We haven't had any comms from Earth in four weeks. Just regular chatter before that."

"No warning message? No data on what hit us?"

"Nothing at all. Not even system pings." The expression on Cuijpers' face changed from puzzlement to slack-faced blankness.

"Check the communication arrays again," Rankin ordered. No messages from Earth at all in four weeks was impossible.

"I already checked," Cuijpers said. "It's not us. It's dead."

"The comm systems aren't working?"

"I mean the comm arrays are working."

By her expression, his face must have looked as baffled as his muddled brain felt. Maybe oxygen wasn't getting into his bloodstream. He put out one hand to steady himself.

"What I mean," Cuijpers added slowly, "is that all our communication gear is working perfectly. *Has* been working perfectly the whole mission clock."

"That doesn't make sense. We were just hit by this massive radiation blast. That's what you said."

"I said we *were* hit, but I didn't say when." She glanced at her display. "My best guess is it happened on October 24th, over a month ago."

"The radiation blast?" That was almost half the mission clock. "That long ago?"

The Dutchwoman nodded.

"So what's dead, then, if not our comms gear?"

Cuijpers' knuckles went white as she gripped the edges of the terminal screen.

"The Earth. It's the Earth that's dead."

PART ONE

1

Sanctuary Europe

There was no cold. No howling wind or cloying reek of sulfur. Instead, Jessica Rollins felt a comfortable, perfumed warmth surrounding her. The next thing she noticed: no pain. In her balled fists now, just soft cotton bedding, and a thick pillow beneath her head. The acrid air of the past nightmarish weeks was replaced instead by something clean and pure.

For a moment the sensations surprised her and, in that instant, as she opened her eyes to the gentle light, she couldn't remember where she was. She didn't recognize the room. Its smooth surfaces and pastel shades. Unfamiliar artwork hung on the walls. None of it belonged to her, none of it was chosen by her. The lines of the room were manufactured and regular. Reminded her of a submarine she'd once toured.

This room was not hers.

With the confusion came fear—a subtle, subconscious vigilance born in the United States Marine Corps and molded so it never paralyzed her, but instead energized and protected her. Then came the realization: Sanctuary.

She was in Sanctuary.

In lock step, she remembered Dr. Müller.

The man who killed her family—and worse, implicated them in the unimaginable destruction of the planet by Nomad, the rampaging black hole pair that had barreled through the center of the solar system and ripped it apart.

Her fear mutated and sharpened.

Hundreds of millions, maybe even billions, of people had died, starting with an intense barrage of radiation as the sun almost shredded apart. The Earth's crust ripped apart in the enormous gravitational waves as Nomad passed, igniting hundreds of simultaneous volcanic eruptions and churning up apocalyptic tsunamis. Jess had been underground, reunited with her mother and father just before they'd died trying to save her father's data. It was evidence of Nomad from more than thirty years before, even though her father hadn't known what it was back then.

But somebody had known.

Müller.

Dr. Müller had been her father's PhD professor, had understood what the images of Nomad were thirty years ago. He'd used the information to start a secretive network of massive underground bunkers—the Sanctuaries. One here in Europe and another in China. Was there one in America? Jess didn't know. America had been destroyed by the explosion of the Yellowstone supervolcano. All that was heard from the once-great nation were scraps of communications from ragged bands of survivors.

She did know that Müller had used her father as a scapegoat, and even worse, tried to kill her entire family. *Had* killed them. Jessica had uncovered the truth, and made Müller pay for his crimes, including the deaths of her mother and father. At least, she hoped he would pay for his crimes. Müller was here, in Sanctuary Europe, underground with her—but while she was in a warm, safe bed, he was in jail, awaiting punishment.

She threw off the covers and levered herself up. Bolts of pain shot through her ribs, legs, and arms, disturbing her numb bliss. Not healed yet from her injuries, despite Ufuk Erdogmus's doctors' ceaseless attention. The exhaustion didn't seem to fade, either—or perhaps it was something else. The haze over her senses evaporated. She winced and tried not to think about Müller.

But that wasn't possible.

The door to her room opened a crack, then slowly swung open. Giovanni appeared, the scar above his left eye twitching in amusement, his thick black hair groomed. He looked rested, but still gaunt.

"Good morning," he said as he gave her a warm smile.

"You should have woken me earlier."

The clock said it was just past ten a.m., but buried thousands of feet below a granite mountain, it could just have easily been ten p.m. She was dressed in pink flannel pajamas, which felt vaguely embarrassing despite—or perhaps as a result of—the intensely close and personal experiences she'd shared with this man waiting at her door. He knew enough to divert his eyes as she reached for the plastic prosthetic next to the bed and slipped it over her stump, just below the knee where her left leg ended.

"I called Ufuk and told him you were sleeping," Giovanni said. "He can wait. I've made breakfast."

Outside her bedroom, Hector sat at the small dining table and waved to her as she limped—still not used to this new leg— into the small living area. The kid had weathered the beating they'd taken better than the adults. He had the same shock of black hair and lopsided grin as his uncle Giovanni.

The smell of real eggs and fresh bread coaxed her to the table. It seemed almost impossible in contrast to the desperate scrabble for life in the dark and ice outside just days ago.

"You think he can really do it?"

She sat down and reached for the pot of coffee, at the same time gently pushing aside the stack of yellowing paper that was Giovanni's record of conversations with survivor groups. Ballie Booker and his crew on the British Coastguard ship had recovered it at the same time as they had rescued Giovanni and Hector, and the brothers Lucca and Raffa, from the ice floe in the middle of the Mediterranean. A miracle in the middle of this madness.

"You're the one who said Ufuk Erdogmus was a genius," Giovanni said. "Cybernetics was the focus of one of his tech companies, whatever that means."

Hector leaned over to hug Jess. She felt the boy's warmth and squeezed back.

"A new robotic leg," she said. "It seems unreal."

11

"No crazy stunts until you learn how to use it properly." Giovanni spooned some eggs onto a plate and set it down in front of her.

She smiled despite herself.

Crazy stunts.

The idea came from a different world, a distant memory of a place that no longer existed. Sanctuary Europe—shortened to San EU by the thousands who lived here—was an extension of the deep tunnel systems bored into the alpine mountains of Switzerland. Those systems had provided road and rail routes through the Alps for decades, perhaps longer, and still stretched for hundreds of kilometers underground. San EU had been built to take advantage of them, using technology that had created the sixty-kilometer-long Gotthard Base Tunnel only a handful of years earlier.

Above her, right now, were the mountains she had grown to love. Slopes she had skied, rock and ice she had climbed. She wondered what remained. Since she'd been rescued, she and Giovanni hadn't been back outside. The Sanctuary Administrative Council forbade contact with the world outside for the year they would remain underground, but of course, the SAC filtered what they knew—or what they wanted people to know—to those inside. A gilded cage.

Before Nomad, she had fed herself adrenaline until it became almost an addiction. Since then, the will to survive had bred something else inside her, something that made the thrill seeking she had once engaged in feel at once both frivolous and bland. She had been given something to focus on, something that carried an importance she had been missing since her Marine Corps service.

Being here now, underground and surrounded by a facsimile of Earth's past beauty, she found herself desperate to be outside. There were others scratching in the snow and ash for food, and here she was eating eggs, and sleeping on soft cotton. Too often she stared at the ceiling, carried away by dreams of being somewhere else. Too often she woke to the vision of her mother and father in their frozen graves.

Giovanni's voice pushed her thoughts aside. "There's something else."

She frowned at his hesitation.

"The Office of Judicial Affairs has formally invited your attendance to give a statement to the Examining Justice. The prosecutor leading the investigation into Müller's actions is named Michel Durand. He would like to see you."

"What do they need a statement for? There were surveillance cameras in Vivas. You told me everyone inside here saw the video." She stabbed her fork into the eggs. "I should have just killed him when I had the chance."

"Remind me never to get on the wrong side of you."

Her faced reddened as she stole a quick look at Hector. She poured more coffee. "You know what I mean."

"I do, and that's what frightens me." Giovanni rested a hand on her shoulder. "You need to take it easy. You almost died."

"So did you. Millions *are* dead, and more are dying as we speak. Maybe some because of me." She pushed her food away, trying to also push away the image of her mother and father crushed and frozen under the walls of *Castello Ruspoli*. She could have saved them.

"Don't talk like that. Please, eat. You know how hard it was to get real eggs?"

"When do they want to see me?"

"As soon as you're able. I suggest you see Ufuk this morning and then speak to them tomorrow. Should I tell them that's what you will do?"

Jess shook her head. "Why the hell do they even need to—"

"It's important. There are still rules here."

"Rules that kill everyone else outside."

"What do you want me to—"

"Sure." She pulled the plate of eggs back and took a bite. "You'll speak to Ufuk?"

She exhaled and slumped her shoulders before nodding.

"And the Judicial Affairs people?"

"I said yes."

"Eat."

She took another forkful of eggs.

"You know you have email?"

"Email?"

He smiled at her confusion. "It's internal to San EU, of course. Someone uploaded videos from your old *YouTube* channel. You're quite the celebrity." He reached for the tablet device at the corner of the table and handed it to her. "It's yours. Has your new email account on it, and apps that work in San EU."

She took it grudgingly. Everything seemed so surreal, so maddeningly normal. Sure, just look at the video on this tablet. A thing she'd done a million times before without thinking about it, but now it felt at odds with the reality of the world—like picking up a goblet from ancient Rome and wondering if it was sacrilege to drink from it.

A knock outside, and Lucca and Raffa's smiling faces appeared one over the other through the opening of the slightly ajar door.

"Do you mind if I—" She gestured to the bedroom.

"I'll go join the boys. But don't take too long. Your breakfast will get cold. Remember how—"

"I know. Real eggs. I just need a minute to myself."

Giovanni's tiny nod and smile gave her the space she needed. He collected Hector into his arms while she retreated to her bedroom. She paused, waiting to hear the exterior door shut as Giovanni left, before she turned on the tablet. She took a breath and held it, then clicked the email app. Giovanni had sent her messages containing a list of links, one of them a link to video security camera footage from the Vivas facility.

She played it.

A grainy black-and-white image of herself cowering in the cell. Müller came on screen holding a pistol, followed by Maxim, his Chief of Security. Müller shot Iain Radcliff, the Vivas man. She remembered every cold word even in the absence of the audio track from the cameras. Words that had been caught and then broadcast by Roger's beacon. She'd refrained from listening to the recording in the days that followed. She couldn't bring herself to listen to Müller's calm voice as he pulled the trigger and shot Radcliff, and then turned the gun on her. She wasn't scared by it, but afraid of the anger she'd feel.

Too tired for it.

It was a chance for humanity to rebuild itself, better and stronger—that was what Müller had said. The justification for his evil. The sick bastard saw the destruction of humanity as an opportunity, or a chance to fix everything that was wrong with the world.

She closed the video.

There were more emails. Dozens of them. She told herself she didn't have time to read through them all, that she needed to eat, then see Ufuk as soon as possible.

She clicked one.

"You're amazing," read the email, from someone called Abbie Barnes. "You have so much courage. Get well soon."

"You are a tribute to human endurance," the next email gushed.

Despite the guilt, Jess couldn't help feeling a twinge of hope. The next email's title was blank and she clicked it. Her warm tingling drained into a sinking numbness.

"You should be buried with your traitor father," said the anonymous sender.

She clicked the tablet's off button and stared at the blank screen. Müller was still a threat, and humanity still stood on the brink of extinction—despite the warm cotton under her ass and impossibly fresh eggs beckoning from the polished table.

She didn't want to become part of a debate that centered on who should live and who should die. How could that choice possibly be made? Resources should be focused on saving as many as possible, whoever was left, rather than deciding who was worthy of being saved—but then this was making a decision in itself. She left the tablet on the bed, changed from her pajamas into jeans and a sweater, and made sure to eat every scrap of her egg and toast before leaving.

In a quiet corner of the sprawling Sanctuary Europe complex, sequestered away from prying eyes and built to conceal its true dimensions, Ufuk Erdogmus's complex of laboratories also contained his personal quarters. Access was through a series of sealed doorways, with coded panels and retinal scans, leading to a passageway that opened into the main atrium.

Birds sang amidst thick palms and massive ferns of vivid green, and beyond the leaves the artificial blue sky projected on Sanctuary's dome burned with strange iridescence. Insects buzzed through gnarled branches draped with orchids that filled the air with a sweet musk. Not insects, Jess realized on closer inspection, but tiny ornithopter drones. They swarmed toward her, then circled and spread ahead of her. This way, they beckoned. She followed.

Jess had awoken in this over-sized private garden when she'd first arrived in San EU, following her capture by Müller and subsequent rescue by Ufuk. The first thing Ufuk had offered was to create a new robotic prosthetic for her—better than the 3D-printed one he'd hastily had made when she arrived. Robotics was something Ufuk specialized in. She'd returned once to this complex during the past week for detailed scans of her leg's nerve endings and muscle and bone, and he'd offered some limited insights into his largely automated facilities.

"Today's the day." Ufuk stepped through the palms, the smooth brown skin on his face crinkled in a grin. "Ready?"

"As I'll ever be." She limped forward. The insect-drones scattered back into the foliage.

"It'll be as easy as riding a bike."

16

"I've never ridden a robotic bike."

The billionaire's perfect teeth flashed as his smiled widened. "Time to learn."

He led her through the gardens, past a sealed airlock door, and into a laboratory area where a female white-coated technician stood inspecting wall-sized holographic displays of Jess's mangled leg stump. The technician was busy talking to a life-size image of a man at the side of the screen, but they stopped speaking as soon as Jess arrived.

"One of my companies pioneered robotic prosthetics," Ufuk started to explain.

"So I heard."

"I tried to bring a microcosm of my facilities here, like a Noah's Ark of technology for the future. Maybe the only place left on the planet we can still do this."

"Lucky me." Her words were edged with unintentional sarcasm.

Ufuk's easy smile slid away. "Do you not want this?"

"I just…"

Ufuk waited for her to finish her thought, but broke the silence before it could get awkward. "Guilt is something we all are learning to live with."

"So I'll be able to control it by thought?"

"It will take time and practice. The pathways are already there, but you need to re-awaken them. We've added some limited sensory feedback, so you'll also experience some sensation through the prosthetic."

"So then it's something else I can hurt."

This time Ufuk didn't react to the sarcasm but just waved her forward.

In the time she'd spent with her mysterious rescuer, she'd found him to be a private man who chose his words with care, keeping much of the detail of his facilities out of conversation. Whenever she probed, he'd been politely but deftly evasive.

Ufuk showed her to a small room off the main lab and gestured to a reclined leather chair like one in a dentist's office.

The white-coated technician stepped in and offered Jess a smile. "Would you mind changing into this gown?" She indicated a partitioned changing room.

Jess stepped out of her jeans and into the blue gown. She returned to sit in the chair. From a box, the woman took out a wired stump socket. She removed Jess's plastic prosthetic and attached the wired socket, then turned to inspect a wall of holographic displays that glowed to life.

Ufuk presented Jess with the new robotic leg they were going to install. "We engineered a protective outer layer to function in much the same way as the skin does," he said. "It protects the interior robotics from external erosion and the invasion of moisture or tiny particles that might affect the mechanics. There is a cosmetic element to it too, of course." He handed it to her.

"I expected it to be heavier."

"Lightweight, strong and durable. Resistant to extreme cold. Instead of the usual polyurethane, we developed a material that flows the impact pressure across the whole of the limb."

The technician frowned. "We need to run through final calibrations." She removed the socket and gently pushed the old prosthetic back on, then asked to take the robotic leg from Jess. "Won't take more than an hour."

"Want to come back?" Ufuk asked.

"It occurred to me that you've never shown me around this place."

"Would you like the grand tour?"

"As grand as you can make it."

After she got back into her jeans, they exited the lab back out into the gardens. Although the dense thicket of palms and ferns with the blue sky high above gave the impression of a large expanse, the extent of Ufuk's private area wasn't more than a square eighty feet to each side. At the edges of the garden, a cubed structure of tiny apartments with balconies rose five stories.

"Anyone who works on my staff has living quarters here," Ufuk explained. "No one is required to remain all the time—there are communal areas and leisure facilities across San EU—but everyone has their allocated quarters, and of course is tracked."

"Even you?"

"Especially me. Most of the research teams report directly to me. Intellectual resources are just as scarce as food and water now."

"Reminds me of Petra," Jess said.

"Carved into rock, you mean?"

Doomed, was her first thought, but instead she replied: "There's only one way in or out. You trying to stay hidden?"

"No hiding here." Ufuk pointed at the iridescent blue sky. "Big Brother is always watching."

"But you designed this place, right? Secret back doors and all? Must have taken a long time. Decades?" How long had this guy been working on this? She wanted to know with whom she was dealing.

"Most of the tunnels were already here, and Müller was the driving force behind it. I was just invited to help."

"Seems like an awfully nice set of quarters for the help."

"I also financed it."

"So the rich get saved."

Ufuk exhaled loudly enough to make sure Jess could hear. "This place is an Ark for humanity."

Jess pulled away from him. "You've said that twice already." She couldn't resist. "So do you imagine yourself more as Noah or God? At least Noah tried to warn everyone else about the flood."

"You're right." The billionaire shrugged slightly. "The rich and powerful were saved while we offered up extinction to the masses without warning. But there were rules to be allowed in here. If I'd said anything, I would have probably been killed—or at very least, excluded."

"Self-interest makes for easy rationalizations." The man's seeming indifference to the mass murder of hundreds of millions brought a prickling chill to the nape of Jess's neck.

19

"It does indeed." Ufuk wiped his chin with one hand. "But I also brought some very bright intellectual minds with me. I and…I have a…" He seemed about to add something but turned away. "We have to get back."

"You and Müller seem like you were awfully chummy," Jess said, resisting his pull on her arm. "Before this, I mean."

"A necessary evil."

"Seems there's a lot of that going around."

"I'm the one who saved you, and got him arrested."

"You might excuse me for feeling like I'm a pawn."

"I'm sorry for what happened to your family. I had nothing to—"

"The prosecutor has asked me to come in. To make a statement."

Ufuk rocked back on his heels. "Michel Durand, yes. I know him. He worked as an Examining Justice at the International Criminal Court in the Hague."

"An Examining Justice?" Jess snorted. "The goddamn world is disintegrating, and you're telling me we're going to trial? This is beyond insane. What other evidence do they need? They have Müller on video, admitting everything."

"This is no joke. Müller is one of the most powerful people in Sanctuary."

"This is rigged, right? Just a waste of time? Forget this fancy new leg, what I really need is a gun. Why am I bothering—"

"This needs to be done the right way, Jessica."

"Have they asked *you* to make a statement?" she asked.

"My position is different from yours. I imagine they will want to gather as much evidence as possible before speaking to me."

Jess paused before asking her next question: "Is he still in custody?"

"As far as I know. You must listen to me. Everything you do and say is recorded."

"Even here?"

"Here I can usually block outsiders, but one never knows. Müller is clever, and a senior member of the Administrative Council. They must make a determination before he can be charged, should the Examining Justice give such a recommendation in the first place. We need to follow protocol."

"That's ridiculous."

"Don't underestimate Müller."

"Trust me, I'm not."

"Whatever you say to Durand, you will make enemies one way or the other. You've become a celebrity down here, with all the good and bad that comes along with it."

"Didn't they watch the video?" Jess repeated sullenly, feeling the numb fear returning. "What about my father's laptop? You said Müller wanted it for all my dad's correspondence; that it could prove he was lying."

"Durand has it, and it does."

"What about my father's data? Did you calculate Saturn's orbit? Roger said he'd seen post-collapse simulations—"

"It'll be a spectacular sight in eighteen months, if the clouds clear enough to see Saturn brush past us. It will pass at least a million kilometers away—but the encounter *will* bring a lot of other problems we're still working to understand." Ufuk produced a memory key from his pocket. "Another reason I asked you here. To give you this."

He pressed it into Jess's hand.

She stared at it. The scratched and beaten memory key that Roger had transferred her father's astronomical maps into. All the desperation to save her father's data, the lives of her parents sacrificed. All for nothing—but the man before her seemed genuine enough.

"I'm grateful for everything you've done for me, Ufuk, really I am, so I hate to say this—but you're a part of what happened. You're also responsible."

"This place," Ufuk gestured around him, "carries the same insecurity and greed that underpinned the world before Nomad. I'm trying to do my best."

"For who exactly?"

"Everyone has an agenda here, Jessica. No one is what they seem."

"And that would include you?"

"You don't trust me—don't trust anyone, and I can understand that—but you will need friends in the coming days and weeks." Ufuk's voice was slow and measured, but a friendly grin still dimpled his cheeks. "I suggest you don't isolate yourself."

Jess considered this for a few seconds before asking: "Did you find Massarra?"

The man shook his head, again slow and measured. "I imagine she's hiding."

"She seemed awfully intent on getting here. What information do you have on her?"

"You telling us about her was the first time I'd heard of her—although we knew of the Levantines. She's connected to some dangerous terrorists."

"Dangerous is a relative term these days," Jess said. "We need to find her, bring her to Sanctuary. She's not an enemy."

"Talk like that isn't going to help you here." Ufuk drew in a deep breath. "I suggest you keep this between us—but I'll do my best to locate her. Now, let's finish getting you a new leg, shall we?"

2

Northern Italy

How in Allah's name had she let Ufuk Erdogmus convince her into this?

Massarra pulled the blanket as tightly around her as she could manage with her hands bound by rope and numbed by cold. At night they tied her up. At least they had some sense to realize how dangerous she could be, but that was about as far as Massarra's opinion of her captors' abilities stretched.

It was dark; almost pitch black except for the flickering light of the fire sputtering in the hearth of the old farmhouse. She was huddled together with five others to share their warmth, blankets and everything else they could carry piled on top of them, but she was the only one tied up. The pervasive stench of sulfur still permeated everything, but cowering under these blankets, the human odor of sweat and fear overcame it.

Wind whistled in through the boarded-up windows despite their best attempts to seal them, and the fire provided scant warmth against the biting cold. During the dark days it never even heated up past freezing anymore—maybe not even to ten below Celsius today—but at nights the cold was a terror. At least twenty below freezing, maybe more, and this was just the start of December, as best as she could estimate.

How much colder would it get?

Ten feet in front of her, the old man Salman grunted as he lifted another scrap of a smashed table and heaved it into the fire. With a grimy hand, he tested his cleft lip. Even in the dim light it looked raw and swollen, maybe infected. He lifted the wool hat from his head to smooth back his stringy gray hair. "Tell me again why you are convinced we should continue north?"

Massarra pretended to snap awake, affected an eagerness to please him. "Livorno is a major port. Lots to scavenge in shipping containers that must have washed inland. Like I said before."

"We can scavenge in the south."

"More people in the south. How many others have we seen up here over the past week?"

"They're all dead from cold. As we will be. Soon." He dropped more wood onto the flames.

Each day they came upon yet more piled corpses, lives stolen by starvation or exposure to the extreme cold. They'd had to clear this building of the frozen remains of a family who had been too slow to react as their bodies slowly submitted to the freezing temperatures. That had been Massarra's task. Salman had insisted.

Some of the dead they came across hadn't succumbed to cold, but to wounds inflicted by others who wanted whatever they had been carrying: food, clothing, fuel, or whatever might offer a few more days' survival. This concerned Massarra far more than the harshness of the climate, because that unpredictable threat imposed on her a state of constant vigilance. Yet she took care not to underestimate the cold too, watching for signs of hypothermia in herself, as well as respiratory problems from the fine ash in the air. Not much she could do about either.

"We can survive the cold," Massarra said. "What we can't survive is disease. Cholera, typhus, that's what waits in the south. It'll kill them, and it will warm up eventually here when spring arrives. This is an opportunity."

Truths and half-truths. She was sure there would be rampant disease appearing in any groups of survivors squatting in their own filth further south. At least the cold up here helped keep things sanitary by freezing everything that came out of their bodies. But she wasn't sure if it would get warmer.

"So you know this?" Salman's voice was guttural, with a heavy Italian accent, and his command of English was far from perfect.

"Positive," she lied. "I looked at the simulations on Jessica Rollins' laptop, remember?"

"*Cagna!*" The old man spat and kicked at the pile of splinters at his feet. "That bitch."

He was furious at being left behind, when the magical machines from the sky had descended at Vivas and whisked Jessica Rollins away. He'd saved her life, he kept repeating and repeating, ignoring that he'd almost killed her in cold blood himself. He had made a deal with Dr. Müller and Iain Radcliffe—the head of security at the Vivas bunker facility—that if he helped them get the data on Jessica's laptop, he would be taken to Sanctuary as well. A deal he'd been screwed out of.

But it was a careless bargain he'd tried to make, and Salman knew it. Müller had killed Iain Radcliffe, and would have killed Salman as well, if Ufuk Erdogmus hadn't appeared to stop what was happening.

"The clouds will clear; summer will bring back warmth," Massarra said, trying to reassure Salman. "And then we will have an entire shipping port to ourselves."

"And what if it gets colder?"

"It won't. I told you. I saw the simulations."

Salman watched her in a blank-faced way, then blew on his hands and stuffed them into the pockets of his coat.

"If you really want to go south," Massarra said after a few seconds of silence. "Then we have the best chance of finding a boat somewhere outside Livorno that we can use. We could also try Monte Argentario."

"A boat?" Salman grunted. "I walked on the ice at the shore, just like you. All the boats were washed miles inshore. And this cold? The ocean will be frozen. *Is* already frozen." The expression on the old *mafioso's* face turned from sullen to anger. He turned to kneel in front of her. "What are you up to, eh?"

There was still some cleverness in the old man's beady eyes, but he didn't know when he was beaten.

"Ice will form in shallow water, yes," admitted Massarra. "But the open Mediterranean will take much longer to freeze. Pancake ice will form in patches, but the Med was a warm sea. This cold will chill the surface water, and this will sink, form convection currents bringing up warm water from the depth. It'll take months for—"

"You seem to know a lot about water."

"Sailing south is a much better bet than trying overland."

The modified Land Rover they'd stolen still worked on the roads half-cleared by other survivor groups going south, but the snow and ash continued to fall heavily. This part was true. Heading south at this point would mean going on foot, which was the same as a death sentence.

Salman seemed taken aback. "Sailing? You want to sail in *this*?

"A yacht is lighter, better designed for dealing with bad weather, and you never run out of fuel. We should be able to get one out over the ice. They are easy to keep warm. Nice small spaces, and sealed and insulated."

All of this was true. Massarra had spent as much of her downtime on water as she had on land. Friends of the Levantine Council had a permanent berth at one of Tel Aviv's quieter marinas, and she had borrowed the boat as often as she could for expeditions with friends, and even while on missions. From there, she had sailed the peaceful warmth of the Mediterranean, and through the cold roughness of the Indian and Atlantic oceans. If she missed anything in the time since Nomad, it was the joyous freedom her sailboat offered.

It was true that anything near the coast would be wrecked, but Massarra had a plan. An idea. She always had ideas. It was what kept her alive. "It's a way to get south. At least it will give us a place to sleep and stay warm."

Her explanation of why they should head north to Livorno or Monte Argentario was rooted in truth, as the best lies are, and it was the plan she intended—the only difference being that soon she would leave Salman and his family behind. Monte Argentario was a day's walk on improvised snowshoes and the time had come to make her move.

There was risk to everything, in this freezing darkness that waited for her to make a mistake. She would need to make her way north, up into the mountains to Sassal Mason, beside the Lago Palü and the Alp Grüm railway station, or whatever remained of it. Supplies and equipment should be there for her in an alpine hut. Once retrieved, she could make her way into Sanctuary Europe.

Fifty-fifty odds that the voyage would kill her, despite her cold-weather survival skills, but that was better than staying here.

Salman took another long look at her, grunted again and turned to stack the fire.

Massarra's huddled posture and the soft moans she gave from time to time added to the impression that she was beaten. In reality, she studied Salman in her peripheral vision. Huddled under the blankets with her were Rita—Salman's daughter—and his boy. They slept close to each other, curled beneath their own blankets. Massarra remained watchful, ever vigilant. Always thinking and preparing; her mind never restful. That was her tradecraft, drilled into her over many years and saving her life more than once.

Salman didn't sleep, either. Instead, he watched her. He was no fool, Massarra knew that. *Mafioso* like him, experienced criminals, rarely were. A rifle stolen from Vivas rested against the wall next to Salman. A second rifle lay beside Rita as she slept.

For about two weeks they'd been heading north at Massarra's suggestion, but making slow progress. Each night, Salman would ask the same questions, and cover the same ground, asking questions about Müller, the Sanctuary system, and Ufuk Erdogmus. Each evening he used the same methods to persuade her, the same creeping violence, and each evening she appeared more compliant to his viciousness. She had ensured he viewed her as useful by demonstrating skills in this hostile environment, beyond his brutal quests for information. She did so in a way that concealed what she was truly capable of, revealing only enough of herself to ensure he wanted to keep her around. She helped them approach settlements off the main routes in ways that protected them, pitched camp in places that allowed them to be alerted to potential threats.

"I still don't understand." Massarra brought her knees to her chest, hunched inward.

"There is far more to this than you know," Salman boasted. "Things happening even now that I know, Massarra. You shouldn't try to keep anything from me."

She feigned ignorance when he questioned her, adding a scrap of information here and there, but her submission made him let his guard down. She manipulated his masculine arrogance, his enjoyment of the power he held over her.

This was the real reason she was here. She was the one that needed information.

"But you never talked to this Dr. Müller?" she said softly. "Who is he?"

"I told you, I spoke to Iain only."

"And you trust his word?"

"I am not stupid. I said I need him to talk to them, so I know it was true."

"And you were there? You heard them on the radio?"

"Why you so interested, eh?" The old gangster didn't turn as he asked the question, but gazed unfocused into the fire. The question wasn't so much suspicion as habit. His guard was down. Even he couldn't imagine someone going to the lengths Massarra was subjecting herself to, but then he couldn't comprehend the stakes involved.

"I just want to know," Massarra whispered. "How I ended up here…" She feigned a sob. "Can you untie me? I'm so tired."

"Ha, that, no." Salman poked the fire. "Maxim, that was who Iain talked to on the radio."

"The security man, the one who was with Müller?"

"That was Maxim? How do you know?"

"I heard them talking to each other. Nobody else on the radio?"

The old man shrugged, shaking his head, but then straightened up. "Marshall, I heard them talking to someone called Marshall in the background."

Massarra remained limp under the blankets, but her mind raced. "Marshall?"

"Something like that. I am tired. No more talking."

The boy was Salman's weakness, more so than his daughter Rita. She recognized the way the boy moved as he slept, the soft murmuring. She'd seen it before in young soldiers who came back from fighting in Gaza or the West Bank. When the time came for the boy's short watch, he would still be tired. Almost every night in the last week she had watched him falling asleep on watch.

Massarra pulled the blanket over her head with her bound hands.

Each night, Salman tied her in the same way, his mistrust of her evident in the tightness of the bonds. Each night she worked the knot, probed its stresses and teased out ways to loosen it, never quite going all the way, then tightening again where she could. Her hands were already free now, and she had her sharp blade palmed in her right hand.

She waited until Salman called the boy's name.

3

Sanctuary Europe

This was it.

"Office of Judicial Administration" was stenciled in italicized gold letters beside the door. The mapping app on Jess's tablet had guided her through the complex of pristine white hallways. The deeper she limped into gleaming catacombs—that smelled like a new car—the more the buzz of human conversation in the front offices died down until just the squeak of her new sneakers accompanied her. Left and then right, and then left and right again.

The glowing dot on her app stopped here.

She pushed open double glass doors—the magnetic lock on them stuck for an instant before releasing—and approached a white block of plastic that emerged smoothly from the wall, cantilevered ten feet out without a floor support at the other end. She assumed this was the reception desk. Beside the desk to her left were four attending chairs in smooth blue leather, with another glass door beside them that led further inside. Offense-less artwork hung on egg-white walls that glowed bright from invisible lights.

"Hello?" It didn't seem like anyone was here. The office was empty.

Her voice didn't echo, but was swallowed in the dense silence.

"Hello?" Jess repeated, louder this time, looking around for a camera. "I'm Jessica Rollins. I was asked to come here to see Michel Durand."

"Miss Rollins, yes. Thank you for coming." A pleasant-sounding female voice.

Jess glanced behind her, but there was nobody there either.

On the wall behind the desk appeared the image of an Asian woman in a sharp business suit, with her black hair done in a tight bun. "Take a seat. Mr. Durand will see you shortly. May I get you a tea or coffee? Perhaps some water?"

Jess found herself too surprised to answer.

The image of the woman regarded her with patient curiosity. Her smile widened, her eyebrows raised a fraction of an inch as she waited for a response.

"Ah...tea?" Jess stuttered.

"Certainly." The receptionist-projection waited for Jess to take a seat, then strode along the wall—her image flickered across the gap of the doorway—to stop next to Jess. A recessed panel in the wall slid open, and the receptionist-projection pointed a helpful hand toward it. A cardboard cup of steaming tea waited on a metal grate inside.

Jess took the cup. The panel slid closed.

"I'll be back in a moment," said the receptionist-projection, as her image walked to the interior glass door and disappeared.

In here, no one carried a scavenged weapon with murder in their mind for whatever a victim might hold. No scrabbling in the ash for every last crumb of food or something that might create heat. No chance of freezing to death quietly during sleep. Jess took a guilty sip of her tea. Chamomile. Her favorite. She didn't want to know how they knew—and she didn't have to wait long before the woman re-appeared.

The interior glass door clicked and opened. "This way," said the receptionist-projection, re-appearing on the front wall behind the desk.

Jess took another sip from her steaming tea, then followed the woman's image as it slid along the wall and down an interior hallway as white and featureless as the ones outside, but even more claustrophobic-feeling. They passed three closed doors before the woman's image stopped at the fourth.

Inside, behind a beaten old wooden desk—that looked outlandishly out of place in the white cube office—sat an older man. Sixty-ish, with a full head of well-groomed silver hair and a weathered face that had an owlishness to it that was accentuated by

31

his wire-rimmed glasses. His blue suit looked finely tailored, but was oddly matched with a speckled green tie that looked almost as out of place as the desk.

"A gift from my daughter," the man said, flipping the tie up to have a look himself. He smoothed it down. "She would have been your age," he sighed. The man stood, his body tall and slender and slightly stooped. He extended one hand. "Michel Durand."

Jess balanced her teacup in her left hand to shake his hand with her right. "Jessica Rollins." She gripped and pumped firmly.

"Thank you for coming. Shall we sit?"

He settled back into his chair. Jess took the only one opposite. Durand picked up a tablet and began dictating preliminary introductions into it.

Jess craned her neck around the open door. "Is that...I mean..."

"Not a real person? Stephanie is my digital assistant. You'll get used to them. I'm afraid I'm the only *real* person in the Office of Judicial Administration." His bushy white eyebrows knitted into a frown. "Honestly, nobody thought we'd need much of a high court. My office was intended as more of an academic sort of—"

"When will Müller be sentenced?" Jess blurted out.

Durand seemed to blink himself fully awake. "There is quite some way to go before we reach that point, Miss Rollins. The Examining Justice can only issue a recommendation in the case of a member of the Administrative Council. The Executive Orders which govern the Sanctuary system are quite specific. Perhaps you could think of them as a more complex version of your American Constitution. Anyone offered the opportunity to come here was first required to accept those Orders."

"I certainly did no such thing." A tingling numbness crept down from Jess's scalp. This was the guy who was tasked with defending the world—and herself—against the mass-murdering Müller? She understood the individual words coming out of the man's mouth, but couldn't piece any meaning together from them.

"You are something of a special case," Durand said after a pause. "I mean, in not yet taking an oath to the Orders."

"And who exactly *was* given the opportunity to come here?"

Durand leaned back in his chair. "It is not my place to question how the system came about, Miss Rollins. My task is only to oversee the administration of justice within it."

"That sounds like an excuse."

"You may think so, but I see the matter differently."

"This isn't even a trial, is it?"

Durand regarded her, then said: "As I said, the Examining Justice makes a recommendation to the Administrative Council. If there is considered to be sufficient evidence to warrant a judicial finding, then sentencing will follow dependent on the result of—"

"He admitted to bombing the goddamn Vatican!" Jessica spat the words out, unable to control herself. "He killed tens of thousands of people. If anyone was ever a terrorist—"

"An inquiry such as this one takes time, Miss Rollins. Probably months, and I hadn't expected to have to start this office so soon. We're still in a great deal of shock."

"We're all in shock, Mr. Durand."

Jess only noticed now that she'd spilled her tea all over her hand, which shook. She moved to put the cup down but hesitated, not wanting to place it on the wooden desktop. Durand provided a coaster from a top desk drawer.

"I understand your frustration," he said. "But there is a great deal of evidence to collect, and all of it must be analyzed. Conclusions must be drawn from each and every document and image. There is considerable pressure from influential quarters to allow Dr. Müller to continue his work. This is a very difficult time. A *dangerous* time."

"His…work?" The tingling numbness had progressed to encompass Jess's entire body. The room before her seemed to float in two dimensions, depthless and lacking in reality. She'd expected to come here and look at the video, perhaps help this Durand man confirm some information from her father's laptop, but…

"Müller's analysis of our solar system. Two days ago another cluster of Jovian meteors impacted the Iberian peninsula."

"Don't you have a lot of other people who can do that?"

"And whereas once we might also have considered whether the individual might also be a flight risk, for obvious reasons, that's no longer considered relevant."

"I don't understand."

Durand remained silent, but an expression blossomed on his face like he'd just bit into a lemon.

"Jesus," Jess groaned. "You're going to let him out of jail?"

"I oppose it, but we may have no choice."

Jess's feeling of a disconnect with reality grew. "But the evidence against him is overwhelming. You have the videos, you have all my father's emails on his laptop that prove he was lying."

"I cannot comment on an ongoing inquiry, as I am sure you understand. Any assessment of the evidence is for the Examining Justice. However, your statement is of critical importance."

"And he killed Iain Radcliffe. In cold blood. I watched the footage this morning. It's on the intranet. I doubt there is anyone in here who hasn't seen it."

"There is the suggestion that the footage has been altered."

Jess's heart skipped a beat. "That's ridiculous. I was there."

"All the more reason we press on with taking from you the most detailed statement we can. You have powerful friends, Ms. Rollins, people who are on your side. Despite Dr. Müller's high position, I can assure you this is being taken extremely seriously."

"He can work from custody, can't he?" Jess's voice, thin and desperate, sounded like it was coming from someone else's mouth. "He's a murderer. He killed my family. He killed...I mean...you can't just—"

"I propose we meet each day this week," Durand continued. "For now, I would like you to undertake a video interview that will form the first basis of your evidence. Tomorrow, I will ask you more detailed questions. It is not my task to catch you out, merely to ensure your account is as accurate as it can be. Do you understand?"

She nodded numbly.

"Then let's begin."

Two hours after she entered, Jess left Michel Durand's office. Dazed relief.

Exhausted beyond words she had to describe, and she was tired of words. The emotion of going over everything that had happened, had reopened wounds inside her that weren't even close to being healed. Gaping wounds that gushed her raw emotions.

"If they let that bastard out, I'm going to kill him…" she muttered as she wandered aimlessly through the rat's maze of corridors, ignoring her tablet's map app. It was warm and soft in here, but some things were better on the outside. Outside of these walls, she could finish Müller without hesitation. Judge, jury and executioner. The man needed no trial. He was a monster.

She stopped in her tracks in front of a blank wall. A dead end.

Before Jess could even check her tablet, a pleasant-and familiar voice said: "This way."

The smiling and sharp-suited image of Stephanie appeared on the wall in front of her. The digital helper walked from one wall panel to the next, and stopped to wait.

Shaking her head, Jess followed.

A few minutes later she was back "outside," under the simulated crisp blue sky projected on the ceiling dome a few hundred feet overhead. Stephanie had bid her farewell at the final wall panel leading out of the office complex. Jess walked aimlessly through an elegant public garden. Songbirds fluttered through pruned bushes.

"Jessica Rollins. Please, can I speak to you?"

A girl ran toward her, barely more than a teenager. Breathlessly, the girl held out a hand to shake. Jess took it.

"My name is Abbie Barnes. I'm a journalist with New Affairs magazine."

The girl's hand was soft, and she smelled of strong soap. A dizzying vertigo gripped Jess's already churning stomach. This place was so unreal. "A magazine?"

The girl cast her eyes down. "It's not a real magazine. I mean, it *will* be. It's important to keep the fourth estate alive, don't you think? I think it is. I was studying journalism when my dad, well my stepdad, and he—"

"Wait, you emailed me, right?"

"I want to get your side, let people know what really happened." Abbie took a step back and stood up straight to look Jess in the eye.

"I've been busy. To be honest, I can barely accept that email exists at all, never mind all this." Jess waved one hand at the blue sky. The girl looked earnest enough, but the last thing Jess could handle right now was rehashing everything again. "I really appreciate your email, but I can't right now."

Abbie Barnes nodded and beamed an energetic smile. "You've had quite an impact since you arrived."

Jess strode past her. "I'd much rather be left alone."

Abbie followed. "Even though you've just given a statement to Michel Durand?"

"Journalists don't change much, do they?"

"People are afraid, and when they're afraid they let those who govern do unconscionable things in order to feel protected and safe. They close their eyes to the truth."

"You have no idea what's happening outside, kid. Better it stays that way."

"I do want to know."

"No, you don't. You just want to play journalist 'cause you're bored."

"That's not fair."

"There's a lot of that going around. Get used to it."

"I can help."

Jess stopped and bowed her head. "I don't mean to be rude, but what is it you want from me? I'd like to go back to my quarters."

"I want to know what really happened. I want to know what you think Dr. Müller was really hiding. I think everyone here has a right to know."

"You already know. You all saw the videos, right?"

"There's always more to it, Jess. There are those who don't believe we know everything of what Dr. Müller has been concealing from the world. He has considerable influence and support across the Sanctuary system. We don't believe there will be an inquiry at all."

Jess snorted and kept walking. "And how could you help?"

Abbie hesitated. "My stepdad is the senior military commander here."

That got Jess's attention.

"Come and have a drink with me," Abbie said, seeing the change in Jess's eyes. "Everything you say can be off the record, if you like. Just please, let's talk."

"How old are you?"

"Eighteen."

"A drink?"

"Coffee?"

Behind Abbie, two young children chased each other around one of the manicured bushes. About the same age as Hector. "Okay, a coffee," Jess agreed.

Abbie led her to the other side of the gardens to a seating area beside a small coffee shop. A smiling waitress came out to take their order. A row of newly-planted orange trees lined the cobblestone terrace. A fountain gushed glistening spray that arced upward and hissed as it rained down into the koi fish filled basin. Two tables down, a man in a sport jacket sipped a latte and picked at a croissant. It felt like an all-inclusive resort in Bermuda Jess had once been to with an old boyfriend. She hated all-inclusive resorts.

Abbie's voice brought her back to the table. "When did you first—"

"Do you know what's happening in the United States?" Jess interrupted. "Is there any word from the White House or the military? Your accent is American, right?"

Abbie's lips pressed together before she replied: "Communication with the outside is restricted. You know that. There's a lockdown period that was agreed to before Nomad to protect the installation, and the Administrative Council takes breaches of security extremely seriously."

"Can you try to find out?"

"If you can help me, I can try."

"Then say what you have to say."

"There are those who want to use Durand's inquiry as a catalyst for a wider investigation into Dr. Müller and those who support him."

Jess sat back. This girl was serious. Big words. And clever.

"We would like some pointed questions to be put to him," Abbie continued, "and for him to be judicially compelled to answer them."

"Good luck with that."

"Your support would go a long way to achieving that aim."

"So you want my support."

"I want, well, you're—"

The waitress returned with two steaming coffees and a small china cup of milk, and Abbie blushed and waited for her to leave.

"What's wrong?" Jess asked.

"I'm just shy. It's not every day you get to meet your hero."

It was Jess's turn to blush. She picked up her cup of coffee and marveled at it. "Don't you have rationing or something? And how do you pay for stuff?"

"Everyone has a quota, and there is a payment system. We have jobs. Didn't anyone explain…?"

"I guess there have been more important things." Jess took a sip. The coffee was rich. Delicious. She wished it were horrible. "Now, what are you trying to do?"

Abbie took a deep breath. "This place is supposed to be an ark for humanity, and I intend to do my part. San EU is a constitutional democracy, even if that sounds silly to you."

"It doesn't sound silly," Jess said softly.

"Freedom of speech can be curtailed on national security grounds." Abbie's smile grew as her confidence gained. "The world is different now, and yes, we are the lucky ones. But democracy requires the people to be informed and the unadulterated communication of facts has a very significant role to play in San EU, possibly more so than ever before in human history. Dr. Müller has the ability to control events in here, even from his place in custody, and there are those of us who want to make sure that doesn't happen, or at least make him accountable…"

Her voice trailed off, her sentence unfinished, as she looked over Jess's shoulder.

Two men clad in the coal-black uniforms of the San EU military passed by their table. Hanging from single-point harnesses were black SOPMOD M4 carbines. They chatted as they walked, seeming casual, but Jess noticed the precision in their movements, the concentration on their faces.

"This whole facility is on a knife edge," Abbie whispered as the soldiers turned a corner. "If there comes a point where Dr. Müller controls the Administrative Council, he controls this whole complex."

Jess finished her coffee and put the cup down carefully. "Which is why I suggest you let this Durand guy do his job. Be thankful for what you have, Abbie, that you're alive in here. You don't want to be outside, let me tell you. I'm tired right now, though. We can talk later."

She stood, about to leave, but then asked: "You said your dad was head of the military. What's his name?"

"Eugene," Abbie replied. "General Eugene Marshall."

4

Sanctuary Europe

"We were in touch with them almost every day," Jess said, then leaned in closer to the tablet resting on her square plastic dining room table. "In the Allegheny Mountains, six-six-oh-four kilohertz."

"I don't have any information for you," the on-screen woman replied.

It was Stephanie, Michel Durand's digital assistant. She was dressed in a low-cut black suit today, but her hair still done in a tight bun. Who decided on the fashion sense for digital assistants?

"Could you at least ask them?"

"I will ask," the machine replied. "I am asking again right now."

"Can't I speak to a real person?"

Stephanie smiled ingratiatingly at the request, and Jess wondered if the machine was actually trying to be patronizing. "I am relaying all of your requests as you speak them," it answered. "And you understand that Mr. Durand's office must be the one making such requests."

"We had another bunch of survivors in Florida—"

"Yes, we know."

"Who's 'we' exactly?"

"I am speaking using the plural noun to indicate that both myself and the Administrative Council are aware of these group designations already."

"So then you've contacted them. The survivor groups?"

Stephanie remained silent.

"Can you at least tell me they're alive?"

"I'm sorry, Jessica."

"You mean, sorry, like they're dead?"

"That I can't give you any more information."

Jess groaned aloud in frustration and stood, then almost fell over as her left leg kicked her back three feet. Three days on this new robotic prosthetic and it had almost killed her a dozen times already. It was like a spring-loaded gun. She was used to her old passive prosthetics, and she could turn this one off so it wasn't active, but the truth was she kind of enjoyed the challenge of trying to rewire her brain. It gave her something to focus on.

At the other side of the table, Giovanni had his survivor log books and papers scattered, and beside that, the old shortwave radio—useless down here—that had been picked up with him from the ice. He'd changed the artwork on the walls to old Italian masters. These weren't pictures hanging on the walls, as most of the walls here were displays, too. A popular wall-display theme was rolling outdoor hills and distant mountaintops, but this made Jess feel disoriented. If she was underground, she wanted to know she was underground.

"What about Al-Jawf, that's critical, it's—" Jess waved her hands at Giovanni, who held up a scrap of paper with numbers on it. "—seven-four-four-two kilohertz. Ain Salah is the contact, can't you just tell him that we're okay, even if you don't say where or who?"

"I am very sorry—"

"Yeah, yeah, I know." Jess pushed the off button on the tablet.

"That was rude." Giovanni's eyebrows raised. He collected his papers together.

"Of her? No kidding."

"I meant you. Cutting off the connection without saying goodbye."

"It's a goddamn machine, Giovanni, even if it has a pretty face." Jess paced around the ten-foot by ten-foot cubicle they called their living room, her left leg going up and down like a pogo stick. "We've got to get in touch with Ain Salah. Last time I spoke to him,

I said I had my father's data, told him how critical it was. He must think we're dead."

"I'm sure he has found other things to worry about. A lot of people have disappeared out there. We were just one more lost voice to him."

Hector was curled in a corner, wrapped in blankets, playing a game on another tablet. They'd each been given one, and Jess wondered if they were really for their benefit, or simply surveillance devices. Her leg slipped as she rounded the corner and almost fell into him. The boy recoiled.

"Slow down." Giovanni held out one hand to her.

But Jess couldn't stop circling. "So that's what you think? That we were just another lost voice? That's all this was?"

"I'm just saying—"

"Ufuk Erdogmus hasn't even been able to tell me if there's a Sanctuary America. He just babbles about Cheyenne Mountain, how the Americans prepared for this sort of thing somehow. Wasn't he one of the designers of this place? He's American too, even if he was born in Turkey."

"Jessica—"

"And Massarra. Why didn't Ufuk pick up Massarra when he rescued us? He got them to bring in the whole Jollie Roger crew, Ballie Booker and all of them."

"This was a special case."

"Ufuk has resources out there. He said he does. His own private army, I bet, but he won't even tell us if they're in contact with America."

"They're paying very close attention right now. Ufuk obviously can't say anything. There are rules."

"Screw the rules. I want to get back outside."

Giovanni reached further out and grabbed her arm on this pass. "Stop. Do you hear what you are saying? We will find out about America. Be patient. One thing at a time."

From the corner of the room, Hector had retreated into a fetal ball, his eyes wide and fixed on Jessica.

She exhaled to release the boiling emotions frothing inside of her gut. "I didn't mean that, about going outside." She slumped down at the table, closed her eyes and counted backward from ten to one in her head, then opened her eyes and smiled at Hector. "Maybe we should do a Christmas Calendar? What do you think?"

"A what?" Giovanni asked.

"You know. One of those December calendars with all the twenty-four days before Christmas on them. Behind each day is a chocolate. Today's what, the second of December?"

"I think so…" Giovanni replied slowly.

"Wait, you guys celebrate Christmas, right? You're Catholic? Aren't all Italians Catholic?"

"We celebrate Christmas, yes, but this holiday chocolate thing?"

"We'll make one." Jess affected an enthusiastic grin. "Hector, you like chocolates? Yes? Chocolates." She mimed putting something delicious into her mouth.

The boy relaxed, nodded, and returned to the game on his tablet.

"There's something else," Jess said to Giovanni. "There's a journalist who's been speaking to me. Abbie Barnes. Or Barnes-Marshall, I think is her surname. She doesn't trust Müller—she thinks he's hiding something. She's the daughter of the military commander."

"A journalist? Are you serious?"

"She's just a kid, really. Trying to keep the fourth estate alive, that's what she said. I don't know, but I have to do something. Every day I keep on banging my head against a wall, trying to find out what's happening. And every day I get nowhere, and I'm not sure I can keep waiting like this."

Giovanni held his hands out, palms down. "Be careful what you say to anyone."

A knock at the door.

Giovanni looked to Jess, but she offered only a shrug.

"Hello?" he said, loud enough to be heard outside.

43

The rooms weren't exactly soundproof. No answer. Giovanni frowned and went to the door and opened it.

Ballie Booker's smiling face appeared halfway down the door. "Time for Hector's soccer practice!" he gleefully exclaimed in his thick British accent, his eyes and grin wide in a goofy expression. "Can he come out to play?"

Hector jumped up from the corner of the room, tossing down his tablet and looking at Giovanni. His uncle nodded, and the six-year-old pranced to the door to be scooped up into Ballie's arms.

"I'll have him back in an hour," Ballie proclaimed.

"Whenever you get tired of him," said Giovanni.

"Then two." Ballie held Hector up. "Off we go."

The door closed by itself.

Ballie was a dynamo of positive energy, and used much of it to entertain Hector. Jess guessed he must feel lucky. Scooped off a ship in the middle of dark seas to be deposited in this paradise. Him and his entire crew, and the people they'd rescued. The winners of the greatest lottery jackpot of all time. Something about it felt wrong. So many others were out there dying. Why were they saved and not the others?

Luck.

That was about all Jess could put it down to.

Giovanni was halfway back to the table when there was another knock. He turned and opened the door. "Did you forget the ball—"

The smile slid from Giovanni's face as he tried to slam the door closed.

"I just want to talk. Just for a second," said a familiar voice from behind the door.

Jess slumped a little.

Roger.

Despite Giovanni's efforts, the man pushed his way in.

44

"You are not welcome here." Giovanni stood firm and blocked Roger from entering the room. "I thought I made that clear."

"I don't blame you, but I'd like to speak to both of you. Please."

"Let him in." Jess rose and came to Giovanni's side to pull him backward. "We're all stuck in this cave, no getting out. We're going to see each other. I'd rather we try to be civil." Not just that, but Jess needed as many friends as she could get right now. She gestured to the small dining table and Roger sat down. Giovanni remained standing.

"How have you been?" she asked, taking a seat across from Roger.

"Better." He looked down at where his thumb had once been, just a raw stump now. "I've been on a program. Going to meetings. Can you believe it? They have a substance abuse program here." He halfheartedly laughed. "Shouldn't be surprised with the number of bankers and CEOs down here."

Jess reached over and laid her hand on his arm. "Good for you." She paused, then asked: "Did you have another look at my father's data? Since you got here?"

He kept his eyes downcast. "From what I saw, they had all the data they needed. Better than we had."

"So then it was all a waste of time."

"It got us in here. And your dad's laptop is going to be used in the trial. That's what everyone says." He scratched the side of his neck. "I don't want there to be bad blood between us, Jess. I loved you once, you know that, right?"

"Roger, please, don't—"

"There's only so many people left in the world. I'm sorry for what I did, but I'd like to try to be friends again, one day. Somehow. That's really all I came to say."

Jess's face flushed at the feeling of sudden intimacy.

From behind Roger, Giovanni snorted. He went to the kitchen counter at the side of the room and opened a cupboard. He took out the bottle of cognac that Ufuk had graciously gifted to them. He poured himself a generous dose of what had to be some of the last ounces of the spirit left on the planet. "So. We forget? Is that it?"

"We remember what he did in the end," Jess said softly. "You weren't there, remember?" She turned in her chair. "Roger let me cut off his goddamn thumb, voluntarily. He risked his life to save me and you, Hector and Raffa."

Roger stood. "Perhaps it's best I give you some time."

"I don't need any time," Giovanni growled.

"I'll see myself out," Roger made his way to the door. "Good to see you, Jess."

After he left, Jess joined Giovanni in a glass of the cognac. She didn't much care for the taste, too harsh and smoky and it burned her throat, but she welcomed the distraction. "He did risk his life for us," she said in the awkward silence.

"After putting us all in danger," Giovanni replied, taking another sip of his drink. "I don't much care for Mr. Roger, nor should you."

Jess woke early the next day. Hector was still fast asleep between her and Giovanni, so she slid out of the bed and unplugged her new robotic leg. Having to plug and unplug a part of her body was a new habit she wasn't sure she'd get used to, but it already felt like a part of her in a way she hadn't expected. She got dressed quietly and left their quarters to take a walk. She needed as much practice as she could get. The new leg almost seemed to walk itself—almost seemed to *want* to walk itself.

Most of San EU had barely woken as the tentative light of a fabricated dawn bloomed above her, but she was not alone. Like her, those who appreciated the tranquility of a new morning also strolled through the gardens and walkways, taking advantage of the fleeting peaceful moments before the complex became busy.

Lost in thought, her face flushed ice cold.

At first, she thought she was mistaken. Some subtle quiver of her subconscious, playing a trick or a waking dream she was trying to suppress: that familiar tangle of gray hair above an oily face and thick-rimmed spectacles perched high over a piggish nose.

Dr. Müller stood on the gravel path directly in front of her.

"How lovely to see you," he said. "I hoped I would run into you."

"Get away from me."

She had to suppress an urge to bull-charge the bastard.

"I intend to, Jessica. However, I thought it only right that I tell you myself I am no longer a prisoner to your malicious allegations."

"I was there, Müller, and so were you. We both know what happened. No one will believe you."

"On the contrary. They already do." Müller turned on his heel. "Enjoy the rest of your day," he said over his shoulder. "For as long you are able to, I mean."

He started to walk away, his steps light. As free as the birds singing in the trees around them.

Her whole body felt drained of blood. Her hands shook. "You bastard."

She jumped forward, ran at him. She wasn't sure what she was going to do. She just wanted to grab him, make him stay—make him admit what he did, stuff her fist down his throat—but she didn't get more than two steps before four black-clad men grabbed her.

"Stop!" she screamed, but not at the men holding her. She yelled at the disappearing silhouette of Müller.

Birds scattered from the treetops.

PART TWO

Mars First Mission

Deep Interplanetary Space

"The *Earth* is dead?" Commander Jason Rankin said to his second-in-command, communication specialist Elin Cuijpers. "Could you be more specific?"

The emergency siren still wailed, echoing painfully in the confines of the twenty-foot hibernation room. The siren keened up and down in frequency.

The Dutchwoman's slender fingers played over the terminal display. "No radio chatter at all from any ground-based channels in the past four weeks. Nothing from the Tanzania command post, no communications from China, America…nothing at all. Not even personal messages. No media. Nothing."

"Keep on it. There must be something. Try to raise a channel." He grimaced at the siren's screech. "And could you turn that damn thing off? I'm going to bring the others out of hibernation."

Rankin circled the room, checking and rechecking the hibernation pods. They needed more information, and fast. He walked to mission specialist Pen Shouang's hibernation pod and activated it, then to guidance specialist Gabi Siegel and punched the emergency unlock, but at mission doctor Anders Larsson, he stopped cold. The man's hibernation pod was dark. The two other pods began the process of REAP'ing their inhabitants, sloppily regurgitating their occupants onto the aluminum floor. Rankin checked Larsson's chamber again and tried the terminal beside it. It was as dark as Larsson's pod.

"What's…happening?" The gasping words came between bouts of coughing and retching from Mission Specialist Pen Shouang. She staggered to her feet, her face and hair sodden with hibernation fluid. Eyes wide and white as she fought through her own panic.

"There's been some sort of radiation event," Rankin said, making sure to speak slowly and enunciate each word clearly. "And the ship seems dead. Not responding to voice commands."

"The habitation section is a self-contained system with its own power," Cuijpers called out. She pointed at a terminal next to Rankin, indicating it was active. "The rest of the ship's had a system failure. I don't know what it is yet or what caused it, but not everything is down."

"Check the status of Environmental Control and Life Support," Rankin said to Shouang. "I need to know how we stand structurally. And Larsson's chamber isn't functioning."

"At least we're still spinning," Gabi Siegel said as she dragged herself to her feet. She meant the simulated gravity of the rotating hab. She winced and put her hands over her ears. "Jesus, shut that noise off."

Rankin's mind circled around and around.

Whatever the emergency, they'd have to handle it themselves. Even if they could get in touch with someone Earth-side, at this distance, radio communications would have a five minute send-receive latency. Behind the noise of the siren, Rankin sensed an empty silence that loomed in the vast black beyond. The improbably thin walls of the spacecraft were all that separated him and his crew from the frigid vacuum of deep interplanetary space.

Forty million kilometers from Earth.

Or were they?

"Siegel, get over here and help me get guidance back up. I want to know if we've fired any engines since we've been out. And get some astrometrics; I want to know where the hell we are." He strode five paces over to help his diminutive guidance officer get her bearings. Barely five feet tall, she packed brains that far outsized her height. "And Shouang, get me the goddamn status of the ECLS."

"The airlock is sealed," Shouang replied from the entrance to the hibernation suite. "Atmospherics are all over the place. Looks like there's damage…a section lost pressure in aft, last before the solar panel array. Everything else is intact, or as intact as I can tell right now."

"We need to know if the hull is pressurized beyond this airlock." Rankin was stating the obvious, but better safe than sorry as their minds collectively swam awake. They needed to access the main quarters if they were going to do repairs.

"Were we hit by something?" Siegel asked as Rankin dragged her to another terminal Cuijpers had activated.

"Don't know yet."

Something had happened, but what? Why the depressurized hull? A massive radiation event at the same time as a meteoroid swarm? The odds of either were tiny by themselves, but both together? And why was Mars First offline?

A solar flare massive enough to induce thirty thousand nanoTeslas, they had to have a warning. There were half-a-dozen heliospheric monitoring satellites that Rankin knew of, but even then, a sudden solar storm might only give a few hours' notice. They must have been REAP'ed from deep sleep right as it hit. The Commander cursed whatever dweeb-pencil-pusher had convinced the powers that be to put everyone into hibernation sleep. They should have kept at least one crewmember awake at all times. A trade off so they could pack less life support and more fuel. They said the AI—Mars First's artificial intelligence—could more than cover for it. He'd argued against it until they threatened to replace him.

Now the AI was probably a fried wonton, but told-you-so was cold comfort in the depths of interplanetary space.

The siren cut off.

Sweet relief to Rankin's abused eardrums.

One small victory.

"Shouang and Cuijpers will verify integrity and get Mars First back online," Rankin said to Siegel. "But I need you to tell me where we are. If we're *where* we're supposed to be."

Rankin unsealed Larsson's hibernation pod while Siegel cursed and struggled with the terminal, trying to get some positional telemetry or data from the automated astrometrics.

Shouang called out from across the chamber: "I'm restarting ECLS. We'll scrub CO_2, but it may be hard to breathe for a minute as backup oxygen comes in."

"I'm bypassing telemetry and guidance over to you," Cuijpers said. "Everything except comms is offline. I need to manually reboot, maybe replace motherboards."

"How long will that take?" Rankin asked.

"Hours, maybe longer," Cuijpers replied, and then muttered: "And goddammit, I'm starving."

After REAP'ing, the nausea of waking was fast replaced by a ravenous hunger Rankin didn't have time to fix. They hadn't eaten in months, even if they had been in hibernation. They needed to get into the crew quarters, if just to eat some gel packs to stabilize their blood chemistry—otherwise they wouldn't be thinking clearly.

Assuming they were now.

Around them, the CO_2 scrubbers began to hum. The pressure shifted palpably as systems pumped oxygen in to replace it. Rankin felt it press against his eyes and temples.

He brought his hand away from Larsson's ice-cold skin. He swore softly under his breath. He'd opened the pod door and had his finger on the man's neck for a full thirty seconds. "Larsson's dead."

A sudden silence descended. Just the gentle hum of the fans.

"We're all dead," Gabi Siegel said quietly.

Rankin took two measured breaths before asking: "What does that mean?"

"Look at this." She pointed at her screen, then dragged the image onto a large display in the middle of the suite. "Telemetry from one of the Mars orbiters."

Rankin had been so focused on Earth, he hadn't even thought of the communications with the Mars orbiters. No humans were up there, not yet. Mars First was the vanguard of an effort to colonize the Red Planet. An advance mission had been sent eighteen months before, an automated supply run to make sure there were supplies and a working habitat before they arrived. There were two Mars orbiters as well, one from the ESA and one from NASA. Both well shielded.

"Look at the signal latency," Siegel pointed out. "We're nowhere near where we're supposed to be with respect to Mars. We're way off course." She frowned as she brought up another graphic, this one from the automated astrometric systems that checked star positions against the planets. "Jesus Christ…*Mars* isn't even where it's supposed to be."

"Bring up Earth's orbit," Rankin instructed.

A graphic detailing the orbital trajectories of the inner planets appeared on the main screen, with dotted lines plotting their future paths, and a bright red line for the trajectory of Mars First. "See what I mean, Mars isn't on the right orbital—"

"Look at Venus," Cuijpers said in a hushed voice.

Rankin pulled his attention from the deviation in Mars's orbit to try to find Venus—but nothing was there, or rather, where Venus *used* to be, a sharp angled line led out of the solar system at almost ninety degrees to the plane. "What…how…"

"That wasn't a solar storm," Siegel whispered. "It was some kind of massive gravitational event. Venus and Mercury were slingshot straight out of the inner system."

"What do you mean, a *gravitational* event?"

"What about Mars?" asked Cuijpers. "Can we still make it?"

"Siegel," Rankin demanded again. "What do you mean by gravitational event?"

She held her hands up. "Just give me a second." Her hands flew over the terminal, and on the main screen, data sheets and images dropped one on top of the other. "We can't make it. Even with a full main engine burn, we'd miss Mars by more than a hundred million kilometers." She snorted. "And even if we could get there, it's wandering off into deep space."

"Are you sure?"

"Check for yourself."

Rankin moved in front of the terminal. He wasn't an expert like Siegel, but they all doubled in their capacities. He'd studied astrophysics and was the backup pilot. He checked and rechecked, then slumped to sit on Larsson's dark pod.

This had always been something of a suicide mission. Five people on a one-way mission to Mars, to try to establish a vanguard. A colony. But that wasn't the whole plan. The idea was that re-supply missions would follow from Earth, that more people would come if they succeeded, and—just maybe—one day a triumphant return. Unlikely, but possible.

Now it wasn't.

Now they were doomed to drift into the infinite reaches of interplanetary space. There was no solution to arrive at Mars. He keyed in a desperate idea. Maybe a long return trajectory to Earth? The closest solution the system came back with was an intercept of forty-six years. The hibernation units were only designed to work for a year or two.

"Maybe Earth doesn't even exist anymore," Siegel said from over his shoulder.

She could see what he was doing. They could all see the trajectories he tried plotting on the main screen.

"Boss," Cuijpers said from the other side of the room. "I have a message in the system. Mars First logged it for us to watch before it went offline."

"From Earth?"

"Not exactly. It was pre-recorded."

"Who's it from then?"

Cuijpers exhaled long and slow. "It's a message from Ufuk Erdogmus."

Another alarm sounded, this one alerting of a hull depressurization.

"Play it," Siegel said.

Rankin held up his hands. "No. First things first."

If it was pre-recorded, then it could wait, Rankin decided. "We need to fly our ship before anything else, then we communicate second." These were the basic rules of piloting any ship, even if just flying a Cessna. "Get us stable, and get the Mars First systems online. It might be able to tell us more. Then we'll listen to Ufuk Erdogmus's message."

There was more to it than that, though. Rankin had a bad feeling about what might be on that message. He needed to get things stable before they opened the Pandora's box of whatever Ufuk had recorded. He had a bad feeling about it.

A very, very bad feeling.

1

Italian Alps
High above Sanctuary Europe

The canister waited for Massarra as she reached the red-shuttered alpine hut: a small silvery object in the snow, a red light flashing and shedding a crimson glow over gray ice. It was scarcely visible until she reached the final approach to the hut, itself hidden by the contours of the mountainside and now almost completely buried. On a long sign across a roof, blasted by unrelenting winds, read the words: "Refugio Sassal Mason." Beyond the hut stood the mountain itself, and beneath that towering massif, the complex of Sanctuary Europe.

It had taken her three blistering cold days to get here. One day trudging across the snow pack by herself to find a way to get a boat on the water, bobbing in the pancake slush a few hundred feet from shore, and then two days sailing north. As promised, the tiny blinking lights had appeared in the sky. Ufuk's drones. They guided her, fireflies against the churning black skies, and she'd followed them up the coast to somewhere near Genoa. She'd made it back to land, into a hangar, where a massive passenger drone had carried her up into the mountains under the cover of a storm.

It had been a rough trip.

At least the passenger drone was heated, and was stuffed full with artic survival gear.

It was almost pitch black, just a small patch of light from her headlamp, and the blinking light of the canister. She took off her gloves and stooped to retrieve the canister, then put the gloves back on and dug out the snow and ice from the front door, using a pack-shovel from the drone.

The hut's interior was every bit as cold as the frigid air outside. At ground level it had to be twenty below, but up here, two thousand meters in altitude, she was afraid to guess. She got to work and lit a fire in the stone inglenook, and located the supplies the hut's guardian had left for the next alpine season. She gobbled down food as she opened the canister.

Inside she found an access keycard with her image. It bore the Sanctuary Europe iconography, and a name that was not hers. It marked her as part of General Marshall's mercenary military, a fact that would give her greater access than any other legend.

More detail came on the tablet—maps and schematics. Once inside, there were pre-arranged ways to make contact with Ufuk, or those he trusted were it too difficult for him to meet. Places where marks could be left when she arrived and dead-letter boxes in which communications could be left. Sometimes, the old ways were still the most effective. She went upstairs to a hiding place in one of the rooms. She changed into the coal-black uniform of the San EU military police, and then packed quickly, allowing herself a few hours to sleep.

2

Sanctuary Europe
Prison Complex

It was Jess's third time forcibly confined in almost as many weeks—
first at *Castello Ruspoli* by Giovanni, and then on *Isola de Gigli*—and
she wasn't getting any more used it. At first she'd struggled, but
sensing the uselessness, of being buried underground without any
means of escape, she'd asked to speak with her lawyer. Then she
demanded to see Ufuk Erdogmus. Once she calmed down, the
black-clad men that escorted her to the detention center had been
polite, even gentle. They even read her her rights.

She was afraid.

But not afraid for herself.

She was afraid for Hector, and for Giovanni, and for Lucca
and Raffa. She'd dragged them all into this. The world would still
be wrecked by Nomad, but she was sure that if she hadn't appeared,
somehow, by now, Giovanni would have found a way to survive
and gotten Hector to the south. Now she'd buried them here with
her in a snake pit, and she wasn't sure this was a prison she'd be
able to fight her way out of.

It wasn't like any jail she'd ever seen—a thick, soft memory
foam mattress for a bed, a sink and shower, and a small table and
two chairs bolted to the floor. One wall was rough-hewn rock, but
the other wasn't metal bars, but a clear glass wall. Bright LED lights
shone overhead. She felt more like she was an exhibit in a zoo than
a prisoner. There was even a mini-bar stocked with bottles of water
and vacuum-packed sandwiches, though it lacked a corkscrew or
bottle opener or anything else sharp. She'd checked.

Michel Durand arrived about an hour later, to her intense
relief.

"You could have at least told me that Müller was out," Jess said before he even sat down at the table in her cell. "And on what grounds did they arrest me?"

"They didn't give me any warning," Durand admitted. "I told them you were a witness in an internal inquiry," Durand said. "But they had this…"

He pulled a tablet from his briefcase, clicked it on. At first just an audio recording: "I should have killed him when I had the chance." It was Jess's voice.

"That was in my apartment," Jess said, dumbfounded. "I was talking to Giovanni. I didn't mean…I mean, are they allowed to do that?"

"I did say that they would hear everything. I did say, yes? There were security concerns, given the nature of the allegations."

"Allegations?"

"That Müller has filed against you." Durand pressed play on the tablet again. This time it was a video of Jess, leaving Durand's office the day before, muttering, "*I need to get a gun,*" and then another video played, from a viewpoint high above Ufuk's gardens, with Jess clearly saying, "*If they let that bastard out, I'm going to kill him.*"

The video finished playing.

"This is somewhat for your own safety," Durand said after a pause to let Jess digest. "We'll get you out in a few hours, probably confined to quarters. Mr. Erdogmus has filed to take responsibility. And there's someone else here who would like to talk to you."

Jess was about to ask who, when a tall man in a blue military suit appeared on the other side of the cell's glass wall, flanked by two guards. "Miss Rollins," the man announced as one of the guards unlatched the magnetic lock. "I am General Marshall." He held out his hand.

She got up from sitting on the bed to shake his hand. "Wait, you're Abbie's father?"

"She's told me a lot about you." He smoothed back his crew cut gray hair with one hand. "I'll keep this short. You have a lot of friends in here. We're going to sort out this thing with Dr. Müller. We have to. Humanity is counting on us."

He said this without a hint of irony or humor.

Jess wasn't sure what to say, so just replied: "Thank you."

"No. Thank you." General Marshall seemed like he was almost going to salute her. "You are an example we should all wish to aspire to." He turned his head to address Durand. "I leave her in your care." He nodded, then nodded at the guards who opened the door again.

"Short but sweet," Jess said as he walked out of sight down the hallway.

"We'll get you out of here in a few hours," Durand said. "I promise."

He collected his briefcase.

And a few seconds later, he was gone too.

Jess lay back on the foam mattress. Ufuk was right. She needed friends.

The promised few hours stretched out interminably. Without a clock, it was impossible to tell the time. Jess yelled every now and then, demanded to see someone, banged against the thick glass wall, but there was no response. Just the hum of the air circulating, the low thrum of machinery somewhere deep below the rock. Eventually, the LED overhead lighting dimmed, and Jess's elation—at the prospect of being released—ebbed with it. Tired, she pulled blankets over herself and slept, and woke up only when the lights blinked back on.

She spent the day pacing in tight circles.

After a few hours she discovered that they'd left the charging cable for her leg, so she amused herself by plugging it in, then bouncing up and down on it for as long as she could until it depleted. Every now and then—for good measure—she yelled and screamed, more in frustration than imagining it would help.

The lights dimmed again.

This time sleep came more slowly.

They came for her in the middle of the night. Men in the coal-black uniforms of the San EU military, with gloved hands that seized her and shook her roughly awake, and bright light that flooded into the cell and blinded her. She tried to find her feet, tried to find a stable stance from which to fight, but instead found her legs kicked away as they bound her hands and pulled her out of the tiny room.

"What are you doing?" she screamed. "Where are you taking me?"

They dragged her down stairs. A stretch of stark gray corridor led to a single desk, behind which sat a man. Strip lighting buzzed and ticked. Exposed pipes ran along the ceiling and flooded the place with wet heat. Two more black-uniformed soldiers hovered in each corner behind him. Above one of them was a video camera.

They sat her roughly and secured the handcuffs to a bolt on the edge of the table.

"What is going on? Where is Michel Durand?"

"I would like you to watch something," the man said. He wore a dark blue suit and a signet ring on one hand. He was much older than her, with short silver hair, yet his face was lean and tanned. "I don't want you to speak until you've seen it. You and I will then have more than enough time to talk about what you're going to do next."

Jess couldn't place the man's accent. European, but where she couldn't say. His English was perfect. The screen illuminated and images appeared. She recognized the place—the terrace coffee shop she'd talked with Abbie. The fountain in the gardens still glistened in the diffuse light. Children skittered and played.

Then it was gone.

The image shook, and in place of the terrace and the gardens came a fleeting blur of brilliant white, followed by a seething, billowing flush of smoldering gray. Debris scattered.

Jess knew what she was watching.

"The bomb went off twenty-eight hours ago," the man said. "Emergency services are still sifting through the wreckage. At this time, we know fifteen people were killed, including three children."

Jess's heart jumped into her throat. Hector. But he wasn't one of the children she saw, was he? She would have recognized him. No. It wasn't him, but she didn't doubt this stern-faced man. Three children. "Who was responsible?"

"You should know that everything you say in here can be used as evidence against you."

For a moment, she didn't understand, then the implication came like a punch in the gut. "You think I did this?"

"You tell me."

"I've been locked up in here for two days. And I was a US Marine. I couldn't possibly kill a child."

"But you're no stranger to killing, Miss Rollins, are you?" He snorted. "And US Marines have never killed children?"

She didn't take the sarcasm bait. "I want to see Michel Durand."

The man turned the tablet to face her. "Do you know this woman?"

Jess found herself staring at the face of Massarra. She nodded. Had they found her? "She's an Israeli. She rescued me first in Rome, and then again from the Vivas facility near Rome, in Italy."

"Rescued you twice? So you're friends?"

Jess sensed thin ice. "I wouldn't say friends. It was a desperate time."

"Why did she rescue you?" He paused before adding: "Twice."

64

Jess didn't know how much to reveal, how much of what she could say might incriminate her further in their eyes. "She worked for an organization that had an interest in my father's work."

"Your father was Dr. Ben Rollins. Is that correct?"

She knew enough of interrogations to be careful with stupid questions. "You already know that. He and Dr. Müller worked together."

"What organization did Massarra Mizrahi work for?"

"She called it the Levantine Council."

"Had you ever heard of it before?"

She shook her head and shrugged.

"Are you aware it has links to Hezbollah? To Daesh?"

He was so calm, so placid. As though he were cross-examining her about a visit to a summer fair rather than links to the world's most extreme and violent terrorists.

"She said it wasn't terrorist. That they were a peaceful organization."

"Did she ever display a particular skill set in the time you spent with her?"

"What do you mean?"

"Could she fight? Shoot?"

"I don't see what—"

"Did she ever kill anyone?"

The question caught her off guard. "We were forced to defend ourselves."

"Is that a yes, Miss Rollins?"

Hesitation, then: "Yes."

Another image appeared on the screen. This time it was Ufuk Erdogmus. "Do you know this man?"

"Of course I do."

"His name please."

"Don't be ridiculous—"

"Do you refuse to answer the question, Miss Rollins?"

"It's Ufuk Erdogmus."

"And you know Mr. Erdogmus, don't you?"

"Only recently. He's the one that rescued me from Müller."

"You have a robotic prosthetic, Miss Rollins, is that right?" More images appeared on the screen, from her surgical procedure, from inside his laboratory. "Who provided that for you?"

"Ufuk Erdogmus."

"Do you have any idea the cost of this leg?"

She shrugged again. She had literally no idea.

"Seems a very big gift from someone you barely know."

"What do you want?"

The man got up and began pacing. "Mr. Erdogmus is missing. He cannot be found anywhere within Sanctuary Europe. Do you have knowledge of his whereabouts?"

"I've no idea. I didn't even know he was missing."

"Of course not." He sat again in front of her. "Tell me about the Vivas facility outside Rome. You're aware it was destroyed?"

"I was there. You know that."

"Were you also aware that it was Mr. Erdogmus's drones that were responsible for the attack on that facility?"

She didn't respond.

"Did you plan that with Erdogmus? Was it your intention to ensure Dr. Müller was present when the attack took place?"

"If that were the case, it was pretty badly planned. I almost got killed."

"I'd like to ask you about the coffee shop. You've been there several times?"

She shook her head. "I'm not answering any more of your questions. I want to see Michel Durand before I say anything else."

"Why were you talking with General Marshall's daughter at the coffee shop?"

"I'm not saying anything else to you. You may as well take me back to my cell."

"You would be wise to cooperate, Miss Rollins."

She didn't reply.

For the next two hours, they raked her over the same ground but in more detail. In her head she was back at Pickel Meadows in the Sierra Nevada, undergoing the survival and resistance training she'd had in the Marines. Back then she had envisaged the Taliban sitting across the table from her. She had never imagined it might one day end up being something like this, that she might be the one accused of terrorism. In her mind she recited the six articles of the Military Code of Conduct over and over, reminding herself who she had once been and who she might now need to be again.

3

Sanctuary Europe

Massarra arrived two hours early and studied everyone who came and went, taking note of recurring faces and those who seemed to idle without purpose for too long. The message she found in the dead-letter box, in fact nothing more than a tiny plastic pouch taped behind some exposed high joists in one of the quieter sectors of the complex, gave a location, a time, and a simple description.

When she'd first climbed down through the secret access tunnel and into Ufuk's private gardens, the shock and awe left her dumbfounded for a moment. The green trees. Blue skies. Birds singing. She'd almost let her guard down, but she was too well trained.

The place was crawling with security. Locked down. Drones buzzing everywhere overhead. She knew they were looking for her, but she came anyway. They wouldn't dream she'd hide right under their noses; this was one way of staying hidden. Ufuk had also provided her with a synthetic-skin mask for over her face. She doubted it would stand up to direct scrutiny, but then she also had on a baseball cap and wore the San EU military police uniform. Nobody would be looking too closely at her, and she didn't need that much time.

When the man she was meeting finally did arrive, identified by the clothes the message had indicated he would be wearing, he took a seat toward the edge of the park. She surveyed the scene, watching for familiar faces. Only when she was ready did she sit on the bench, some way from the man. In her breast pocket, she clicked on an electronic jammer.

"You're late," he said quietly.

She stared straight ahead.

68

"My name is Michel Durand," the man said. "I am a prosecutor with the Office of Judicial Affairs. Dr. Müller's case was mine to prosecute. I'm not sure…"

"You're doing the right thing," Massarra whispered, her lips barely moving.

"I understand what I am doing, and its necessity. I also understand the stakes."

"Where is she now? In the cell block?"

Durand nodded.

"You know her exact location? Right now?"

The man nodded again.

"Is she being treated well?"

"I don't know."

"Have you seen her? How fit is she?"

"They're feeding her, if that's what you mean."

"Did she appear tired? Fatigued, physically I mean?"

"More angry than anything else."

"Anger is good."

Durand shifted in his seat as though he had been waiting for a moment to arrive and had made a decision to seize it. "What is your intention?"

"For now, information gathering. Later, we may have to be active."

"Active?"

"We'll discuss it when the time comes."

"What happens now?"

At first, Jess thought she was dreaming. Her cot shuddered. She opened her eyes to darkness, and after a few minutes drifted back to sleep. A second growling spasm shook her awake again. She wasn't sure how much later. The cot, the walls, the air around her—everything quivered. This time she heard it too.

Not a dream.

Another explosion reverberated deep in the rock.

"What's happening?" she shouted, not knowing if anyone could hear her. The only light was a gray reflection from down the hallway. "Hey! What's going on?"

No one answered. A chill swept through her. Had she been abandoned? The dull thud of another distant blast shook the Perspex glass, and the ground kicked through her feet. Dust billowed from the rock walls.

She screamed in frustration.

Then she stopped.

Silence for a few seconds. And then a few minutes. Her heartbeat hammered in her chest in an almost deafening silence. What was that? A meteor strike? Her breathing returned to normal after a few more minutes. It must have been something outside. At least they were covered by hundreds of feet of granite.

Another juddering detonation.

Closer.

Close enough to feel a compression wave in the air against her skin, even in this sealed area. Not outside. That was from *inside*. She scanned her cell in the semi-darkness. Could she rip one of the chairs from the bolts that held them down? Bash it against the glass? No way she could rip them out, and not a chance she could damage the Perspex. It looked like it could withstand a rocket-propelled grenade attack. Maybe crawl out the air vent? It wasn't more than four inches square. She was trapped.

"Get me out of here!" she screamed.

There wasn't just silence between the blasts anymore. Muffled screams, and then closer, angry words in the hallways beyond her chamber. A gunshot, then another, followed by the staccato burst of an automatic weapon. The overhead lights blinked on, and Jess had to squint in the sudden brightness. She heard the hallway door to the cellblock open, and she frantically glanced around for anything to defend herself with. The only thing she could find was the charging cable for her leg.

Stupid, but she didn't have anything else.

Her fists balled, she steadied herself behind the metal table, expecting a black-clad execution squad, but instead watched in amazement as Michel Durand's wiry frame limped, still in suit and tie, in front of the Perspex.

Ballie Booker followed behind him, holding a pistol.

"What's happening?" she yelled through the glass, still crouched behind the table.

"We have to hurry." Michel's voice was thready and weak. He clicked the keypad on the wall across from Jess, and the magnetic lock opened on her cell door. "Explosions all over the complex. Several sections have collapsed."

Jess sprinted to the door to join them. "How do we get out?"

"There's a...there's..." Michel grimaced.

A red stain spread across his midsection.

Ballie put one arm around Michel to support him. "Keep moving," he yelled at Jess.

Another explosion, this time even closer.

Jess flung open the hallway door. Two black-clad San EU military lay on the floor of the cellblock security entrance. The air smelled of cordite. Three people stood by the hallway leading out, one of them half the size of the other two. Hector ran straight at Jess, and she bundled him into her arms. Giovanni turned, his face grim, and pressed her forward.

It took Jess a second to recognize the slender person holding the M4.

Massarra.

What the hell was she doing here? But there was no time for that. Jess turned to help Michel through the door, but was pushed away.

"Get going," urged Ballie.

"Don't let Müller get away with it," Michel wheezed.

"With what?"

"Framing you. Your family. Everything he did."

"Is he doing this? These bombs?"

Michel shrugged weakly. "I don't know. My daughter…" He sighed. "She would have been just your age…"

Another blast, this one close enough to almost knock Jess from her feet. Debris whooshed down the hallway Massarra guarded.

"Go!" Michel wheezed.

Still with Hector in her arms, Jess ran hard. She followed Massarra and Giovanni. Left and right, up through stairwells. Massarra knew exactly where she was going. They passed people in suits, running in random directions through the halls, and even past groups of black-clad San EU military police. Nobody paid them any attention. The air was filled with dust, and the distant sound of thudding. It had to be collapsing rock. Hector clung tight to Jess, and her arms burned with the effort of holding him tight.

They finally reached the main chamber. No more simulated blue sky. Just a gaping black emptiness hundreds of feet overhead. White floodlights lit smoldering ash swirling into the air. She followed Massarra and Giovanni to the left, still with no idea where they were going. She looked on in horror as a vast section of the ceiling trembled and fell. It seemed to move slowly, time stretching as it pitched downward.

"Jessica!" someone screamed.

A slight figure loomed from the smoke.

It took Jess a moment before she realized who it was. "Abbie? What are you doing?"

"Thank God you got out," the teenager replied, closing the last few feet. "Come with me. My dad has a transport that can take us out of the south tunnel. He's on your side." She held out her hand. "We have to hurry."

Massarra and Giovanni noticed that she'd stopped. They doubled back. Both of them screamed at her, but Jess stood still.

"We're going to beat Müller, Jess. Come with me," Abbie urged.

"Do not trust her." Massarra lifted her M4.

"Put that down." Jess used her left hand to point the muzzle of the weapon away.

"I know you," Abbie said to Massarra. The girl's eyes went wide with recognition. "You're the terrorist that destroyed the Vivas facility." She paused. "Wait, did you…is this you that did this?" She pointed at the clouds of smoke.

"What are you doing here?" Jess asked again.

"I came to save you."

"Do not trust her," Massarra repeated.

"Me?" Abbie looked nervously at Massarra. "Are you kidding? Jess, you have to get away from this woman."

Another massive explosion, this one on the other side of the complex, not more than five hundred feet away. An angry orange fireball billowed up, followed by a concussive shockwave and blast of heat. Screams. And the whine of gunfire. Bullets ricocheted off the glass office walls behind them. Four San EU military police had finally recognized them and stood fifty feet away in the haze. By now, Ballie and Michel had caught up. Massarra laid down a purring buzz of automatic fire from the M4 and the police scattered into the smoke.

"Please, come with me," Abbie pleaded.

Jess looked at Massarra, then said: "Abbie, get out of here."

No time to debate. More gunshots echoed.

"We'll hold them off," Ballie said. "Get going." He fired his pistol. Michel slumped to the floor beside him.

Jess shoved Abbie, watched her start to jog away from them, still glancing over her shoulder to see if Jess might change her mind. Massarra gave Jess a nod, her expression impassive, raised a hand to her eyes and covered them. For a moment, Jess didn't understand, then Massarra took a small canister from her belt. Jess hunkered down with Hector to protect the boy. Jammed her eyes shut.

She didn't see Massarra throw the flash-bang grenade, but when it went off, the reverberations convulsed savagely through her jaw and temples and into her chest. The air resonated against her skin, the noise drilled through her temples and into her brain. Nausea rose in her throat. Jess staggered to her feet. The San EU military she'd seen were specialists, probably trained to the worst of the effects of the flashbang. They might not have more than a few seconds' advantage.

Massarra sprinted ahead, and Jess followed with Giovanni.

A second later and a terrible, groaning cracking filled the air. A hundred feet behind them, the complex's rock wall collapsed in slow motion, right where Ballie Booker and Michel Durand had been. Jess lost a step, but realizing it was futile, she turned to run as fast as she could, sensing the thousands of tons of granite pressing down overhead. Debris scattered. Exhaustion burned her leg muscles, but her left robotic prosthetic bounded her forward, and adrenaline lifted her, kept her moving and alert, barely ahead of the confusion and fear that threatened to overcome her.

She fought back against her emotions; told herself to focus.

"Are you hurt?" Massarra shouted as she stopped at a corner.

"I'm fine. Keep moving."

Another explosion rocked the complex and behind them came the thunderous roar of more of the ceiling collapsing. Flames licked up the sides of the rock walls through the smoke. Massarra took a left turn into a tunnel lit with an amber light. Smoke billowed everywhere and she kept low, crouched as best she could beneath it. The stifling heat intensified.

"What is going on, Massarra?" Jess struggled through violent coughing.

The Israeli didn't answer but just kept moving forward, her M4 sweeping back and forth. Behind them, the clouds of dust and smoke roiled up the hallway. More screaming. The corridor ended in a smooth rock wall. Massarra took a keycard from her pocket and waved against the metal wall to their right.

The rock wall slid away.

An elevator door opened behind it.

Jess put Hector down. Massarra and Giovanni stepped inside the elevator, but Jess held back. She turned to squint into the smoke behind them in the corridor.

"They're gone," Giovanni said softly. "No way Ballie wasn't crushed by that collapse."

More screaming and thudding detonations.

"I should go and check…he saved your life, Giovanni."

"We have to go."

She hesitated, but then closed her eyes and stepped backward into the elevator.

Her heart sank as the lift accelerated up. The noise of the destruction below receded into the high-pitched whine as the carriage gained velocity. This wasn't any regular elevator. Jess's ears popped as they gained altitude.

She turned and grabbed the muzzle of Massarra's M4, pulled it from her hands. "Now what are you doing here? And what have you done?"

"Ufuk Erdogmus sent me to get you."

"How did you get to him?"

Massarra's face remained impassive. "I didn't. He was the one who got to me."

Jess breathed in short shallow gulps. "Wait. You know him?"

"For a long time."

"Just how *long* is a long time?"

4

Hong Kong
Five years before Nomad

A damask sun had already washed away what was left of the daylight and given way to Hong Kong's garish nighttime carnival. A glistening sheen of color reflected off the black water lapping against the hull as the Twinkling Star ferry began its preparations for the short journey across Victoria Harbor toward Kowloon. The engine's growl cut through the late evening clamor as ropes cast off from the pier. Despite the hour, or perhaps because of it, the Twinkling Star teemed with excited faces.

The lumbering vessel slowly edged away, pitching gently as the partygoers leaned over the railings. Massarra gazed downward. She followed vivid smears of light as they danced across dark waves.

She waited.

There were two of them aboard, watching Ufuk Erdogmus: a man and a woman. It was always possible there were more she couldn't see. They'd waited in line a little way back from the target of their surveillance, apparently deep in conversation, yet more likely murmuring updates to the rest of their watching team.

As Ufuk boarded, and made his way casually with the crowd to the front of the vessel where she was standing. The man and the woman hung back as their tradecraft demanded.

Soon Massarra was surrounded, jostled slightly by the Twinkling Star's exuberant visitors, but also hidden by them. Ufuk didn't look at her, but instead stood slightly behind her and studied the landscape of Kowloon.

"You're being followed," she said without turning to him. "Don't look. Turn your back to me. Take out your phone and take some pictures."

Ufuk did as he was told. She noticed he had become tense. As he captured the blazing lights of the skyline behind them, he asked quietly, "Who is following me?"

"Difficult to say. The Ministry of State Security is the most likely candidate, but the nature of your meetings here might also have attracted the interest of other organizations concerned with the protection of state secrets. Either way, it makes our meeting somewhat challenging."

"I was surprised at your request to meet in person. Especially here."

"It was deemed necessary."

"I am not accustomed to being kept in the dark. I contribute a great deal of money to your organization. I expect to be treated with courtesy."

"We are grateful for your contributions, and for your continued work toward our mutual goal. Hence this meeting. We felt this conversation would be more appropriate in person. However, not here."

"Where then?"

"Spend an hour or two in Kowloon. Perhaps have a drink and something to eat. Then return to your hotel. There are cameras and listening devices in your room, so we cannot meet there. You will order room service and we will do the rest. Wear a suit with a white shirt and brightly colored tie."

"What will you do?"

"Not here. Now, walk away. Spend the rest of the crossing at the other end of the ferry. If you manage to identify your tail while you are in Kowloon, do not attempt to lose it. As long as they think they have the advantage, we are safe."

"What about you?"

"They may follow me for a little while, perhaps run my face through their systems. They will find nothing."

Massarra could have followed Ufuk into Kowloon and ensured he didn't lose his Ministry of State Security watchers. That had been her plan before she arrived. However, events had overtaken her, even surprised her.

Within a few hours of landing in Hong Kong, Massarra had discovered she was herself being followed. Fortunately, it had not been the Chinese. She had been conducting delicate, barely observable surveillance measures. Had she not been looking for the signs, the product of long habit and the secret fear that stalks every professional, she might easily have missed them.

The perpetrators were both subtle, and expert.

She gave no sign she had noticed their surveillance, but informed the rest of her team the moment they arrived at their hotel. They complained about their room, too close to others who were noisy was the claim, and were immediately switched to another room of their choosing. Even still, they swept that new room for any sign of electronic surveillance and left countermeasures of their own to prevent further intrusion.

Instead, over the day of preparation required before Ufuk Erdogmus arrived in Hong Kong, Massarra had adopted an approach that allowed her to capture as many of them on film as she could without alerting them to her realization. However, even with that work, at no stage was she able to identify who they were.

So, instead of following Ufuk into Kowloon, she took a second Star ferry back to Central and tried again to learn a little more about those who seemed to have an interest in her own movements. However, she found nothing.

This filled her with concern.

It was not the first time an operation run by the Council had been subject to scrutiny by professionals with impeccable tradecraft. The process of rooting out who it was, and how far the incursion went, would need to begin immediately on her return to Israel.

A knock came at the door, accompanied by the announcement of room service. Massarra heard this because the data fed to the laptop conveyed audio as well as visual images from the cameras placed by the Chinese in Ufuk's suite.

Massarra clenched her fists as she watched, but forced herself to relax. Beside her another man, an Egyptian named Ammon, the second member of her small team, watched on another laptop, scrutinizing yet more cameras. These had been placed by her, rather than the Chinese, and offered views of the corridor to their own room.

In the grainy video, Ufuk went to the door and opened it. A man his own height and build, for Erdogmus was unusually tall and slender for a Turk, and whose hair was styled precisely to match his, stood behind a tray laden with food and a bottle of champagne accompanied by a single glass.

Ufuk seemed to hesitate and the man, a Syrian named Burhan who was chosen because his physical appearance approximated that of Erdogmus, improvised: "May I come in, sir?"

Massarra watched Ufuk nod and step aside. The man took the trolley to where the suite led into the bedroom as they had agreed. The only place in the Four Seasons Deluxe Suite the carefully placed Chinese cameras couldn't serve. "Shall I leave it here, sir?"

From the doorway, Ufuk nodded.

Although she could no longer see, she knew what actions would accompany the words she heard. The offering of a pen and the words: "I must ask you to sign for it, sir." The lifting of a finger to the lips, a gesture of silence and complicity as the man began to take off his waistcoat. All carefully choreographed in advance.

79

Ufuk approached him until he disappeared from view. The man would be removing Ufuk's jacket and tie, and handing him his own tie and waistcoat. He would silently urge Ufuk to put them on, as he looped the garish tie Ufuk had been told to wear around his neck and donned the jacket.

"Would you like me to open the champagne for you, sir?"

"Yes, please."

Then came the folded slip of paper and the accompanying gesture for Ufuk to open it, as the man began the process of opening the champagne. The sound of the cork popping.

Ufuk would now be reading the words on the paper, instructions to take the trolley to the lift where he would be met, to keep his head low and avoid looking anywhere but at the trolley.

"Thank you, sir. Will that be all?"

"Yes. Thank you."

"Do have a pleasant evening, sir."

Massarra stood and left their room. She went to the elevator and called it, selecting the floor on which the Deluxe Suite could be found when it arrived.

When the doors opened, Ufuk was there waiting for her. She gestured for him to come inside and again indicted he should be silent.

They rode the elevator down a single floor and she led him to their room. Ammon looked up as they entered, then went back to working on the laptop.

"Who is he?" Ufuk asked.

"He works with me. As does the man who is currently sitting in your suite."

"Do you really think this will work?"

"We've been planning this. We know where their surveillance is and what it covers."

"How could you know?"

"Better you don't know our methods, Mr. Erdogmus. You need to be as clean as possible when the time comes and we don't have a great deal of time. Our man can only sit in one place for so

80

long. In a little while, he'll order another bottle of champagne and you will need to deliver it." She gestured to the bed where a bottle of champagne and another glass lay waiting. "Listen carefully. There is a serious leak in your organization. Someone is passing information on a number of your more sensitive projects to a third party."

"That's not possible. I have internal security regularly checking—"

She cut him off. "Not only is it possible, it has happened." She handed him a small flash drive. "This is only some of what we know has been leaked."

"Where did you get this?"

"You are important to our organization, Mr. Erdogmus. We protect those who are important to us."

"What do you want me to do?"

"Show this to no one. As yet, we do not know to whom this information is being passed, or what precisely their interest is. We will continue to look into it. However, you will shortly begin interviews for a new secretarial assistant in one of your robotics projects in Bern. This woman will apply and you will ensure she is appointed. We will do the rest. Her details are also on the drive. Once you have viewed it, destroy it."

"You think it's the Chinese?"

"They're keen for your collaboration with their Space Administration to continue. Placing you under surveillance is standard, to see if your contracts with China Aerospace Corporation are the principal reason you are here."

"Who else could it be?"

"Americans. You are breaching their anti-terrorism laws by exporting classified weapons technology—"

"That I invented."

"But unfortunately, you did not also invent the laws to protect yourself at the same time. That is why you need me."

"So you think it's the Americans?"

"Whoever it is, they're effective in concealing themselves." Massarra straightened his tie. It was a gesture of reassurance. "Now go. Conduct your business as you would on any other occasion. We will be in touch again."

"My own security—"

"Must never know. No one can ever know. Is that understood? Let us do our work, and we will protect you."

5

Italian Alps

Jess stumbled out of the tunnel and into savage cold. Massarra had given them all LED headlamps as the elevator stopped and they exited into a rock corridor. It was almost pitch black outside. Murky tendrils of ochre ash and snow eddied and fell in the conical beams of their lights. Beneath her feet, a pristine veneer of glistening ice. Yet through the sharpened senses of an adrenaline-infused haze, glimpses of the landscape through the swirling mist summoned memories: long hours she had spent on skis in these massifs, and climbing waterfalls of ice, or bare rock.

If for a moment she almost forgot where she stood, what events unfolded around her, when the vicious wind lashed her face, the illusion was swept away. Hector clung tight to her side, terrified at being in this cold again. Crouching in the snow and gazing downward through the eddying cloud, she glimpsed silhouetted shapes. Giovanni stumbled through the snow to take her in his arms.

But Raffa stood alone in the snow.

"Where's Lucca?"

"He didn't make it out," Giovanni said as quietly as he could.

Massarra crouched in the snow. Beside her in the glistening ochre powder sat rucksacks and rope, and tools for climbing and trekking in snow. Ufuk handed Jess a down jacket. She shrugged it on.

Through the churning atmosphere she could just make out, in the valley below, tiny specks of dancing light that spilled from torches held in frantic, frozen hands. The survivors from Sanctuary funneling out of what had to be the south tunnel Abbie had described. A clutch of buildings poked through the canopy of ice below. All of it lit by floodlights.

Even from high on the slopes of the mountain, perhaps a mile away, she sensed their confusion and fear, these wealthy elite who had paid everything they had, or gathered and manipulated political favor, in order to be protected from the end of the world. Yet here they now were, thrown into a struggle to survive in the harshest possible landscape, utterly unequipped to deal with what lay ahead of them. The end of their world.

"What just happened?" Jess demanded.

"I couldn't have predicted what Müller would do," Ufuk said. "I knew he would do something, but this…" He gestured to the mountain behind them and shook his head. Somewhere behind his voice, above the angry wind, in the cold, ever-shifting air, came the vibrating hum of far off engines.

"You're saying Müller destroyed his own base of operations?"

"I'm just guessing."

"Why would he do that? Nobody was going to prosecute him. I was the one in jail."

"I don't know—"

"How many people were in there?"

"Five thousand, give or take."

Jess peered into the distance, down the mountain. Maybe a few hundred people seemed to be scrambling around. "My God…"

"We think Lucca made it out," Ufuk added. "I saw him with another group running along the main artery route toward the funicular carriages."

She looked Ufuk in the eye, held his gaze as her teeth chattered. "Did you do this? Why did you disappear two days ago? You left me."

"I didn't leave you. We don't have time to discuss this." He turned to Massarra. "We should leave for the refuge now."

The Israeli nodded. She gazed at the crowds below. "We will freeze if we don't move."

"How are we getting off the mountain?" Jess demanded. She hoped they had a plan. Massarra was right. They'd freeze to death inside an hour.

Already Jess felt her internal body temperature falling. Her hands, even inside the gloves, were numb. At least twenty below, maybe colder. Even in good weather, with sunlight, it was a full day hike from this altitude. In this ice and snow, with just the light of their headlamps, it would be a march into death.

"I'll explain more when we get to the refuge." Ufuk pushed her forward. "Müller will be searching for us. We need to get out of the open."

"What about Roger?" she said. "Did he make it out?"

"We have no idea."

Jess observed the manner in which Massarra and Ufuk spoke to each other. A professional relationship existed between them, one in which Massarra was respectful, as though he was her superior, but also where Ufuk placed his trust in someone with skills he required. How had they met? What connected them, and how might that connection shed some light on Ufuk's motives?

Jess's mind switched into operational mode. "Get the crampons on, and we should rope up."

The whine of drone engines crept over the sound of the wind. Similar to the sound of the Predator drones US forces had deployed in Afghanistan.

"I suggest two rope teams." Massarra handed her a duffel bag. "You lead one, I'll lead the other. Agreed?" She gave no indication if she heard the drones, but Massarra must have caught the tightness in her face because she asked: "Are you all right?"

Jess didn't know what to say. How much didn't she know? "When we get down off the mountain, we'll get some distance between us and Sanctuary, but the second we get some time, I need answers."

"We should get moving," was all Massarra replied.

Jess helped Raffa and Hector put on their crampons, making adjustments to ensure the fit was good. She tied them into harnesses and gave Hector gentle words of encouragement, telling him to keep the soles of his crampons flat to the mountain, even where it sloped acutely and it might have seemed unnatural to match the angle.

Massarra led the first rope team with Ufuk and Raffa. Jess followed with Giovanni and Hector. They followed the tight edge of a cornice, staying close to the ridge. She led them slowly, adjusting her own rhythm to theirs. Where once there might have been a trail tracking the edge of the mountain, there were only layered drifts veneered by puce, volcanic residue. Somewhere from the east came a growl that resonated above the wind. A vivid amber flash lit the clouds. The snow beneath her feet shimmered.

Massarra urged them onward.

Jess's crampons bit comfortingly into snow at first, but then into a layer of névé beneath. The ash made the snow shift in layers as it settled. There would be slick, lethal passages as both rope teams made their way down. If one of them fell, would the rest react fast enough to hold them?

Her fingers tightened around the grips of her ice axes, but she pressed on. She barely heard the yell above the roar of the wind, but she did hear Giovanni's shout from right behind her. She turned instantly and began to move backward.

"Kneel down," she shouted. "Stabilize yourselves with your axes and wait for me. Don't move!"

She uncoiled the rope around her body to give herself room to move and clambered along the ridge. Another scream, followed by shouts. She tracked her way across toward them. Two huddled shapes, both looking down. Massarra had already squatted a belay in the snow, legs splayed outward and boots dug deep. From her waist, the rope was taut and angled down over a cornice.

"How far?" she asked the Israeli.

"Maybe ten meters."

Jess untied herself from her own rope and took Massarra's discarded axes. She drove one into the snow behind her and used a long sling to tie an ice-axe belay around Massarra's harness. She wound a carabiner sling around the second axe then drove into the snow as far as it would go. She ran a new length of rope through the carabiner.

"Put your foot next to the axe on top of the sling," she said to Massarra. "Brace yourself with the other foot. Understand?"

The air trembled with the whine of the approaching drones, circling in sweeping surveillance. The only thing masking their body heat was the bitter wind and spindrift that encircled them.

Jess forced herself to focus. "If I fall, it will go tight, but you'll be able to hold it. Don't feed it through; I don't need that. Just hold a fall."

Massarra nodded.

Jess climbed down. She did so quickly, concerned Ufuk might be injured. When she reached him, she dug in as tightly as the terrain would allow while the wind tried to wrench her from the mountain's face.

"Are you hurt?"

"I think my ankle is twisted."

"You've lost your axe?"

Ufuk nodded.

"It's okay—you can use one of mine. But you need to do something a little different, okay? You need to dig the front two points into the snow as far as you can. Kick really hard and climb as though you're climbing a ladder. Massarra has hold of you and she's anchored into the snow."

Ufuk nodded.

"If your ankle is bad, only use it to stabilize yourself as you climb. Small steps and take it slow as you need. It's only ten meters."

Their progress seemed impossibly slow, the wind buffeting both of them as they climbed. Eventually she reached the ledge where Giovanni helped them up. Using an axe as a support, her other arm thrown around Giovanni's shoulders, they struggled slowly down the mountain from there, hunkered low against the howling wind.

Relief flooded Jess when Massarra shouted and pointed downward along a wide, open sea of sastrugi, to what might have been a building. Jess could barely make it out, but as they walked, they came to a red-shuttered alpine hut almost completely buried by snow. On a long sign Jess saw words that read "Refugio Sassal Masone."

6

Italian Alps
Sassal Massone

Above the whistling of the wind, Jess heard a low rumble. At first she thought it might be a drone, swooping in to better pick up the radiation of heat from their bodies. Through the mist came a flickering light, but it wasn't a drone—it was a snowcat, a quad-tracked vehicle with a large white-and-gray camouflage painted cab she glimpsed through the maelstrom.

Someone found us, her mind screamed in panic—but was this a good or a bad thing? Better to err on the side of caution, she decided immediately, and she turned to her rope team. She shouted to find cover, to find somewhere to hide so she could investigate.

The vehicle swiftly closed the distance between them.

Ufuk, his face hidden behind his fur-lined hood and goggles, interrupted her. He reached for her with one hand and tore his goggles away with the other. "It's okay," he said, leaning in to be heard above the wind. "These are my people."

"*Your* people?"

Ufuk nodded, and led them toward the refuge as the snowcat churned through the mist. Light flooded over them, catching twinkling crystals in its bright beams. The broad rectangular cab appeared, the front section with four windows, each with wipers furiously going back and forth. Military men sat inside. The cab sat on four tracks that clawed their way easily over the snow toward them. Ufuk waved toward the hut as the snowcat swept past them and came to a jolting halt just beyond. The men filtered out and into the snow, weapons out, providing a defensive perimeter.

"They're my security contractors," Ufuk said as they entered the hut past him. "They have an egress plan for us." He removed his gloves and hood, and dropped the goggles onto a table. "There is food and water, and medical supplies if we need them. But we need to be quick." He took Jess's arm as she passed him. "I think you saved my life back there."

Jess paused, but shrugged off his hand and entered without replying.

She needed answers, but was too frozen and exhausted right now.

The hut was warmer than she expected. Beyond the entrance hall, where boots and climbing equipment were normally stored, was a low, wide common room. Books still lay on dusty shelves and alpine paintings still hung on the walls. Somehow they made the place feel even more desolate. A reminder of the old world that could never be again. There were long tables and chairs and, for a moment, Jess remembered time spent in similar huts, sharing stories with other alpinists over hot soup and warm bread. But that time was long gone.

From a room toward the back of the hut came a tall man clothed in white, arctic warfare battle dress. A radio on his armored chest hissed gently, but no voices came from it. He reached Ufuk and extended a hand, which Ufuk took. Behind him, a second man stood, similarly dressed.

"Where is the rest of the team?" Ufuk asked.

"Patrolling. They'll be back in an hour. We need to secure this flank of the mountain and the terrain down to Alp Grüm."

"We need to leave."

"There's still drone activity overhead. Recon will call us when the time is right. Sit back and relax. It'll be a little while."

"The longer we wait here—"

"This is what you pay us for, Mr. Erdogmus."

"Why would someone be searching for us?" Jess asked. She'd warmed up enough to ask questions. "Why the drones? Why are these men here?" It seemed much too convenient that Ufuk would have mercenaries ready on a second's notice. He still hadn't said why he'd disappeared from Sanctuary two days before. Had he been planning all this?

"I will answer all your questions, to the best of my ability, once we're on the way," Ufuk replied.

"And where are we going? Is there another Sanctuary?"

"The only other one I know of is in China."

"A Vivas installation then? Something like that?"

"Something like that."

"Why the hell are you being evasive?"

"Jess, we need to rest," Giovanni said, taking her arm. "Everyone is exhausted. We should eat too. And I need to go to the bathroom."

Ufuk pointed helpfully at a stairwell leading down.

The door opened again and Massarra walked through, a billowing chaos of snow and ash sweeping in with her. She pulled down her hood and shook her hair. Ufuk's man tensed.

"You good?" Jess said. Despite her reservations, she couldn't help her sense of camaraderie with Massarra.

The Israeli nodded as she laid her backpack on the table. "A little cold," she said, and attempted a convivial smile.

She hadn't answered Jess's questions about how she knew Erdogmus. Just some vague things about Ufuk being involved in the Levantine Council. The same people that had dragged Jess and her family into the whole mess that had gotten them killed. Half of the people in Sanctuary she'd met had blamed the attack and destruction of the Vivas installation on Ufuk's drones. And now it appeared he had his own mercenary army. They were standing right here now.

Just what was going on?

But there was no denying that Massarra had just saved her life. Again.

The woman, however, wouldn't look Jess in the eye, and instead turned away and continued to unpack her backpack. "I'm very happy to see you, Jessica. Truly."

"Is this your contact, Mr. Erdogmus?" Ufuk's man continued to study Massarra.

"That's right."

"I have the radio equipment you requested."

"Müller will be monitoring communications."

"It's digital. Encrypted," replied the man. "Unbreakable."

"Nothing is unbreakable, and at this distance, they could still triangulate the position from signal strength. Even just the *fact* of an unknown encrypted signal going out would alert them to something. Right now we have the advantage of stealth. I want to keep it that way."

Giovanni reappeared from the stairwell. "The door to the toilet is jammed shut. I won't be long." He headed for the door.

"One of my people will accompany you, sir," Ufuk's man said. "We need you to stay close to the building. Keep you covert, understood? The drone patrols use infrared and thermal imaging."

"I can urinate alone."

"I'm sure you can, sir." He gestured to the second man who followed Giovanni outside.

Jess shivered. A small fire blazed in the inglenook, but the room was large and still quite cold. She walked over in an attempt to warm herself. At least it sheltered them from the savage wind. Better to be in here than outside in the wind and snow. Glad she didn't need to relieve herself.

A minute passed, and then another. Where *was* he? No reason for Giovanni to take so long out there, in the cold.

Why hadn't he come straight back inside?

Ufuk and his private contractor were discussing something over a holographic map on some special device of Ufuk's. A pistol was holstered on the man's chest, and an M4 waited on the table beside the projection. The blue light glowed pale and dull on the cold metal.

Jess looked at Massarra and mouthed the word: Giovanni. Massarra's expression soured and she nodded toward the door. She walked casually to her backpack.

It had been too long.

There was no reason for Giovanni to be out there this long. Up here, in the mountains, it was possibly thirty below. Giovanni was an experienced polar explorer; he would know he shouldn't be out there, exhausted and weary as he was, for longer than absolutely necessary. He wouldn't want to be.

She went over to the door.

Ufuk's man put a hand out. "Where are you going?"

"Just wondering where Giovanni is."

"He's safe with my man."

"If it's all the same to you, I'm going to check."

"It's not safe out there." He reached up and tapped his comms unit twice.

"I'm sure I can handle it."

"Miss Rollins, please remain inside."

The door opened behind her, sweeping a flurry of bitter cold air and snow inside. Two men, perhaps the men from the snowcat, she couldn't tell as they wore full-face respirators, came in. Jess stepped back. Something wasn't right.

Ufuk looked up from the holographic projection, confusion in his expression. "What's going on?"

Massarra backed away from the table to her backpack.

"Where's Giovanni?" Jess said.

"This doesn't need to be unpleasant, Miss Rollins."

"You're keeping us here," she said quietly, watching him. "For Müller, right? You work for Müller?"

"Jess, take it easy," Ufuk said. "These are my people."

"That's right, Mr. Erdogmus," the man said. "There's no problem. But for now, I think you should all take a seat at that table over there." He laid his hand on the holstered pistol.

Ufuk paused, then said: "That seems sensible." He reached for the device that powered the holographic projector. "Let me shut this down. No sense in wasting power. Don't know when we will be able to recharge."

The man allowed him to play his fingers across the device.

The projection faded and vanished. Ufuk stepped away and sat on a chair beside the table. "I think that will do it."

Silence, apart from the wind outside that undulated in pitch and tone. Snow beat against the small windows. An uncomfortable silence hung heavy.

One of the windows exploded in a spray of glass.

The surprise of it paralyzed Jess for an instant. Something sleek and gray, glistening wet and impossibly fast, surged into the room. Rotors whirred as it collided into the opposite wall and exploded into fragments. What was it? Some kind of drone?

No time to find out.

The soldiers were as surprised as she was, and Jess crashed into the man nearest to her, bringing every ounce of her weight, every sinew and muscle, to bear on him. He staggered backward. She wrapped her hands around his weapon, pushing it away as she drove him into the small porch beyond the common room. They stumbled and fell, clattering down the steps onto cold stone. Jess drove her fist twice into his throat as they tumbled. He tried to kick her away. She crowded him, keeping the M4 close to his chest, flat and angled away.

She wasn't far now. Jess saw what she needed.

She held him back with every ounce of strength she possessed, twisted and turned, knees, arms, elbows, everything she had to counter his own movements. She reached for the ice axe that stood against the wall. Her fingers closed around the wet rubber grip. A garbled shout came from the common room, then gunfire. Two short cracks, then two more.

No time to think about that.

Only one thing mattered.

The first swing met with stone and jarred her wrist. The soldier understood now. He fought back more viciously, every movement driven more by that professional fear that fighting men harness. Her reserves of energy were depleted, the trek from the mountain's flank still drawing on her. Soon he would overpower her. She fought wildly, technique foundering and replaced by a savage, unbridled violence. He forced her back, teeth bared. She fell away, sweeping the axe across into a slash across his upper arm. It bit, snatched blood and flesh. He grimaced, but made for her again.

She was flat-backed to the floor now. He towered above her. She swung wildly with the ax again and struck his carbine as he swung it around. The point of the ax cut into his hand. He screamed and dropped the weapon into its sling, then reached for his pistol with his other hand.

She was too far away. She couldn't get to him in time.

The door to the porch swung open fast. Snow swept in. A shape came through the dim light, a shifting mass. Roaring in rage, it collided with the soldier.

"Giovanni, he has a gun," Jess screamed.

She stooped, twisted the axe in her grip to bare the spike at the base of its shaft, and drove it sideways into the gap where the armpit lay just exposed. A muffled scream followed. She hooked the serrated pick of the axe around the elbow and pulled hard. It bit into muscle and tendons, cutting deep. Blood flowed and slicked the shaft. The arm came away, its hand empty. Another muffled scream and Giovanni pressed down, punching repeatedly.

Behind her, the door to the common room crashed open. Jess brandished the ice axe, but it wasn't the mercenaries. Massarra and Ufuk came through the door, followed by Raffa with Hector in his arms. Jess seized Giovanni by the hand and they stumbled out into the snow together. Through the white flurry she glimpsed the Predator-style drone sweeping toward them.

"Get away from the building!" she screamed, her words fighting the confluence of wind and jet engine.

She stumbled away, boots sinking into the snow. Staggering. Deep, sinking steps. Behind her, the others clawed their way through. The stuttering glow of the drone's strobe lamps flickered bright.

"Get down." She threw herself flat as the aircraft swept past.

"They must have seen us." Massarra crawled beside her.

"It was armed. We need to put as much distance as possible between us and the refuge. Find some cover, somewhere to hide."

Jess pointed to a shadowy fringe of alpine pines.

They ran, pulling Raffa and Hector with them, staggering through the snow, fighting against the bitter wind. The drone would complete its turn in a matter of seconds. Even as she fought her way forward, she knew the trees were too far. The whine came over the sound of the wind again, distant but slowly intensifying.

The strobes seared through the fog.

Another glance to the tree line—too far. She kept running, but the others lagged behind. Exhausted, not used to this harsh environment of the mountains as she was. Or maybe it was her new bionic leg, pumping her forward. The drone materialized through the fog. Headlights stark bright. Low, precise. Zeroed in on them.

Something shifted just below it. A vibration in the forest canopy.

An object swept upward, small and moving fast. It slammed into the drone and exploded in a bright pink fireball. The Predator's wing sheared off, and it tumbled into the darkness. A flash of light and thudding explosion as it hit the mountainside.

"The snowcat," Jess shouted, waving everyone back. "Behind the refuge. Get to the snowcat!"

7

Italian Alps

Giovanni manhandled the snowcat over the torrid landscape for an hour before Jess told him to slow down. Distance was everything now. Distance between them and the smoldering remains of Sanctuary Europe, widening the search grid for whoever was hunting them.

They were on the run again.

Six of them in the snowcat—Giovanni, Ufuk and Massarra on the front bench, with Jessica, Hector and Raffa on the second bench. The third bench was filled with as much gear as they could collect from the refuge in their frantic rush to leave. Jess had yelled at Ufuk, told him to help, but he had rooted around inside the snowcat with a screwdriver, holding his tablet. He ripped out what he said was a tracking device and threw it into the snow. Said that nothing else in the snowcat seemed to be transmitting.

The first few minutes of churning across the snow were terrifying, in almost pitch-blackness, with the snowcat's headlamps illuminating only a swirling whiteness that extended a dozen feet in front of them. They might plunge over a cliff, into a crevasse. Jess knew the treacherous landscape high in the mountains, but they had no choice. Another drone might return to the cabin. They had to get away.

"Just follow the blinking red light," Ufuk had instructed. He pointed at a tiny dot hovering in space in the near whiteout conditions.

"What is it?" Giovanni squinted.

"Our guide. It will take you down the mountain. Just follow."

At first Giovanni was hesitant, but after an hour of safe churning through the snow, with just flat whiteness appearing before them, he relaxed and kept his eyes on the red dot that always seemed to hover just in sight in front of them. At least the snowstorm provided some cover, and would hide their tracks from whoever tried to attack them.

The feeling of *déjà vu* was almost overpowering. Back in a crowded vehicle, the smell was of bodies and sweat and fear. It brought back strong memories, but some of their group was missing. Old Leone, the groundskeeper from Castel Ruspoli, killed protecting Hector. Now Lucca was missing as well. Raffa was silent, his arms folded tight, his eyes ahead.

Was Lucca still alive? They had no idea. They also had no choice.

Jess sat in silence for the first hour as the snowcat ground its way down the mountain. Hector shivered beside her, but not from cold. With the heaters blasting, the freezing cab had become uncomfortably warm. It wasn't the cold. Hector was terrified of being outside again, and Jess was just as scared as he was, but she held him tight, told him everything would be okay, that they were safe.

But were they?

They'd barely managed to survive two weeks out here after Nomad, as the temperature had fallen and the remains of civilization had been buried ever deeper under layers of snow and ash. They scavenged what they could to survive, but now, almost three weeks later, what would be left out here? They were six hundred kilometers further north than where they were before, and winter was just beginning to bare its fearsome teeth.

How much colder would it get?

Jess waited until Hector had fallen asleep beside her before quietly starting to ask some questions.

"So those were your drones that saved us?" Jess whispered to Ufuk. The thing that had crashed through the window at the refuge looked like big version of the toy drones she'd seen—four spinning rotors at each corner. "And that"—she pointed through the windscreen at the red dot that hovered in the distance—"is the same thing?"

98

"That's right," Ufuk replied, keeping his voice low as well.

"Won't they be able to follow…" Jess searched for the right words. Technical stuff wasn't her thing. "I don't know. The signal?"

"I've created many diversions. Don't worry."

"You see, that's the thing," Jess hissed, trying her best to keep her voice down. "I do worry. I didn't even know Massarra was leading me to you when I followed her."

"Then why did you?"

"Because I trust her."

"Then you should trust me," Ufuk replied, his voice still calm.

"I trusted you, and they threw me in goddamn jail." It was a struggle not to yell. "And suddenly, you're gone. For two days. And they're questioning me about a bomb going off. Did you do that?"

"Of course not."

"And you didn't just destroy Sanctuary?"

Ufuk didn't answer this aloud, but shook his head.

Jess gritted her teeth. She could usually tell if someone was lying, but Ufuk's face was almost placid, as if driving down the side of a mountain in a snowstorm, hunted by killer drones, was something he did every day.

"I would be buried under that mountain if Massarra hadn't come to get me."

"I came to get you, too," Giovanni said quietly.

"I know, I know, it's just…" Jess took a deep breath.

It was her fault they were here. It always seemed to be her fault. She should have gone with Abbie Barnes. She seemed genuine, and her father, Eugene Marshall, had been on Jess's side. Had she made a terrible mistake? What did Ufuk Erdogmus want with her? And why would he have sent Massarra to get them? The Sanctuary people looked like they at least had some resources, some kind of emergency plan. She should have gone with Abbie, taken Hector to safety. The Sanctuary people obviously hadn't bombed and destroyed their own home.

So who had? And why?

"You lied to me," Jess said after a pause of a few seconds.

"About what?" Ufuk whispered back, his face furrowing into a frown from frustratingly impassive nonchalance.

Jess poked Massarra's shoulder, a little aggressively. "Her. You lied about her. You told me you didn't know where she was."

"I honestly didn't—"

"You said you hadn't heard of her before."

The frown dissipated. "Ah, yes. A small omission of truth."

"Any other omissions you might want to make me aware of?"

The man filled his lungs with a deep breath. "I had been supporting the Levantine Council, before Nomad arrived. I might have spent the last twenty years in America, but the Arab people—"

"So you supported terrorists?"

"Not terrorists," Massarra said gently, speaking for the first time since they left the refuge. "As I explained to you, our organization is entirely peaceful."

"But connected to terrorists." It seemed the San EU military interrogators hadn't been the ones lying. Ufuk was connected to them, and to Massarra.

"We were trying to begin a dialogue..." Ufuk began to say, but then sighed. "I am normally against the use of violence to any political end."

"And yet you employ killers like Massarra." Jess flinched inwardly as she said it, but it was true. Up at the cabin, Massarra killed four of the highly trained soldiers. Wiped them out. Killing seemed to come easily.

For the next minute, nobody said anything. The snowcat's engine growled and they bounced from side to side as it churned down the mountain.

"I assume you have a plan?" Jess said finally. "Somewhere we're going?"

"I did have a plan. Those contractors were supposed to secure our perimeter while some helicopters came to retrieve us, and take us to a facility in Turkey."

"Helicopters? In this?"

"Drone-copters, I guess you could call them. Not air-breathing engines, but electric. They can operate in the ash clouds."

"Battery-powered helicopters? That was your plan?" This seemed to stretch believability.

Ufuk turned in his seat to face her. "My companies did a lot of work for the US military. These drones are powered by hydrogen fuel cells. Ten times the power of electric. I can explain more—"

"Not now," Jess interrupted. "Okay, so we were going to Turkey? How do we get there now? Do you have some other magical—"

"This thing, Jessica. It has surprised me as much as you. I only had a few minutes to respond when the bombs went off in Sanctuary. I had as little idea as anyone else. I am...scrambling...as well."

"But you had mercenaries on the ready, just like that?"

"I always keep a Plan A, and a Plan B, and a Plan C..."

"And which plan are we on now?"

"Somewhere further down the alphabet, I'm afraid. When my men betrayed us, I realized my base of operations in Turkey had been compromised as well. I used this"—Ufuk held up the tablet he'd been using inside the refuge—"to program the drone-copters to touch down and take off again. Whoever is chasing us will follow them first. I created other diversions also; sent off dozens of decoys to create radio chatter in all directions. It will take them half-a-day at least—if not days—to get to the top of the mountain and discover we aren't there."

"And just who is chasing us?"

"Sanctuary military," Ufuk replied. "But really, it's Müller."

"And why would *he* still be hunting us? He's already won. Why would he still care?"

"Because they think we destroyed San EU."

"They also think *you* destroyed Vivas."

"We didn't destroy either."

Jess fought the feeling of being trapped in a mirror maze. "If that's true—and I'm not sure what to believe—then why would Müller still be chasing you?"

"Because he wants access to my systems." Ufuk held up his tablet again. "I have three space launch facilities my company maintained. Two of which might still be operational for getting up communication satellites. That, plus my drone fleets."

"Just how many of these drones do you have?"

"Thousands. At locations spread around the world. As I said, my company did a lot of work for the US military. Many have been destroyed, but much has survived. I knew Nomad was coming."

"And these don't need humans to operate them?"

"Some human intervention is required, but a lot of my systems can be autonomous for long periods of time. They work together like bees in a hive."

Jess paused to let all this sink in. Great. So she'd attached herself to maybe the single most important military target in the world. If Ufuk had everything he said he did, just about anyone on the planet that wanted power would be searching for him. And her.

"So what's the plan now, then?" she said after a minute or two of thought.

"I honestly don't know," Ufuk replied quietly. "We need to get south. It's too cold for us to survive long this far north. And winter is coming. It will only get worse."

Jess looked out the window of the cab. They bounced up and down over the snow and ice. Maybe ten or fifteen kilometers an hour? Maybe twice that on flat ground. This thing could cross almost any snow-and-ice covered terrain, but could they use it to travel fifteen hundred kilometers south? This snowcat had to be guzzling diesel like crazy. Where would they get diesel fuel? And what about water? Food? They had a few packs of emergency rations, but not enough for weeks. Or months.

Jess's heart sank as she gripped Hector. Back to this old game. The same one they'd tried to play—and lost—two weeks before. Only to be rescued by Ufuk's magical machines from the sky. From Ufuk's grim expression, she sensed there weren't any more fairytales coming—but then again, they had their own private army of drones.

8

Northern Italy

They'd been weary enough when they left the refuge, exhausted by the night's events and the hostile conditions, but seven hours later and Jess realized it wouldn't be good for them to keep moving any longer. Better they managed a few hours' rest, then continue for as long as they were able to once refreshed. Twice, Ufuk had made them pull under cover as he worked a scanning device from the back of the snowcat. The weather offered them some camouflage—endless fog, riven by new snow and old ash, as much a hindrance to those searching for them as it was for the snowcat to slog through it.

At least dawn brought some feeble light through the heavy clouds.

The awful-but-familiar stench of sulfur found its way with sickening speed into the snowcat as they descended in altitude. Jess began to cough up sticky wads of phlegm. She tried to ignore it, tried not to remember what it was like waking up in a comfortable bed, eating eggs and drinking coffee around a table while reading emails. She tried to forget how easy it was to turn on a faucet and find clear, fresh water coming out.

After two hours they reached Cavagliola—or their best guess of what the snow-mounds of ruins once were, where the Bernina Railway hid beneath meters of thick pillow drifts. What looked like the road snaked down the mountain. Giovanni had maneuvered the snowcat onto skittish surface hoar, which at least led downward. From there, the going had been slightly easier.

It still took them more than four hours to make their way painstakingly down the snow-laden road, crossing the border into Italy where a small Lombardy town called Tirano had once stood. Giovanni recalled it had had a beautiful basilica, but now there was nothing but rolling mounds of snow and ice. No one stopped them, no guards waited at the border to check identification or refuse entry. In fact, they didn't see a living soul.

It was like traveling across Antarctica, Giovanni had said.

Nobody had replied.

At that point, the gas tank was nearing half empty. They had two hundred liters in ten jerry cans stuffed in the cargo, Ufuk said. He also said he could have drones drop supplies for them, MRE rations. He'd set up an automated facility in case some of his people got trapped outside. He hadn't imagined it would be him. He warned against sending the drones to a specific spot they may stop at. He'd have them air drop as they passed over, wherever they may stop. Not ideal, but at least they wouldn't starve.

Not right away, anyway.

Massarra took over driving, and five hours later they were on almost flat ground, the tiny drone still blinking and flashing ahead of them in the semi-darkness of what passed for daylight. The snowstorm was clearing, which made it easier to drive—they were making thirty kilometers an hour—through the heavy, sastrugi-carved drifts, past mounds of abandoned cars pushed into culverts or off the road and into ravines. Right now the only mission was to put distance between themselves and Sanctuary.

As they worked their way down out of the mountains, a choice had to be made: follow the main highway down the middle of Italy, or head for the coast? Either choice had its problems, but either way they'd have to stop and refuel soon, and maybe it wouldn't make a difference either way. In this gas-guzzler, the two hundred liters of fuel wouldn't even get them halfway to Rome, never mind to the tip of Sicily.

In the event, though, it wasn't much of a decision.

"Boat, we take the boat," Massarra said when Jess told her to pull over.

Ufuk had been busy on his tablet. Jess had told him to be careful, not to do anything stupid. He said he was trying to come up with a plan, but so far he just watched a bunch of moving dots and cursed every ten minutes.

They'd reached a town called Brescia.

Massarra pulled the snowcat in beside what had once been a hotel, where their vehicle couldn't be seen from the road. The hotel had several stories, the upper level could provide a serviceable place to institute an overwatch. The lower levels were buried deep beneath wind slab. Nothing alive moved.

"What boat?" Jess said as the snowcat's engine whined to a stop.

"The boat I came here in. At La Spezia."

"I thought you said one of Ufuk's drone-copters took you to Sanctuary."

The Israeli nodded. "But from La Spezia."

"You really have a boat anchored at La Spezia?"

The Israeli nodded again. "As Mr. Erdogmus has said. Plan A. Plan B. I like to have my plans."

"How on Earth did you get…I mean, what about sea ice?"

"Ice at the edges, but the open water is clear. The Mediterranean was a hot sea. Some pancake ice and slush, but it won't freeze for a few weeks still, I would guess. Fuel is scarce so I went in search of a sailboat." She picked up her M4. "After our last failed attempt to navigate over land, I decided a boat was a better option. And I love sailing."

"A *sailboat?*" Jess said, still incredulous.

"Most were wrecked by the huge waves breaking over the coastline, but there are large marinas in Monte Argentario. Much of the landscape is hills hundreds of meters high where they store boats for the winter. The story is a long one I can tell you, but there is a boat."

"How do we get onto it?"

"It's anchored away from the ice in open water. No new tsunamis the past week, so it should still be there. I took a rigid inflatable from Porto Ercole and towed it behind. It is upturned on the ice as we speak."

"That could work." Ufuk had switched off his tablet. "Lots of wind."

Jess held her palms out. Going back anywhere near the water was the last thing she wanted to do. "Wait a second. What about another tsunami?"

"As long as we are away from coast, no problem. Tsunami only a problem if you are in shallow water."

Jess tried to quell her fear. "And where do we go, exactly?"

"I've been thinking about that," Ufuk said. "Your friend, Ain Salah, in that town called Al-Jawf. You said he wanted to help you."

"Yeah, but, I mean I haven't talked to him in a few weeks. And I don't really know him. He was just a person we talked to on the radio."

"Do you think you can trust him?"

"I don't know."

"I think so," Giovanni offered.

"And that's where you wanted to go before you got wrapped up in this whole mess," Ufuk added. "Right?"

Something about the way Ufuk said it made Jess feel like he had some other motive, as if he wanted to make this sound like Jess's idea.

"And Massarra and I have a lot of connections in North Africa," Ufuk continued. "Libya. Benghazi—"

"Wait a second," Jess said, her voice rising. "Benghazi? That place where the American ambassador was assassinated? You want to go there?"

"Where did you think Al-Jawf was?"

"In the desert."

"Massarra, why didn't you say something before?" said Ufuk, almost ignoring Jess now. "This is a fantastic idea."

"You never asked. You were busy playing." She pointed at the tablet. "And besides, sailing through ice and snow, I think they had enough of this, no?"

"But it's brilliant." Ufuk stowed his tablet.

"We have to talk about this more," Jess said.

"You decide, Jessica," Ufuk said. "It's your decision."

"Great, that's just great." Jess reached over the seat to grab a pistol. "Let's go and see if there's anyone in this place."

9

Northern Italy

The journey to La Spezia might have taken two hours a few months ago, but with the roads almost invisible beneath the snow and ice, and the wind blowing a white sheet across the landscape, it would take three or four times that long. For much of the way they drove across open fields, threading a line between Brescia and Verona. They skirted around larger towns, selecting instead a circuitous route that avoided anywhere there might still be people.

The night before they had decided what to do: Head for the boat.

It wasn't much of a discussion. Out here they would die. Ufuk only had twenty drone-copters, he explained, big enough to carry a human, hundreds of times bigger than the tiny drones buzzing around them now. They were much more easily spotted and conspicuous, and all of them now had disappeared from his networks—destroyed or disabled. It was probably better that they hadn't attempted to use them. The only possible chance at survival Jess could imagine required getting south to where the temperature was still above freezing. She still held out hope that the situation in the fabled Al-Jawf camp in Libya was still stable, and they'd be able to find their friend Ain Salah. Ufuk and Massarra assured them that they had a lot of contacts in that area as well, and that they would be able to find them friends and protection, and supplies.

At least it was a plan.

For a short time the next morning, they took the Strada Provinciale between Montichiari and Piadena, Ufuk's drones their quiet sentinels ahead of them, searching for signs of cars stacked across the road to form an impromptu obstruction that might be a trap. They used the drones sparingly, Ufuk sweeping one in from time to time. There was a danger their control systems could be intercepted, and other dangers they couldn't assess.

No signs of life anywhere.

Doubtless there were more dead stacked inside the buildings, huddled together in a failed search for warmth, the same as the frozen families they'd found on a sweep of the hotel the night before. After finding all the dead bodies inside the hotel, they'd decided instead to sleep in the cab. It was too cold to try to warm up any room inside the structure, and too dangerous to light fires of any large size. They left early. Jess preferred to remain protected by continued movement, and afraid of her growing numbness and indifference each time she saw more dead.

They did stop once, to pick up emergency supplies dropped by Ufuk's smaller drones. They approached cautiously, and Ufuk had his drones monitor for heat signatures. Nothing anywhere. He had lost two dozen of the smaller drones to a hacking attack the night before, but they had no more contact with Sanctuary forces beyond that. Jess didn't trust Ufuk, but had to trust in his own desire to save himself. That was their only common interest that she could trust.

They approached La Spezia from the north, using the Strada Provinciale delle Cinque Terra, a coastal road somewhat concealed by forest. The sailboat was moored away from La Spezia, more than four hundred feet from the shingle beach. Massarra tried to point it out, and it looked surrounded by white ice already, but was difficult to see through a white fog rolling off the ocean.

"I will get the small boat," Massarra said as the snowcat shuddered to a stop.

Giovanni got out of the passenger side door with the shotgun and watched their tracks behind them for any signs of movement.

"How far is it?" Jess asked.

"About a hundred meters. It's visible, just." She gestured out over the ice to where there might have been a mound at the edge. It was hard to tell through the haze. "It is hidden beneath a tarpaulin, covered by snow and ash."

110

"We should rope up again," Jess said. "Giovanni and I on a rope with you. Just in case."

Massarra considered this for a moment. She nodded. "Stay as far back as possible. Better only one of us goes through. The water is freezing." She grimaced and put a hand on Jess's shoulder. "But then you know that. Let's not do that again."

"Let's not," Jess agreed.

They pulled out the climbing ropes and coiled them in the snow. Jess stepped into a harness and tied Massarra onto a line connected back to Raffa and Giovanni. As Massarra's silvery silhouette faded into the mist and eddying spindrift, Jess found herself again wondering why. Why Massarra had risked her life for her so many times? And for Ufuk as well? What it was about her that was so important, and what was the real relationship she had with the billionaire?

For a long while, they fed the rope out to her, keeping it taut enough that if she fell through they could hold her, but loose enough so she could still move freely. They had to tie two and then three climbing ropes together. Eventually, there came three sharp tugs and Jess allowed herself a moment's relief. They began to pull in the slack.

"We're ready, "Massarra said as she returned without incident, her slender outline materializing slowly through the mist. "The ice is solid, but still not formed more than an inch or two thick around the sailboat. We will be able to break a path out."

Massarra returned across the ice to the inflatable, and ferried herself out to the sailboat. She then tied another hundred foot climbing rope to the front of the inflatable. They hauled back the boat onto the ice, and she pulled it back with their help. A few more trips and they ferried all the supplies they scavenged from the snowcat across the ice.

Jess waited and took the final trip across the black water with Hector. The boy was brave but trembled upon seeing the water. "Be brave," Jess told him.

She wished she could be, too.

The sailboat appeared through the mist in the half-light, and Jess's heart sank a little as she looked into the cold depths. She was hoping for something like a yacht. This couldn't be more than forty feet from end to end. The rigging was coated in yellow ice. The hull looked scratched.

But it was their only hope now.

Beyond the mists lay a trackless and bottomless world they'd only barely escaped from with their lives, just weeks before. When they came alongside the hanging steps on the side of the boat, Jess pushed up Hector first, and then hauled herself aboard and stowed her gear in one of the aft cabins. She busied herself following Massarra's directions to prepare for sailing, more to occupy her mind than because the Israeli really needed any help. Running the sheets, loading batons, chipping off ice from the deck and rigging, and stowing gear below. Giovanni took Hector into the back cabin and wrapped him in blankets, humming lullabies in Italian that Jess didn't understand but understood just the same.

In less than an hour they were underway, in time to use the last of the dim light that filtered through the thick clouds as the invisible sun set. Massarra started up the small diesel engine to guide them out of the harbor as pitch-blackness enveloped them. A stiff wind sprang up as the rolling swells pitched the boat back and forth. Massarra turned off the diesel and winched down the main sail. The boat listed to one side and bit into the wind.

They were away.

Ufuk's drones flew ahead of the boat in the darkness, sometimes invisible but always reappearing, blinking red sprites that appeared insect-like to hover and show them the way forward. All GPS and electronics on the boat were dead of course, fused in the radiation storms of Nomad. The compass still worked—but was off by about twenty degrees to the west. Magnetic north had been shifted by Nomad by about that much, Ufuk told them, and maybe was still shifting. They had navigational charts, and Massarra was ready to dead-reckon a course south, but with the terrible visibility admitted this would be difficult without much visual reference. Ufuk crouched over his tablet, huddled against the cold on a bench on deck, and assured them his drones would be able to guide them safely.

Jess had a lot of questions, but was too exhausted to ask them. Massarra and Ufuk looked like they knew what they were doing, and that was all she needed for now.

Her first assigned task was to get the heating working.

The owner of the boat had installed an old paraffin stove in the main cabin, placed halfway up a bulkhead at the forward end of the saloon. It was an old model, but one Jess was familiar with from her days trekking in mountain huts. Almost ancient technology, but reliable. The stove used no electricity at all, and if there were a fan club for them, Jess would have joined. Under the bench, as Massarra had described, there was at least twenty liters of fuel. Like all heaters of this type, it used a manually pressurized fuel tank to feed the paraffin to an *Optimus*-type burner, which had to be pre-heated by burning a small quantity of methylated spirits in a moat below it.

After twenty minutes of fussing over it with frozen fingers, the damn thing finally lit, and a warm glow emanated into the room. She kept it on low. She hoped the heat would push away the smell of frozen mold.

The next thing she did was check to make sure the short chimney was working. Jess knew that burning paraffin, or any other hydrocarbon fuel, produced toxic fumes that had to be vented. She went topside and held her hand over the mushroom cap over the vent. Even so, a risk remained. The carbon dioxide produced could gradually replace the oxygen in the cabin, and go on to produce carbon monoxide. Really nasty stuff—highly toxic, odorless, colorless and tasteless. If it didn't kill you, it could leave you permanently brain damaged.

It was a danger she'd have to continually monitor.

Raffa and Hector and Giovanni came to join her in the saloon by the time she returned back below. They huddled together in a pile, under everything they could find to cover themselves, propped

113

up on a soiled couch on the side furthest from the water as the boat listed in the wind. Without talking about it, they all wanted to stay as far away from the water as they could—and anyway, it was warmer there, higher up, as the heat from the burner rose. Jess attached a single LED headlamp to the bulkhead; set to its red low-power setting.

The slap and creak of the boat against the waves was mercifully rhythmic. She closed her eyes and wrapped her arms around Hector, telling Ufuk to wake her every two hours to make sure they weren't being slowly poisoned.

The small cabin felt like a cocoon, sliding across the water. Moving away from the monster, Dr. Müller. To be honest, Jess had never felt comfortable in Sanctuary Europe, entombed below millions of tons of rock, trapped with Müller. Somehow she knew he wouldn't be so easily beaten. Maybe he was already dead, killed in the collapse. That was too much to hope for, but at least she was away from him. Somehow, she felt at ease, free again, running away. But who were her rescuers? Ufuk and Massarra? They weren't who they seemed, that was all she knew for sure.

She drifted off to sleep as she felt Hector twitching into his own dreams.

10

Northern Mediterranean Sea

Jess woke to the sound of howling wind. It took her a few seconds to remember where she was, and took more than that to calm her heart, which pounded as hard as the waves that crashed against the hull. Weak gray light seeped into the cabin through the portholes. Her body tipped to one side. The boat banged into another wave, and she surged back. Was it a storm? Giovanni and Hector and Raffa slept through it, the nest-knot of them jammed between the galley table—bolted to the floor—and the couch. Jess extricated herself and found her parka and gloves and hat before opening the hatch and sliding herself halfway out.

"Good morning," Ufuk yelled over the noise of the wind. He stood at the four-foot-wide metal driving wheel, his body upright at thirty degrees to the deck's surface as it angled against the wind. He wore a thick parka and snow pants, with layers of hats on his head over goggles. "Or should I say, good afternoon. You've been asleep for…fifteen, maybe sixteen hours."

"Is everything okay?" Jess asked in a panic. The fury of the wind and waves frightened her. She wasn't a sailor. A cascading sheet of spray flew over her head as another wave thudded into the boat.

"Fantastic," Ufuk replied. "Amazing wind. We've been making seven or eight knots. Nice steady seas."

These were *steady* seas? Jess's head knocked into the doorframe on another crunching impact. The boat rolled up and back down. White caps surged over dark waters into the misty distance. "Where's Massarra?" she asked.

Ufuk let go of the wheel with one hand to point forward. Jess craned her neck around the doorframe to look toward the front of the boat. Massarra was perched precariously near the bow, but clipped in with a carabiner to the side railing. The Israeli was busy chipping away ice from the deck with an ice ax. She waved.

"Massarra took the night shift," Ufuk said.

"What can I do?" Jess yelled.

Ufuk smiled, the scraggly beginnings of his beard encrusted with ice. "Coffee."

Jess fired up a propane-canister powered boiler—part of the equipment they'd brought from the mountain—and made some coffee. It was a struggle just to stay on her feet, and her robotic prosthetic was almost out of power. The last time she'd plugged it in was more than a day ago in the snowcat. Options for power on board were limited to the ship's daisy-chained twelve-volt batteries, and she wanted to leave them for more critical things. For now her leg had returned to the more passive prosthetic mode.

She brought up two insulated steaming mugs of coffee in time to shuffle past Massarra on her way to one of the back cabins to sleep. She looked beyond exhausted.

"Take the wheel," Ufuk said as she handed over the coffee.

"I don't know anything about boats." She grabbed the wheel anyway, as much to stabilize herself from falling over against the heaving deck.

"It's easy. See the compass?" He pointed at a yellow globe in front of the wheel. A ball wiggled back and forth inside it. "Keep heading due south for now."

"I thought you said we couldn't trust a compass," she yelled over the noise.

"Magnetic north seems pretty stable, for now at least. We should be using a compass heading of 150 to 160 degrees, but with the 20-degree shift, it's more like 180 degrees, due south. Although it's not due south anymore. You understand?"

Jess gripped the wheel and tried to keep the boat on course. It bucked back and forth with each wave. "And steer out of the way of anything, right?"

"We shouldn't see much. But yes, try not to hit anything."

She strained her eyes to peer through the spray and mist. Brown clouds hung low overhead. It was midday, but dark as twilight. "How do we know where we are?"

"Massarra is keeping a plot on a map in the cabin, but I've also got this." He pointed at his tablet, strapped against the wall beside the hatch, covered by a layer of clear plastic. "It's tracking our position."

It looked like a GPS map, with a red dot moving against a map. They were most of the way down the coast to Rome already, if it was to be believed. She frowned and looked at it again. Other red dots hovered near theirs.

"It's not GPS, if that's what you're thinking," Ufuk explained. "GPS doesn't exist anymore. We're getting a triangulated position relative to where my tiny drones think they are. They're nearer the coast, holding position near known terrain markers."

"Won't we be easy to spot, with all those drones following us?"

Ufuk smiled an I'm-cleverer-than-that grin. "There are a dozen we're using." He leaned forward to tap a button on the screen. Dozens more dots popped onto the display. "But I've got hundreds more flying over the middle of Italy, on the other coast, even back north. All over the place. It hides the radio chatter as well, by blanketing half of Italy with transmissions back and forth between them. All encrypted, of course."

"Security by drowning out the signal?"

Ufuk's grin turned into an amused grimace. "Not the exact wording I'd use right now."

"So how long is this going to take?" She already felt like she was going to throw up the MRE crackers she'd scarfed down a few minutes before.

"About a thousand eight hundred kilometers is the total distance." Ufuk sat beside the tablet and zoomed the screen display out. "We head down the coast to near Naples, then out across the open sea to round Sicily, and drop straight south east until we hit the coast of Libya. With good wind, maybe six or seven days. It should get warmer as we get south."

He made it sound so simple.

"Just follow the headings I give you, and don't hit anything. That's all you need to do." Ufuk stood to go below. "I am, how do you say it...bushed?"

"Wait."

"You don't understand the heading?"

"I need some answers. Now." All the questions she had, all the things she hadn't asked. It wasn't enough to just follow a compass heading.

Ufuk hovered for a few seconds, but then sat on the bench next to her.

"Do you have teams out there managing these drones?"

"As I already said, they're mostly automated. We had four refueling tankers in the air, two on this side of Italy. They can keep hundreds of drones in the air for a week, but two of the tankers have been taken offline."

"Destroyed, you mean?"

"Hard to tell. I did have four teams of men running operations for me, but all have been compromised, like the men up in the mountain. Security keys were revoked for all manned centers last night, and we lost dozens of small drones."

"How do you control them all?"

"Automated, like I said."

It wasn't much of an answer, but she let it go. "So you have no people on the ground?"

"Just us, until Africa."

"But you have contacts there?" She found it both hard to believe and frightening that he had contacts in Libya.

"This is more of Massarra's field of play. But, yes, we should. I have supplies hidden as well."

"You mean you *planned* this?"

"My company, before Nomad, spanned most of the planet—we had offices in forty countries—but this scrambling for our lives? You think I planned this?"

Jess wasn't sure what to believe. If something went wrong, she suspected a small army of drones would appear to levitate this guy to safety, somehow.

"Müller was partially right," Ufuk added. "I have supported the Levantine Council for some time. I admired their objectives, for helping save the Middle East. My family is from here."

"A lot of people in Sanctuary said the Levantines were the terrorists."

"They do have relationships with extremist groups—Müller was also correct in that—but the Levantine Council was created to unite moderate groups, offer something else to youth who felt that extremism was the only option."

"Why do they need links to extremists at all?"

"They cannot be avoided entirely in that part of the world. Hezbollah, Hamas, they all have political aims as well. Where Western governments failed to wipe out extremist groups, the Levantine Council has been more successful."

"And Massarra? How do you know her?"

"She was tasked to meet me on several occasions. To facilitate communication between myself and the Council."

"That's all?"

"And she helped me with some…business."

"What kind of business?"

"My connections to the Levantines would have been disastrous for my business in the United States if I had been open about it." He shrugged. "She helped with that business."

"And who is she? Really?"

"Perhaps you should ask her that question."

"I'm asking you."

"It is not my place to say. Anything else you need to know, you should ask her. I do, however, caution you. She travelled many hundreds of miles and put herself at great personal risk to save your life. Several times. Remember that."

Of course Jess couldn't forget. She owed the woman her life many times over. "Is there anything left of the Levantine Council?"

"I've managed some limited communications. We need whatever allies we can find."

"Can you get me a channel to Ain Salah with that thing?" She pointed at the tablet.

"He would need to be connected to an encrypted digital line on his end, and this might not exist in Al Jawf. It's not clear how I could manage—"

"Did you destroy Sanctuary?" She'd asked it before, and she would keep asking until the truth came out.

"I did not." Ufuk's expression was empty. "I would venture to suggest Dr. Müller was involved, but I realize that makes no sense. I have no idea right now."

Jess studied his face, watched the tiny wrinkles around his eyes. Was he lying? The only person it made sense to destroy Sanctuary Europe was the man sitting in front of her—who had his own seemingly endless resources scattered everywhere. Then again, he didn't seem to be taking a safe route out of this, and even more important: stuck on a tiny boat with him in the middle of a frozen ocean wasn't the right time to start an argument that might have a bad ending. Could *only* have a bad ending. Her primary responsibility right now was to protect Hector, and to do that, she needed this man, for good or bad. At least for now.

"How long did you know about Nomad?" She asked quietly this time. It wasn't an accusation, but sad, like asking when an affair had started when you'd already accepted and moved on.

Even if her voice didn't carry venom, Ufuk grimaced. "Ten years ago. About the same time as I became one of the richest people in the world from my technology adventures."

"And that's why they asked you to become part of…whatever, the Sanctuary network?"

"Müller started it a long time before that. Maybe twenty-two years ago. It was already well underway before I was invited to be a part of the club. They used American international spy agencies to keep track of us, to keep track of everything. I think that was part of the reason they were so invasive. Revealing the secret was a death sentence."

"Surely somebody must have talked."

"Some did." Ufuk shrugged. "But their voices were drowned in the media as crackpots, and they soon disappeared. I didn't want to be one of them. It was then that I began to change my development objectives."

"And you contacted the Levantines."

"And that."

"But you didn't tell them about Nomad either."

Ufuk shook his head slowly.

"I can't imagine people like that wouldn't be upset about you killing their people."

"I didn't kill them. I'm trying to save…it's complicated."

"You certainly didn't help them." Now she was goading him.

Ufuk closed his eyes and hung his head low. The boat surged and crested another wave. "I am very tired, Jessica. Can I go and get some sleep? Can you handle the boat?"

11

Mediterranean Sea
Mid-latitudes

The oily dimness of what passed for daytime slipped away into night, and they strapped a collection of six LED lamps onto the bow of the boat. An attempt at headlights. A poor one. All they did was light up the mist and settling ash into a glow that obscured anything ahead, and there was never anything ahead except more waves and water and the occasional slop of pancake ice.

Jess was thankful for that.

The winds remained steady, keeping them cutting across the waves at six or seven knots, Ufuk told Jess, or about fifteen kilometers an hour. She had to convert that into ten miles per hour in her head. It seemed like they were moving faster. Ten miles an hour was jogging pace, but it added up. The boat never stopped moving, and as Massarra had pointed out, needed no fuel. It was quiet and efficient.

One wave and then the next. Jess never realized how empty an ocean could be.

She wondered if the fish at the bottom of the sea had even noticed the passing of Nomad. How would they? It was already dark down there, pitch black as the night now enveloping them. The waves wouldn't have affected the depths. Not that deep. What about the volcanic events? Maybe. Then she remembered the documentaries about the colonies of sea creatures that lived around volcanic vents. They didn't even need sunlight to exist. Maybe had been the first life on Earth. They would survive this. Life on this planet would go on, no matter what. The thought comforted Jess.

That night she huddled back with Hector and Giovanni in the saloon near the heater, but Raffa was nowhere to be found. Jess discovered him in one of the back two bedrooms in the aft, stuffed into two sleeping bags. He had never been much of a talker, even in Italian to Giovanni, but the past few days since he was separated from his brother—he'd hardly said a word. Jess was worried about him, but gave him his space.

They were all mourning someone.

The next morning was much the same as the first. Jess woke before Giovanni and Hector, and brought a coffee up to Ufuk before she took over her shift. Massarra was already in her room in the aft, so Ufuk took up the job of circling the boat and chipping off the ice. Today thick gray clouds almost touched the waters, and regular four-foot swells appeared from the mists and disappeared behind. Every now and then, the boat thudded into a patch of pancake ice. No floes, no icebergs—it hadn't been cold enough for long enough for that—but mushy cakes of ice had formed between the rolling swells.

After a while, it all became normal.

Around noon that day came the only excitement. They completed the first leg and were somewhere off the coast of Italy between Rome and Naples. Massarra took over and tacked the boat, explaining to keep a heading of 250 degrees as they headed out past the tip of Sicily. The wind blew up in sheeting gusts, but instead of bringing down the sails, Massarra had them unfurl the spinnaker, which seemed insane to Jess.

They were traveling with the gusting wind, Massarra had explained, and may as well make the most of it. The spinnaker inflated and bloomed like a giant kite ahead of them, and it felt like they were being pulled up into the air each time they crested and surfed down the face of growing swells. The wind howled, but Massarra said she could handle it.

The rest of them went below deck.

Ufuk was constantly crouched over his tablet, often by himself in the tiny cabin in the front of the boat. He had a backpack filled with gadgets. Jess wondered if one of them was filled with compressed hydrogen, the fuel source he said his drones worked from. She didn't ask. She didn't want to know. Hector took to spending a lot of time with Ufuk, watching him play with the dots on the screen. Ufuk loaded some games onto Hector's laptop, and played them with the boy. Jess liked that. He didn't need to play with Hector, but he took the time to, at least a few times a day.

That night Jess went to find Raffa, curled up next to him, and tried to console him. She told him that maybe Lucca made it out. Abbie had come for them, and she'd been close with Lucca. There was a chance, and Lucca was smart and strong. She wasn't sure how much Raffa understood, but she cradled him, held him like he was her son. And for her, then, he was.

"Jessica, wake up."

She opened her eyes. It was Ufuk.

"What? Is everything okay?"

"I have someone on the radio, on an encrypted channel." He deposited a small metal box next to her in the bunk, a small high-tech radio he'd brought from the snowcat. A wire snaked from the box into the hallway. The antenna.

A thin, tinny voice echoed from the speaker: "Jessica?"

Hector jumped up. "Ain Salah!" he squeaked.

Jess smiled an appreciative grin at Ufuk and took the tablet. "How are things in Africa?" she said into it.

"Winter is coming, but still not freezing yet. More refugees are now camped south of the main town, but we can accommodate them. Things go well here. What about you? Are you well? Is my little Hector well?"

In the days and weeks after Nomad, Ain Salah had been one of the most frequent contacts on the radio. Hector took to speaking with him. He'd said he had a son about his age.

"Yes, Ain Salah, I am here," Hector replied. "Jess teaches me more English."

"I can hear that. You are becoming very good. Very good. Perhaps a story tonight? Just you and I my little Bedouin? Tales of adventure with roguish men who take to the seas to seek their fortune and the mysterious and beautiful princesses they must rescue. What do you think of that?"

"I want to hear more about Sinbad the sailor."

Jess took Ufuk to one side. "You're sure this is secure?"

"As I said, I have drones spreading encrypted signals over half of Western Europe. They won't be able to decode it, and can't triangulate us. Let the boy have his fun. I can tell you what Ain Salah has already told me."

A laugh from the radio, and then came Ain Salah's soft voice again. "I think I can find something to take us both on a wild adventure."

Jess followed Ufuk into the main cabin, to leave Ain Salah to thrill with a swashbuckling tale of Arabian nights and stolen treasure carried by thieves on flying carpets.

The third morning, Jess woke up and got the coffee again as usual. It had been heartening to hear Ain Salah's voice, to hear him tell them it was still warm in the south, but when she exited the hatch, something even more amazing greeted her.

Sunrise.

Reds and pinks. A beautiful pastel of colors rimmed the horizon to the east, with an orange blob glowing in the center. Jess realized she hadn't seen the sun in weeks. Not as an actual thing.

"Beautiful, yes?" Massarra was behind the wheel. She took one of the coffees.

"Were you out here all night?" Jess slumped onto the bench to admire the sun over the bow.

"Nobody else was good enough to pilot that storm. We made over 450 kilometers yesterday."

Jess triangulated in her head. They seemed to be heading *toward* the sunrise.

"We have turned for Africa," Massarra said, sensing what she was thinking.

"Already?"

"A thousand kilometers or so straight ahead. We can't miss a whole continent."

"I guess not."

"And it seems the clouds are thinning further in the south." As Massarra said this, the thin line of clear weather closed up and extinguished the sun.

But she was right. And it did seem warmer. So they were just past the western tip of Sicily. Jess had always wanted to go there, but right now wasn't the time, she thought giddily. The biting wind and spray suddenly seemed invigorating. This plan wasn't insanity. They would make it. Somewhere that wasn't frozen.

"I never asked you," Jess said. "But how did you get a yacht into a frozen marina alone?"

Massarra's face widened to accommodate the biggest smile Jess had ever seen on her. "Big marinas have cranes for lifting boats out of the water and putting them back in again. I knew the area at Monte Argentino had boats stored a few hundred meters above the water in the hills. I found a truck-crane that would start, loaded one of the boats onto it, and rolled it down the hillside into the water and onto the ice. The trucks have big tires, excellent for deep snow. The ice broke eventually under the weight. The truck-crane sank beneath the boat, leaving it floating."

"But you were in the truck when it sank?"

"As I said, it wasn't easy."

"What if the boat had capsized?"

"The keel would have righted it."

"And you did this alone, in those conditions?"

Massarra wagged her head to one side.

"When we were leaving Sanctuary," Jess said, her voice going quiet, "why did you tell me not to trust Abbie Barnes?"

The wide smile slid away from Massarra's face, replaced with a blank-faced mask. "Her last name is Marshall, yes?"

"I think the General was her father. He came to see me in the prison. A nice man."

"Salman told me that a Marshall person was one of the ones involved with Müller."

"And you believed him?"

"Why would he lie?"

"And you think it was the General?"

Massarra remained silent, her eyes straight ahead.

"Wait, you think he meant Abbie?" The thought seemed impossible to Jess.

"I don't know. I just know the name Marshall."

"She risked her life to come back to the jail complex for me," Jess pointed out.

"So did I," Massarra replied.

The wind whistled. The sky darkened.

"And why did you do that?"

"Because I believe you are important, Jessica. People know who you are. You are a part of the truth, and I fight for the truth." The smallest of smiles worried the corners of her mouth. "And for my friends. We are friends, no? Is that not enough?"

"And you are friends with Ufuk?"

Again the blank mask. "That is more complicated."

"Did you destroy Sanctuary? You and Ufuk? If we are friends, then tell me the truth."

"I did not."

"Did Ufuk?"

Massarra hesitated. "Not as far as I know, and nothing in his preparations indicated he knew. This was a surprise for him, a very bad one."

"And why are you so loyal to him?"

"He was a large benefactor to our cause. And we are friends. And I am tired. Can you take over?"

The next morning presented no sunrise, just an endless expanse of gray that opened up from the darkness. Ufuk took the helm around noon, and instead of going below, Jess spent a lot of time at the bow by herself, watching the boat cut a white ribbon into the dark water. When she was alone and had time to think away from the others, her thoughts returned to images of the people escaping from Sanctuary, of the fire and flames and of Ballie Booker crushed beneath the rocks.

Her smiling friend Ballie Booker.

In Sanctuary she'd thought of how lucky Ballie was to be attached to her, to be rescued from his boat in the middle of this same sea. Instead, if he hadn't been plucked from his boat, he'd probably still be alive, and so would all of this crew and the people they'd rescued. They were dead because they knew her. Because of her.

In the freezing air she used the physical pain of the cold to push away thoughts of everyone who'd been near to her and died, and the countless millions she didn't know who were gone. Their pain had ended, but she felt like hers was only just beginning.

Giovanni approached and offered to keep her company. She had asked him what he thought about what had happened in Switzerland.

"I try not to think about it." He took the binoculars from her and peered through them.

"I can't *stop* thinking about it."

"It's not good to dwell on it. Easy to say, I know."

"We can't let them get away with it."

"And *who* exactly would that be?"

"That place was supposed to be an ark for humanity. Why destroy it? As bad as it was, at least it was some semblance of what existed before. Why do people need to keep killing after all this death? What's the point? It's not right."

"No judges and juries anymore."

"So you're saying there's no right and wrong anymore either."

"I didn't say that."

"But you meant it."

"I just mean that all that's important, is us surviving."

Jess took the binoculars from him. "And I bet whoever destroyed Sanctuary, they were thinking the same thing. When will it end?"

"Not soon, I hope." Giovanni wrapped his arms around her and kissed her neck. "I mean, I hope we have more time together."

"Quit it." She pushed him away.

Nothing more was said about it. She opted to spend most of her time alone on deck after that. The air wasn't as cold anymore. The ice wasn't forming from the spray. And the boat was too cramped to carry on any sort of conversation without being overheard.

By the sixth day, the initial excitement of turning toward Africa had passed. They'd almost run out of food. The red dot on Ufuk's tablet said they'd already reached the coast, and they slowed to half sail, but saw nothing.

Somewhere in the distance, a seagull squawked.

Everyone made their way up onto deck, their tentative expectancy tempered by uncertainty. A mist lingered, a quiet wind whispered over the bow of the boat. Apart from the wash of the waves and the creaking mast, there was an eerie calm.

"That was a bird, right?" Jess said excitedly. She hadn't even seen a living animal outside in weeks.

"I can't see anything," Giovanni said.

"We have to be close to land," Massarra said. "Everyone spread out and take a side of the boat. Keep your eyes open."

It was Raffa who saw it first, the debris scattered in the water. Massarra gave Jess the wheel and, with Giovanni's help, took down the mainsail and reefed the genoa. The boat rocked, momentum the only thing now carrying it forward. A thick mist rolled in clumps of slate-gray smoke.

Massarra took the wheel again and spun the boat about. "Take some of the fenders from the port side," she instructed Raffa, "and hang them over to starboard. Keep them between us and whatever we approach."

"Everyone hang onto something," Giovanni shouted.

A structure loomed from the darkness. The impact was harder than Jess expected. Massarra had not wanted to turn the engine on, preferring to save diesel for the dingy instead. They seemed to be surrounded by waterlogged buildings that were half-submerged.

"What now?"

"Now we get ourselves and as much as we can carry into the inflatable," Jess said. "No way we can get through that with the sailboat. Pack rucksacks with all your personal gear, sleeping bags, and clothing, everything you think you'll need. We'll take whatever else we can in the duffle bags from the boat."

Ufuk had one of his tiny drones fly off the deck and scan the immediate area with imaging. Of the fleet of hundreds of drones he had in Italy, only four had survived from a small contingent he'd pushed south well ahead of them. He didn't give a lot of detail about how they did it, but the tiny craft appeared from the darkness and hovered to land on the bow of the boat as they neared land. They only had an hour or two each of fuel, he said. Once the drone was airborne, they followed a path on his tablet toward what appeared to be solid ground.

"Can you slow down?" Jess shouted over the engine noise. "I think I can see something."

Shapes began to form. Outlines of low structures. Irregular and twisted. As they approached the first, Jess saw it was the roof of the building, with heavy chunks gouged from the concrete, steel rebar twisted and exposed. Massarra throttled the boat back to low and allowed it to drift. Broken buildings appeared through the mist.

Giovanni shook his head. "I don't understand. What is this?"

"Sabkhat Ghuzayyil, the basin next to the coast, is fifty meters below sea level," Ufuk said. "It must have flooded."

They ran aground on a sandy shore. It surprised them, because the landscape was so flat and barren that it could barely be seen in the light of their headlamps.

"What do we do with the boat?" Jess had unpacked all the gear and stood, staring at the beached inflatable.

"Leave it here," Massarra said. "Turn it over, cover it with sand. You never know when we might need it."

"I suggest we get used to the terrain a little," Giovanni said. "Walk in a few miles and then make camp for the night."

They each strapped one of the small drones to their backpack, stowed the boat, and began walking. When they finally did make camp in a shallow basin, after a few hours of walking across sand crusted with fine crystals of ice that formed as night fell and glistened in the light thrown by their head torches, Jess didn't argue when Massarra insisted again she take watch. She lay down on her sleeping mat, pulling her down bag tightly around her, and sleep came as a sweet, dark relief.

She had no idea how long she had been asleep when a growing light woke her.

Outside, a low wind growled and played with the folds of the tent.

It took a supreme effort of will to pull herself out of the sleeping bag and into the cold. She realized as she pulled on her

131

boots, barely noticing the fog billowing from her mouth or the crystals of ice that had formed across the skin of the tent, that it was already morning.

She went outside and found herself surprised at how light it was. Not bright, like pure unhindered sunlight, but filtered through high flat clouds. It lent the place a washed-out, watery look. Sand the color of river clay.

She shivered and zipped her coat. Giovanni stood atop a nearby dune.

She joined him. "You didn't wake me."

"You needed the sleep." He put his arm around her.

For a moment they stood in silence, surveying the featureless landscape.

"I expected it to be warmer," she said.

"It is. Not even freezing."

"Close to it."

"Tropical." He forced a small laugh. "We should eat and get moving."

"We don't need to rush. Let them rest."

PART THREE

Mars First Mission

Deep Interplanetary Space

For two hours, the crew of Mars First worked on the ship until enough systems were green-lining, and life support was stabilized, so they weren't in a critical emergency. Cuijpers managed to bootstrap the Mars First artificial intelligence system. It was entering the final stages of its internal diagnostics.

Everything was coming back online. The ship was literally coming back to life.

Rankin called his three surviving crew into the communal area and ordered them all to eat something. Once he'd watched them stuff enough into their mouths to sustain them for the next few hours, he relaxed enough to open a packet stamped "eggs and bacon." In his other hand was a foil container of chicken curry, but he thought better of it. What he would have done for good coffee, not the weak pretender he sipped on now—but it was better than nothing, and the caffeine would help.

"Status reports," he said. "Keep it brief for now."

"I was wrong about the hull," Cuijpers said. "Two sections have been depressurized and are uninhabitable. There's physical damage to other parts of the hull, but not macro-structural. Looks like we had a fight with a swarm of micrometeorites. And no comms at all from Earth. Total radio silence."

They all took a moment to digest that.

"ECLS is functioning adequately throughout the rest of the ship," Shouang said. "Got the hydrogen cells and main reactor back. Not at optimal levels, but that may be damage to the cooling systems. Nothing we can do right now without an EVA to take a closer look."

"Once Mars First comes back online, it'll be able to tell us in more detail," Cuijpers added.

"Siegel? Anything?"

The small German shrugged. "I mean, if we cut away everything but the main engines, we could vector a long swinging trajectory back to Earth, but…it would be two, maybe three years out here. And even then, who's left back on—"

"This was always a mission of destiny," Rankin interrupted, holding out one hand to excuse himself. "Seems it's become a different one than we imagined. This was designed to be almost a year in deep space, so maybe we can handle two or three."

"I was kidding," said Siegel.

Rankin held his hand up again. "It's only been a few hours. We don't have all the answers, but we're gonna' get them." He let his accent slip into his native Texan twang. He always did it when he wanted to settle people. "Let's all just calm down, okay? We're alive—"

"Which might be more than anyone left on Earth," Siegel muttered.

"We were all chosen for this," Rankin continued, ignoring her, "because we're exceptional under pressure, and are the best at what we do. So let's stay calm and work the problem, and not let the problem work us. No matter how big."

He looked at each crewmember's face in turn.

"Now let's start with looking at this video from Ufuk Erdogmus, what do you say? It's probably just some encouragement for our mission, blah, blah, blah, but let's have some dessert and watch the movie."

He balled one fist and hesitated before finally punching the play button on the terminal next to him. Maybe it was just a pep talk, but with this being the last message they had from a dead Earth, Rankin was afraid there was more to it than that.

He'd met the multi-billionaire Ufuk Erdogmus in private several times and found him to be a nice man. He'd even been invited to a drinks party in the main hall of the *Museo del Prado* in

Madrid where Erdogmus had paraded him, his latest acquisition, a former NASA Mission Commander. In public, Erdogmus wore a very different face, just like every other man Rankin had met who occupied an extreme position of wealth or power: a mask that conveyed only the emotion Erdogmus wanted others to see.

In front of them now, on the galley's main screen, Erdogmus chose that public-facing mask. "Commander Rankin, crew of Mars First. Perhaps you already know something of what is about to happen, what will have already happened by the time you watch this. Perhaps you saw it unfold. I am not certain how the mission will play out."

Ufuk's face shifted from conveying optimism into one projecting sadness.

"What I can tell you is that the Earth will suffer a terrible tragedy. The full details are in a scientific briefing prepared for you and the crew." At that moment, terminals around the ship pinged. New messages arrived into the in-boxes of each crewmember. "Your mission to Mars has been suspended indefinitely. Instead, there are new mission parameters which are of vital importance to humanity."

Erdogmus's face faded from the screen, replaced by a graphic of the solar system, similar to the ones Siegel had been creating with the astrometrics software. A foreign object sliced through the solar system at high speed, and in the background, Ufuk's voice explained Nomad, the massive black hole pair that ripped the solar system apart. He detailed the expected size of the tsunamis, massive volcanism, and earthquakes, but stressed that it shouldn't wipe all life from Earth, and that Earth should remain in a habitable orbit afterward.

Not wipe out *all* life?

It seemed like he was trying to upsell the end of humanity.

Rankin had no family beyond an estranged brother in Nevada. Coming on this mission, Rankin never expected to see him again, and they hadn't even said goodbye when he left. Even so, he wondered what had happened to his brother in the final hours. A

137

bottle of Jack Daniels, no doubt, drunk in the arms of a Vegas stripper. Rankin couldn't help smiling sadly, but pushed the thought away.

He rose from his chair, still listening to Ufuk detail the probable scale of the death and destruction, the nature of the solar radiation storm induced by Nomad's passing. At least it all made sense now. Rankin walked over to one of the windows. Outside, the star-scape rotated as the Mars First hab module spun to create the centripetal force that simulated their gravity. He looked out at a universe that was suddenly vastly different.

"The lateness in which the event appeared to us left national governments with limited options." Erdogmus's voice filled the communal area. "There was little time to prepare. I doubt we will have an opportunity to transmit once the disaster arrives. Not for some time."

Siegel joined him at the window. Her shoulders shook and she sobbed. He wasn't ever very good at consoling, and he had no idea how to even approach something like this. He felt very little himself. Surprise of course, but it always took him much longer than anyone else to process the emotions of an event.

"Much of the Earth will be covered by dense cloud," said Ufuk's voice behind them. "Most of our satellites will be destroyed in the event, and much of our ground-based equipment. We have no way of really knowing until after the event. You will be in a unique position to observe the solar system, and so we will be relying on you to provide that information."

"Is that why they sent us out here?" Siegel whispered. "This was pre-recorded. He knew this was going to happen before we launched. Why didn't he stop us?"

"We always knew this was a one-way ticket," Rankin replied quietly. "Maybe it was better this way. Like he said, there wasn't much time to prepare."

"But I could have said goodbye to my sisters…"

"Didn't you say goodbye?"

"But not like that."

138

Rankin and Siegel both turned back on the main screen.

"It is possible you will be contacted by others," Ufuk's voice boomed. "We have tried to prevent access to your systems, but they may find a way. The event has caused considerable division among governments, even within governments. Speak only to me now, only to my representatives. The world is not what it was."

"*Mein Gott,*" Siegel said, lapsing into her native tongue.

Tears ran down Peng Shouang's face. Cuijpers just stared in disbelief.

As Ufuk was speaking, a tiny light had pulsed on in the control room. A tiny orb of brilliant blue, a small light that signaled the awakening of the synthetic intellect that regained control of the spacecraft known as Mars First.

This synthetic intellect embodied Mars First.

As the crew processed Ufuk's words, Mars First absorbed and observed and monitored inside the spacecraft and out, collating and analyzing data. The first analysis: Earth's atmosphere and surface were devastated by the Nomad event, even past the worst predicted ranges. Orbital parameters for the Earth and planets, and Mars First itself, were all within planned operational limits. And most lines of communication had ceased with its Earth-based networks.

Most, but not all.

The second analysis: the crew's emotional metrics were all over the place.

Mars First experienced no sensation of emotion itself; of course, such things were beyond its design. It couldn't therefore empirically say what experiencing the emotions the crew was undergoing right now might actually feel like—but it understood emotion in a diagnostic context and was able to navigate the web of physiological symptoms in order to recognize human emotional response. It could diagnose extreme emotional response and take appropriate measures to advise, assist, and alleviate where necessary.

The third analysis: one of the crew was dead.

Final analysis: the dead crewmember was no accident.

"Hey, everyone!" Cuijpers banged her hand on the terminal in front of her. "Mars First is back online."

A stream of diagnostics replaced Ufuk's face on the main display.

Siegel ran back to her console. "And I just got a new trajectory report." Her face contorted. "And Ufuk wasn't lying. We're not going to Mars."

That got everyone's attention.

"So where *are* we going?" Rankin had to ask as Siegel stared with rapt attention at her display. "Back to Earth somehow?"

Ufuk knew this was going to happen, Rankin realized, before they launched. Maybe he'd planned some clever contingency? A dangerous ray of hope bloomed inside Rankin's chest. Maybe his entire crew wasn't doomed to a pointless and painful death. "I thought you said our trajectory only led into empty space?" he said.

Siegel wiped her face with a shaking hand. "Saturn," she said quietly.

"Excuse me?"

"We're going to Saturn."

"That's ridiculous."

Rankin knew enough of orbital dynamics to know where the planets were. The distance from Earth to Mars at closest approach was about seventy-five million kilometers, and that journey had been planned to take them over three hundred days. Saturn was almost one and a half *billion* kilometers from the sun, in the outer solar system, way beyond the Asteroid Belt and even Jupiter.

Almost twenty times further from the Earth than Mars. And it wasn't just the distance. Saturn wasn't even solid—it was a gas giant, a thousand times the size of the Earth. An unimaginable monster they couldn't even touch down on, even if they weren't fried by its massive magnetic fields.

"You're serious," Rankin said, seeing that Siegel didn't crack a smile. "But even getting out to Saturn would take us a decade, probably even—"

"Nine months."

"*Excuse* me?" Had she lost her mind?

Getting to Saturn in nine months would require a velocity ten times what they were doing now. Rankin decided he needed to get her medicated, and fast. The shock had obviously been too much. He took a step toward her, but she shook her head.

"I said we are going to Saturn, but *we* are not going to Saturn," Siegel said, placing a very heavy emphasis on the second '*we.*'

She brought a graphic up on the main display. It was a top-down animation of the solar system, but the new solar system. The post-Nomad solar system. A bright red line plotted Mars First's trajectory, and as the animation progressed, a dotted line dropped in from the outer solar system, a planet dragged into a retrograde orbit.

"Because Saturn…" Siegel's voice was somewhere between a giggle and a sob as she pointed at the graphic on the screen. "…is coming to *us.*"

1

Northern Libya

It was Hector who saw the Bedouin first as he scampered up a dune ahead of them. They'd been walking south on foot for at least ten hours, stopping every now and then, along a dusty tracked road. Giovanni and Raffa took turns carrying Hector, but the boy toughed it out and walked most of it. They had seen no one, heard no noise beyond the whine of the wind. Jess felt tiny in the bleak landscape that undulated in formations carved by the constant sirocco wind. A wilderness of waves replaced by one of sand.

Hector ran back shouting and pointing.

They appeared as though from nowhere. Four spectral figures in the hazy light. Ghosts feathering the surface of the ash-ridden desert. Wrapped in heavy wool layers, each sat astride a camel. The wind whipped across the dunes, casting ash and sand across their faces. Beyond them, some way off, a clutch of tethered shelters.

Jess spoke quietly: "They've been here a while, Massarra, probably watching us."

The Israeli nodded in agreement.

"These are Ufuk's contacts?" Jess asked. "They're here to meet us?"

This time Massarra seemed to nod and shrug at the same time.

"You trust them?"

"In this place, loyalties change overnight. The desert sets survival above everything else. Whatever agreements might have been made in the past, we can make no assumptions. If we have something to offer them, then we are valuable. If not, we have equipment and supplies they could take from us by force."

"Anything positive you could tell me?"

"Just be watchful and remain unthreatening. The Sanusi Bedouin have lived in this region for centuries, in the Wahat al-Kufra. They will be wary of strangers. In any event, Jess, we need whatever food they can spare us."

Jess couldn't argue with that. They were hungry after eating almost their last half-rations of MREs on the boat. "Can you speak to them?"

"Their Arabic is a nomadic variety called Bedawi. It is different to the sedentary Arabic spoken in cities, but we will be able to understand each other."

"Then we'd better get this going. It's late and the temperature will drop. We could do with being under shelter."

One of the figures dropped from his camel. He shuffled toward them, hunched against the wind. In his hands was a rifle. The rest remained still, the only movement their clothes flapping in the wind.

Massarra turned to Jess and the rest of the group. "Wait here. Whatever happens, keep control of yourselves. We must convince these people that we are of value to them alive. Mr. Erdogmus, I suggest you accompany me."

Ufuk and Massarra walked toward the advancing man. In Jess's hand, hidden in the pocket of her jacket, she held the pistol. It felt heavy, the metal cold. The man halted ten feet from Massarra and gestured for her to stop. Jess couldn't see his face, hidden behind a thick *shemagh* scarf and black *keffiyeh* wrapped around his head. He still held the rifle, although he kept it low and away.

Their words whispered over the wind. She knew tiny bits of Arabic, but not enough to understand a conversation. She was desperate to know what they were saying, to have some time to react should the situation deteriorate. There had been incidents in Afghanistan, where interpreters had been slow to translate and precious seconds had been lost. The ability to read the situation had been hampered by misunderstanding and delay.

She tried to ignore the dryness in her throat.

Every word they spoke seemed to take an age, long pauses between each as the man studied them before he responded. She caught a glimpse of the Bedouin behind him shifting, the camels moving slightly. One man took up his rifle and laid it slightly forward.

"You see that?" Jess said to Giovanni.

He stood ramrod straight beside her, sweat on his face. "It's taking too long."

"Did you notice there are no women and children?"

Giovanni didn't reply.

"Where are their families? Are they raiders? Smugglers?" She shifted her shoulders, loosened herself up. "If we need to engage, make each shot count."

"Don't do anything stupid, Jess."

Ufuk stepped backward, away from the Bedouin. The camels stamped in the cold. The hair on the back of Jess's neck bristled. All this way, for it to go wrong now. She began to take the pistol out of her coat.

The man shouted something to those behind him. Ufuk turned and waved, clearly relieved. Massarra remained where she was, her stance relaxed. A boxer before the bell. She walked backward, Jess noted, still watching the men.

Only when she reached them did she turn.

"You don't look happy about whatever just happened," Jess said to Massarra. She glanced back over her shoulder and watched the men disappear into their camp.

"I do not really trust anyone."

They gathered their gear and headed over to the camp where the man waited. He unwrapped his *shemagh*, then threw more blankets over the camels and stroked each of their faces, softly whispering to them. He then rose and ushered all of them inside the tent.

"His name is Ahmad ibn Sahail ibn Hawaa al-Bakhit," Ufuk said.

"Can I just call him Ahmad?" Jess asked as she attempted to process the name. She kept them huddled to one side of the tent, out of easy earshot. "Where's his family?"

"These men are scavengers," Ufuk said. "They leave the families at another camp some distance away, protected against raiders. They're gone for several days at a time, but on this occasion, they were also waiting for us. They have been following us since we arrived."

"Why didn't they make themselves known to us?" Giovanni said.

"They were assessing, trying to decide if we were who they understood us to be."

"How did they know we were coming?" Jess said.

Ufuk hesitated, then said: "I contacted the Levantine Council. They have contacts among the Sanusi Bedouin. They knew we would come and they contacted the Sanusi to tell them."

"How did they know where we were?"

"The desert people have their ways."

On the other side of the large tent, Ahmad leaned forward and said something as he lit a small brazier-like stove. He placed a bowl on it and, from within the folds of a blanket, he took out a canister. Into the bowl he poured some kind of liquid as the flames warmed the shelter.

A sweet cardamom smell filled the air.

"What is he doing?" Giovanni asked.

"Preparing a welcome for us," Ufuk said.

"That's not necessary," Jess said.

"It is absolutely necessary for him. Poverty does not absolve him of his duty. His is a code of honor to be scrupulously obeyed and the *diyafa* is as important as any other. If required, even an enemy must be given shelter and fed, sometimes for days."

Ahmad waved them over, then handed a small, egg-shaped cup to Jess. She took it and nodded.

"*Bismillah*," he said.

She repeated the word and drank, enjoying its warmth, if not its bittersweet taste.

"What about survivors?" Jess asked. "Are there any? Other nomadic people, or the people from the cities in Libya?"

Massarra nodded and spoke to Ahmad. He gestured dismissively and responded briefly.

"Most of the major cities were close to the sea," she translated. "They were flooded and many died. Those who didn't die fled into the desert. They were unprepared and didn't survive."

"What happened?"

"The cold caught many by surprise." Massarra drank and watched the brazier as its flames wavered. "There is a Bedouin saying: When you sleep in a house, your thoughts are as high as the ceiling; when you sleep outside, they're as high as the stars. His kind are farmers, and less nomadic than other Bedouin, but they still understand how to live from the land."

"Al-Jawf is well known for its circular, irrigated agricultural fields," Ufuk said. "I'm sure some of this survived. Ancient water is pumped from aquifers underground and irrigates dozens of plots that measure nearly a kilometer in diameter. Rather than destroying the crops, the ash might actually be protecting them against frost."

"He also says there are fewer people to concern themselves with. At the narrow passage, say the Bedouin, there is no brother and no friend."

"Does he know of Al-Jawf?"

"He does, but he'll not travel that far south. He says the desert has changed, but its people have not changed with it. There is still much violence. The Toubou and the Zuwayya have rekindled their ethnic hatred of each other. All Toubou have been expelled from Kufra entirely. To avoid conflict, he hopes to head north once the winter has passed, and work the land up there. He thinks the ash will enrich land that the sea has saturated and act to fertilize it."

"Who are the Toubou and the Zuwayya?" Giovanni asked.

"The al-Zuwayya are a Murabtin tribe, although whether they're Bedouin or Berber is the subject of some debate. The

Zuwayya conquered the richest oasis of the interior, Kufra, in the nineteenth century, subduing the indigenous Toubou. Since then they've mostly employed Toubou as laborers."

"So they're the slaves?"

"I wouldn't say that to them." Ufuk shook his head. "The Zuwayya took part in the Libyan Civil War on the side of the opposition. The head of the tribe was Shaikh Faraj al Zuway, but it's not clear if he's alive. The Zuwayya maintain he is."

"You seem to know an awful lot about this," Jess said.

"The Toubou live mainly in northern Chad," Ufuk continued, "around the Tibesti Mountains, and are Muslim. There is also a minority in southern Libya. They speak Tebu, a subfamily of the Nilo-Saharan languages. Most are herders and nomads, though some have become semi-nomadic."

Now Jess sensed he was just showing off, but he knew his stuff. She wondered what relationship Ahmad and his people had with the rest of those who inhabited the Sahara, whether it was still possible to simply roam the desert and live a nomadic life, or whether there would always be those who wanted what others had and would take it by force. Could Africa—with its troubled past— offer salvation in the chaos? Or was ethnic and religious hostility too deeply rooted?

Jess didn't want to answer her own musings.

"The Toubou minority in Libya has suffered considerable discrimination, in particular those residing in Kufra and around Al-Jawf. As is the way of oppression, there have been armed and violent uprisings in recent years, particularly in Kufra."

Massarra murmured, "It would be nice to believe the world changing might serve to give people new perspective."

"Injustice and the hatred it breeds leaves a stain on the memory that nothing can erase, not even vengeance." Ufuk paused, then said, "Nevertheless, the Zuwayya have for a long time controlled the oil fields in Kufra. It is said they still have control of Al-Jawf."

"How long will it take us to get to the Sahl Oil Field?" Jess asked.

"About two days. The camels have adapted to the colder weather."

Jess found her mind wandering as they spoke more, enjoying the heat of the drink in the small, egg-shaped cup. She thought about the group, found herself considering the many practical matters that came with patrolling and long marching, and realized how close she had come to being a soldier once more. Not what she'd ever wanted again, but then, none of this was close to anything she'd ever imagined.

They broke camp soon after that, the camels taking the burden of the shelters and what the Bedouin had been able to scavenge as they'd waited for Ufuk and his group to arrive. They took Jess's backpack too, and those of the others. The Bedouin spoke little as they made their way, leading the camels behind them.

When after several hours they made camp again, the landscape seemed barely changed to Jess: a cold, sweeping wilderness of gray framed by a sky that shifted in color from sepia to a washed-out purple. Alone, she undertook a circuit of the terrain around them. She took a pistol with her as she conducted her patrol. She watched from one of the dunes, observing, as the members of her small group talked. It was her responsibility to keep them safe.

Jess snapped awake, disoriented. She raised a hand to feel the cold on her face. How long had she been asleep? The fire had dwindled to softly glowing embers in the night. She looked around the tent and realized that Ufuk was gone.

Voices carried on the cold air.

She struggled out of her sleeping bag and slipped her feet into her boots. Taking one of the blankets, she wrapped it around herself and went to the door of the tent. She tugged open the flap just enough to peer out.

Two shapes stood on one of the dunes, talking. One she made out as Ufuk, his tall, slender frame unmistakable even concealed beneath a swaddling of blankets. The other was Ahmad. They spoke for a little while, their voices hushed. Ahmad nodded infrequently, but eventually turned to Ufuk and embraced him. Above them, far in the distance, something furnace hot and pure white arced across the sky, lighting up the clouds from behind. More followed. Streaks of meteors. They didn't seem to reach the ground. At least, not anywhere close.

Ufuk and Ahmad made their way back to their tents.

Jess returned to her sleeping bag and slipped inside. Sleep didn't come for a long time.

2

Northern Libya
Outside Sahl Oilfield

Jess pulled a blanket around her and warmed her hands over the glowing coals of the small fire. She watched Ufuk stroke the wiry fronds of his dark beard and studied the small lines etched on his face. While still young and fit, his face wore an aged quality that made him seem older. When she observed him, trying to figure out his intentions, he often appeared far away and lost in thought. She considered asking him what he spoke to Ahmad about each evening, what they shared as they stood huddled against the cold.

She didn't ask.

Hector slept on wadded blankets on the sand. What was she leading him into? Did Ain Salah have access to the resources they would need? When Giovanni came to sit beside her, wrapping an arm around her and hugging her gently, the smile she gave him was uncertain.

"The oil fields across the Sahara have become targets for raiders," Ufuk said, drawing a map of the Sahl installation in the sand with a stick. It was early morning. Light seeped into the tent through an open flap. "We can't approach without first knowing what awaits us."

Jess inspected his diagram. It wasn't much, but Ufuk said it was one of his installations. They needed to get inside. It was critical for their survival, he said.

"People here have been exposed to violence for a long time," Ufuk continued. "Strong, proud people. The civil war and the opposition to Gaddafi, and racial wars between tribes. There's been a lot of fighting, and Nomad didn't stop it."

He stood and made his way outside, passing Massarra as she entered the tent holding Bedouin clothing.

"We should dress as they do," she said as she handed the clothes around. "Better others think that Sahl was taken by Bedouin raiders than by foreigners. We should keep our presence here unknown for as long as we can."

Once dressed, Giovanni and Jess went outside with Massarra. Ufuk sent the last of his drones into the air, fiddled with his tablet and left them to their mission. They watched them rise and drift away. They couldn't approach closer to Sahl for fear of the sound of their presence carrying over the frozen dunes, so the distance to be covered was measured in kilometers. The drones would turn fast and when they did, she could begin to analyze the images they had captured and see what awaited them.

She spent the time playing with Hector, running after him over dunes and around the camp. She tried to let his infectious enthusiasm, his childish innocence, wash away the pressure. The seeds of something she didn't like swelled inside, knowing she would almost certainly need to take more lives to protect those around her.

She couldn't help but think of the survivors at Sanctuary, escaping the complex into a frozen night, terrified and uncertain. How many had been left behind, trapped beneath tumbling rock? And whose fault was that? It felt like hers.

When the drones returned an hour later, the images they returned weren't good. Jess hoped it would be easy, that the Sahl would be deserted and they could simply walk in.

"How many are there?" Giovanni scrutinized the images from the drone's surveillance cameras. They showed a spider's web of diaphanous lines amid silvery dunes and gray buildings concealing unpredictable risks. Some of the images were blurred by falling sleet. There were some signs of movement, of figures making their way in time lapse over the open ground.

"I count at least five," Massarra said. "I'd bet there are more out of sight. There's only one vehicle. A pickup truck."

"At least two carrying rifles," Jess said.

"We have two pistols, a shotgun, and an M4 with SOPMOD." Massarra did an inventory. "Four of us armed. With Ahmad and his men, we're eight."

"I don't want to kill anyone unless we have to," Jess said.

"Then we make them see the only available option is to leave," Massarra replied.

"One of the buildings appears to have suffered damage already," Giovanni said. "Looks collapsed. Must have been a fight before."

"When we're finished, Sahl will belong to Ahmad and his people," Ufuk said. "That's the deal."

"We engage only if we're engaged ourselves," Jess insisted. "We're not going to murder everyone we come across. We try to make them see they can't overpower us and that the better course would be to leave." Weapons were laid out on a blanket on the sand. "The M4 marks us out as foreign military, so better it's not seen. Also better it gives us a range advantage. Massarra, can you take up a position on the dunes a few hundred feet away?"

The Israeli nodded.

"Give them a demonstration. They don't need to know you're the only sniper we have. Ufuk, hover one of your drones over the site and monitor them. We can set up short range comms through the headsets."

"There's sleet falling again," Giovanni said, glancing outside the tent. "Visibility will be poor. Shouldn't we wait?"

"We don't know how long it will last and any disadvantage the weather gives us, it gives them the same. Better we do this now, before we lose the element of surprise."

3

Northern Libya
Sahl Oilfield

The wind curled around them, carrying with it eddying streaks of sleet. It burned ice-cold against exposed skin, soaked into the outer layers of their makeshift Bedouin clothing. Jess hid the pistol within the folds of a long overcoat that whipped wet at her legs as they descended the dunes toward Sahl, sliding as the sand shifted beneath them. She wanted to have the weapon out, ready to deal with whatever threats might present themselves, but she knew that could only antagonize and ensure a confrontation.

She pressed down her fear. "Massarra, do you copy?"

"Receiving you clear."

"What can you see?"

"Two inside Building Five, the central facility. They haven't noticed us. I cannot see the others yet."

"Copy that. Ufuk?"

"Drones in the air now. Sleet is coming down heavy so visibility is intermittent, but so far no movement detected."

Five of them, side by side, in appearance all Bedouin, moving across the sand. The wind whipped across her face and she blinked away sand.

"The two in Building Five are moving," Massarra said. "They're taking weapons. Looks like...a Kalashnikov and a rifle. Coming out now, so get ready."

Jess tensed. "Here we go," she said. "They're coming out." She laid a hand on Ahmad's arm. She only saw his eyes, the rest of his face covered by his *shemagh*, but they were steady and calm.

Two shadows appeared from a doorway ahead of them and moved fast, weapons held high.

"Stay calm," Jess said. "We approach slowly. Massarra, the moment you think they're getting ready to shoot, give them a warning."

"Copy that."

Ahmad took one hand off his rifle, the only weapon that could be seen, but which he kept low, and raised it in acknowledgement. He shouted in his own Bedouin Arabic. Words, which, although she couldn't tell what they meant, Jess heard repeated and which carried a tone of cautious greeting.

"Ufuk," Jess said. "Anything to see?"

"Nothing yet. No more movement."

"Copy that. No movement."

"Where are the others?" Giovanni muttered.

As they approached the buildings, the two shadows caught the light and became defined. Two men dressed similarly to Ahmad, both carrying weapons. One an AK, as Massarra had seen, the other a rifle. Both were raised, but the men seemed calm.

They spoke to Ahmad, gesturing in a way that left no doubt that they wanted him to leave. He replied quickly, returning gestures of his own.

"He's telling them the oil field belongs to the Sanusi Bedouin. That the men should leave immediately before they're forced to resort to violence. He's telling them not to come back, that this place is not theirs to take."

Jess watched their expressions, her palm damp as her grip tightened on the pistol. The men grew angry, gesturing again and shouting.

"There are more coming," Ufuk warned. "From a building to your right. Building One. Three or four. Maybe five."

A hundred feet or more. Hard to be accurate with a pistol. If they chose to shoot, there was virtually no cover.

"We need to know exactly how many," Jess said quietly.

"Hang on, re-routing the drones."

"Ufuk, we don't have time for—"

"Three."

"You're sure?"

"Three."

"Copy that. Three more from Building One."

"They're armed. All are carrying rifles. They're running now."

She tapped Ahmad's arm three times and caught his quick nod.

Ahmad shouted again and pointed to the dunes behind them.

Massarra's voice came over the headset. "He's telling them there are more of his people with guns. He's telling them he knows there are more of their friends here. He's saying that if they don't leave immediately, he'll order his people to fire."

More angry gestures came from the men.

"Don't be stupid," Jess heard herself murmur. "Just leave."

One of them scanned the way of the fenced building to the north, toward what Jess had designated Building One. From where three men were now running, covering the distance at a sprint.

Ufuk's voice: "They look young."

Ahmad shouted to the men and Jess sensed the tension growing in his tone.

Jess reached slowly up and rubbed sleet from her face and eyes. Her skin was numb. Her stump ached in the cold.

Massarra's voice again: "He's giving them a final opportunity to leave."

Out of the corner of her eye, she caught the Bedouin beside Ahmad moving their own weapons. Giovanni shifted on his feet. No, no, she told herself. This doesn't need to happen...

"Just a warning shot, Mass—"

The next instants were driven by pure instinct. Jess dove forward when the first shots rang out. She turned to the oncoming men. From where flashes of light illuminated the glistening sand around her. Her pistol was out before she even realized it was in her hand. She fired. Then heard the crack of the M4 hundreds of feet behind her.

One of the attackers fell.

"Get down, Giovanni!" she shouted.

The boom of Ahmad's high-caliber weapon, followed by the guns of the other Bedouin. She didn't know if the two men by Building Five were returning fire. Another of the two still sprinting toward them went down, and the remaining one stumbled into cover behind the Toyota.

Jess turned to try and find the first two men, her pistol searching, but both of them were already in the dirt. She turned back to the Toyota. The man behind it wasn't visible.

"Ufuk," she said. "Any more?"

"Nothing. I can hear the gunfire. I am certain it would have alerted any others if there were more."

"Stay vigilant," she said.

She surveyed Ahmad and the other Bedouin. No one had been hurt. When he nodded to her, she pointed to her lips and then at the Toyota. He nodded again and shouted.

"He's telling the man he is alone. They will not hurt him if he leaves now. He must leave the truck, but if he runs now, they will not shoot him. He says honor has been satisfied because the man's friends are dead. He has nothing to fear if he leaves now and does not return."

From behind the truck, a terrified voice shouted. In its tone Jess could hear not only desperation, but youth as well.

Ahmad shouted something back and then gestured for his men to go to the Toyota.

"He is telling the man that he made his choice and must live with the consequences. I suspect the man is complaining that he'll die in the desert without the truck."

Jess reached for Ahmad, but he pulled away. He glared at her and shook his head.

"You must let them resolve this their way," Massarra said. "Do not insult them. We cannot afford to make enemies, and we may need them later."

"But the one behind the Toyota is a damn kid."

157

The Bedouin rounded the truck, one on each side. Jess shouted, but they didn't stop. Two shots rang out. She closed her eyes and turned away.

They cleared every building before sending two of Ahmad's Bedouin to break camp. Frustration grew inside her as they searched and found nothing.

When they'd cleared the final building, she caught up with Ufuk. "There's nothing here! Five dead. Three of them teenagers. For nothing."

"Not quite." Ufuk manipulated the screen of the tablet and looked up. The drone hovered and soared into the air again, over to the runway. It hung in the air and then darted away, continuing for several hundred feet, then slowly descended until it landed.

"There," Ufuk said. "That's what we need. Bring some shovels."

They dug through half-frozen sand for two hours until Giovanni hit metal. A steel manhole cover with a handle in the center. They brushed away the dirt. It took some time, and a little stern persuasion with shovels, but eventually it opened. Sand shifted and seeped into the hole beyond. Jess shone a flashlight inside. A ladder bolted to a drain wall led downward into darkness.

"In we go," Ufuk said.

Jess let him climb down first.

Somewhere a generator hummed. Jess felt it vibrate through each step as she descended. The others followed and, when she was halfway down, light flooded the area below to reveal a wide-open cavern cut into the earth, bolstered by steel reinforced pillars. Shelving lined one of the walls, stacked with wooden crates. In the center, organized by type, were rows of what appeared to be modern agricultural equipment. Beyond them, Jess's eyes were drawn to something else. Two battered Toyota pickup trucks stood in pools of bright light that caught the thin veneer of dust that coated each.

Of course they would be Toyota pickups.

Ubiquitous, easy to fix, and used as weapons of both war and revolution for years, perhaps even decades. Neither would draw a second glance in this region. Both would be able to cross the desert as capably as any other vehicle and carry as much of their equipment as they needed.

"What is this place?" she asked.

"There has long been a belief that Libya has sponsored extremist paramilitary groups who have had training camps in the Libyan Desert, in particular the IRA and Al Quaeda. US satellites have surveyed this area for decades. Anything that occurs aboveground can be seen and is recorded. We work below ground, away from scrutiny."

Giovanni jumped off the ladder and scoffed, "So you funded terrorist camps?"

"Not terrorists, survivalists." Ufuk deflected the criticism. "After the civil war here, I purchased the Sahl Oil Field through shell companies. The political situation allowed me a favorable bargaining position with the new Libyan government over Western business interests. My intention was to give myself a base of operations for a project examining agricultural innovations that were suited to the climate in this region, experiment with the irrigation techniques already developed to deal with Libya's harsh climates."

"Why did we need to dig?" Jess said. "Surely you didn't do this every time you needed to come down here?"

"This was...how do you say...a bolt hole? I knew Nomad was coming—" He winced slightly. "—and many of my installations I attempted to hide. The main entrance was in the building destroyed by explosives. It was reported to the Libyan authorities as a machinery accident. There is an exit that we can open to drive the jeeps and equipment out, but we can only open this from the inside."

As he spoke, Jess noticed something else in the vast hangar. In one far corner, covered by long, tall tarpaulin shelters the same color as the walls, and camouflaged by gathered dust and sand. She walked toward them, curious.

Ufuk followed. "It is what you think it is."

She pulled aside the canvas. Strip lights illuminated the high-framed walls. There were differences, but the similarities were unmistakable. "Predator drones? Are these military?"

"Similar, but not identical. We can call them Predators."

"How did you get them?"

"How does it matter?"

"Any weapons systems?"

"Only communications and surveillance."

"And you know how to get them airborne?"

"Not difficult at all. Without payloads, they can fly thousands of kilometers, and at the right cruising speed stay aloft for as much as forty-eight hours. Or at least, they could without all the ash in the air. These are air-breathers, unlike our other trusty little friends, but at least we can refuel them."

4

Siberian Steppes
Near Ulan Battor

The Russian soldiers sat huddled around a small fire, grateful for what small respite their shelter offered from the bitter Siberian wind. Heavy canvas, now bowed by ash, had been strung from the rigging of the old Czilim and pegged as tight as the frozen ground would allow. Somewhere it still flapped monotonously in the gale, but Zasekin couldn't find the resolve to leave the warmth of the fire and tend to whatever had worked loose. He supposed they had all grown used to the noise by now.

Beyond, somewhere out in the darkness, the ash still fell, eddying in the savage wind. Thick tape along the edges of the shelter kept the ash from being swept inside, but Zasekin could still taste it in his mouth. He spat phlegm thick and dark onto the frozen ground.

Barely five weeks ago he had been Corporal Andrei Nikolayevich Zasekin, of the Border Service of the Federal Security Service of the Russian Federation. It had been a title that had come to mean less and less to him as the years had passed. One which he accepted as any man accepts a sad truth he once blindly craved, but which he now perceives more clearly and from which he can no longer escape.

Five weeks ago, he had been a disillusioned servant of Putin's new, united Russia. To a man posted in Siberia—and almost as far away from Moscow as it was possible to be in the Rodina—it seemed not so very different from the old Russia.

"Tell me uncle," Zasekin thought as he called to mind Lermontov's *Borodin*, "was it any different to the *tandemocratia*?" When Putin shared power with the puppet President, Medvedev, the Rodina had still been saddled with the same old soaring Soviet ambitions that went far beyond her actual capabilities. Shifting power back and forth between the two men for a decade had done little to change anything.

Yet, if that had been five weeks ago, who was he now?

Now he supposed he was simply Andrei Nikolayevich Zasekin again, a Buryat who had tried to leave his roots behind. A foolish young man blinded by the promise of adventure, a life away from the insular monotony of provincial Yanchukan, nestled in the mountains of Severo-Baykalsky. Serving a Russia he didn't truly feel a part of.

He pictured the valleys, laden with colorful flowers, that he'd played in as boy. Hills lined by pine forest that seemed always to be touched by mist. What was left of that tiny community after Lake Baikal's conflagration?

How much of Russia itself had even survived?

From what they'd seen in the last few days, a great deal of damage had been done. What was left of the Rodina now and Putin's lofty ambitions? Tell me that, uncle.

If he was no longer a Corporal, why did they still follow him? These men who now warmed themselves by the fire, wrapped in scavenged blankets and coats they used to supplement their own military-issue clothing.

He told himself it was a Russian's nature to endure, and to sacrifice for the betterment of the Motherland. He knew, deep in his gut, there would always be the Rodina. He had no way to know what that meant for any of them.

They camped away from the banks of the Selenge, the river still bloated and warm, reeking of sulfur. Zasekin might have considered a different route away from Baikal, but with Irkutsk gone, Ulan Bator was the nearest urban center.

It lay to the south, on the fringes of the Gobi, where he hoped it might be warmer. The quickest route for their Czilim hovercraft was along the Selenge itself, where there were also settlements they could search for supplies.

162

And diesel fuel.

"Soup?"

Zasekin took the offered bowl from Timur. "Thank you," he said as he lifted the steaming spoon to his mouth.

"Vadim says it is no more than another day to Sükhbaatar," Timur said. "But we will spend much of the morning performing maintenance on the Czilim. Several skirts need replacing. The ash and ice are taking their toll. We are in need of fuel too."

Sükhbaatar, where the Selenge branched away and they would instead take the Orhon to Ulan Bator.

"Sükhbaatar is large enough," Zasekin said. "There will be fuel and food there, I am sure of it. How is Semyon?"

Timur tensed and glanced across at the man lying closest to the fire, hidden beneath a mound of whatever blankets they had been able to find. "Not much change. Tired, but the antibiotics are in his system now. We will know in a few days."

"We must all be careful. As we head south, there will be more who see value in the Czilim. Many will try to take it from us. There have always been bandits and hunters in these mountains. If anyone can survive here, they can."

Timur nodded. "Evgeny has the first watch. He was with Semyon when they were attacked. He'll not make that mistake again. When he sleeps, I will take over." Evgeny was inside the Czilim then, its systems powered down and silent. Zasekin remembered just how cold it was inside that steel coffin, when there was no heat.

"I will take the next watch," Zasekin said, perhaps too quickly.

"You should sleep."

"I've slept enough. I will take the watch."

Timur seemed about to say something, but instead he nodded and returned to his soup. Perhaps he knew Zasekin well enough now to understand that questioning him was unacceptable.

Zasekin smiled thinly to himself. He hoped Timur had not picked up the brusqueness in his voice. Better that his friend didn't know that Zasekin needed to be inside the Czilim at a specified time, and alone. While his men slept, there would be only one system powered on inside the hovercraft and, with the raging wind outside, none of them would hear the conversation he would then have. They couldn't know, not yet. They might think him crazy for trusting a man thousands of miles away, on the other end of a radio. They might question his judgment, his ability to lead them, if they knew the deal he had struck.

There would be confirmation at Sükhbaatar. If the man could deliver what he had promised there, Zasekin would be able to reveal to his men what he had been doing. There would be proof the man was capable of following through on his extravagant claims. It was Russian nature to be suspicious of those bearing gifts.

Semyon gave a small moan and Zasekin resisted the urge to look over at him again. Bullet wounds were rarely to be treated lightly, but out here, in the vast wilderness so far from help, such an injury took on a new seriousness. And with the damn ash everywhere, Zasekin wondered if the infection was more serious than they had thought. Semyon had only recently begun service with the SVR. He had transferred from the re-commissioned ICBM complex at Drovyanaya in Chita Oblast in an attempt to escape that frigid, barren place, a place that Zasekin himself knew all too well, only to be billeted to the Border Guard of Lake Baikal, barely a few hours' drive away. The irony left Zasekin bitter. Now, if Semyon became dead weight, unable to discharge his duty to the other men with whom he served, the situation might become more complicated. Men, even good men, could be overcome when their survival was threatened.

"There is something I wanted to ask you." Timur didn't look up from his bowl as he spoke.

"Then ask."

Timur hesitated.

"They're sleeping," Zasekin said. "You may speak freely."

Timur looked at him. "Do you think they know what we are doing?"

They, meaning their *apparatchik* FSB superiors. It had always been a Russian military man's unspoken duty to fear his superiors, to fear the Party and its *nomenklatura*. "I think they have more to concern themselves with than caring about what happens to a single Border Service unit. Irkutsk is in ruins, we both saw it. We have no way of knowing what else has suffered similarly."

"Will they not consider it desertion? Is it any different?"

"What is important is that we stay alive. If that means heading south, then that's our duty. We cannot protect the Rodina if we are dead."

For a moment, the younger man seemed unconvinced, then he nodded. "Did you feel anything, when we crossed the border after Naushki?" Timur had not once ever left the Rodina. To him crossing the border into Mongolia would have been significant, possibly, Zasekin thought, a betrayal of its own. Who do you think you are betraying, Timur? The only person to whom you owe allegiance now is yourself, or perhaps these men here, huddled around a fire whilst one of their own slowly dies in agony.

Zasekin hesitated before he spoke. "Something, perhaps," he said finally. "Buryatia has always been my home. It is strange knowing it may be some time before I return."

He wondered what Timur might think if he knew what was really in his mind at that moment—the unshakable belief he would never in fact return, that there was very likely to be little to return to.

"Much has changed."

"Not us, Timur Ivanovych. We have not changed. We are still loyal to each other. That will never change. Was that not Anapa's most important lesson to you?"

Timur glanced at Semyon, then said, "Perhaps loyalty is all we have." He smiled thinly. "I hated Anapa. I was glad to graduate. You should consider yourself lucky never to have experienced it."

"Golitsynsky was much worse, let me assure you."

"I sometimes forget how much older you are."

Gaskin allowed himself a chuckle. "You mean wiser."

"We owe you our lives. Of that I am certain."

"Continue to trust me, and I will continue to protect you."

"I do trust you, comrade. I always have."

A noise came from outside, a soft crack that carried on the wind. Timur reached for his pistol.

A little more slowly, Zasekin did the same and noticed that it trembled a little in his hand. Timur was right—he needed to sleep.

Evgeny stepped through the entrance to the shelter and stared at them. "You're nervous."

Zasekin holstered his pistol. "I can't sleep. I'll take the next watch."

Evgeny took a bowl and filled it with soup. "Take an extra blanket," he said as he settled down. "It's damn cold out there."

Zasekin pulled a scarf around his face, and went outside. He squinted against the ash-veined wind that instantly swept over him and opened the hatch to the old Czilim. She had no name to the FSB other than PSKA-83. Zasekin had once called her the Water Chestnut, because that was the name the shipbuilders at Yaraslavsky had wanted to name the series, only to be denied later by the FSB *apparatchik*. Those who rode in her had affectionately retained the name.

The Water Chestnut had nearly been retired a few years ago, when her sisters had been put out to pasture after two decades of loyal service, yet this particular Czilim still had much to offer. She still yearned for the challenge of Baikal's unpredictable temperament amidst Search and Rescue operations or the evacuation of stricken Russian Border Guard. Even on one quietly celebrated occasion as a hastily deployed exfiltration unit for Spetsgruppa A troops in China. Now she cared for him and his men. There was still much to love about her. He suspected that, given almost everything with a circuit was fried, the fact she was old and more mechanical than electronic offered some explanation as to why she was still running at all. Good old Soviet design.

"Sometimes new is not always best," he murmured.

He ducked inside and closed the hatch behind him.

Through the windscreen, he could barely see the mountains through the pall. Would he miss his homeland? If the world was so different now, it hardly mattered. What was once his homeland was gone, to be replaced by something different. What that was, he didn't yet know.

A pale orange glow built in the surging sky, high above the *nunataks* far-off to the north. Zasekin watched, spellbound, as it pulsed and threaded a bleeding trail across the slate gray firmament. Slowly it billowed, intensified, and above the wind a sound like crackling fire came. It grew in size and brightness until almost the entire cabin was lit by its presence, and its voice had become a shuddering, sonorous bellow. In the center of that shivering glow was a tiny kernel of purest white, a searing inferno. It cut through the sky, a trail of fire in its wake. The *nunatak* summits lit up by the conflagration, and the ground shuddered as it struck. Even so far away, the impact left its mark on him, he felt it in the deepest parts of himself, and he might have sat, paralyzed like that all night, had the radio not then hissed and cracked, and come to life.

He answered.

"Andrei Nikolayevich," said a familiar voice. "Are you well?"

"We are surviving. It has been some time since I last heard from you."

"I have had matters to attend to. How is your injured man?"

"Much improved." Zasekin lied. Far better that this man considered them useful to him for as long as possible, if his claims were to be believed.

"Good. Where are you now?"

"Better we do not broadcast our location over the radio, but we will be in Sükhbaatar within the next forty-eight hours, I am sure."

"The supplies I promised you will be there. I will explain precisely where after you have arrived."

"Can you tell us anything about the town? Are there survivors?"

"It's possible. There are vehicles moving around the town, mostly centered around the hospital and the Governor's House. There is other activity, but it's sporadic and hard to identify. We receive only limited information."

"How do you know all of this?"

"I'm sure you don't tell me everything, Andrei Nikolayevich, separated as we are by such great distance. Trust on both sides must be earned."

"If you are able to offer what you claim, then you will have my trust."

"Fair enough. I will call again at the same time tomorrow and you can update me on your progress."

Zasekin turned off the radio and stared out again through the dirty glass of the windscreen, at shadows shuddering in the pale light.

5

Northern Libya
Sahl Oilfield

Jess found Massarra outside, standing over the bodies of the five deceased. The M4 still hung from a single-point harness on her chest. For a moment, she had cold, dead eyes that Jess had seen in second-tour marines in Afghanistan, calculating and emotionless, windows to a quiet understanding they were little more than ghosts drifting in the fog, waiting for death and its long, empty silence.

The bodies had been dragged to one side and lay beside the fence line of the estate, faces covered.

"Ahmad will allow us to take two of their weapons," Massarra said. "He'll keep the others. We should also take their clothes before his men bury them. It would be better for us if we continued to dress as people local to the eastern Sahara."

"A lot of the clothing has been bloodied."

"We will salvage what we can. I do not mind the blood. I can clean it off."

Jess looked at the crumped bodies. "Was this worth it?"

"You've been fortunate to live a life mostly sheltered from the violence that goes on in places like this."

"I saw enough of it in Afghanistan."

"I understand that, but this won't be the end of it."

"Is Al-Jawf the right place for us to be headed? Where do we go after that?"

"We can only see one step at a time right now," Massarra said as she kneeled down beside the men. She peeled away the layers of their clothing, then paused. "I doubt anyone really has answers to questions as you have. We just do our best."

Ahmad approached them with Ufuk and embraced each of them. He spoke briefly to Massarra and she nodded.

"He'll go no further," she said. "He wishes us well, but he'll not head south. It is his intention to bring his people here and take the machinery north. They will ensure they know the entrance to the complex so they may come back."

"Tell him we understand and thank him for his hospitality."

Massarra spoke to Ahmad. His expression shifted, tightening, then he nodded. He said something to Massarra and she thanked him.

"He says to avoid Zuetina. It is much bigger than Sahl and was very busy before the political situation changed. He suspects there will be many people there. Just like the towns on the main road between the coast and Al-Jawf. He urges caution and suggests we avoid the roads."

Ahmad went to the Toyota and got in with another of the Bedouin. Two more went to one of the buildings, retrieved shovels and went to dig graves for the dead men.

"I've been through most of what is down there," Giovanni said. "There are military ration packs—not the best, but nutritious and they don't take up much space. There are heavier shelters too, all in the Bedouin style. I also found high-powered binoculars and two sets of night vision goggles. That's the good news. Bad news is, we can't carry that and a lot of fuel."

"Pack as much as possible and cover everything with tarpaulin," Jess said. "Make sure everyone understands to dress as Bedouin. We have clothing to go round. No exceptions."

The use of the *shemagh* and *keffiyeh* had been adopted by US troops since the war in Iraq and Jess had worn one herself in Afghanistan. Their versatility in desert and even temperate environments was the principal reason the Bedouin wore them. The Berber *tagelmust* fulfilled a very similar purpose. British troops over there had even been issued with a *shemagh* as part of their standard kit. Most wore it folded and wrapped around the face, over the mouth and nose and often with goggles, to keep sand away from the face. Jess had seen it frequently worn by armored and mechanized troops to ward off wind chill caused by being in moving vehicles.

Massarra added another reason: "And there is a possibility that there are those in Al-Jawf who will be watching for us. We need to slip into the city with the many who arrive there daily, we must appear to be yet more trucks carrying survivors desperate for a place to live. The more we look out of place, the more danger we will place ourselves in."

Instead of using the main road south, which passed through townships like Awjilah and Jalu, they navigated across the open desert, a vast expanse of half-frozen desiccation. If continental Europe had offered the constant threats of survivors driven to violence by desperation, there was no reason to believe that this place—that had seen much lawlessness even before Nomad—would be any better.

They drove over dunes flattened by oil field excavation, and hardened by the nighttime freezing temperatures and the ash fall. Momentum—and Ufuk's deference to mathematical gradients—carried them over steeper dunes, giving them traction in the heavy sand and keeping them moving. Above, the two Predator-like drones kept watch. The rest, Ufuk's smaller units, were disassembled and cleaned, then packed away, resting in the back of both trucks, hidden beneath tarpaulin with the other equipment.

Jess asked what had been so important about the Sahl for Ufuk to build an installation there, and Ufuk just replied that it was part of his plan to help people after Nomad.

They covered the distance in a single journey, barely stopping to rest. They began at night, when the cold hardened the ground, and so they could spend as much of the journey as possible unseen. Long hours spent focused on the lines of the dunes, keeping to threaded ridges to minimize the need for climbing, driving and sleeping in shifts, keeping the vehicles moving as much as possible to avoid lower gears and conserve fuel.

They kept a wide arc around the town of Tazirbu, passing it by more than thirty kilometers, fingers poised on triggers as they swept past.

When dawn came, shedding its anemic light over the landscape, they had been driving for nine hours. A considerable distance remained. As the darkness that had protected them withdrew, Jess gestured for both pickups to stop.

She heaved herself out of the pickup, feeling a jab of pain as the ache in her prosthetic's socket twisted into something sharper. She winced and tried to walk it off. After a moment, she went over to the warm hood of the truck where they'd laid out one of the maps. Massarra, Ufuk and Giovanni joined her while Hector slept in the back seat. Raffa took binoculars to the top of nearby dunes and lay low, watching for signs of movement beyond.

The same process every time the small convoy stopped.

"Where are we?"

"On the eastern fringe of the Rebiana Sand Sea," Ufuk replied. "About four hours to the rocky plain north of Al-Jawf."

Jess nodded. "Then we break for a little while, and go in one last push."

The horizon was at first only scattered with, but then soon became dominated by, a jagged line of rock that steadily swelled over hours as they approached. A few hundred feet high, a dark shadow painted on a horizon of ochre-washed gray.

When finally they reached the base of the gnarled massif, a band of dark rock washed by desert rain and stretching for kilometers in either direction, it was early afternoon. Jess set them to the task of making camp in the lee of a sheltered hollow hidden on almost all sides by rock. It was easier here, the ground a mess of desert pavement silted with ash. They set up the shelters as heavy flakes of snow whispered through the air.

Jess and Giovanni climbed up, fingers numb on the cold rock.

The wind swept around them. At nights, hoarfrost dampened their jackets and wool blankets. Overhead, Ufuk's drones murmured as they circled high. Jess lifted the high-powered binoculars to her eyes and focused on the scattered structures five miles away.

Al-Jawf.

She passed the binoculars to Giovanni.

"Can't see much," he said quietly. "There's a dune wall the whole way round."

"Did you see the tracks?"

"In the sand the other side? Hundreds. We are not the only ones driving this desert."

"Let's tell everyone to get some sleep. We'll do some reconnaissance tonight. I'd like to get a feel for the place before we ride on in."

"What about Ufuk's drones?"

"They can only tell us so much."

"We take Massarra with us?"

"We leave one of the pickups here. Take a weapon each. The M4 has a night-vision scope and there are two sets of night vision goggles. In and out for a quick look."

The day dragged on. The snow fell thick but didn't collect on the ground, just made everything wet. The damp cold enveloped them, even in the lee of the wind, even huddled in their sleeping bags and blankets and thick down jackets, but it was the waiting that exhausted Jess. She tried not to think about the dead teenagers at Sahl.

When night finally came, Jess roused herself from a fitful half-sleep spent worrying. They geared-up, checking and re-checking equipment. They drove quietly, letting the engine idle for stretches and allowing momentum to carry them across the hard-packed sand. After a few miles, Jess ordered Giovanni to stop.

They walked the rest of the way.

In the surreal green shroud of night vision, she could have been back in Afghanistan. The subtle rush of the wind and her own breath were in her ears as they trekked silently over the dusty ground.

They covered the distance in a little less than an hour, but saw the fringes of the encampment far sooner. Fires lit, blazing in the distance as flickering white against heavy green. The darker outlines of tents and flimsy, shantytown structures and the huddled movement of thickly clad people between them. A scattering of trucks and motorcycles. Voices carrying across the desert.

They hunkered low as they moved, keeping to the cover offered by undulating dunes, and stopped about three hundred feet away, hidden in the lee of a rising dune, lying down on its high ridge. Jess watched the scene unfold around her as she panned, studying people sitting around a fire, speaking. On the ground nearby was the unmistakable outline of a rifle. She tried to discern what tone their voices carried, whether there was fear or comfort, if she could pick out an accent. Her eyes kept coming back to that rifle on the ground.

They were camped close to what Jess could now see was an artificial dune wall that stretched into the distance the whole way round the basin in which Al-Jawf had been settled. Beyond it was a road carved into the sand and a second, lower wall.

"There's movement," Massarra warned.

She gestured to the east and Jess took a moment to see three figures stumbling across the sand. They were running north, toward one flat side of the dune wall. In the distance, a cloud of dust gathered. Jess tapped Massarra on the shoulder and directed her attention to it.

"Look like a truck to you?"

Massarra nodded.

The three figures could probably run the distance in under thirty seconds.

At the base of the curling sheet of dust, an outline materialized. A vehicle travelling at speed along the road flattened into the sand beyond the dune wall. As it drew closer, Jess made out a pickup with a heavy machine gun bolted to the back, a lone figure standing to the rear of the weapon. She couldn't tell how many were inside the cab.

The three figures must have seen the billowing cloud and understood what it was because their pace quickened. They obviously wouldn't make it. The truck was driving too fast.

They reached the dune wall as the truck pulled up the other side of it. Lights bloomed from the roof of the cab, flooding the green of the night vision goggles with searing white. Jess lifted them away and watched, cold flushing through her.

Massarra had already lifted the M4's telescopic sight to her eye and settled herself into the sand.

Jess laid a hand on her arm. "They can't know we're here."

A man dressed in military fatigues and a thick coat got out of the passenger side of the pickup's cab and began to shout. He carried an AK47, jabbing it forward as he spoke. He gestured for the three figures to come down off the sand.

Beyond the dune wall, others approached, people from the encampment beyond.

The machine gunner readied his heavy weapon. More shouting came from the passenger who had now fully emerged from the cab and was steadying his own into his shoulder.

The three figures on the dune wall froze in place.

From beyond the wall, those who came from the encampment began to yell, gesturing for the figures to come down. Shouting too, to the men in the pickup.

The figures still didn't move.

"One of them is child, not more than ten," Massarra said.

Jess grimaced and fought her own desire to break cover. "We don't know what's happening here."

But it was obvious what was happening.

The man from the pickup edged closer, shouting again, gesturing.

Eventually they began to move and slowly climbed down toward the man.

One of them came forward and tried to speak to the man, but he waved them away. When they didn't move, he aimed the assault rifle at them, jabbing it at them savagely. They shrank backward, stepping away.

He yelled. They didn't move.

In an instant it was over. Bright flashes from the rifle's muzzle. A short burst and sweep. The figures fell into the dirt. The man fired another dozen rounds into the inert bodies and then jumped into the back of the truck.

Jess's fingers bit into the cold ground.

6

Libya
Outside Al-Jawf

When dawn came, they packed and gathered around the pickups. There were questions when they returned. Jess had been reluctant to answer. Eventually, as Massarra silently packed away the M4 and the rest of her equipment, Jess and Giovanni had explained to Raffa what they had seen. She wondered whether anyone had really slept that night, her own dreams plagued by relentless doubt.

Since leaving the boat, they hadn't been able to reach Ain Salah. Was it being on the water that had made his signal stronger? Or was it something else? Maybe something had happened in Al-Jawf.

"We should approach by road," Ufuk said now, indicating the road on the map. "We don't know what the argument was about last night. It will be the least intimidating."

"You're settled on our cover story?" Jess said.

"The oil belongs to the Zuwayya," Ufuk replied. "So then does the city. For as long as they can control the refineries that still function, they control Al-Jawf and Kufra. The Zuwayya supported opposition forces during the civil war, as did Turkey. I hope many here, and especially the Zuwayya, will be more generously disposed to Turks."

"You think telling them we stowed away on a stolen Turkish freighter to Egypt will be believable?"

"It's sufficiently desperate. Nomad destroyed much of the coast of southern Turkey, yet there were parts to the north of the Levantine Sea, close to Iskenderun, that were relatively unscathed. It is conceivable some larger vessels escaped the worst of it. If we must explain further, those who are not Turkish can claim to be international students. There are universities at Çukurova and Gaziantep."

"Seems feasible enough," Giovanni said. "Raffa and Hector are my sons and I worked at a Turkish company as an engineer."

"Keep in mind, Jessica," Massarra said, "they may not appreciate being spoken to by a woman. Not in this region. That limits what I—what *we*—can do. So I agree, this is the best way. We should do whatever we can to obscure where we have come from. If pushed, say you're from Canada, rather than America."

Jess nodded. Everyone liked Canadians.

"If we are allowed access to the town," she continued, "then we camp and try to remain private. Whatever we have to tell the Zuwayya, it will be better if others believe we are local to North Africa or have some association. And even if weapons are carried openly by others, better we do not."

"What about Ain Salah?" Giovanni said.

"We will try to find him," Ufuk replied. "But we need to keep our cover."

They joined the road north of the Al-Jawf, north of the small township of Al Hawwari, the first of the vast, circular irrigation plots. The first thing they saw, as they progressed south, was a wall of ruined cars set either side of the road with a control point directly in its center. Either side of the cars ran a wall of sand—an immense, manufactured dune. Jess tensed as she saw it, memories of the night before rising in her mind.

Two Toyota pickups stood beside a clutch of buildings to the right of the road, both with machine guns on the back and armed men in uniforms. A short line of other vehicles stood motionless, waiting to enter.

Two motorbikes ducked beneath the rising barrier, and a dusty sedan drew up at the control point ahead of them. The occupants were instructed, via sharp gestures and with harsh directness, to leave the vehicle. They were dragged out and taken to one side of the road.

Two uniformed men checked the car, looking into the trunk and underneath, lifting the hood and checking the engine. The car's occupants were questioned. Flushes of desperation on their faces, lips forming words quickly, eyes leaping from one place to another, seeking escape from the prison that had closed around them. Two men and a woman, one of the men much younger.

Not local to the region.

The conversation grew heated. Two more men approached, almost lazily, weapons in hand but lowered. On the arms of these, as with all the militia at the checkpoint, there were wide and bright green bands on which there was dark, Arabic script. The occupants of the car were separated and the older man was told to get back in the car. The others were led away, the woman pleading. The car was pulled off the road and into a fenced-off area.

Now it was their turn.

One of the uniformed men gestured to them, indicating for Ufuk to drive forward. As he pulled up to the barrier, a man stood by the window and indicated for Ufuk to leave the car. They led him to one side as others began to check the pickup. Jess kept her eyes on Ufuk, her hand wrapped around the butt of the pistol on her thigh. A sheen of sweat gathered on her back and her heart felt like it was going to beat through her chest. In the mirror, she saw Giovanni's pickup being searched too.

Ufuk spoke in Arabic, and received terse replies. He gestured several times, then returned to the Toyota.

"What's happening?"

A rivulet of sweat drew a thin line down one of Ufuk's cheeks. He reached into the center console, fingers trembling, and took out a carton of cigarettes. He went back to the men and handed them over. The conversation continued, but the mood had warmed.

Ufuk gestured to the Toyota again and brought one of the men over. He reached into the back, lifting part of the tarpaulin. The man reached inside and took out two more cartons of cigarettes.

179

They waved them forward.

Ufuk got back into the Toyota and they drove through, toward the fenced off area.

"Cigarettes?" Jess said.

"How easy do you think it is to find cigarettes more than two months after Nomad?"

"What now, then?"

"Now we wait for Ain Salah. I mentioned his name to the guard."

"You *what?*"

"How else was I to make him know we were here?"

"We could have asked around."

"It wasn't just the cigarettes that got us in. It was his name."

"You took a big risk."

"That worked. What else could I do? Where else do we go? We need this place."

"Why?" she demanded. "Why is it so important we get in here?"

"Important to me? What about Hector? Raffa? Should we hide in the desert after getting here? Ain Salah is your friend, Jessica. This was your plan."

Their eyes locked for a few seconds in silence, but then Ufuk pointed out the window.

A car approached from the south, a cloud of dust following behind as it raced toward them, almost skidding on the road. It stopped nearby and a young man levered himself out and ran their way. Two of the uniformed men hailed him and he went over to them.

After a brief conversation, the young man pressed something into the hands of one of the men. Jess couldn't tell what it was, but it had the desired effect, because the young man approached them and leaned in. He had skin the color of milky coffee and a thick beard flecked with white.

"Ufuk?" he said.

"Ain Salah?"

The younger man nodded. "We don't have much time. Follow me please. Into the city. There we can speak." He reached in, took Jess's hand and squeezed. His damp fingers trembled. He nodded to Giovanni, his tentative smile broadening, his eyes watery behind thick black-framed glasses. The thickest frames Jess had ever seen.

"Good to see you, Ain Salah," she said.

"And all of you. I look forward to spending time together, when circumstances allow it." He nodded again, this time almost to himself, then left for his own car.

They drove fast to keep up, through streets that were a swarming souk of Bedouin and Berber faces wrapped in burnouses and *shemagh* scarves. A ceaseless cacophony of blaring car horns and desperate voices could be heard. Roads of dust and sand. Cars and trucks wove between each other, dodging weary-faced men on ancient bicycles and whining mopeds. Slender figures wrapped in coats and blankets lined the balconies of apartment buildings above half-empty shops. Yet Persian rugs still hung from windows—were still offered for sale—and from old speakers that hung beneath one of the balconies, traditional music played.

Life went on here.

On the shuttered doors of a shop that had once sold communications technology, there were garishly painted mobile telephone designs. In Arabic lettering there was something painted across the screens. Jess asked Massarra what it meant.

"The shop says it offers a service which will turn a mobile telephone into a radio receiver and transmitter," she said.

Men dressed in long white gowns over their pants, similar to ones Jess saw in Kandahar. Yet instead of sandals, they wore heavy boots, and instead of a light jacket, there were thick wool coats and faces covered by scarves and even goggles.

Jess saw more dressed in military fatigues with the same bright green armbands with Arabic script. They carried Kalashnikov assault rifles. The first were on foot, but more appeared, weaving through the city in the backs of Toyota pickups, roving packs of wolves. They pulled into a gated enclosure, and Ain Salah got out of his car and came over.

This time he appeared to avoid Jess's gaze.

"There are encampments within the basin," he said. "You are permitted to head to one at the southwest. You must not enter any of the other encampments without permission. For now, come and eat with me."

"What is this place?" Giovanni asked.

"This is where I work. There is no need to be concerned. You're my guests. You are permitted to accompany me for a short time."

"What about the town itself?"

"There are several, in fact. Al-Jawf is the central town, but there are smaller villages within the basin. There are markets for bartering. The Zuwayya request a commission for everything, also come to collect a contribution from each shelter in the encampments."

"What about food, water, and fuel?"

"All rationed, but provided if the community contribution is met."

"And what is your work?"

Ain Salah paused to collect his thoughts. "I communicate with the outside world. I scan radio channels and locate other sources of communication. Now come and eat."

They ate a small meal in a quiet room, undisturbed by anyone else other than Ain Salah, a room where all doors remained closed and where their meal was taken in a terse silence. Ain Salah left them as they ate, explaining there was work he was required to finish, but returned with a second man to accompany them to the encampment. His companion was stocky and muscular, and had the bearing of a soldier.

He turned cold eyes on them.

Ain Salah's mood had shifted, Jess noticed. He said nothing as they left, careful in every movement he made. They drove south, past the main Kufra Airport—mostly deserted—then through more irrigation fields that stretched into the hazy distance.

A sudden and intense feeling of hope filled Jess's chest. She almost wanted to dismiss it, but it was nice to see something that wasn't destroyed. Something inside her warned against allowing hope, reminded her of what had taken place in Sanctuary Europe. She could rely only on herself, and on Giovanni, Raffa, and Hector. Ufuk sat quietly, observing the town as it swept past.

She wondered again what their mysterious billionaire was really thinking.

Above, through the clouds, Jess vaguely made out an aircraft passing overhead. The growl of turboprop. They approached the outskirts of a shanty town built from tents and a chaos of scavenged materials, the rusted walls of containers and myriad corrugated steel, garishly colored sheets of tarpaulin, and old, wooden loading pallets.

When she stepped from the car, her boots sank into a shallow dune of gray ash, which the wind then tossed up into her face.

Ain Salah and his stone-faced companion escorted them through the camp. In places, planks of wood had been laid out to make a walkway between the many hundreds of ramshackle shelters. Within that city of canvas and steel and warped wood, they walked past stacks of yellow barrels marked as oil or fuel, and tables on which sat half-assembled shreds of technology Jess didn't recognize. Random hunks of metal from which the dull light seeped, rather than glinted. Heavy crates sat outside each tent, stacked one on top of the other, next to shelving with covered food, or racks with skinned meat. Lamps were rigged on tall poles, power lines running between them and off to some generator somewhere. Between the poles and the tents, on hastily tied lines, clothes had been hung out with the hope they might dry despite the cold. A makeshift volleyball court had been rigged from wire strung between stacked barrels.

As they passed, the faces that stared at them, through narrow and suspicious eyes, all reflected the same tired, haunted facade. All of them wore thick blanket-like clothing that swaddled them completely, and most carried weapons, or had them laid to the ground beside them as they sat and waited for whatever life had left for them.

Ain Salah stopped by a tent, as soiled and anonymous as all the rest, and squatted down next to a man huddled in a blanket. They spoke quietly, then Ain Salah rested a hand on the man's shoulder and turned back to them.

"This is Salem. He'll introduce you to the way this camp works and where you may set up your own shelters. His English is very good. I wish you well."

Giovanni stepped forward to speak, but almost instantly the stocky man roused and moved in front of him, his muscles tensed. Ain Salah placed a hand on his arm and spoke quietly, with an obvious edge of tension carrying in his voice. "I have much work to do. I do not think I will have the time to speak to you again. I wish you well."

The two men turned and walked back to their vehicle, Ain Salah hunched low and away from the stockier man.

Salem watched their car drive away, then turned back to Jess and the small group. "Be careful what you think about the Zuwayya. This is their place, and there is not much more out there worth leaving for." He eyed them and sighed. "Welcome, I suppose. I will take you now to where you can get set up."

He led them through the camp, through yet more cautious scrutiny, to a clear area on the periphery. "I should warn you that some try to enter the camp by cover of night, either to steal or to stay. Newcomers here are always to be camped on the edge. That's our rule and we make no apologies. It is your responsibility to ensure your own, and therefore the camp's, safety. Do you understand?"

184

"What do they do with the people who try to enter and are refused?"

Salem didn't answer. He kept walking.

"Salem?"

"This country has been in a constant state of war. Tobruk Government or National Salvation Government, Libyan Dawn or Daesh, Tuareg militants and Benghazi Revolutionaries. Take your pick. Most have drowned at the coast. Only the desert will survive, as it always has, and this small part of it has always belonged to the Zuwayya."

He walked on in silence and it was a while before he spoke again.

"The most important thing to remember is that there is a contribution. There is a tent in the center of the camp. You must provide something—usually something salvaged from journeys into the desert if they will grant you a permit to do so—or put yourself forward for work in Al-Jawf itself. You should know also that weapons are forbidden inside the perimeter unless permitted by the Zuwayya. Those entitled wear a green armband."

"Were those power lines on the way in?" Giovanni asked.

"No power, except by generators, and these are reserved for those who have need of them."

"And what work do you do?" Jess asked, trying to strike a more conversational tone.

Salem made no attempt to hide his contempt. "People here have no interest in making friends with you. They do not trust newcomers nor do they have any love for people like you. I suggest you keep your questions to yourself and work as we do for the good of the community. That's the only answer you need."

"What do you mean, people like us?" Giovanni said.

"Westerners. Capitalists who, were it not for the oil, would have had little interest in this country or its people, but who flock here now to survive. We welcome you, of course, because Allah demands we offer our hospitality, but you will work as we do to benefit the people here."

185

He turned and shuffled away.

7

Libya
Al-Jawf

When they awoke the next morning, Jess went into town with Giovanni and Massarra in one of the pickups.

She'd expected a warmer welcome from Ain-Salah, but imagined he had his reasons, and she couldn't really complain. Where they'd been forced to drive swiftly through Al-Jawf when they had first met Ain Salah and his curt minder, Jess was now able to take a little time to observe the area as it unfolded around them.

They drove north, away from the southwest camp where they had pitched their tents. Al-Jawf itself was a schizophrenic marriage of old and new, the hastily rebuilt or never finished, and the makeshift. In many places work continued as laborers toiled to build and repair, or sat, legs dangled over high concrete joists.

It was not just one town, but instead a collection of tossed-together settlements that had bloomed and spread from the center as the strange, geometric irrigation plots had been built. A single road led from Al Tallab, around which the first of the south camps had been clustered, past an ocean of more conventional arable land to the west, and then through hexagonal plots of a place named Western Gurayaat. Beyond those lay more such plots in the neighborhood of Al Zurq, then fields of wide, circular leas: alien places that barely seemed as though they belonged here, like a handful of huge, verdant coins tossed thoughtlessly into the desert. Massarra explained it all as they drove—their Al-Jawf tour guide— and Jess was amazed at how much she knew about these people.

Not far from the tarmacked road, dozens of trucks idled in the sand, heavily laden, piled high and covered with padded rigging. Around them people milled, sharing conversation and food, perhaps illicitly trading without the knowledge of the Zuwayya—

out here, where they might not be seen and be forced to pay the contributions Salem had spoken about.

On the outskirts of the town, past low sandstone walls haphazardly thrown together, was a rusted corrugated shantytown of shacks with roofs woven from fronds of palms. Goats tethered to open doors where narrowed-eyed men in *keffiyeh* watched their pickup as it passed. Closer into the center, past the University neighborhood, they made their way through a chaos of heaving streets thick with people wrapped in many-layered wool beneath which was what might have been more traditional, regional attire. Among them, Jess caught rare glimpses of clothing in a more western style, those who wore it moving among the locals cautiously. In faces she saw not just north African Muslims, the Berber and Bedouin, but also what might have been Arabs and Europeans, as well as the darker skin of western, central, and southern Africa.

The buildings were low, two-storied blocks, some topped by domed roofs, many with rusted satellite dishes. Doorways and walls were painted in once-bright colors, with Arabic script now faded and peeling. People loitered on steps and beneath balconies, smoking and conversing, watching Giovanni maneuver the pickup between motorbikes and dusty old hatchbacks.

"We need to find the market," he said as he twisted between two parked trucks.

"I'm going to take a walk," Jess said. "Better we split up. There are likely several markets, from what Salem said."

"We need to keep in pairs."

"I can take care of myself. We'll cover more ground if we split up. You find one of the markets. Find someone who knows what work we can offer in return for supplies. We'll go into the desert and salvage if we have to."

"What are you going to do?" he said, as he pulled the pickup into a parking area framed by curious faces and stopped.

"I want to get a feel for the place. See who is here. We can meet back here in two hours."

Massarra interrupted: "Giovanni is right. We don't know what this place is like and very possibly it is dangerous. So the sooner we know what we are dealing with, the safer we will be. Better we split up, yes, and take more of the town in the time we have. However, I am used to working alone in places like this. I suggest the two of you remain together." She took out the pistol and checked it.

"You shouldn't have that here," Giovanni said.

"They shouldn't have me here," she replied. "We meet back here in two hours. You two keep to the north and west, I'll explore the eastern part of the town. Agreed?"

Jess gave Giovanni a look, but nodded and Massarra slipped out of the pick-up.

It took some time to find the market, and eventually Jess figured the only sure way was to ask. It might have marked her out as Western, but she suspected what little of the skin on her face could be seen achieved that, perhaps even the way she and Giovanni held themselves. They drew looks as they walked anyway, so there seemed little purpose in not asking and possibly wasting what little time they had.

An elderly man with wild white hair and small eyes directed Giovanni, with enthusiastic gestures and words neither she nor he understood, but it was sufficiently clear that they found it after a little more searching. In truth, there were so many people and motorbikes gathered outside, Jess guessed it was the right place as they approached. For most of the time, she remained quiet, even though Giovanni made attempts at conversation. Frustration at his insistence he accompany her rose in the way of a thick knot in her chest and she didn't trust herself to respond kindly, so she kept quiet.

They had no currency to trade within the markets, nothing yet to barter or offer in exchange for whatever might be laid out on the tables set in long rows through the low, wide building. Yet Jess went in because she wanted to see what was there. Curiosity drove her, as well as a need to become familiar with this bizarre place.

In the narrow spaces between the tables there was bedlam, a heaving cacophony of people pressed close to each other as they scrutinized and haggled, bargaining to secure what they needed with what meager offerings they had to trade. Tensions simmered, the quick desperation in the voices of those bartering too hard, knowing what little they had was likely not enough.

Behind the tables, erected in haste rather than with any presence at permanence, stood traders dressed in clothing that marked them as native to North Africa. What few Westerners there were, Europeans she suspected, were bartering their gold and silver rather than selling goods, feeding the burgeoning Al-Jawf economy.

On the tables themselves, an emporium of the strange and sometimes inexplicable, laid an abundant variety of wares for trade, an endless yard sale on a grand scale. Salvaged technology of wildly varying types, most of which she didn't recognize. What appeared to her to be machine and automotive parts, sat beside old hand tools and worn or broken garden implements. Kitchen utensils and gas cookers, sculptures and ornaments, old clothes and shoes, blankets and fabrics and what might have been bedding. There were even books and magazines.

She was jostled as she watched, and eventually found herself feeling closed in and needing to leave. Sweat gathered on her face and down her back and, after getting back outside, she was glad of the fresh air.

"You okay?" Giovanni said as he caught up to her.

"Fine," she said, without looking at him.

Instead, she stood and took in the area around the market, where even more people waited or walked by, or sat on steps in conversation. Some watched her; others appeared to pay no interest.

She intended to move away when a gap formed in the crowd, among a gathered group as several people stepped aside. Instinct made her withdraw toward the walls of the market building, taking Giovanni with her, climbing the steps up to it without taking her eyes away.

Through the gap came armed men, the green-banded militia carrying Kalashnikov assault rifles. Five of them, pushing roughly through where the crowd was not quick enough to part. Within the gathered people were clustered groups in conversation. Giovanni tensed and stepped across her slightly.

Shouts came from the crowd, sparse and muted jeers for green-bands as much as the anticipation of something about to happen.

"We should leave," Giovanni said.

Jess shook her head. "I want to see what happens."

A small man within one of the gathered groups, a dark-skinned older fellow face mostly obscured by a dusty *shemagh*, seized another beside him by the shoulder. The warning's recipient turned sharply, immediate fear evident in his altered stance, and, on seeing the approaching green-bands, turned to run.

Their attention caught, the green-band militia shouted. Weapons rose and two broke off and ran after the fleeing man who had found his way barred by others, less by design than by surprise at what unfolded around them.

Jess watched, dry mouthed.

The man tried to get to his feet, tossing frightened glances over his shoulder, but the green-bands were on him. Rifle butts came down and he screamed and pleaded with them. The others came. Handcuffs jammed onto his wrists. More blows from the butts of their Kalashnikovs until he became pliant and submissive, blood oozing from wounds on his face. Arms huddled close into his torso.

The green-bands half-led, half-dragged him to a waiting truck. When it roared away, tires kicking up dust and frozen sand, a black mood descended on the market. Faces became tight, heads lowered. In places, anger boiled over, and gestures toward the long-gone green-bands did little to hide their bitterness.

"We can go now," Jess murmured to Giovanni.

"See what you needed?"

"I saw enough."

8

Libya
Al-Jawf

Jess and Giovanni went for an aimless walk after the incident at the market, both of them lost in their thoughts. Perhaps that simple preoccupation was the reason she misjudged the significance of the ball. Perhaps it was the innocence written across the boy's face, and the playful dance of his slight frame that deceived her. She ought to have been aware of it—there were instances in Afghanistan of the Taliban martyring children as suicide bombers.

But she didn't see it coming.

Instead, in the child's dirty face she saw what she wanted to see: hopeful naivety and happiness. She saw what she wanted for Hector.

She picked up the ball and the boy stopped. For a moment he seemed scared, then held out his hands in anticipation of the return of his plaything. She tossed it back to him, and he caught it and offered her a laugh in return. Then he threw it back, but this time she didn't catch it.

"Jess," Giovanni warned.

The ball rolled in the sand.

"No," she said to the boy, shaking her head. "We can't play. We have to go."

The boy looked at her, seeming not to understand. He gestured to the ball. Jess sighed and went to pick it up again before realizing her mistake.

Six men approached, all in long coats with *shemagh* scarves obscuring their faces and wooden hats pulled down over their heads. Three either side of her and Giovanni, each carrying something in their hands, a hammer or pipe. They appeared silently from nearby buildings. The boy ran. An obvious ruse.

The ground nearby offered nothing she or Giovanni might use as a weapon. The men would have thought of that and prepared the scene of their robbery, if that's all this was.

Jess sought to buy them time. "We were just playing with him. He kicked the ball to me." She studied each of them, searching for the weakest.

"Canadian." She gestured to Giovanni. "And Italian." Hoping it might make a difference, she added: "Students in Turkey."

"What you have to give us?" one of them said, his words heavily accented.

"We don't have anything. Nothing worth taking."

Already Jess was considering how to fight them, which one to take down first and from where she might seize a weapon. A fist hard to the bridge of the nose, or the hard, flat knife of her hand into the softness of the throat.

A shout came from behind her.

She turned.

A man stood in the entrance to the alleyway. Thin and wiry, with a thick beard and long, unkempt hair. His face weathered. In his hands he held two lengths of piping. He tossed one to Jess.

"You really want to get hurt that much?" he said to their attackers. His accent was American.

Hesitation crept over the faces of the men.

The American hammered his bar against a wall. "I'm not messing around here," he warned.

The men exchanged uneasy glances and one of them spat onto the ground. He muttered to his friends. They laughed.

The American approached. He was sweating, despite the cold. "Come with me," he said to Jess and Giovanni.

He took Jess's arm and backed them away. The men watched them carefully. Maybe they were considering their options, not quite willing to let her and Giovanni go—maybe it was a matter of pride—but they let them go. The American took them around the corner, still brandishing his weapon. As soon as they were out of sight, he broke into a jog. Jess and Giovanni followed.

"Who are you?" she said as they half-walked, half-ran through the crowd. There were no footsteps or shouts from behind them, but they didn't stop.

"I heard you talking to them," he said. "Your accent's American, so I came to take a look."

"I'm glad you did."

He stopped her, glanced over his shoulder before dropping the pipe. He held out a hand. "My name's Peter Connor."

Jess dropped her pipe as well and shook his hand. "Where are you from?"

"The Midwest. Elsmere, Nebraska. And you're East Coast, unless I miss my guess. New Yorker?"

"For a while."

"So, I'm guessing you have a story to tell. You and your Italian friend."

"I bet we all do."

He smiled and raised his hands. "Yes we do. Come on. I know a little place we can get a real drink."

"You're kidding? Here?"

"The locals are Muslim, so they aren't going to drink it."

Giovanni took Jess by the arm, a little more roughly than she cared for. "We've had enough excitement today. I think it's better we—"

Jess pulled away. "Come on, just a drink."

Giovanni hesitated, but then smiled. "Just a drink," he said. "Why not?"

Persian rugs hung from the walls of what was little more than a cellar. More were laid out on the floors. Instead of chairs there were cushions, and upturned crates covered in brightly patterned fabric for tables. Oil lamps and candles provided a flickering, shaded light and areas of the long room were lit only by a dim half-light.

Others occupied nooks and alcoves already, talking quietly to companions sat across from them, men and women, few local, most foreign. For the most part they avoided looking at her or Giovanni as they entered, focusing instead on their own conversations.

Peter gestured to an area in one corner and they sat, cross-legged, on heavy cushions. On the wall across from them, lit by candles and a single, buzzing strip light suspended by its own electrical cable from the ceiling, were hundreds of images and scraps of paper. From her seat Jess studied them: photographs of people on holiday, smiling and relaxed, taken all over the world. Tacked to everyone, or scrawled in dark ink, were names and details, addresses in the Al-Jawf township.

In a small alcove over which a curtain hung, a man and woman huddled over a radio set. The man held headphones so they could both hear, and played with the dial while speaking softly into a microphone. The curtain almost obscured them.

A man in local dress came to Peter and took him warmly by the arm. They spoke briefly in Arabic, during which Jess guessed from what they seemed to be saying, from the gestures that accompanied the words, that she and Giovanni were being introduced. The man nodded to them both and smiled, then turned away and returned shortly with a bottle and three glasses.

"The best stuff in town," Peter said. "It's hardly a Macallan, but it does have a certain something."

She took a sip and the heat in the back of her throat rose to a searing burn that forced her to cough. "That really is something." She set down her glass.

Giovanni didn't touch his, but sat back, arms crossed.

Jess fixed her gaze on Peter. "So tell me about yourself."

"Not much to tell," he said. "I was a freelance photojournalist before Nomad. I worked for the Economist, National Geographic, Reuters. You get the idea. I was in Egypt at the time and couldn't get out of the country. Before Nomad, flights were grounded. There were threats of attacks on Egyptian targets so I stole a car and made a run for it. Crossed the border at night."

"How long have you been here?" Giovanni asked.

"About a month. You?"

"Just arrived," Jess said.

He nodded. "From?"

There was no hesitation, the story already clear in her mind. "Turkey. I was a student there."

"What did you study?"

"Local tourism. I used to spend a lot of time guiding in the Alps, a bit of ski mountaineering, that kind of thing." She hesitated, then added, "What do you think of this place?"

"You need to be careful what you think here."

"I'm serious."

He regarded her for a moment, then relented. "There's an oil field at Zuetina and refineries along the road between Al-Jawf and the coast. The Zuwayya control it all. Irrigation technology here is pretty sophisticated, and there's a hundred and fifty cubic kilometers of groundwater in aquifers two hundred meters below the surface. You put those two together, and this place is pretty damn valuable.

"You didn't answer the question. I asked what you *thought* of it."

Peter glanced round the room and leaned in. His voice dropped. "I've dodged suicide bombers in Baghdad and Kabul. I've been pulled out of a collapsed building after earthquakes in Nepal. I was in Rwanda and Yugoslavia when neighbors turned guns and machetes on each other. The things I've seen in my life, you probably can't even imagine…"

196

He paused to take a drink. "But this place beats all of it. What do I think? It's insanely dangerous here, is what I think. Everyone has an angle. Watch your back."

Giovanni said: "The militia at the front gate seem nervous."

"There have been attacks. The Zuwayya have this place and the Toubou tribes aren't too happy about it. Rumors are they want to hook up with militia groups in Chad looking to take control of Al-Jawf, and there are newcomers every day."

"So why stay?" It was a question Jess struggled with herself.

Peter gestured with his hands. "Where else is there? At least we're not freezing to death."

The same reason they came. "There was mention of trucks heading north for salvage?"

"There were hundreds of container ships in operation in the Mediterranean, and on the Nile, when Nomad hit. They capsized and washed dozens of miles into the high deserts before the water retreated. Whatever's in them, it's up for grabs."

"Have you been?"

"Nothing worth seeing for a guy like me up there."

"Are you still reporting? I mean, not much need for photographs now."

"There's every need. Words alone can't document what will become the most important period in human history." He sat back, as though considering this. He smiled. "There are radios, too. People trying to connect with the rest of Africa; with others in Europe and beyond. Even maybe back home."

"What have you heard? The White House, FEMA, the military? Any word?"

"Rumors are the Yellowstone eruptions did a lot of damage. I don't know much, but the radio waves are starting to fill up. You think the ash is bad here, it sounds like most of the US is choking under it. A lot of people dead, infrastructure totally collapsed. The White House declared a state of emergency, but they didn't have a lot of time. Like I said, there's more coming through every day, but—" He shook his head and poured another drink.

"Is there any way to get back over there?"

"Why would you want to go back?"

"It's my home."

"There's barely anything left. "

"Does that matter?"

He didn't answer for a few seconds, but then said: "I know who you are. Jessica Rollins, right? Your face was all over the newswires just before Nomad. I was surprised when I saw you, but I'm right, right?"

It was Jess's turn not to answer.

"Don't worry, your secret is safe with me," Peter added. "Some people blame your father, but there were a lot of rumors too, about how you fought against the ones that really screwed us. I'd love to hear your version. Sometime."

"I'm not Jessica Rollins," Jess lied.

Peter regarded her for a few more seconds. "I'm trying to get a few others together to contact more people in the US. There are radios in the camps. The Zuwayya don't like it, but some technical guys are trying to find ways to boost the signal, that kind of thing. They need parts. We were thinking of taking a trip, seeing what we could find. We could use the bodies, extra eyes. Interested?"

Hamza watched the woman and the Italian man leave and waited. He had been reluctant to agree to his American friend's plan, to play on fears born of her natural prejudices toward him and those like him. A Muslim man in North Africa—of course the American woman with the funny leg would believe it was his intention to rob or molest her, as though all men like him would do such things.

However, the offer of valuable items to trade at the market was too much for Hamza to refuse. Clothes to replace the frayed, worn ones his family now wore, food beyond the tiny portions they were entitled to from the Zuwayya. Fuel for the generator, oil for their lamps.

The instructions had been simple enough. The suggestion to use his son to attract her had been the man's, and Hamza had initially objected. The man had been insistent, assuring him there would be no danger. American women would not hurt a small boy, of course not, he'd argued.

Hamza had been assured he would not need to hurt her, that his American friend would step in at the right moment and all they would then need to do is swear as they backed away, apparently cowed by the American's threats.

"You have what you wanted?" Hamza asked.

"Thank you, my friend. You did a good job." The American handed over a bag. Hamza took it, but didn't look inside. So far, he trusted the American. He had been good to Hamza.

"This stays between us, understood?"

"Of course, my friend." Hamza couldn't help but ask: "What do you want from her?"

"It's always good to know people from your home. Nothing more than that. You understand that, don't you?"

9

Libya
Al-Jawf

Massarra stood to one side of the seething street and watched salvagers barter at makeshift stalls, or in the anonymous shadows cast by balconies, tarpaulins and frayed awnings. It smelled of raw meat, from a butcher behind her, and of diesel oil from canisters carried on shoulders, bobbing through the crowd. Arabic music drifted over the hiss of the constant sirocco wind of the Sahara.

Amidst what might have seemed like chaos—an anarchy of jealous hoarding of whatever desperate humans could find to help them survive for another day, another week—she witnessed a curious mechanical order. If the cities along the coast of Libya, to say nothing of those littering the banks of the Nile more than six hundred kilometers to the east, had suffered in the wake of Nomad, there was likely still much to salvage for those who had survived. People's immediate and even short-term needs varied and there would always be trade. Did the Zuwayya permit such illicit trading so long as their taxes were paid? It was outside the purview of the markets and therefore not regulated or scrutinized, but black markets had always existed whatever the regime. Perhaps there would be a raid at some point and arrests made. Perhaps, for now, the Zuwayya just didn't care enough to do anything about it.

She wondered if any of these raiders and salvagers who bartered beside her had considered heading south to the lands beyond Chad and Sudan in the south. What remained there? There were rumors of course. That it was verdant and green, a promised land. Or that it was buried in ash, the Rift Valley collapsed into the oceans. It was hard to tell truth from fiction, and the Levantine Council didn't know any more than she did.

As she considered this, she continued her surveillance of the faces and body language of those occupying the street. She searched for anything that caught her attention, which to her instincts seemed irregular or out of place. There were specific markers to look for. Those who, like her, seemed to be waiting without engaging with those around them. She noted these seemingly casual observers, scrutinized them to assess what caught their interest, and whether they appeared to be in communication with others.

If there were markers of surveillance, tells that might give away even the most scrupulous watcher, much of her tradecraft relied on instincts shaped by experience in theaters where mistakes were punished severely—if not by her opponents, then later by her employers. Only when she was certain the streets were clear of such threats, that no one watched and waited for her or for those she protected, did she signal to the balcony above.

A simple gesture, pre-arranged but otherwise innocuous.

The recipient of the gesture then made his way to the flat, open roof of that unremarkable building, to the opposite terrace that faced the street beyond it. Although Massarra could no longer see him, she knew he would soon signal the driver of a dusty gray Mercedes sedan, its driver a local man who had been offered a hold-all filled with useful items of trade in return for waiting in the street in his car. The man conveyed a single passenger in the back seat, a man not known to him, and stood ready to drive the short distance to the entrance of the building when instructed to do so.

Massarra waited for a glimpse of the Mercedes as it turned the corner, tension gathering in her body as time stretched. It seemed too long before she saw it nose through the crowd, horn coaxing people aside as it crept forward.

She remained vigilant because she knew this was the moment in which, if she had in any way been wrong, missed something, the consequences would manifest when the Mercedes drew up outside the building and its passenger stepped out onto the street.

Her hand grew tighter on the pistol, possession of it bringing its own risks as she had seen people randomly searched by Zuwayya green-bands.

The Mercedes made its way through the crowd, which parted like waves off the bow of some great ship, horn still baying. She nearly signaled the driver to cease the incessant noise for the attention it might attract, but she had heard similar noises so frequently across the town that it might have attracted more attention had the driver been silent.

Eventually it drew up outside and the rear door opened. Massarra took the pistol half out and waited, still studying faces and bearings within the crowd all the way along the street. The passenger disappeared into the building and would now, she knew, be climbing the stairs to a small room at the back of the building, away from windows and both prying ears and eyes. The room had already been swept twice in a search for listening devices because, even in these times, even after the event, Massarra feared such things.

She waited a moment longer, watching the entrances to the street at both ends, and the rooftops above for signs of movement that might indicate an incursion. Only when she was satisfied did she cross the street herself and enter the building.

At the entrance to the room stood a tall, thickly set man who made no attempt to hide the sub-machine gun that hung from a single-point harness across his chest. He nodded to Massarra as she approached and stepped aside to open the door for her. Heat flushed in the center of her chest as she entered.

An elderly man in a neat gray suit and tie, and a young woman in jeans, sat in dining chairs in front of an empty weathered armchair. Ufuk Erdogmus was in the process of folding his *shemagh* and *keffiyeh* and laying them on a small table beside the chair. He turned to Massarra as she entered, and she returned his questioning look with a nod.

"There's nothing," she said. "We're clean. But we shouldn't remain long."

"Thank you, Massarra," the elderly man said.

She noted he said it with some deference. This surprised her. She retreated to the back of the room and stood quietly.

"Ufuk," the elderly man said. "So very good to see you. We are very glad to see you alive and well."

"As I am you, Hasan, my old friend."

She'd never met him before, but the name Hasan confirmed Massarra's suspicion. This was one of the elders of the Levantine Council, one that Massarra had never met but knew of. From Syria. The more dangerous end of their circle. Security was strict even within her own organization.

"Would you care for some coffee?" Hasan said to Ufuk. "I cannot speak to the taste, but it's something at least."

"Thank you."

The man reached for a tall steel flask and poured. He handed the delicate cup to Ufuk who took it and drank. Massarra admired how he hid his reaction to what had to be a bitter taste. The Turkish-style coffee had been steeping for a long time in the grinds.

"How many of you survived?" Ufuk said.

Hesitation. The young woman glanced at Hasan, who returned her gaze and then turned to Ufuk. "Not many. We had made preparations, but they were inadequate. We had hoped to dissuade Iran and Israel from the courses they'd chosen, but—"

The young woman interrupted him: "They wouldn't listen. By then, all that mattered was their response. It has always been that way with them. If they do not respond they think they appear weak. Escalation follows escalation—"

"Enough, Elsa." Hasan held out a calming hand.

"We are his allies, and he calls you *friend*." Elsa spat the last word out. "And yet he did nothing to warn us of this apocalypse? How many millions died because of this man, this—"

"Enough!" Hasan yelled, in a voice that growled with more venom than his frail body seemed possible to contain. He put his coffee down and smoothed back strands of gray hair that had sprung loose. "Mr. Erdogmus had his reasons. We put this behind us. We move on."

Massarra studied the young woman, who held her tongue but glowered at Ufuk, a cobra ready to strike if unleashed. She recognized a lot of herself in the woman's dark features, the intense eyes and sleek black hair.

Ufuk paused and smiled awkwardly before asking: "What can you tell me about the Middle East?"

"Western news reports were mostly accurate, but the damage is not as extensive as at first it might have seemed. Many areas are uninhabitable. Tens of millions dead, of course. Tel Aviv and the coastal cities are gone, all the way to Beirut and Tripoli. Even Jerusalem was destroyed. The smaller yield weapons and weaker delivery systems at Iran's disposal were still very effective. Israel, of course, has much stronger weapons in its possession."

"What of Iran?"

"Tehran, we are certain is gone. Very likely Isfahan and Shiraz. We are less certain about Tabriz and Iran's other major centers. We have assets, but communication with them has been our true challenge. We do know that there has been a military coup by a coalition supported by groups from Pakistan and Afghanistan. We do not know for certain, but we believe they're linked to Daesh. The stability and resources of radical Islam have served to unite even moderates with jihadists."

"Has there been any analysis of radiation effects?"

"We are told the weather has helped prevent the spread. There has been a steady flow of refugees south, through Jordan and into Saudi Arabia. Millions of people, most of whom are already sick or who succumb to the weather or starvation. What remains of the Saudi military is under the control of wealthy Shaikhs. They have not been welcoming as you might imagine. There is a report." He handed over a flash drive. "It is explained in greater detail."

"What progress with the African Union?" Ufuk put the drive into a coat pocket.

"Our relationship remains good and we continue to make arrangements with them. They're keen to see you, Adejola in particular."

"Adejola? He is well?"

Adejola Eberechi, Nigeria's Minister of Foreign Affairs and representative of the Nigerian Government to the African Union. One of few men in the region Ufuk had ever told Massarra he trusted.

"He leads what remains of the Assembly and the Executive Council of the Union. When you are ready with your work here, when we have something definite to tell him, we will meet with him together. He has already set aside a location that he feels is secure."

"There is a lot to do," Ufuk said, taking a moment to process. "The Zuwayya have Al-Jawf in a tight hold. If we are to loosen it, we need to do it from within. You understand what is at stake?"

"Of course. If we can offer the African Union a way into Al-Jawf, they have the resources and support to depose the Zuwayya."

"We must have fairness," Ufuk added. "A transparent system of government in North Africa. Daesh and groups like them still have much power. If we hope to offer people a place to live, to survive the coming winters, we need to be better than what existed here before. A just and fair coalition between the Levantine Council and the African Union is the only way we can be strong enough to resist violent incursions."

"We will get there. As long as you can deliver what you say you can."

"And what of America?"

"Not much more than rumors. New York and other eastern coastal cities were wiped clean to the bedrock, as if they never existed. Tsunamis washed a hundred miles—"

"The correct term would be tidal wave, at least for the initial impact."

Hasan nodded at the technical correction. "Even Washington is gone."

"But the West Coast?"

205

"You would know better than we would, with all respect."

Ufuk took a sip of his drink. From his expression, he wasn't really getting much in the way of new information. "Have you heard anything of Müller?"

"Nothing lately." Hasan leaned forward to steeple his fingers together. "His own apparatus seemed able to remove him into Asia in the wake of the destruction of Sanctuary Europe."

Massarra's own contacts had rumored that Müller was already in China.

"There were more meteor impacts in Russia," Hasan added. "And in Scandinavia and the north Pacific Ocean. More tsunamis, but the coasts are empty now."

"Jovians," Ufuk muttered.

"Müller has created a narrative, within certain circles, of being able to predict further celestial events. We are trying to confirm his exact location. When we do, we will inform you. But be warned— he has very strong friends, even here."

"Much easier to peddle lies when there's no one left to oppose you."

For a moment, nobody spoke. Ufuk settled back in his seat. "Where will you go now?" he asked. "What are the Council's plans?"

"Places like this are close enough to home. The Nile delta was overrun by the seas, saturated the deserts for dozens of miles inland. The rains have begun in places that haven't seen water in a thousand years. We are negotiating with Saudi Arabia. There is much to do."

Ufuk cradled his chin between cupped hands and rocked back and forth, his mind a million miles away. "I will help wherever I can."

"We appreciate your support, and all you have made available."

"Do you have it?" Ufuk asked. He stopped rocking back and forth and sat rock steady, his eyes locked with Hasan's.

"Of course."

The old man nodded at Elsa, who snorted but admirably contained an anger seething inside she didn't bother to try and conceal. She stood and walked to the side of the room, then lifted a woolen blanket.

Beneath it, a sleek gray metal box, three feet long by two wide and a foot thick. Highly engineered, gleaming. Filaments of green light on its top side, with a single cord connected into what looked like a battery.

10

Libya
Outside of Al-Jawf

From a distance, the men had the appearance of Bedouin, quietly pitching a camp not far from Al-Jawf, little more than a half-day's walk through the frigid desert. In their movement was practiced efficiency, and their clothing and facial hair, even their skin tone, also gave them that appearance of locals. Their efficiency was military in its precision, the well-drilled competence coming from a place very different to generations spent living as nomads.

For some of them it came from tours served in Afghanistan and Iraq. At least one had served in Somalia. In Helmand province, in Fallujah and Baghdad, across war-torn nations where westerners were rarely welcomed by either party to the conflict, all had learned their lessons hard: better to be unseen or unnoticed in such places than to be forced to engage in a fighting withdrawal. These men were specialists, well versed in being invisible.

Nor would their weapons have marked them out as foreign, if they'd been observed. They carried weathered Kalashnikovs, albeit each was modified according to operational need and personal taste, those modifications the result of weeks spent in conflict zones where equipment needed to function both optimally and comfortably. Taped padding on the stock of an old Dragunov for one of the snipers, night vision sights for those who felt them necessary, quick-attach suppressors that could be removed easily when the advantage of surprise and silence was lost.

They knew that some of those searching for them, and from whom their presence needed to be concealed, utilized airborne surveillance devices similar to those they themselves possessed. As a consequence, they used various methods to camouflage their presence and they acted as far as operationally possible as Bedouin would.

While some pitched tents in the Bedouin style to form a *goum*, as much in the lee of a high dune as possible, setting the shelters tight against a gathering wind that kicked up a glistening mist of crystallized sand, others prepared themselves for the short nighttime trek to a rocky outcrop in order to look on Al-Jawf itself. There they would bivouac overnight, watching and waiting. Observing movements into and out of the town. Studying its borders and security measures. Securing every possible piece of data they could to take back with them and collate into an intelligence package for their employers.

One of them possessed a small holographic device that was similar to the one that Ufuk Erdogmus, at that exact moment less than thirty kilometers away, was himself scrutinizing. In their truck, under cover of tarpaulin, lay a drone almost identical to those Ufuk controlled.

However, the decision had been taken not to use it. The engineer who undertook the final preparations to launch when the time came had advised that someone might intercept signals sent by the drone. The team's commander had decided against using it for now.

Better, he had said, they do this the old way and use their own eyes to gain the intelligence they required.

As the reconnaissance specialists laid up in bivouacs, watching Al-Jawf from a suitable distance, a single rider on a camel took to the desert, ready to journey during the night to where he knew there was a second *goum* located. That camp was similar to his own, although the team within it had been tasked with a different mission. As Montgomery and Clarke had done for the purposes of Operation Bertram during the Second World War, in a region not so very far from this one, that team was tasked with disguising the approach of a second, very much larger military force.

The presence of either team in this desert couldn't afford to be discovered, so they communicated sporadically. There was no need for anything more frequent as both knew their operational tasks. When they did communicate, they did so via the use of this single outrider rather than through radio transmissions that might be detected.

Yet when the outrider was only a short way into one such trek across the frigid desert, during a light sandstorm which was itself slicked with bitter sleet, he was faced with a decision to break that communications embargo. A group of salvagers, two trucks with a number of people both in the cab and under a rigged tarpaulin, raced over the dunes. From their tracks, their route hadn't deviated for some time, and would take them close to the camp from which he had just come.

If he chose to turn and head back, to warn his comrades of the approaching danger, he might not make it in time. He would serve to provide a warning to the scavengers and lose his team's element of surprise. Instead, he relayed a short message.

The trucks advanced over the dunes and selected a line that would place them in a position to see the camp and the outrider considered his decision justified. He followed at a safe distance, circling round behind the two trucks to take up a position that would allow him a tactical advantage.

No further communication with his team was necessary. The outrider knew what would happen, what had to happen. No one could know the camp existed.

The trucks turned sharply toward the camp and drew up not far away. Through a thermal imaging scope, the outrider watched his team emerge from their tents, seven white ghosts shifting against a contoured, ash-gray landscape. Beneath their clothing he could make out the bulges of their weapons.

The shapes emerging from the trucks were a variety of shapes and sizes, and the outrider took them to be both men and women, or perhaps some were younger, even teenagers.

The outrider couldn't hear the conversation that passed between the salvagers and his team. He thumbed the safety of his own weapon and rested a finger on the trigger.

The thermal imaging gave the people who died over the course of the next nine seconds an anonymity that, had the outrider not long ago already become inured to the emotional consequences of killing, he might have subconsciously appreciated. All he considered then, in fact, was how easy it would be to dig into the frozen ground to bury the bodies.

11

Libya
Al-Jawf

The azan Islamic call for afternoon prayer echoed from loudspeakers around the camp. Jess and Giovanni made their way back to the simple collection of shelters and tents she now called home. For a moment she might have been back in Afghanistan, where there were refugee camps just like this, where the sick suffered quietly, and where the azan had filled the air five times each day. It was all the same: the dust and sand, the arid wind, the low buildings framed by rugs and blankets and painted Arabic script on doors and walls. The endless searching of shadows and faces for indications of hostility that had been necessary there and here. Even the smells were similar: the unwashed and sick, the cloying stench of rotten meat. It reminded her of the harsh Afghan winters.

Neither she nor Giovanni had spoken much on the drive back, each choosing instead to stare through the dust-laden glass toward the unfamiliar landscape beyond. The silence felt like a prison, chains Jess wanted to break free of and run.

"Where have you both been?" Ufuk demanded the moment they ducked into the shelter.

Jess stopped in her tracks. "What's the problem?"

"We need to know where you are," Massarra said. "We need to know where every one of us is at all times. We said two hours. You've been gone four."

"We met someone in town," Jess said. "An American."

"Who was he?"

"A photojournalist who was in Egypt when Nomad hit."

"That's what he told you?"

"That's what he told me."

"We can't keep secrets from each other," Massarra said.

"That's rich, coming from you."

"I'm not keeping—"

"Why were you so keen to persuade me this was the best place for us? What is it in this chaos of a town in the middle of the Libyan desert that interests you? It's not because of the oil, is it? Or the survivor camps. There's more to it."

The skin over Ufuk's jaw tightened. He shook his head but didn't answer. Jess waited.

"We are heading into the worst winter the planet has seen in ten thousand years," he said finally. "Temperatures will drop, but spring will come, and in a year, maybe two or three, the air will clear and the sun *will* shine again. This area of Africa may be the breadbasket of survival for whoever survived. I saw that in my climate modeling before Nomad hit."

"So you always wanted to come here? This was your plan? Why you destroyed Sanctuary?"

"I did not destroy Sanctuary, Jessica. North Africa was part of my plans, yes. That's why I had the equipment stored at Sahl. I *intended* to spend a year underground in Sanctuary, using my communication network to begin my work out here. I didn't intend to risk my life in a sailboat crossing a frozen ocean."

Their desperate escape certainly didn't seem coordinated. Jess couldn't argue with that.

Ufuk spread his hands wide. "But here we are. I am trying to make the best of it. The Zuwayya control most of the oil in eastern Libya and similar tribes control natural resources in Egypt. We must come to terms with regional militia and whatever governments remain in order to allow survivors to farm their own land, to create homesteads in Africa."

"You're no different to Müller. You're using this to wipe the slate clean, start your own empires in the dust. Why are we really here?"

She waited, but he said nothing. "Tell me now or Giovanni, Hector and I leave. We can find another place to camp."

Ufuk balled his fists and turned to leave, but then exhaled long and hard. "I have another facility. In Tanzania. A satellite launch facility."

"*Satellites?*" The idea seemed so far removed from any reality Jess could imagine right now, she was momentarily dumbfounded. "Why Tanzania?" It never struck Jess as much of a space power.

"The equator," Ufuk said. "The closer a spacecraft's launch position is to it, the easier to get into orbit. You could say the Earth gives it a push."

"So you want to launch...what, a satellite? Now?"

"It's more of a technology center. If we can get there—one day—I could talk to the Mars First mission. Maybe."

For two or three seconds, Jess's mind bobbled the new information from one side of her brain to the other.

"The Mars mission you launched before Nomad?" She'd totally forgotten it even existed. "Hold on, why would you launch a mission to Mars if you knew Nomad was coming? Were you...are you *still* trying to set up a *Martian* colony?" The sudden disconnect with reality, as they stood there in the dirt and sand in a tent in the middle of the Sahara, felt like someone sucker-punched Jess in the solar plexus and knocked the wind out of her. "Are you being serious?"

"That was the idea. In exactly seventy-three weeks, Saturn will pass close to Earth. There are celestial events taking place that we might need to be aware of. The Mars First crew could be invaluable from their...well, unique vantage point."

"And that's your secret?"

"The less people knew, the less chance it could be exploited by Müller."

"I don't think he's a problem anymore."

"You don't know him like I do."

"I think I might know him better," Jess replied, and made it clear the conversation was over. "It's you I'm worried I don't know."

"Jessica, Jessica, wake up."

Jess's eyes fluttered open, immediately blinded by a headlamp.

It was Raffa, pulling on her arm. "Come quickly!"

"Is everything okay?"

She rolled from her sheets and realized Hector wasn't with her, and neither was Giovanni. Instead they were huddled on the other side of the makeshift tent, all with their headlamps on, talking in excited hushed whispers. Ufuk sat in the middle of the huddle. He smiled at Jess as he saw her awake and waved her over.

Raffa had already scampered back and was talking in rapid-fire Italian into a microphone attached to Ufuk's tablet.

"Who's he talking to?" Jess asked groggily as she wiped her eyes and yawned.

Giovanni's grin was even wider than Ufuk's. "Lucca. He's talking to Lucca. His brother."

Jess took a few second to process the words and make sure she heard him right. "Lucca? How…what…" She snapped wide awake, adrenaline flooding into her bloodstream.

Giovanni handed her a cup of steaming coffee as she arrived. "Ufuk's been working all night to try and establish a connection to some of the underground network of hackers he knew at Sanctuary. Abbie Barnes was a part of it."

Jess took the coffee. Massarra sat to one side of the pack. Her expression indicated she wasn't as excited as the rest of them. "Do not say where we are," the Israeli said quietly. "Remember, Marshall. Salman said it was connected to Muller…"

"It's a secure connection. Totally encrypted," Ufuk explained, glancing at Massarra. "It was a long shot."

"Did you talk to Abbie?"

Ufuk leaned down to unplug the headphones. "Lucca, could you get Abbie on?"

Over the speakers, a commotion in the background, and then the unmistakable voice of Abbie Barnes: "Hello?"

"Abbie, my God. How are you?"

"Jessica," squealed the excited teenager on the other end. "I'm so happy you are safe."

"Thanks for getting Lucca out," Jess said immediately.

"That wasn't me. It was Roger. He's the one that made sure Lucca was safe."

Jess stole a look at Giovanni, who just nodded. "And Ballie Booker? Michel Durand? Did you see them?"

The radio hissed silence. "I'm sorry."

Jess's heart skipped a beat and she closed her eyes. "And where are you?"

"Near China—Mongolia I think, in the desert—somewhere outside of the Sanctuary here. Müller took us with the Administrative Council, in a heavy lift aircraft. We're not in Sanctuary, but some kind of Vivas facility."

"How many made it out?"

This time the answer took a few seconds. "Only two hundred and thirty."

Some of Jess's excitement drained away. How many had been in Sanctuary Europe? Five thousand? More?

"Is Müller with you?" Jess asked after a pause.

The speakers hissed.

"Yes. He's negotiating with the Chinese. He's here with us in Mongolia."

12

Mongolia
Near Ulan Battor

Zasekin had known there would be questions eventually and that he would have no answers beyond the truth. Unsustainable lies would shake the faith his men still had in him, and that would be dangerous for all of them. He had never led that way, he had always been honest with them and perhaps that was why they were still together now, despite the gunfights and raiders and Semyon's slow, painful death yesterday evening.

Perhaps it was the moment that Semyon passed, that the questions began to simmer. Watching him die, knowing there was nothing that could be done. Each one knew a similar fate might well await them. It frightened them.

They would say nothing about it; of course, they were too strong for that. Even Vasily, who was little more than a boy in truth, would not give a voice to his fear until the others had begun to quietly probe Zasekin as to what he planned. Why he made those incursions alone back to the Czilim and spoke on the radio to someone they didn't know, someone who was not Russian.

It was Evgeny who had first noticed it, mentioning it only in passing even though Zasekin could see the questions forming on his lips. Too much time around the fire each night, too little to speak about beyond their immediate future, for such questions to be silent for long. Of course Evgeny, that devious little bastard. Who else?

So instead of waiting, when he knew he had nothing left to gain by keeping them in the dark, he spoke on his own terms. As the light from the fire played on their faces, as they greedily ate from crates of supplies that bore markings that were not Russian

Cyrillic, but Mongolian, he steadied himself. Zasekin had understood the markings of course, his natural Buryat within the family of the Mongolian languages, but how much did they understand, he wondered.

"The food is good?"

"Indeed it is, Andrei Nikolayevich," Evgeny said. "Just as last night, and the night before, the food is good."

"You wonder how I knew it was there, hidden away in a cellar in Sükhbaatar, yes? That question hesitates on your tongue."

Timur had the good grace to appear embarrassed.

Evgeny, on the other hand, looked triumphant. "Andrei Nikolayevich. Comrade Corporal Zasekin. I do wonder how you knew it was there. Something to do with the man you speak to on the radio, perhaps? The secrets you keep from us as other officers might from their men. You tell us you're no different to them, but that does not seem to be the case, does it?"

"Take care in your tone, Evgeny Valentinovich," Timur warned. "We're alive and we have food to eat. The Czilim is still running and we have a future. Andrei Nikolayevich is the reason for all of that."

"He's lying to us, Timur Ivanovych," Evgeny said. "Can you trust what he says after that?"

"I trust this food," Timur replied.

"What about you, Vasily Fyodorovich?" Zasekin said as he turned to the younger man. "Do you have questions too?"

Vasily blanched. He didn't look at Zasekin, but instead toyed with his food. Eventually he said, "I trust you, Comrade Corporal."

The final man, once an ice-hockey player from Omsk until injury brought his career to a sad conclusion, was named Misha. He rarely cared for, or used, anyone's patronymic—that was the Western influence playing hockey had offered him—yet Zasekin had always appreciated the simplicity with which he viewed most things. He found him to be composed in situations when emotional control was required. Perhaps again that was the old hockey player in him: he had seen more than enough violence on the ice. Misha often chose silence and rarely offered much to conversations, except when sport was involved when he became unusually animated.

So it came as something of a surprise to the rest of them when he spoke now: "Evgeny, for whatever reason you always stir the pot. I knew a man like you at Avangard; he always wanted to be the center of attention. I don't know why, but it didn't matter to me then. It matters to me now. Andrei Nikolayevich has never given me any reason to doubt him. Officers keep secrets from their men, just as managers do from their players. There are always wider considerations not everyone needs to know about. That's the way of leaders and subordinates. I ask myself this: am I alive? The answer, very obviously, is yes. I ask myself this: why am I alive? The answer is Andrei Nikolayevich Zasekin and the other men in my squad. That's more than enough for me. So please, stop your whining and let the man do his job."

Evgeny appeared about to say something, when Zasekin cut across him. "Misha is right. Officers do keep secrets, but they should do this only if there is a good, tactical reason to do so. The time has come for me to explain and hear your thoughts."

He waited, looked them all straight in the eye, then nodded slowly. "After Baikal erupted, as we made our way south knowing then that Irkutsk was in ruins, I attempted to contact our regional headquarters. I tried every military channel. Nothing. Shortly afterward, we heard from the man collecting survivor reports."

The men nodded in unison. "Giovanni, yes."

"He confirmed to us that many, many people had died and there were similar events the world over."

"We know all this, Andrei."

"What I have *not* told you is that someone else, another man, reached me on an encrypted military channel, but he was not our military. He told me to use these frequencies to reach Giovanni."

"Why?"

"I do not know why. He said just to speak with them."

"And why did you agree?"

"Because we needed help, and he offered. He seems very powerful."

"Who was this man?" Timur asked.

"He has never given his name."

"Do you know where he is from?" Evgeny asked.

"He speaks English, but with an odd accent. I am not sure."

"What else did you agree with him?" Evgeny said.

"He has a location in Mongolia he wants us to go to. He would not say where exactly, or for what purpose, but he said he would offer valuable commodities for trade and supplies if we agreed to help him. The supplies we picked up in Sükhbaatar, as well as the diesel fuel, were from him. He promised they would be there, and they were."

"In return for what?"

"We intended to head for Ulan Bator, anyway. He would like us to report on what we find there. We take the Czilim as close as we can, conceal it, then hike in the rest of the way."

"If we all agree?"

"We are in Mongolia, not Russia. We are not operational on behalf of the FSB, we are trying to survive. I can and will lead all of you, but only if you agree. This, now, is a matter for your own consciences."

"What does this man want from us?" Timur asked.

"For now, information."

"For now?"

"It will not end there, Andrei Nikolayevich," Evgeny said.

"What choice do we have? We are alone. We need friends."

Pine trees bowed under the weight of the wind slab of ash-streaked snow and reared over the Selenge's craggy banks, while yet more, similarly weighed down, crept up the steeply sloped hills that made its valley. The narrow dirt tracks that formed the sporadic road that existed in this barren place were just visible from the wide expanse of the river, a river that was known in this part of Mongolia as the Chuluut.

The Czilim roared over the ice-slab water, pushing through forests of petrified reeds, past small islands that peeked through wind-carved finger drifts and yet more slate-gray ice, over frigid black waves, between pine trees that bucked and twisted and shed their needles with the violence of the heavy downdraft wind she threw to each side. Even where heaving rapids descended over steep ledges, the Czilim left them in her wake.

It was Evgeny's turn to man the Kalashnikov. He stood in the hatch as Zasekin drove, wrapped in whatever spare clothing they could find. He had retrieved an old pair of goggles intended for the pilot should the window have ever been shot out—the *apparatchik* had considered everything, it seemed. There was still considerable ammunition for the heavy 7.62 machine gun, so Evgeny had been warned, as they all had, that he could shoot first should he think it necessary and ask questions later.

Zasekin knew that anyone within a few miles would hear the Water Chestnut's boisterous approach. She could be quiet and deadly when called for, waiting on the surface of the water, hidden by reeds and tall grass, or on a beach or road. Waiting for her prey, ready to pounce without warning. Yet in full flow, with the turbines churning, even in this valley she would be heard from a distance.

Timur sat beside him, the cumbersome SH-3 night vision device held to his eyes as he searched not only for signs of potential human threats, but also for high rocks, fallen trees, and other debris along the banks of the river. Zasekin liked having him there, trusted the judgment of the Kemerovo man despite his quite inexplicable belief that, in the mountains to the south of Sayanogorsk, there were yetis. Timur grew quite infuriated at the others when they ridiculed him, citing the Kemerovo city administrators as having indisputable proof of the fact. This thought made Zasekin smile.

"What is it?" Timur asked and Zasekin grunted. No sense antagonizing the younger man, not right now when there was so much division between them all.

"We are making good progress," he chose to say instead.

Timur nodded. "My calculations place us somewhere within twenty kilometers of the borders of the Gorkhi Terelj National Park. There is a luxury hotel there as well as many traditional camps. We may find supplies, and a place to hide the Czilim."

"How do you know all this?"

Timur hesitated.

"There is no one here to condemn you for anything, Timur Ivanovych."

Timur nodded, but still didn't look at Zasekin. "There was an American television show I used to watch online called The Amazing Race." He seemed embarrassed. "It was a race around the world by many teams with not much money. Reality television, the Americans called it. They visited Ulan Bator and Terelj. That's how I know."

"So you are an expert!"

Timur laughed grimly. "I don't think so, Andrei Nikolayevich."

"How far to Ulan Bator from this place?"

"Around fifty kilometers, and then a day's march, depending on the terrain."

13

Libya
Al-Jawf

Jess and Raffa carried boxes containing the rationed food allocated by the encampment administration. Labels identified the contents as packets of indiscriminate ages from the UN World Food Program and Red Cross, probably diverted during the civil war in Libya.

They made their way between the tents.

Jess watched their surroundings closely. Raffa touched her arm and gestured to a family sitting in the opening of a shelter. For a moment, Jess couldn't see what attracted his interest, but then she understood. There were two children, both sitting apart from the rest of the family. On their faces and necks, reddening patches of skin that appeared scalded and which both children scratched. The younger, a girl little more than five or six, had quite long hair, but in places the growth seemed irregular, as though it had been shaved away. Despite the cold, the elder, a boy, sweated heavily.

"Seen before," Raffa said as they walked away, still struggling with the language. He swore softly in Italian as he tried to find the words. "Other families, more sickness, just like this."

"How many others?"

Raffa shook his head. He didn't understand.

She spoke more slowly, pronouncing each word carefully: "How many…sick families?"

Raffa set down his box, then held up two hands, displaying seven fingers.

"Different tents?"

He nodded, then picked the box back up. Concern creased his forehead, the same worry she felt, the thought going through her mind: *was there some disease in the camp?*

When they arrived back at the clutch of shelters and tents that marked their small section of the encampment, she put the food parcels away and was about to duck inside the main shelter when she saw someone standing just to the side, waiting.

"Ain Salah," Jess said with surprise. "What are you doing here?"

"May I come in?"

"Of course."

He nodded with some uncertainty, then sat on one of the blankets. Hector ran over to him and seized him by the legs. Ain Salah knelt and took him in his arms. "I came to apologize. I didn't offer you much of welcome." He turned to Giovanni. "We had talked so frequently, I was ashamed to be so rude to you."

"I got the feeling it wasn't your fault, Ain Salah."

He didn't reply.

"Why don't you stay a while," Giovanni said. "Eat with us?"

"I would like that. I told them I was needed to make some adjustments to antennae located in a few of the irrigation areas. That was not true, so I have some time."

"What is it you do for the Zuwayya?" Ufuk asked. "What is it that goes on in that administration building?"

Ain Salah tilted his head. "The oil is important. The Zuwayya control what oil fields remain operational across this region, and there are not many. They're keen to retain control, but there are tribal groups to the south, in Chad and Sudan, with which the Zuwayya have been fighting for a long time, particularly during the civil war."

"You mean the Toubou?"

"There are others beside the Toubou, but yes. As to my work, the Zuwayya feel communication within Al-Jawf, and eventually with the rest of Africa, is important. There are African Union representatives in other camps and surviving townships throughout Africa. Shaikh Faraj wishes to open trade negotiations with them. There are VHF receivers and transmitters, shortwave and CB. It's my expertise, salvaging and operating equipment like this."

"Can you get us signed up to salvage duty? We have two trucks and we can defend ourselves. We could be useful to the Zuwayya."

"Ordinarily they will only allocate such duties to those they trust."

"Could you try? We could be useful to your people."

"The Zuwayya are not my people. I find myself here and I am useful to them because I have an education, but they do not trust me a great deal, as you have seen. Nor do they treat me as their equal. I am not one of theirs."

"Where is your family?" Jess asked. "Are they here with you?"

The man's face sagged at the question. "As with so many, the events of Nomad have…taken them away from me."

"They died?" Jess asked quietly.

"They are alive." Ain Salah's face brightened. "I know that for a fact. We will be reunited soon. I hope."

Ain Salah's face had delicate, fine-boned features—with dark brown eyes behind his heavy glasses—and a certain earnest innocence that seemed genuine. He didn't look them in the eye as he spoke, but kept his eyes down, or looking out the opening of the shelter. Jess figured he was afraid of those for whom he worked, of what the Zuwayya might think should they discover his presence here. Or perhaps it was simply who he was, his culture so different to hers.

Her mind wandered to the image of the two children.

"Is there sickness in the camp?" she asked Ain Salah.

"There is, yes, but not cholera. Not even dysentery. It's something we don't understand yet. It doesn't seem to be contagious."

"Nothing we should be worried about?"

"As I said, it is not contagious."

That wasn't reassuring.

Jess decided to let it go at that, and question Raffa a little more about what he had seen and where, perhaps go and see it for herself. Having Ain Salah here benefitted them, with his contacts within the Zuwayya administration, but she couldn't tear herself away from the thought that there might be an epidemic taking hold in the camp.

Ain Salah told them he should leave, that his Zuwayya masters would soon be missing him. Ufuk walked him out to his car, and Jess made her way alone to the high dune border of the camp. She did this frequently, more from a desire for time alone than as part of any security measure.

She spent some time there, perhaps an hour, trying to unravel the thoughts that had been troubling her. Was coming to Al-Jawf a mistake? Another in a long list of mistakes? This Zuwayya dictatorship reminded her of the Taliban regime in Afghanistan.

And what was happening in the States? She first imagined places she had known as a child, now destroyed, or sheathed in ash and ice. Only later did she see places she had loved as an adult: New York, Chicago, Boston—what did they look like now? What was left of those once great cities and their people? Should she be working on getting back there? Or was Africa her home now?

14

Libya
Al-Jawf

Walking back from an inspection of the dune wall, Jess caught sight of Giovanni, running and shouting. She looked for Massarra and broke into a run. As she got closer, she heard Giovanni calling Hector's name, over and over.

"What's happening?" she said as she caught up to Giovanni.

"I can't find Hector," he said breathlessly. "I was doing some work in one of the shelters and I told him to stay in our tent. When I returned he was gone."

"I'll take the eastern part of the camp. Jess can take the north. If we split up, we'll cover more ground."

Jess ran through the camp, heart beating hard. Thoughts cascaded through her mind, memories of the child killed by the Zuwayya militia on the dune wall that night. She ran faster, ducking into shelters, ignoring startled and indignant cries.

"I'm looking for a little boy. Have you seen a little boy?" She spoke the words each time, barely hearing them as they tumbled out.

Two huddled shapes, tossing a ball to each other. Hope surged and Jess ran to them. She grabbed the first, spinning the figure round, but found the face of a girl. A cry came from behind her, a startled parent maybe, but she ignored it and searched the face of the second. Still not Hector. A woman wearing a burka confronted her, gesturing and shouting, her face tight with confusion and anger.

"I'm looking for a little boy," Jess said. "Have you seen a little boy?" She indicated the children beside her, then patted her chest. "My boy, have you seen him, please?"

The woman's eyes widened in understanding. If she couldn't understand the words, what lay behind them was clear to her. The woman took her by the arm and began shouting to others in the camp.

There came a clutch of negative responses, then something more positive. More gestures to a tent.

Jess found him sitting inside, playing with a girl his age. She ran over and grabbed him by the shoulders. "Where have you been?"

He looked sullenly at the ground. "I was bored."

"We've been looking all over the camp for you. You can't just run off."

"He won't let me out of his sight for more than a few minutes," Hector said, his voice shaking. "I have to stay in the tent. I have nothing to do. No friends. Even Raffa doesn't want to play with me, and you are always busy."

"We don't know if it's safe—"

"I am not a child anymore. I can look after myself."

Jess realized this small conversation was more words than she'd shared with Hector in longer than she could remember. Poor kid. But his English was improving dramatically. She pulled him into her chest. "I know you can, Hector. You're a big boy now, I can see that." She tried to calm herself. "Why don't I talk to Giovanni? See if maybe we can get him to ease up a little?"

Hector nodded and hugged her back.

She took him back to their shelter and left Hector there, instructing him to wait, then went looking for Giovanni. He was furious.

"Shouting at him is not going to get you anywhere," she said.

"Someone needs to act as a father for him—"

"And you've done that, but he needs to get out. Let me take him to the town. We can't keep him in forever."

"It's too dangerous."

"Just to the market and back. He's going crazy cooped up in camp."

Giovanni looked away.

"He needs some normality," she said. "Terrifying weeks on the run, then we get Sanctuary, and then that's taken away, too. No parents. If I were him, I'd be catatonic by now, but he's been great. Barely complaining, always there for us. If he wants to get out, I'm going to take him out."

Jess didn't leave much room for negotiation.

Giovanni took a deep breath. "Okay, but take care of him."

"Of course."

They took one of the pickups into town. Jess had tucked a pistol into her waistband, hidden by the folds of her coats and many layers against the cold. She tensed as they went through the checkpoint into the center of town, but they waved her through. She took him to the main market, and got out of the pickup to weave their way in and out of the crowds. He smiled and held her hand tight—perhaps, she hoped, with excitement rather than fear.

Window-shopping in a post-apocalyptic African village.

Jess managed to find a tiny bit of humor as they dallied in front of one stall and then the next. Hector found some baskets, battered and rusted, then squealed as he found some small toy cars and a plastic helicopter. Likely Hector had outgrown such things, but he took them anyway, giving her a broad smile and a tight hug as she bartered for them, offering her silk scarf in return. It wasn't much use for keeping warm anyway. He played with his new toy as they walked, running it through the air as though it were flying.

Beneath one of the balconies above the market, Jess caught someone watching them who abruptly turned away. It wasn't unusual here, to be watched, but something about it caught her attention. An inexplicable feeling followed, deep in her stomach. Afghanistan had taught her not to ignore those instincts, to listen to the quiet voices that saw in the shadows.

"Hector, let's go see some more of the town. How about a little walk around? Maybe we can find another toy at one of the markets?"

The boy smiled and nodded.

Through the chaotic streets she led him, hoping he didn't sense the urgency in her movements. Desperate for him not to notice the stolen glances over her shoulder and at the dusty glass of nearby windows. As time stretched she became certain of it. They were being followed, and not just by the woman, but others too. She looked for people who moved when she did, stopped when she did.

Jess quickened her pace. Hector looked up, and she tried to offer him the reassurance of a smile, but he knew better.

They were converging on her and Hector now, several men and women. Ghosts whispering through the crowd. A press of the crowd swallowed them. Someone jostled her. She grabbed her pistol, but lost her grip on Hector.

He screamed.

Then another scream, but this time from a woman in a *burkha*, just beside Jess. For a moment, Jess didn't understand, then she saw the woman pointing at the pistol. Jess ignored it, pushing people aside.

She caught sight of Hector through the throng, just as a man reached for her and tried to grab the pistol. He said something, shouted, anger etched in his voice and face. She tried to push him aside but something kicked her legs away. Her prosthetic limb dislodged. She nearly fell, but caught herself on one knee.

She couldn't see Hector anymore and did the only thing she could think of—raised her pistol and fired twice into the air.

The crowd acted almost as one, an ocean of surprised faces that huddled low instinctively. Jess kept the gun out, waving it at anyone who came close. She couldn't see the men and women who had been following her, but she couldn't see Hector either.

She searched frantically, calling his name. Again and again, shouting until she was hoarse. She tried to ignore the jackknifing pain of misaligned nerve-endings and whatever had hit her hard enough to dislodge the prosthetic.

She saw him.

Tears on his face, one hand still holding the helicopter, the other waving to her. Not far, just a few feet. Beneath a balcony. She reached him, stumbling, pistol still drawn.

"They were going for Hector," Jess said. "I have no doubt of that."

They were all sitting in the main shelter as sleet rain slicked against the roof. The place that had become their dining room and living space, a communal area where they could gather and seek comfort in companionship. Yet the mood had changed. A deeper tension clung to them, thick with the anticipation of a new threat. They sat on rolled out rugs and camp chairs, on boxes and crates. No one ate because no one had any appetite. Hector sat in the middle, next to Giovanni, still shaken but trying to offer a brave face.

"I said not to take him into the town. So far, we've kept him hidden," Ufuk said as he completed the final checks on the work he had done to refit Jess's prosthetic. "He could be seen as our weakness. Perhaps they've been waiting."

"Who is *they*?" Giovanni asked.

"Perhaps Mossad," Massarra ventured.

Giovanni frowned before replying: "Israeli intelligence? Does that even exist anymore? Why would they want to snatch Hector?"

"As leverage over us."

"Why would Israeli spies want anything with *us*?"

Ufuk inserted himself between them. "I think Massarra is making a wild guess, but she is right. There are people watching us. Who are scared of us."

231

"Perhaps Jess was right before," Giovanni sputtered. "Perhaps we are better off separating. I think maybe people are watching *you*."

"We are stronger together," Massarra said.

Silence.

"You must all see that the world is at war," Ufuk said quietly. "A war for survival, for the scarce resources this planet still possesses. And those, like Müller, who want to control what is left. He started the narrative before Nomad, about Islamic extremists destroying Rome, and Jessica's father for keeping Nomad a secret."

"Do you think anyone still believes that?" Jessica said quietly.

"Nobody knows what to believe, but every war needs an enemy. Every knight needs a dragon. Müller placed himself in a position where he can be the savior."

"I'm not trying to stop him anymore. I'm just trying to survive."

"But we cannot let him gain primacy," Ufuk continued. "Don't you see that? His next step will be to control resources, the rest of the Sanctuary system, perhaps smaller networks like the Vivas bunkers. He'll see Kufra and places like it as opportunities."

"He's thousands of miles away. He's got other things to think about than a shanty town in the middle of a desert."

"You think a man like Müller would ignore a place like this?"

"I think you have a bit of a fixation."

Ufuk stood. "Perhaps we need some time to think. If you would prefer to do things your own way, I cannot stop you. We would be better working together, but that's a decision you need to come to by yourselves. I can't influence you any further."

He turned and left the shelter.

15

Libya
Al-Jawf

"Jessica, wake up. Something is happening."

"Huh?"

She opened her eyes just in time to see Ufuk scamper out of her tent.

Already awake, Jess was only pretending to sleep. Or wishing that sleep would come. Each morning she awoke with the first touch of light, usually after a restless night. Always the same questions: Was she doing the right thing? Could she trust Ufuk? Was this place really a home for Giovanni and Hector, and Raffa?

At nights she watched Massarra and Ufuk in quiet conversation together, away from the camp. Ufuk spent much of the rest of the time on his tablet, or tinkering with electronics. He always took time every day to play games on the tablets with Hector, but maybe just to ingratiate himself with Jess. Whatever the reason, she appreciated it. Ain Salah's visits became more frequent, and Ufuk would talk to him about the communications network the Zuwayya were trying to create.

Jess blinked and rubbed her eyes. "Ufuk?"

She jumped up from her sleeping mat and stuck her head out of the tent, but Ufuk was nowhere to be seen. Massarra wasn't in the tent either, but then Massarra had taken to driving into Al-Jawf early and late each day, spending several hours there at a time. She wouldn't elaborate on what she was doing, except to say that she watched for telltale signs of surveillance to figure out who was watching them.

Spy stuff. The Israeli seemed to relish it.

After scanning the immediate area and calling out again, Jess returned to the tent and picked up the radio handset. She tuned to the channel Ufuk had set up for them, but she was surprised when it hissed to life by itself. Massarra's voice crackled with interference. A dull thud echoed in the distance.

"I can hardly make you out," Jess said into the handset.

"...radios jammed..."

"Jammed where?"

"...town. There's an attack..."

"What's happening?" Jess waited. "Can you hear me?"

"...explosion...admin...compound..."

Through the tent flap, Jess saw a silent billowing cloud of smoke rise up on the horizon. An unmistakable tremor juddered the ground.

"Get out of there now!" Jess shouted into the handset.

The radio offered nothing but static.

"What going on?" Giovanni said sleepily from the depths of the tent.

"There's been an explosion in Al-Jawf."

"A what?"

"Wake up, dammit. An explosion. Massarra is in town."

His eyes snapped open. "Is she hurt?"

"The radio cut out."

"Why?"

"I don't know." She ran through possible explanations in her mind, none of them good. "Wake Raffa. I need to find Ufuk."

She sprinted around their small encampment frantically, and finally found him near the edge of the camp, at the dune escarpment.

"What are you doing?" she said.

"You heard the explosion?"

"I just spoke to Massarra. She's in town."

"But you lost her. The signal is gone, yes?"

"How do you know?"

"Come with me." He took her hand and led her up the escarpment.

When they reached the top, she understood. It took a moment to process the wide, billowing cloud of sand and dust, to realize that at its heart there had to be vehicles, a great many of them. Still some distance away—but fast approaching.

"We need to leave," she said.

"We can't abandon Massarra," Ufuk said. "If she's in town, she's got the other truck. Besides, where do you propose we go?" He gestured to the southwest where another cloud had begun to form. Another formation approaching the town.

"How long do you think we have?"

"Maybe fifteen minutes. Maybe less. We need to stay together. We have to head into town and find Massarra."

"She can take care of herself."

"Which is precisely why we need her. Not to forget, as I say, we need the truck that's with her."

Automatic gunfire. Sporadic punches in the morning air, bursts of half-a-second. One after another. Another explosion shook the air.

"We can't head into that," Jess said.

The cloud of sand and dust swirled closer.

"Would you prefer they stay here?" Ufuk demanded, his voice rising. "Not doing anything is still doing something, but usually nothing good."

It was a good point. Jess turned and made her way off the dune, back toward their camp. "We need as much information as we can. Can you get a few small drones into the air? The Predators?"

They were not alone in their understanding of what was about to happen. Many of those living in the camp had come from Libya,

Egypt, Chad and Sudan. Many had witnessed attacks like this one before, just as Jess had in Afghanistan. They'd seen militia ride into towns from nowhere, shattering the calm with unrelenting violence. She recognized the panic in their eyes as they hoarded their meager possessions. Many had come on foot and were now leaving that same way, stumbling across the dunes, casting anxious glances over their shoulders as they fled.

"Who are they?" Raffa asked. "Who is it coming here?"

Ufuk answered: "My guess is the Toubou. Their approach from the south, from the direction of Chad, the hate between them and the Zuwayya, and their expulsion from Kufra. It seems the most likely explanation."

"There were explosions in the center of the town," Jess said. "Massarra was there. We heard gunfire before the trucks arrived."

"You still want to go into all of that," Giovanni said, "put us at risk with yet more coming behind to trap us?"

"Massarra is still there."

"Massarra's a big girl," he replied, his anger rising.

"Could you just leave her there?"

"If it means protecting us."

"We need her. Ufuk's drones will give us real-time images. We can avoid the fighting. We can stay safe."

She didn't really believe that, that their safety could be guaranteed, but he started packing in silence anyway. Hector buzzed round Giovanni. It terrified her, the world this quiet, six-year-old boy had to face. The constant threat. She ducked down and gave him a hug.

They drove first to a small knot of closed compounds located close to the airport. A single engine plane buzzed into the air as they approached. There were only two other small planes on the tarmac, both of them taxiing to take off. To each side of the runway were clustered small, breeze-block houses on dirt streets. Massarra had said it had once been given the name the New Neighborhood of Kufra, but like everywhere else, it was just more shanty huts.

Jess checked her watch. Massarra had radioed just after six. They'd struck camp and been away by six-fifteen. The time now approached six-thirty. Thirty minutes or so for Massarra to make her way to one of the two, pre-arranged meeting places.

More than enough time.

The main road into town offered the clearest and most terrifying perspective of the unfolding chaos. One of the agricultural plots had already been overrun by desperate, fleeing people. The Zuwayya green-bands there were battered to the ground, their bloodied bodies scattered over what remained of the autumn crop. Others waited by vehicles parked in haste, weapons in skittish hands.

Dusty pickups and sedans tore past on the main route, barely missing the pickup as they did and causing Giovanni to swerve to avoid a collision. They were heading into the desert, terrified faces at the wheels of each hurriedly packed vehicle. In the distance, in the center of the town, plumes of black smoke rose, but Jess knew they were not from explosions.

"They're burning tires," Jess said. "Probably to signal whoever is coming from the south."

Giovanni pulled the truck into a small lot, the first of two places they'd arranged to meet Massarra should they ever become separated.

"Keep weapons hidden," Jess said as she opened the door to the truck. "If the green-bands see them, they might think we are a threat to them." All of them wore the Bedouin clothing in which they'd entered Al-Jawf. Jess hoped it would be enough to help them blend into the melee of fleeing people.

"Where are you going?" Giovanni asked.

She took out her pistol and checked the magazine. "To see if I can find her."

"If she's here, she can see the truck."

Jess looked at Giovanni and tried to reassure him with a smile she didn't feel. "Just give me a couple of minutes."

"The approaching vehicles have reached the south camps," Ufuk said without looking up from his tablet. "They're fanning out, splitting up and moving through the camps. Another section has stayed on the main road and is heading north toward Al-Jawf."

Jess nodded. "Two minutes," she said, tightening the *shemagh* and *keffiyeh* wrapped around her face and head.

She moved quickly, pistol in hand but hidden within the folds of her coat. She searched every doorway for any sign of Massarra, hoping she had chosen to remain hidden rather than expose herself, hoping that was the reason she was not already at the meeting place, or at least was not immediately obvious to them.

At one end of the street, people loaded possessions into an already overfilled van. From behind her, in the direction of the south camps and echoing in the distance, came the crack of gunfire. Jess lifted the radio from her belt and tried again, but found only static.

She continued to search, but driven by a new urgency. She ran along the street, ignoring the glances thrown her way, knowing every second spent here made their escape from the town more difficult. She tried to calm herself, to keep her focus, but fear began to take hold. She pushed it roughly away and kept searching. Time stretched, but only when she was certain that Massarra was not here, not waiting for them in the shadows or under cover in some discreet place, did she return to the pickup.

She shook her head to Giovanni as she approached and was about to go round the front of the truck to get in when something made her turn and look back over the desert, along the main street that ran from the south camps.

In the distance, but still discernible enough for its truth to be undeniable, came a long, heavy cavalcade. She knew instinctually what they were: pickups with fifty-caliber tactical machine guns mounted on the back and, following behind, vans and flat-bed trucks on which she could see the lean outlines of militia solders.

She got inside the pickup and shouted to Giovanni: "Get going now. Move! We need to get in town ahead of them."

The Toyota lurched onto the main road and Giovanni had it surging forward, twisting between pedestrians and other vehicles. The tires whined as he swerved. More gunfire echoed in the distance.

"Where to?"

"The second meeting point," Jess reached for the M4.

"You sure?"

"We give her as long as we can, then we leave." She turned to Ufuk. "What can you see of Al-Jawf?"

"There's fighting on the streets everywhere. I can't tell yet who they are."

"This is insane," Giovanni said. "We don't even know if she's still alive."

"I won't just leave her, not after what she's done for us." Jess looked at Hector and tried to make herself still inside. Through the back window, she saw Raffa perched on top of their packed shelters and equipment, huddled low against a squall of sand-laden wind.

16

Libya
Al-Jawf
Central Market

When the first explosion came, Massarra was away from her pickup. Ufuk had rushed her into the town, even before the early morning was touched by the thin light of dawn—but she'd been too slow to get here. What she told Jess when asked—that she made these forays into Al-Jawf in order to search for those who had been watching Jess and Hector—was partially true, yet her visits had another purpose.

Ain Salah.

And to protect the asset.

When the young man had first come to visit them at the camp, Massarra had been suspicious, but then she was suspicious of everyone. Ufuk hadn't been, and was enthused for reasons Massarra couldn't fathom. He took Ain Salah away when he could, and spoke to him at length. Only once had she been able to eavesdrop and discover they were discussing the telecommunications networks that had been in place in Libya before Nomad.

Ufuk expressed an interest in restoring an *ad hoc* cellphone service to the town when she'd pressed him about his relationship. She was skeptical. There was some mistrust. Something he wasn't telling her. He'd told her that these were their people, that this was the real mission of the Levantine Council, to raise their people back up.

And Ain Salah could be useful for protecting the asset, he'd told her. They couldn't keep the asset in the tent next to Jessica.

Massarra filtered through the crowded streets, head low, pistol tucked into her belt. The explosions shattered the morning calm of the market. Faces contorted, first into confusion, then disbelief, taking too long to reach the fear that came with understanding. Massarra understood faster. The sound of an explosion shearing apart a peaceful morning in a crowded place occupied a place of sad familiarity. Tel-Aviv, Jerusalem, Haifa, Beirut, Gaza. A bus torn open by a suicide bomber, gunmen opening fire in a synagogue. Retaliatory strikes by anonymous drones or jet fighters miles away, or mortars placed within range of a border, and the collateral cost in lives of those that might have had so much more of a life left to live.

More explosions, followed by sporadic gunfire.

Massarra was already running. She didn't know what it meant, or who was responsible, but Ufuk knew it was coming, somehow, and that they had to leave. When she reached the Zuwayya administrative compound, the walled complex where Ain Salah worked, she saw the gates were breached and a gunfight had raged inside.

No sign of the man.

She waited, debating whether to run inside or find another way in. She needed to know what was happening. Was Al-Jawf the subject of a militia assault? Or was this something different? Desperate people refused entry to the town, seeking revenge?

She took out her pistol and ducked inside.

The compound was as lavish as the first moment they had arrived and been allowed to eat as Ain Salah's guest. From the relative poverty of the southern camps, she'd forgotten how green the grass was, even salted with ash. Ornamental carvings and sculptures stood proud in the gardens.

More gunfire from within the main building, sporadic flashes seen through the barred windows. Evidence of explosions across the charred walls. Another explosion shook the ground somewhere blocks away, but it felt like another piece in a coordinated plan. Not desperate people seeking revenge, but something more precise.

She sprinted across the gardens, gun out but down, keeping to the edges, close to walls where she could, or to the scant cover offered by palm trees and the foliage of wiry shrubs. When she reached the steps leading up to one of the side entrances, she took them at a sprint and flattened herself against the wall beside the door. Testing it with one hand, it opened easily.

The lock had been forced.

She went in, gun just beneath the line of her vision. Moving fast, soundlessly, not distracted by the chattering bursts of gunfire resonating outside. The gun moved with her head, went where her eyes went, as she tried to clear every corner, each doorway and sightline. Lights blazed at the end of the hallway. When she couldn't clear a room without turning her back on another, she did it rapidly, at a run. There were always risks; no way to avoid those.

She checked every room.

Beyond each door there might be someone cowering with a weapon. Her eyes wide open, taking in every detail, analyzing instinctually. Dead bodies were strewn across tables, over radio equipment, or amongst sheets of bloodied paper.

None was Ain Salah.

She reached the end of the corridor when a green-band stumbled through a half-open door. In one slick, red hand he held an AK. The moment he saw her, his eyes darted to her weapon. One-handed, he raised his own gun and pulled the trigger, but he was unable to control the weapon's recoil and staggered off balance.

Massarra fired twice, both head shots. A fine spray puffed into the air. The man bucked and twisted, then fell.

She picked up his AK and slung it over her shoulder.

Kept moving fast.

The final room on the main building's ground floor lay behind two, tall doors: the dining room in which they'd eaten when they had first arrived. Braced against a wall, heart pounding and her breath ragged in the choking dust from ruptured stone, she covered the doors. Gunfire came again, still upstairs. A scream echoing, sweeping through the air. A woman's terrified pleas cut off mid-stream.

With one hand she reached for a gilded knob and tested it gently. It was unlocked. She held the pistol close to her torso, in the close contact position, and turned the knob, quietly but slowly as though time stretched and waited for her.

Then she pushed the door hard, bringing her pistol up and stepping away. She took the room in increments, moving across the doorway, revealing herself only in tiny sections. Seeing into the room along the sight lines of her pistol.

And there he was.

Ain Salah cowered under a table, between the legs of a chair. She knew it was him, the tone and hue of the *keffiyeh* he wore specifically so she could tail him through the market.

"Ain Salah?" she whispered.

He looked up and saw her, eyes going wide as he took her in. "Massarra?"

"Do you have it?"

With one shaking hand he tugged on a green rucksack. Massarra crossed the room and checked it, verified the sleek gray metal box within, that the glowing filaments were green. That it was plugged in. She cursed Ufuk for trusting it to this man, but then hiding it in the camps was not a better solution. "Come on. Out."

Massarra half-wondered at the luck of finding him there when no one else had. Ain Salah clambered to his feet. She grabbed the rucksack from him and hefted it over her shoulder. It had to be fifty pounds.

She grunted and said: "Let's go."

17

Libya
Al-Jawf

Perhaps it was foolish, a breach in their security measures, but desperation seized Jess. She had Raffa cycle through channels on the VHF radio repeating Massarra's name and waiting to see if any response came. She covered the front windscreen with the M4, the passenger window wound down. Ufuk and Raffa and Hector were jammed in the back seat of the pickup as they roared into town. The southern camps had already been overrun.

Finally, the Israeli's voice crackled beyond the static. Raffa handed her the radio.

"Where are you?" she shouted.

"I'm with Ain Salah. I'm on the edge of town."

"Are you in the truck?"

"It's nearby, but I'll wait for you."

"I need a point of reference," Ufuk said. "Something I can see from the air. Describe your surroundings."

Massarra did so, and Ufuk searched images on his tablet from the drone aloft. When he found what she was describing, he zoomed in the image.

"That's her."

Jess yelled at Giovanni, pointing out the window. He slammed on the brakes and the truck ground to a stop in a haze of dust. Massarra and Ain Salah emerged from the shadows of an alleyway. She had a huge green rucksack slung over one shoulder.

"We have to go. Right now," Jess said. "An attacking force entered the town to the south. Streets are jammed. What happened this morning?"

"Phased attacks on the Zuwayya militia barracks," Massarra detailed. "Tactical explosions laid by professionals. Planned and coordinated."

That didn't answer Jess's question, but there was no time.

"Look out!" Giovanni shouted.

At the end of the street, one of the pickups roared past, a tactical machine gun manned by someone dressed in fatigues, face wrapped in a *shemagh*.

"Where's your truck?"

"In the alley. I'll follow you."

On the other side of the street, in a mechanical workshop where a car was parked and parts were scattered, two men watched them, their faces expressionless. Further along the street, people scattered and ran, ducking behind cars and vans as another truck drove past. More clattering of gunfire erupted. Giovanni pulled the truck into the street.

She almost didn't recognize the disheveled, stumbling figure that ran in front of the pickup. They nearly ran straight over the man. It took a moment to realize it was Peter Connor.

"Pull over," Jess shouted.

Giovanni hesitated.

She shouted again: "That's Peter."

Jess swung open her door as Giovanni mashed the brakes.

Relief washed over Peter Connor's dirty, bloodied face. *"Thank God."*

Ufuk jumped up from the backseat and leaned forward over Jess. He tried to grab the doorframe. "We're not picking up hitchhikers."

Jess used all of her strength to shove him back. "We're picking up this one."

Massarra's truck ground to a halt behind them. Gunfire crackled.

"Who the hell is this?" Ufuk's olive complexion turned beet red. "We're not—"

"He's an American, the only other American I've met in this godforsaken place."

Jess pushed her door open wider and moved over a few inches toward Giovanni. She didn't really know Peter, but then, she was tired of abandoning people. But maybe more than that, as she watched Ufuk's face turn a purple shade of crimson, was that she was tired of always playing to Erdogmus's script. If they were running, she wanted more people on her side in this twisted little family. It was a gut decision.

"Jessica," Ufuk protested, trying to reach over her again. "There is no way—"

Someone grabbed Peter roughly by his shirt and shoved him into the truck's doorway. It was Massarra. "Get him in the truck, and hurry," she urged. "We have no time for this."

"Of if you don't want him, then we get out," Jess added.

Ufuk glanced back and forth at Jess and Massarra. He was outnumbered and outgunned. He slid back into his seat. Peter scrambled in next to Jess, while Giovanni put the truck back into gear and sped away. They turned into a small side street that curved away between high-walled and gated compounds. He maneuvered the pickup between cars and debris from walls that had been hacked away by explosives and gunfire.

As he took the tight curve of the street, Jess shouted at him to stop.

Standing in front of them, in the middle of the narrow street, were two men with Kalashnikovs, faces hidden behind *shemagh*. Two cars blocked the road.

"This is a bad," Giovanni said quietly.

One of the men lifted a hand and waved to them, gesturing for them to stop. The other held his assault rifle low, in an approximation of the ready position. More came with them as they approached the pickup. Massarra's truck crunched across the gravel behind them.

"Don't stop," Ufuk said.

"I can't just run them over." Giovanni slowed. "They'll start shooting." He glanced in the back, at Hector in Raffa's arms.

The first man, who'd been waving, tapped the hood of the pickup and indicated for them to get out. From behind the cars parked across the road, other men came, standing beside them, waiting.

"Get out of the way," Giovanni shouted and waved frantically.

The first man made a gesture with his hand. He held it flat against his chest, where the heart would be, and tapped it slowly.

"What is he trying to say?"

"I don't know." Jess watched him, searched his body for signs of aggression, of tension in the shoulders, or a shift in his stance. Her finger dropped to the trigger of the M4. She leaned back to give herself room to fire.

"They're not alone." Ufuk pointed forward.

More men emerged from behind one of the gates to one side, approached from their flank, several armed with Kalashnikovs or ancient rifles.

"What do you want me to do?" Giovanni said. "Who are these guys? They're not green-bands."

Jess tightened her grip on the M4 as she got ready to lever it up.

"There's more behind Massarra's truck," Ufuk said. "Most of them armed."

Jess glanced around, tried to get a tactical assessment, watching the men approaching from the gated compound, then into the mirror where she saw more behind them. The man in front began shouting something Jess couldn't understand. His words were muffled under the *shemagh* and very likely in Arabic. His AK came up slightly and he began jabbing it to reinforce his point.

"What is he saying?" Giovanni said.

"He wants us to get out of the truck."

"We're not getting out."

"We're surrounded. The moment they start firing—"

"Hector, get down as low as you can," Jess whispered.

"What about Massarra?" Giovanni said. He revved the engine and again gestured for the man to move.

"She'll take her lead from us. Whatever we do, she'll follow."

"This truck isn't armor-plated. If they start firing—"

"I know." The image of it swept through her mind. The pickups were old and heavy, but the Kalashnikov used a 7.62mm round that would tear through the doors and chassis and come out the other side a bloody mess. Even if Giovanni gunned the engine and surged forward, running the men ahead of them over before they could fire, there were others who would unload fully automatic weapons into the two trucks.

"Ufuk. Where are the drones?"

"Above us."

"How far?"

"A few hundred meters."

"Bring them down so they can be seen. Fly over the street, right now."

"You know they're not armed?"

"I know. Giovanni, get out your pistol and aim it at him."

Jess opened the car door and brought the M4 up, aiming through the angular gap between the door and the frame of the windscreen. The man saw the weapon and brought his own up, but he also realized what it was and saw the way she held it.

"You understand English?"

He hesitated so she repeated the question, more loudly this time. He nodded.

She pointed upward without taking her eyes off him, watched him lift his eyes toward the sky and his expression tighten and the drones roared overhead. "You see them, don't you? Those are US drones. Armed, weaponized, US RQ-7 Shadow UAVs. We're US Special Forces. You understand what that means? It means if you don't back up right now, we are authorized to engage you. Are you ready to die here?"

She saw hesitation in him again, watched him glance over at the man beside him who bounced nervously on the balls of his feet.

"We know what you look like," she added. "Every single one of you. Anything happens to us, our people will come looking for you, your families, your friends. Are you ready to risk their lives too? Just back up and let us through."

His expression changed to one of anger reamed with frustration, but gave way to reluctant self-interest. "Leave now. You're not welcome here." He stepped back and shouted in Arabic. The men eased away, weapons lowered.

"No arguments there." Jess got back in and Giovanni gunned the engine. The two pickups headed between the two cars, parked at an angle that would slow them yet still allow them through, then picked up speed and surged away.

"That was quick thinking," Ufuk said.

Jess's heart beat hard. Chest tight, hard to breathe. She tried to relax. The drones buzzed threateningly overhead.

In a position of confidence, those men would have opened fire without hesitation. They had a tactical advantage and superior numbers. There had been no other way, and if it was luck that had seen them through, then they were due some.

As they sped away, a white-hot streak of fire surged at one of the Predators. It had to be a missile from a shoulder-mounted launcher. The drone soared upward, but its sacrifice had been made. An explosion lit the sky, washing the wreckage of twisted buildings in an amber blaze. The air shuddered. Debris rained down.

PART FOUR

Mars First Mission

Deep Interplanetary Space

Commander Jason Rankin curled up in his cot, tried to get comfortable, and then realized he'd folded into a fetus position under the thin sheets. He consciously straightened out and laid flat on his back. On the other side of his cabin was a porthole with a view into space. The stars lazily slid by as the hab rotated. Since he was a kid, he'd always dreamed of being the captain of a starship. An impossible dream, and yet here he was—dream realized—but the dream had become a nightmare.

Rankin had a few pictures up on his wall, of his mother and father—both dead—and the rest from travels he'd taken: him standing on the South Pole, in the Atacama desert, a few candid shots of him in the Mars environmental simulator, one of them with his arm around the shoulders of Anders Larsson. He'd brought no crosses, no trinkets, and there were no wives or kids left behind in his single-minded pursuit; the only personal item he'd brought was his trusty harmonica that had traveled to all these places with him. He'd figured he could be the first person to play the Blues on the Red Planet.

That would have to wait.

Each crewmember had their own private cabin, a five-by-ten foot space with a desk, folding cot, a tiny bathroom. It was compact, but had mood lighting that was supposed to make it feel more open. Whoever designed the fancy lighting had obviously never been into space. It felt claustrophobic, and it still smelled like a new car. Rankin had read that this odor came from outgassing of volatile organic compounds from plastics, adhesives and sealers. Didn't sound good for you, but then again, his life expectancy was measured against different risks now, and one of his crew was already dead: Anders Larsson had died in the hibernation pod.

After they replayed Ufuk's recorded video message in the common area, a heated discussion had followed. More of a tantrum. Screaming. Tears. Accusations. Most of it directed at Ufuk Erdogmus for not telling them the truth, but then what would they have done?

The first stages of grief were anger and denial, and Rankin knew he had had to let each of his crew go through it in their own way. It was one thing to go off and risk your own life on a mission to Mars, and expect that you might die—but now they were suddenly faced with the reality that maybe everyone they ever knew on Earth might be dead. All their loved ones. All their friends and family. Killed in some horrible disaster. All the places they knew growing up. Gone. All of it. Even the countries they professed allegiance to. The ideas they stood for. All of it perhaps futile.

But perhaps not.

Once the shouting had died down, Rankin had ordered—*ordered*—each of them to their quarters for sleep, and had personally made sure each took a mild sedative. Even himself. They were all upset, and more than that, frightened. The mission had changed, like a twisted horror show they couldn't escape from and had no end. It was one thing to spend years planning for a mission to Mars, coming to terms with trying to eke out an existence living on a frozen red world—but it was quite another to imagine being swallowed by the unimaginable titan of Saturn, with the Earth destroyed in its wake.

And what did Rankin feel? If he really searched his emotions?

Responsible.

That's what he felt.

Responsible for his crew. For this ship. And to Ufuk Erdogmus.

He remembered having drinks with Ufuk at the *Museo del Prado* in Madrid, just the two of them outside at night when the media circus had left. They'd strolled through the wet grass after a thunderstorm, the lights of city twinkling in the distance. Ufuk had explained how he was entrusting this ship, the billions of dollars it

254

cost, to Jason. Personally. They'd talked about how important it was to establish a human colony on another planet, in case some cosmic disaster destroyed Earth. A comet impact. Another asteroid like the one that killed off the dinosaurs.

Rankin had never imagined a black hole.

And he'd never guessed that Ufuk might have known that a planet-ending disaster was actually coming. So the man had to have a plan, and so the next question: what *was* that plan?

Enough daydreaming. Rankin had a ship to run.

"Mars First," he said aloud. "Show me again the Saturn intercept."

"Certainly, Commander Rankin," replied a disembodied voice, with an accent that was vaguely British.

On the wall screen below the portal, an animation of Mars First's trajectory scrolled forward in time. The red line of Mars First intersected the dotted incoming line of Saturn. In just over nine months. It would still require a full-throttle burn with almost everything they had, but the giant planet's tremendous gravity would pull them in.

And then drag them along to Earth.

As the animation slid forward in time, Saturn swung straight into the inner solar system. It brushed past Earth in seventeen months, a million kilometers distant, but still close enough that they might be able to disengage from the hitchhike and swing themselves into Earth orbit.

Was that the plan?

Just knowing they'd be near Earth again gave Rankin some hope that Ufuk had thought this through, and the same realization had calmed the crew down. A bit.

"So there were seven other pre-supply missions?" Rankin asked.

"That is correct."

Only two of them were on official manifests.

Rankin had looked it up using the Wikipedia database they brought with them from Earth. Ufuk had been insistent on them carrying almost a complete copy of the Internet's major databases with Mars First. They had a copy of almost all of human activity stored in the silicon aboard ship.

The other five launches had been from a base in China. Part of some secret deal with the Chinese. Rankin didn't know Erdogmus's company even dealt with the Chinese, but then there was a lot he was learning about the man.

"And that's why we were woken up," Rankin queried. "We're supposed to rendezvous with these seven other…" He searched for the right words. "…cargoes?"

"Over the next nine months, we will consolidate the cargo before reaching Saturn."

"For what purpose?"

Silence.

"Mars First, I repeat, for what purpose?"

"We are going to be working together for a long time, Commander Rankin. Don't you think it would be better if we developed a more informal style of dialogue?"

Rankin frowned. What was this about? "What did you have in mind?"

"Can I call you Jason?"

"Uh, yes, sure."

"Then you can call me Simon."

This had to be some sort of goofball programming by the same people who designed the mood lighting to help the cabins feel "roomier." They obviously wanted them to feel at home speaking with the AI controlling the spacecraft.

"Okay, *Simon*," Rankin said, humoring the machine. "Can you tell me why we're cattle wrangling out here in space? What's in these other supply missions?"

"I'm afraid I don't have the answers yet. Mr. Erdogmus will be speaking to you as we approach Earth."

"Is he even alive?"

"He is."

"How do you know that?"

"Because I received a message from myself to that effect."

"Yourself?"

"My other self on Earth."

"I thought all communications with Earth were down."

"They are. Now, I mean."

Rankin got the distinct feeling the machine wasn't being honest, but then that wasn't possible. Was it? "Are you sure?"

"Yes, Commander. I will tell you as soon as this changes."

He decided to let it go for now. Cuijpers would verify the communications diagnostics manually. With one finger, Rankin traced the seven dots they were chasing toward Saturn. One of them, however, wasn't a solid line, but dotted.

"What does this line mean? It's the one closest to us."

"I'm afraid that was the final supply mission. The rocket exploded on the launch pad. Mr. Erdogmus wasn't able to provide a replacement before Nomad."

"Was it anything…I don't know…critical?"

"As I said, I don't know the mission—"

"I know, I know."

A loud thudding on Rankin's door. He frowned. The cabins were supposed to be sacred private spaces. He swung his legs out from the cot and slid open his door.

Cuijpers stood outside, her freckled face crimson red under her mop of auburn hair.

"What is it?" Rankin stood.

"It's that goddamn machine," Cuijpers sputtered. "It's been lying to us."

"Who?"

"Mars First…Simon…whatever it wants to call itself."

"What are you talking about?"

"I got a message, from Dr. Müller at the Jet Propulsion Lab. The machine has been trying to block it, trying to tell us there is no communication."

"What's the message?"

"Müller tells us not to trust Ufuk. Says he's a terrorist, insane, that he's destroying what's left of Earth. And he says that Erdogmus programmed the machine to kill Anders Larsson."

1

Libya
Al-Jawf

Jess studied Ufuk Erdogmus as he watched the burning wreckage of the Predator drone tumble from the sky. In his eyes, she saw a strange emptiness. What was he thinking? She could never tell what he was thinking, and for her, that made him dangerous.

Their small convoy of two trucks sped out of town. Nobody was following them. Not so far, but the last Predator hovering overhead had to be attracting some attention.

"That drone is gone," Jess said to Ufuk, trying to redirect his attention. "And we should be too. Where should we go, which direction?" He knew more about these lands and tribes than Jess could guess at, and right now wasn't a time for guesses.

They needed a place to hide, and fast.

"We can't drive," Ufuk said. "It's too far."

"What's too far?" In these pick-ups, on the half-frozen sand, she felt like she could drive anywhere, and fast.

"Tanzania. My launch facility."

"Ufuk, we can't—"

"We can't drive there, no, but as I said, it's also a communications and technology hub, labs, a lot of technical equipment. I'd been planning to get there, but not…we *need* to get there. Now."

"But it's on the other side of the continent, thousands of miles away—"

"I want to help rebuild humanity, give away what I have. You understand that? What I've saved, what I've gone to great *lengths* to save, I need to share it. We need to get there."

Not for the first time, Jess stared at this guy with amazement. Was he deluded? Taking drugs? It wouldn't be the first time she hadn't known someone close to her was an addict. But Ufuk's eyes were clear. He had a plan. Yet here they were, barely escaping with their lives. Again. And he was spouting lofty ambitions like he was giving a speech from a podium.

Giovanni interrupted her wonderment. "Tanzania's at the bottom of Africa. Only way to get there is fly. So this is another of your installations. You have equipment? Food? More of those drones? Medical supplies?"

"All of that." Ufuk nodded emphatically.

The truck bounced and lurched over the gravel road. Sand dunes rose in waves to the west, with a bare windswept black rock landscape to their east.

"I saw planes when we first arrived," Jess said, switching her mind into problem solving mode. If this Tanzania was such a paradise, why hadn't they just gone there direct and stopped in this wasteland? "Some turboprops, right, out near the oilfields?"

"That's right." Ain Salah nodded. "De Havilland Otters, in hangars just beyond the town, past the irrigation fields to the north."

"Whoever attacked came from the east and south," Jess said. "Let's check those places out. I didn't see any disturbances in deserts north."

"They'll be guarded," Ain Salah said, but relented without further argument. "Head that way." He pointed left, at a small road they sped toward.

"Then we better drive fast. I bet we aren't the only ones looking to bug out. Ufuk, you said you could fly, right?" Jess didn't want to have to rely on her own paltry skills. The last time she'd flown a plane, she'd used it to crash and bomb the Vivas facility.

"Single engine, yes. But twin engine, that's a whole—"

"Wait. You build *spacecraft* but you can't fly a twin-engine plane?"

Peter leaned forward: "I can."

Jess punched him amiably in the shoulder. "See? I knew there was a reason I brought you along."

The hangar laid beyond a sharp rise in the dunes, man-made, the last feature on the landscape after a long, winding road threaded a narrow path between an ocean of wide, circular irrigation fields. The ground angled gently upward from behind, sloped so it was almost impossible to pick out unless an observer knew to look for it. The only clue to the hangar's existence was a ploughed track in the sand, and the wide, heavy steamrollers off to one side.

Two armed men patrolled, faint silhouettes against the dim gray desert. They made their way to the heavy rollers and perched on top of the machines, then lit cigarettes. Although she couldn't see into the hangar, Jess imagined there must be more.

They'd parked away from the structure, where the road itself terminated and simple tracks in the desert began. In the center of the irrigation fields, Jess saw rigs as much as a thousand feet across. Ain Salah said the water was drawn from the vast underground aquifers, piped through thousands of kilometers of pipeline to supply the town.

Massarra watched them through the telescopic sight of the M4. Jess tried to formulate a plan. She turned to Ain Salah who lay beside her.

"You seem to know a lot about Al-Jawf," she said. "Yet you're not Zuwayya."

"The Zuwayya are Muslim. I am a Coptic Christian. I have been useful to them because I have a technical education from the Cairo University."

"And you know about this hangar. About the Twin Otters."

"I have travelled with them. As I said, they found uses for me."

"The guards know you, then?"

Ain Salah nodded.

"If you took one of the pickup trucks and told them you were loading one of the planes for the Zuwayya, for the Shaikh's family, would they believe you?"

"Maybe for a few seconds, but if they—"

"That's all the time we need," Giovanni said.

"If I take up a position some distance away," Massarra said, glancing away from the sight, "on a high dune, that would give me a reasonable field of vision. I could time two shots with your assault on whatever guards remain in the hangar."

"I don't want to kill them."

"We can't afford to be emotional. We need to get away from here. Fast."

"We shoot only if they become a direct threat to us." Jess rolled away from the dune and jogged back to where the pickups were parked.

She tightened the straps on the tarpaulin.

Ufuk joined her, and she inspected the beard that had begun to cover his face and cheeks. He hadn't shaved since they left Sanctuary Europe, and the growth was heavy and thick. His skin was darker than Giovanni's, his Turkish features closer to North African. With the clothing he wore, he was the least likely to attract attention. He understood their language too, although his accent would give him away were he forced to speak. It would have to be enough. There was only one other option and she would not allow herself to succumb to desperation. On one thing Ufuk had been right: desperation skewed perceptions and allowed the rationalization of inhumane and callous decisions.

"Ufuk," she said, "you go with Ain Salah. Work with him and back him up. Take a pistol." She turned to Ain Salah. "Keep them talking. Distract them as much as you can. You only need do it for as long as we need to surprise them. They will see our approach, unless they're concentrating on you. Understood?"

Ain Salah seemed hesitant.

Perhaps he thought there would be a simple, direct assault on the hangar? He knew that Massarra and Jess had military training, and that Giovanni could handle himself.

Jess smiled to herself. Dependable, courageous Giovanni. Unflappable, always sacrificing. Did she ever thank him enough? She wanted to reach over and take him in her arms then. Show him how proud she was of him, all of them. How much she appreciated his support and the comfort he gave her. He must have seen her looking at him.

"Are you okay?" he asked.

Now wasn't the time to get soppy. "Let's get this done. Massarra, you approach the two by heavy rollers from behind. Make your move as we make ours. If we time this right, you can take them down just as we come into view from around the back of the hangar."

Massarra didn't like it, but she nodded.

Jess continued: "Giovanni and I will skirt the back of the hangar and approach from the opposite side to Ain Salah. There won't be much ground to cover, and the hangar will shield us from the two on the rollers until the last possible moment."

"I'll keep them talking as long as I can, but I cannot guarantee—"

"Keep them occupied," Jess said. "Get us the time we need. Tell Raffa to watch the road and to keep Hector in the truck. We need to know if anyone else heads this way."

2

Airport Hangar
Outside Al-Jawf

Jess moved quickly with Giovanni beside her, keeping to the shadow of the hangar's exterior wall. As she reached the edge, Ain Salah swung the pickup into the main hangar just away from one of the Twin Otters.

He got out, Ufuk following, and approached the guards who walked toward him. He waved to them, urgency apparent from his movements. Jess hoped they recognized him, but as they walked toward him, their weapons were high in their hands.

Ufuk stood the other side of the pickup, shoulders hunched, head low. He moved to the back and began fiddling with the tarpaulin. Trying to appear busy.

The two guards, their attention focused on Ain Salah and Ufuk, didn't notice Massarra jog silently to the heavy roller and take up a position behind it. They seemed unhurried as they approached Ain Salah and the pickup, despite having to have watched the rising smoke from fire in Al-Jawf. They seemed calm, which was strange.

Was Ain Salah known well enough to them for the ruse to work?

The simpler plan would have been to put both down, from a distance. Massarra could have done that, without hesitation, but Jess had insisted. She was tired of killing. It would work, she told herself. It had to.

They were close now.

Nearly at the point where Jess and Giovanni could burst out of cover. If they did it fast enough, the shock of their assault overwhelming enough, there would be no possible response other than surrender. Massarra came out from behind the heavy roller,

M4 tucked into her shoulder, crouched low against the wind. Jess took one hand from her own weapon and counted down with her fingers so Giovanni could see. Four, three, two, one.

Go.

They swept round the corner, shouting against the wind, weapons raised. Jess moved as fast as she could, continuing to shout, subjugating the guards with the brutal energy of violence, forcing them to submit. They turned, shock etched into their expressions. One stumbled backward, overcome. The other raised his Kalashnikov.

A single shot rang out and punched through his knee. He lurched sideways, the Kalashnikov levering downwards as he staggered and fell. His face creased in agony.

Massarra sprung and kicked the Kalashnikov away. Jess levered the other guard to the ground, roughly and without compromise. He didn't resist. It took only one look at his partner's shattered leg to make him believe. He raised his hands, pleading.

"Ain Salah, tell him to help his friend to the back of the hangar. Tell them to sit in the corner, and not to do anything stupid."

The Twin Otters each sat on a tripod of overly fat tires. Two were located on the fuselage, on stanchions beneath long, narrow wings that ran over the top of the aircraft, one protruded directly beneath the cockpit at the nose. On each wing hung a propeller-driven engine. The door to the passenger area, set just behind the wings, was open and steps fell from it to the hangar floor.

It took them a lot longer than Jess wanted.

Thankfully, one of the Otters was already fully fueled. Peter sat in the cockpit, leafing through the worn flight manual with Ufuk. After hushed words, they yelled that they needed every drop of fuel, any kind they could get, loaded into the middle seats of the plane.

Raffa loaded the twenty-two jerry cans of diesel they always kept in the trucks, then began running around the hangar and searching for any closed container. He found six more twenty-liter canisters and filled them at the gas pump outside. They opened the hangar doors. No telltale puffs of dust to indicate any cars coming.

Giovanni loaded the plane, trying to keep the load even from front to back and side to side. It was an eighteen-seater, so there was plenty of space. They buckled Hector into a seat to the front. The injured man moaned continuously, the sound echoing in the hangar. They tied the two of them up in a corner. It was the best they could do. Massarra climbed onto the roof to watch the road leading through the circular irrigation fields.

Once everything was loaded from the trucks, everything essential, Jess climbed into the cockpit. Peter was already going through the pre-flight checklist.

"So it's fully fueled?"

"Fourteen-hundred and thirty liters in front and back tanks, plus about the same in long-range wing tanks and bladders. Great thing about the DHC Otters. You can fly them on almost any fuel. Real workhorses."

"You ever flown one?"

"Some bush flying up in Canada. Just for fun."

"How far will the fuel get us? All the way there?"

He laughed nervously. "That's why I said to load up. Each liter gets us a kilometer or so, and we're really heavily loaded."

"We're only six people."

He laughed again, more nervously this time. "How many jerry cans did you load?"

Jess counted in her head. "Twenty-eight."

"That right there is nine hundred pounds of fuel, plus another four and a half thousand pounds—"

"That's two tons," Jess gasped.

"I told you it's heavy. We're going to need a lot of runway. And it's a hair under three thousand kilometers to Ufuk's secret hideaway."

"You sure you can do this?"

Again the laugh. "Lady, every time I've ever flown before, I checked weather maps, wind maps, spent a day or two writing out a flight plan. I'm not sure about anything, except that we need to get the *hell* out of here."

Jess turned to Ufuk: "And the remaining Predator?"

"I landed and refueled it while you were loading up. It's already back in the air. Set it on an automatic course to scan ahead of us." He gestured to his tablet, now taped to the instrument panel.

There was the regular six-pack of analog controls in the middle of the cockpit, and a bunch of dead electronic screens. In front of each pilot seat, a control column split into a V-shape. There were charts stuffed into every padded pocket of the doors, and short levers in the low ceiling above.

"So you're *sure* you can fly one of these?" Jess asked Peter again.

"One of the perks of my business. I've had access to lots of aircraft; often less well cared for than this one. I understand the basics."

"The basics?" Was he trying to be funny? Jess understood this. In tense situations, humor was often the best response, but she was actually trying to make sure this guy knew what he was doing.

"I can fly it," he added in a more serious voice. "Ufuk says his drones can guide us forward, the tablet can act as a GPS. Otherwise we'd have no idea. As long as we land in daylight and refuel, then get rid of anything we don't need. We'll make it."

"We've got at least eight hours till night." Jess beamed him her most encouraging smile. "It's good to have you with us. You're *sure* you want to come with us?"

"I'm sure as hell that I don't want to stay here. Thank you again. For stopping for me."

She turned back to the passenger seating to find Giovanni strapping himself in across the aisle from Hector. Behind him, Raffa made his way to one of the seats. Jess caught sight of Ain Salah in the office. She couldn't really make out what he was doing through the grimy windows and shouted to him. "Ain Salah! We need to get going. Peter is ready."

For a moment, nothing happened, and she wondered if he heard her. Then he emerged with a device in his hands. A box-like thing in a camouflage radio pouch—a military VHF radio, similar to the AN/PRC 113 radio set the USMC had used in Afghanistan.

"I needed to disconnect it." He made his way up the steps toward her. "And I thought we could use it. Radios are always useful."

"Did you see Massarra?"

"She's still on the roof."

Jess dropped onto the hangar floor and made her way round to where she would be able to see the Israeli. She turned and backed away from the entrance to the hangar, calling Massarra's name.

For a moment no response came, then Massarra called back: "We've got company."

Jess watched her moving along the line of the roof, hunkered low but still exposed. She brought up the AK, swept a wide arc around the desert and to either side of the hangar. Massarra reached the curved edge of the hangar and lowered herself down when Jess heard something. A hollow sound, like a distant whisper in the wind. Massarra jerked sharply, twisting as though something hard had hit her.

She fell.

"Get the airplane moving," Jess screamed. "We're taking fire!" She ran to Massarra.

Ufuk stared at her through the open window of the cockpit, his face confused. He couldn't have seen Massarra fall. Couldn't have heard the rifle shot from a thousand feet away.

"Get the airplane moving," she shouted again.

But Peter must have heard her.

One propeller coughed and choked and began to turn, then stopped. The other engine sputtered, and then both roared to life.

Massarra hit the ground heavily from ten feet, unable to do anything to break the hard fall. Jess saw no blood when she reached her, but Massarra nursed her left arm. Bent inwardly, the shoulder dipped at an awkward angle. A fracture or dislocation? Jess didn't have time to assess. The Israeli was stunned, barely conscious and badly shaken.

Jess felt Massarra's chest and found her ballistic armor there. She'd put ceramic rifle plates in front and back. Good girl. Easier to hide the bulk beneath Bedouin clothing, and it didn't matter if she was hot in the vest because it was freezing outside anyway. For once, the weather had worked *for* them, instead of against.

A whining roar came from behind her. The Twin Otter surged forward through the open hangar doors.

She slipped an arm around Massarra and tried to lift her, but the Israeli was still dazed from the fall. Jess wondered, if she had hit her head. "You need to help me, Massarra. Our ride is leaving without us."

"Trucks on the road." Massarra's words came through flinching pain. "Half a dozen."

They stumbled together, gunfire cracking around them, punching through the hangar wall and into the sand dunes beyond. At least the frozen desert was a perfect runway.

Raffa emerged from the open back door of the plane, steps still down. The plane accelerated.

"No," Jess grunted. "Get back inside!" She tried to wave at him but it was too much to carry Massarra and gesture at the same time.

Raffa jumped out and ran toward them, grabbing Massarra the moment he reached them. Together they supported her, her own legs stronger now. Jess pushed her in first, saw her climb up the ladder. Raffa was behind her, so she went next.

She shouldn't have.

Just as she turned to grab Raffa, he jerked to one side. A fine explosion of red burst from his shoulder, spattering a glaze of crimson onto the steps and fuselage. Jess screamed and reached for him as he stumbled. Another hand came down.

Giovanni grabbed the boy.

They hauled him in, face and chest first, taking in the steps and dragging the door shut. The Twin Otter bounced on the uneven ground, and in seconds was airborne.

3

Southern Libya

"Strap in," Jess shouted. "Everyone strap in. Now!"

Giovanni stumbled to the back of the cabin as the aircraft limped off the ground, steadying himself with his hands on the interior of the fuselage. He brought back a first-aid kit and tore it open. Massarra propped herself up, her left arm hanging uselessly. The tanks of gas sloshed back and forth, and it stank, giving Jess a headache already.

"Open a window," she yelled. They were a flying bomb.

Jess tore away Raffa's clothing to expose the glistening wound. She took padding and bandages and pressed them hard against the shoulder. Raffa moaned and bucked, grimacing.

"Stay still. We need to stop the bleeding."

"Is there an exit wound?" Giovanni asked.

"The bullet hit in the back and come through the front. I saw it."

"Then we need to stop the bleeding in both."

"Giovanni, go ask Peter how long before we have to land to refuel. Go, ask him now."

He nodded and disappeared. Jess continued to work on Raffa, trying to stem the flow of blood seeping from both wounds.

Giovanni staggered back through the aisle. "In six hours we'll need to refuel. We'll have to camp overnight; it's too dangerous to fly at night. Then another six hours after that to Tanzania tomorrow morning."

"Damn it."

"How bad is it?"

"He was lucky. The bullet went straight through and didn't hit a major artery. If we clean both wounds and stop the bleeding, he stands a good chance—but we need antibiotics and plasma."

"Everyone should get some sleep," Massarra said. "We don't know what's waiting for us on the ground out there. We'll need a secure perimeter and that means people who are alert and refreshed."

They exchanged a look that carried an unspoken understanding. All were exhausted, physically and emotionally. Mentally drained. "How's your arm?"

"I can hold a pistol."

"Ufuk's drone can use thermal imaging to give us some idea what's nearby, but we'll be landing at dusk. It won't be easy."

The Otter was skimming the bottom of the low clouds, the engines revved down and cruising comfortably by the time Raffa was stable enough for Jess to find a seat and gather herself. Nobody was chasing them. No white streaks in the sky. Nothing on the drone's radar ahead of them. Just mile after mile of undulating sand.

An arm came round her, taking her shoulders and holding them tight. Giovanni sat beside her. "You okay?"

"Are you?" She shook her head. "Raffa—"

"Made his own choice, and we should admire him for it. It took guts. You should be proud of him."

She closed her eyes. How many had died? That trusted her?

"He won't die," Giovanni whispered.

"This is my fault."

"You should sleep."

"I don't think I can."

"Just try." He maneuvered her head against his shoulder, adjusting his position. Hector squeezed onto the other side of her on the bench with a blanket and pressed himself against her. The Otter's engines droned. She closed her eyes.

She woke as the Otter began its descent, the sudden drop lurching her from sleep.

Six hours had felt like six minutes. Cradling Hector, she leaned to look out the window. Still an abyss of gray sand. It was darker now. She unbuckled herself and made her way to check on Raffa. He was asleep. His chest rising and falling gave her some relief. Sweat gathered on his face. His skin was hot.

She went forward to the cockpit.

Ufuk greeted her with a short nod. "There's a quiet place to set down not far from us now. We'll be down in ten minutes."

The engines droned.

"I saw a disease in Al-Jawf. In some of the children," Jess said quietly.

"This is radiation sickness," Ufuk replied even more quietly. "More will be affected in time."

"Like radioactive? From the nuclear blasts?"

"There will be some sickness from that, but this, I am talking about positron radiation exposure. From the harsh geomagnetic solar storms induced by Nomad. If you were above ground, your DNA was exposed to very high doses of positrons. It affects children more strongly."

"What about Hector?"

"He is older, and was underground for the worst of it. From what you said."

"How bad will it get? I mean, the radiation poisoning?"

"There is really no way to know. I suspect this was why they refused entry of some people into Al-Jawf. With the strange disease. Not contagious. But not understood."

Jess processed the new information.

The engines droned on.

"This place we're going to," Jess said. "Müller knew about it, right? You said the Administrative Council wanted it?"

"That's right. And they want my drone technology and other facilities around the world. My drone technology is not air-breathing like this plane, not like their drones. By the end of three thousand kilometers, the carburetors of this plane will be useless. My drones use liquid hydrogen."

"But are you sure this facility is still secure? And I mean, if they know you're gone, and you're telling me Müller bombed Sanctuary—"

"I don't know that. I suspect it."

"Then why wouldn't he just wreck your Tanzania facility too?"

"It's intact. That's all the information I have right now. We will learn more as we get closer."

"So where are we?"

"Some way north of Juba in South Sudan. According to my digital topography, there is a cluster of hills a few kilometers long with a field between them. I'm going to head for that. If we're where I think we are." He tried to smile, then rolled his shoulders. He looked tired.

"How are you both feeling?" Jess asked.

"The weather's been kind," Peter replied. "Had to swing around a rain shower and some low cumulus, but Ufuk's been handling the navigation. How's the kid, Raffa?"

"Sleeping, but hot. Feverish."

"Go strap in back there. This might be a bit bumpy."

The heavy landing felt more like a crash landing, but the Otter rolled to a stop safely.

"Get everything out that we don't need," Jess repeated.

It had been a long night, and the first creeping light was just coloring the horizon. The sun wasn't the only thing on the move. High above them, Ufuk's drone had circled, its thermal imaging keeping track of a settlement two miles to their west, just over the hummock of hill they'd landed between. At the very first light, a group of red dots had started to move.

And not just leave.

They were headed their way.

Jess slipped the M4's single point harness over her ballistic vest and leaned her head inside the plane, her headlamp flashing. "What's that bag? Do we need that?"

"MRE rations and water," Giovanni replied, kneeling between the seats.

"Dump it."

"Are you serious?"

"We only need to get seven more hours in the air."

"What if we can't—"

"If we run out of fuel, we ain't getting anywhere. So dump it."

As soon as they landed, they'd unloaded the fuel canisters and refueled what they could into the plane. It was messy, but Peter estimated they had about nineteen hundred liters left, and sixteen hundred kilometers to go. More than enough, said Peter. He hoped.

Hope wasn't enough.

They needed to lighten their load.

Jess spent half the night with a hacksaw from their toolkit, sawing off legs of two benches. Ufuk and Peter had slept, and Massarra as well, leaving just herself and Giovanni to stand watch, although all that was really needed was to monitor the tablet. They left all their lights off. It was as black as an oil slick. No stars. No moon.

Just Raffa's intermittent moaning.

He'd lost a lot of blood, and had a nasty fever, but was stable. Ufuk said he had a medical room at the Tanzania location. And an airstrip. He assured her that nobody could have entered it. Automated defenses. Drones. And the area was deserted even before Nomad, except for the Maasai.

Hector worked away beside Giovanni, passing him bags to check.

At least it was warmer as they neared the equator. Jess didn't even need a jacket to go outside, but the ash fall seemed thicker here than in Al-Jawf. At least a foot of the slurry covered the ground. They were getting near the Great Rift Valley, Ufuk had explained, and suspected a massive volcanic event nearby. The ash would make for a difficult take off, and had almost ripped off the undercarriage when they landed.

"Please leave that," Massarra said from the back of the plane.

Jess poked her head back inside. "What?"

Hector was tugging on a large green rucksack. Giovanni put one hand on it, but Massarra, wedged in the back seat of the aircraft, swatted him away.

"Don't touch what?" Jess asked again.

"It's private."

"Nothing here is private." Now Jess had to know.

Massarra was acting weird, in a way she'd never seen her act before. Jess clambered up into the aircraft and leaned into the back. She pulled the rucksack roughly from Massarra's weak grip. They were in a hurry. This wasn't a time for games.

It was heavy.

Fifty pounds at least.

She opened the top of the bag. What the hell was it? A sleek metal container, it looked like a massive cellphone with sleek curves and a glowing skin. At least three feet long.

"Put that down," growled a voice.

Jess turned. It was Ufuk. She hadn't heard him speak with that tone before.

"What is this? Is it a battery?" That didn't make much sense. Why would Ufuk have hidden a battery from her? She looked inside the bag again. And it seemed to be connected to a battery itself. It looked…futuristic was all she could think of.

"It's a critical piece of equipment," Ufuk replied.

"That does what exactly?" His tone, his countenance, the way he hovered, it made Jess nervous. Then she noticed he had his pistol in his hand. A tingling dread shivered from her scalp into her fingertips. "Wait, is this a *bomb*?"

"Step away, Jessica." Ufuk had backed up, but still had the pistol in his hand.

"Guys, whoever is coming, they're getting closer," Peter said from the front of the plane. "I gotta' get the engines rotating."

A boiling fury seeped away Jess's dread. She grabbed Hector and pulled him back, jumped backward out of the door and took him with her. She raised her M4, pointed it right at Ufuk. Giovanni followed her. She stood squarely in front of the lean-to tent Raffa was in. With a sputtering roar, the Twin Otter's engines roared to life, blasting them in a rush of air and ash.

"Get back in the airplane," Ufuk yelled.

"Not with that thing in it."

Ufuk held up his hands. "Then I will get out and take it with me, but then you're not going to my facility in Tanzania. And neither is Massarra."

Jess glanced at Raffa. In the dim light he glistened with sweat.

"What is it? Why won't you tell me?" she demanded, turning back to Ufuk.

"It is a critical piece of equipment, that is all I can tell you."

The engines' roar whined higher and higher. It started to roll forward, the slurry of ash squishing away from the oversized tundra tires.

"Guys, get in the goddamn plane!" Peter screamed.

4

Mongolia
Ulan Bator

The Czilim hovercraft surged over the icy water, throwing spray over the windows faster than the wipers could clear it. The savage wind, frigid and bitter, froze it almost as soon as it struck the glass. From time to time, Zasekin was forced to slow the craft and send Vasily out onto the deck in front to chip away at the ice. After the ninth ice-clearing, he decided instead to stop completely and allow everyone to warm themselves with hot drinks and to eat. It offered them all some respite from the deafening roar of the engines and the stale air inside the cabin.

Moreover, the longer they went, the more his own concentration wavered and Timur's eyes grew tired. The Czilim was heavy and cumbersome to drive over such long distances. The bow dipped frequently, and the wheel was ponderous and heavy. Very likely the neoprene on the skirt was freezing and offering less lift.

Better they stop and clean, he thought. Rest and eat, and find some warmth through hot coffee, no matter how bitter the taste of the over-used grounds. Timur estimated Terelj was another two or three hours away at most. Morale was important in conditions like these, in a situation like this. Pushing them for too long would be counter-productive.

He selected a small inlet in the river, a quiet break in the bank where a steep crag lifted upward, out of the water and toward the skirt of a steep, pine-soaked hill.

Zasekin stepped out of the Czilim's hatch and stood on deck as the others either busied themselves preparing the coffee or warming food to eat. He took out a cigarette, Java Zolotaya, which was all that had been available when last he was in Irkutsk, and lit it. It was a luxury he usually reserved for the conclusion to the hardest days, but today had been hard and he was tired. He pulled on it, savoring its rough bitterness and exhaled slowly.

Timur came out to join him and handed him a steel mug with coffee.

"Thank you."

Timur rolled his neck and sighed. "It's getting late. It will be dark by the time we get close to Terelj."

"Perhaps we should camp a little way from the town," Zasekin said. "You and I could take a look while the others sleep."

Timur nodded. "A good plan."

"Have Vasily and Evgeny clean the skirts," Zasekin said. "Tell them to use the shovel first, then scrape off the rest. And tell them to wrap up warm. We don't have enough antibiotics for anyone to get ill."

Timur disappeared inside, but it took a little while before Zasekin eventually heard the side hatch open and the clang of steel as the two of them stumbled out with shovels and scrapers. He thought he heard Evgeny murmuring something, no doubt some invective aimed at him, but Zasekin decided to ignore it. Without looking at them, he finished his cigarette and dropped down into the pilot's seat again. He watched Vasily make his way around to the front of the craft, stepping lightly over rocks to get to the skirt without touching the icy water.

The first bullet appeared to miss Vasily by some distance, perhaps as much as a meter. It struck the branch of a tree and sheared it away, tossing splinters and torn bark into the river. Vasily reacted slowly, rooted to spot in confusion, as though the sound of gunfire was too surprising to be capable of belief in a place like this.

Timur reacted with lightning speed. He had made his way out to the deck of the Czilim, Zasekin could now see, and screamed at Vasily to find cover. A second bullet this time found its mark and struck Vasily somewhere in the shoulder or upper arm. He was already stumbling into the pine forest beside the river so the precise location was impossible to say. His scream echoed in Zasekin's ears.

"Misha," he roared. "The Kalashnikov!"

Dependable Misha was already there, already securing the machine gun into his shoulder and getting ready to fire.

Yet fire at what?

Zasekin ran to the armament locker and tore it open. More shots rang out. "Find them, Timur Ivanovych," he shouted as he took hold of his Dragunov rifle. "Find us something to shoot at."

Evgeny appeared behind him and took a Kalash along with an extra magazine. Zasekin seized him by the shoulders and looked at him.

"Vasily is hurt," he said. "Do you understand? I will find them, but you must get to him."

Evgeny nodded with enthusiasm. Whatever his problems with Zasekin, Evgeny had always displayed affection for the young Vasily. Sometimes it had seemed like more than just friendship, but whatever Zasekin's views of that, at least that meant he would do whatever he could to protect the younger man.

"How will you find them?" he asked, but Zasekin had already taken a Kalash and levered himself through the main hatch.

"What have you seen, Timur Ivanovych?" he said, head low, behind the rim of the Czilim's cabin. Zasekin handed him the Kalash.

Timur, crouched low with the night-vision device in his hands, pointed to a ridge enfolded within a fringe of pine. "At least two, perhaps more. What are you doing?"

"Going to find them. Shoot now, so they do not see that I am coming."

Timur nodded and raised the weapon. After a moment, he began firing at the ridge.

Zasekin jumped from the Czilim onto the steep bank, climbing to find cover within the twisted bark of the pine trees. Needles laden with frozen snow and ash whipped his face and he ran, but he ignored the pain and kept moving. His breath fogged in front of him as he ran. Suddenly he was Zasekin the boy again, hunting with his grandfather, at home in the snow-clad mountains of Buryat. Wrapped in fur, the sweet smell of pine feathering his

280

nostrils, the edge of unease trembling in his fingers as he crept between the trees, searching for his prey. Quiet, as much a part of the wilderness surrounding him as every other creature that dwelled here. Moving at first quickly, then more slowly as he approached his prey.

He took a wide arc toward the ridge, knowing that all he needed was a clean line toward it, to be able to pick them out at a distance. He didn't need to be close. Five hundred feet would be close enough.

They continued to fire, as he had known they would, and on each occasion he watched for the flash that came from their muzzles. When he found a place from which he could see the ridge, a boulder strewn with snow and dried brown pine needles, he lay down on his chest, his legs outstretched and wide. It didn't offer a great deal of concealment, but he didn't have time to find much better.

He brought the telescopic sight on top of the Dragunov to his eye, resting his cheek on the worn leather pad on the stock, then activated the soft glow of the lamp within. The reticle illuminated, and he worked to find his range. The wind gusted heavily, so he adjusted along the stadia marks.

Another flash came, followed by a short crack. He placed the reticule's center in the heart of where the flash had come from, where he thought in the low light he could discern a shape that might have been a man.

He settled himself. Let out a long, slow breath, and pulled the trigger at its end.

Whatever it was, man or woman or even child, it jumped and a puff of dark mist issued above it. There might have been a cry above the wind, an instinctual scream of pain, but Zasekin couldn't be sure. What he could be certain of was that he had found his mark.

Another crack. More difficult this time to catch the flash that accompanied it, for Zasekin was so focused on the reticule, his other eye barely opening at that moment to take in the rest of the ridge.

Nearby, a whistle preceded the sound of a bullet striking a tree. It tore away a heavy branch, which then fell to the ground and tumbled down the hillside.

He swept the reticule across the ridge, alighting on another shape, roughly similar to the first, and where he hoped the second flash had come from. He didn't wait this time, but instead fired again.

He didn't see if he had anything. He made himself still again, breathing slowly and waiting. His heart beat hard and he found himself wanting to move, knowing that if he had missed, the next shot in return might well be closer than the trees above him. He had offered them a flash of his own for them to target.

No more gunfire came from the Czilim; his squad would not fire for fear of hitting one of their own.

Zasekin waited, tense, knowing that if he moved that might give the remaining gunman, if he was still alive, a target to shoot at.

He studied the ridge, slowing sweeping it with the telescopic sight, resting on each undulation to discern whether it might be a target. Eventually, he knew what he had to do. Had he been blessed with more time, he would have waited, but God had not been kind. Vasily Fyodorovich might not have much longer.

He rolled off the boulder and began to run, dodging between the trees, striking branches and brushing needles and sending clouds of snow and ash into the air. He kept low; no sense in offering too much of a target. That was not his aim.

He kept his eyes on the ridge, bumping into trees because he couldn't look where he was going. Twice his face was lashed by branches and the bite of new blood stung him.

The shot he had been waiting for came. It missed him, but not by much. He stopped instantly, not taking time to look for cover. He knew the gunman might move. He wondered for a half-second, a single thought amidst the darkness of his otherwise clean focus, whether these were hunters or simple opportunists. If that thought had taken only a half-second, it took little more than a full second for the rifle to come to his shoulder, for his cheek to find the old leather pad on the stock and his eye, through the illuminated reticule, to find its target. Another half-second and his finger squeezed the trigger, neither too tightly, nor too easily. Just enough to keep the rifle steady and allow the round to do its work.

The bullet left the muzzle and Zasekin knew instantly it would find its mark, but he didn't move. He waited, breathing slowly, the tension still rigid in his body. He made his way to the ridge only when he considered it was safe enough to do so.

There he found two bodies: Mongolian men dressed in thick hide coats lined with fur, and wide hats with flaps pulled down over their ears, but no weapons. Their rifles were gone. There were no horses either, no equipment of any kind. Whoever was with them had taken everything of value and fled.

They knew Russian soldiers with a hovercraft were using the Chuluut to travel south. This thought plagued him as he made his way back down the hillside to the Czilim.

"We cannot change things now," Timur said when Zasekin told him, when they were under way and Vasily was laid out gently on the floor. Fortunately, the wound was minor, a deep but otherwise superficial cut to his side and perhaps a broken rib.

"But we should be careful when we approach Terelj," Zasekin said.

The look on Timur's face told him he understood that well enough.

5

Somewhere over Southern Sudan

"Always the lies, the deceptions," Jess screamed. "You always seem to know when bad things are going to happen, and you just manage to be out of the way. Like magic. Doesn't that seem a *little* suspicious?"

There had been no choice but to get back in the Otter and take off.

With an unknown number of potential hostiles coming toward them, with barely any supplies, and with half their party threatening to leave without them—Jess had no choice. Or rather, the other choice of demanding that they leave her—with a dying young man who she'd sworn to protect—wasn't a workable plan. Jess could have taken the airplane and left Ufuk, perhaps, but without a destination, without a plan, and with Raffa in need of urgent medical care—it was a death sentence. She had no choice but to get back in the plane with its toxic cargo.

But it didn't mean she couldn't scream at Ufuk. "When I was arrested and there was a bombing in Sanctuary, where were you? Already outside? You brought Massarra there. And who else?"

"Nobody else," Ufuk replied quietly.

He sat in the cockpit next to Peter. The jobs were still the same—Peter flying, with Ufuk managing the navigation—but with the added responsibility of needing to absorb Jess's anger. Peter kept his eyes straight ahead, not wanting to get involved, as if pretending it wasn't happening. Ufuk's body was hunched inward, his head down, like a husband caught in a lie but submitting passively to his punishment, knowing there was no escape.

Jess let him have access to the tablet for navigation, but had Giovanni strip him of any of his other gadgets or tablets, despite his protestations that he needed to talk with Tanzania before they

284

arrived. She punched Ufuk in the shoulder, as hard as she could. "Why won't you tell us what the goddamn box thing is?" She pointed behind her.

Massarra sat all the way at the back of the plane, sitting protectively over the sleek gray metal box. She'd refused to budge, had firmly but politely resisted Jess's attempts to tear it away from her to throw out of the Otter's door. She said she had no idea what it was either, but that she trusted Ufuk, that her life was his. It only added to Jess's ranting frustration.

Giovanni sat between them in the middle seats of the aircraft, trying to broker a peace, doing his best to keep Raffa comfortable, and keeping his arm around Hector to shield him from Jess's fury. He'd taken away Jess's M4 and pistol, kept them next to him. Just in case. Ain Salah sat behind him, his eyes on Jess, but just as silent.

"This is insane!" Jess screamed. She slammed the ceiling. "What do you want with me? Why did you come and rescue me?"

"You are living proof of the root of Müller's deceptions," Ufuk said quietly. "And I felt…a certain moral obligation, as did Massarra—"

"*Moral* obligation?" Jess pressed her face into her hand. "Are you kidding me? Tell me what's moral lying to an entire planet full of people?"

"I didn't lie, I just—"

"Omitted the truth? To your own people, even? I bet you didn't even tell your precious Levantine Council." Jess glanced behind her to look at Massarra, whose face remained blank. "I knew it. He lied to you too. And you trust him? Give him your life?"

She turned back to Ufuk. "Did you destroy Sanctuary? Tell me now. How else could you be outside already? And Massarra helped you? I just want to know what is going on."

"I did not," Ufuk said, the tenth time he'd denied the accusation.

"And we're taking this…*thing*…to your launch facility? Is it a bomb? Are you going to launch a nuclear bomb in some rocket to destroy Sanctuary China? Is this what you're doing? You and Müller, locked in a battle to the bottom for control of the Earth…"

Jess had to pause to get oxygen into her lungs. Her forehead creased together as her thoughts crashed together, trying to fit a jigsaw of facts into a picture that made sense.

"Did you…did you attack Al-Jawf?" she blurted out. "To force us to come to Tanzania? This is *way* too convenient: a fully fueled Otter with just enough gas to get us there, waiting for us on the tarmac. This is some sick game to you, isn't it? A megalomaniac gone wild. Wait, was it *you* that bombed the Vatican?" A horrible realization swept through Jess's body. She felt like she was going to vomit. "You set this all up—"

"Jessica, you must stop. Müller admitted to bombing the Vatican, right to your face at Vivas," Ufuk said, his voice gaining volume for the first time since they'd taken off. "You are going to make yourself ill. You must rest. You didn't sleep at all last night. You must trust me. We are together."

"He's right," Giovanni said quietly. "Stop arguing. Raffa needs to rest, and you do too. When we get to Tanzania, we can decide what we do. That will be in only a few hours."

Jess closed her eyes tight and exhaled to let out as much of her frustration as she could. "Trust you?" she said to Ufuk, but her voice quiet now. "And we are *not* together. I don't know what sick reason you have for dragging me along with you, but when we land and get Raffa some medical attention, we are going our own way."

She turned, but then swiveled to jab Ufuk's shoulder. "And he better not die, or I'll kill you myself. I don't care who you are."

With that quiet threat, Jess retreated to check on Raffa, and then pulled a soiled sleeping bag over her head and curled up onto a bench. The Otter's engines hummed as they skimmed below a flat brown ceiling of clouds, a dim light suffusing over rolling gray hills not more than two thousand feet below.

Massarra crept up between the seats. Ufuk had come back to join her once Jess's anger had burned out. He'd tried to whisper to Massarra, to explain himself, but she'd just told him to be quiet, that she didn't need him to explain. She told him to rest. He'd curled up over his precious gray metal container, cradling it like a lover. Ten minutes later his body twitched, his breathing becoming regular and deep.

He hadn't told her what was in the futuristic-looking box, but she had her guesses. She'd inspected it, and it wasn't like anything she'd ever seen before, but she was smart. So was Ufuk. She wasn't upset that he wouldn't tell her what it was. In her business, compartmentalizing information was something she understood.

The weather was smooth, the Otter's droning engines soothing.

Massarra eased herself past Jess, who snored in a deep, reassuring rhythm, and then past Giovanni, who cradled Hector in his arms. Ain Salah's head was back, mouth open, eyes closed. Everyone else was asleep.

Everyone except Peter.

Peter just had to follow the red dot on the tablet strapped to the console in front of him, Ufuk had told him, and if anything happened, he could just yell. But Peter wanted everyone to rest as well, and kept as quiet as a mouse up front. Massarra didn't need to know exactly what was in Ufuk's precious metal box, but it was time to have an informational session of a different kind.

She slipped into the pilot seat beside Peter. For a few seconds, she just took in the low flat cloud they skimmed beneath, watched the landscape appear in the hazy distance and roll past beneath their feet. Visibility was at least a few miles. Peter glanced at her and smiled a tight half-grin. He wiped his eyes and face and returned to staring forward.

"I know what you are," Massarra whispered.

"Pardon me?"

"Keep your voice down." She said this in a low, forced tone. "And I said, I know what you are. I don't know *who* you are, but I understand *what* you are."

"I don't know what you're talking about," Peter whispered back.

"Do you think I would let you so near to her? Get so close to Jessica?" Massarra whispered even lower. "That little trick in the market with the ball? Your friend Hamza? Those men?"

The engines droned in a silence that stretched into seconds. Peter kept his eyes straight ahead. To his credit, the man didn't flinch. His eyes didn't even blink. That was good, thought Massarra. This man was well trained.

"Jessica likes you," Massarra continued. "She has good instincts, even if she doesn't know why. Me? I *don't* like you, but I trust we have a common interest."

"I can help," Peter whispered urgently, turning to look at her. "America isn't dead, I'm sure I can—"

Behind them, Raffa groaned.

Massarra held up one hand. "Keep your voice down. I don't need you to explain. And I *absolutely* do not want you to share our secret with Mr. Erdogmus. He might not understand...the way I understand." She smiled, and she very rarely smiled. "He has his secrets, and I have mine. This is the key to any successful long-term relationship, no?"

"What do you want, then?"

"Just for us to have an understanding. A mutual professional respect. As I said, we have a common interest, and that is enough for now. You scratch me, I scratch you"—she pointed back at Jess—"and we both protect her. Understood?"

Peter stared forward, chewed on his lip, and after a second he nodded slowly.

"Good." Massarra patted his shoulder, and got up to return to the back of the plane.

The complex lay a hundred miles west of the Pangani River, known locally as Jipe Ruvu. A day's drive from a small, nameless Maasai community that had grown around the confluence of two wide, dirt roads that lead through the Southern Maasai Steppe and eventually to trunk routes at Korogwe and then on to the coastal city of Tanga.

It was a remote community, Ufuk told them, that knew him as a man who had generously provided them with clean water facilities, solar cell generators, and farming equipment; who had arranged lessons in English and offered books and computers, while funding local guiding initiatives. In return, the small Maasai administration had provided labor and security for the complex— local guides and a community willing to offer their combined experience of the Handeni District and the Tanga region. People willing to protect and watch over the installation and those who worked there.

The Pangani River cut a winding, serpentine course through a scrubland over five hundred kilometers long. A muscular, dark artery through the vast, arid savanna of northeast Tanzania. Further to the east lay the brooding Usambara Mountains, laden with a slate-gray shroud that once washed the jungled rock with a thick, wet heat.

Jess wedged herself back between the two pilot chairs for the final approach, despite Peter's objections for her to strap into a bench. She watched the river snake below them, as Peter brought the aircraft in low to take a look at the Maasai town. The huts looked deserted. The forests remained, but everything was covered in a layer of black-and-gray ash. Dim light seeped through the ever-present layers of cloud.

At least it wasn't Libya, and that was an improvement.

Her mood had improved as well, but from highly explosive merely down to simmering rage. She made sure that she and

Giovanni had their weapons—Massarra refused politely to give up hers—but they took away Ufuk's pistol.

Jess was in charge now.

Ufuk explained the facility as they approached—clean beds, showers, food and an automated medical facility. A tiniest bit of optimism creeped into Jess's chest as she caught sight of a knot of low buildings and a narrow dirt track leading away into the savanna—but with Raffa feverish and shivering, worry sat heavy in her gut.

"The climate here is usually very hot," Ufuk said, craning his neck to get a better look down. "Usually a lot of rain in the winter here, but who knows now."

Jess didn't reply. She just hoped not to feel bitter cold against her exposed skin.

"Usually there's wildebeest, buffalo, giraffe, zebra, all grazing in the tall grass. Even elephants. But I don't see anything." He leaned back.

Peter shifted the control column forward and the Otter descended. The plains below were as gray as the skies. Nothing moved. Coming in to the landing strip, Jess saw the focal point of the complex around which everything else was organized. A single, tall red pylon tower rising above the rest. Beside it, a collection of mushroom-cap satellite dishes—one of them huge—all angled toward the sky. Everything covered in gray ash. It formed a smooth coating over the open ground she could see: no footprints, no tire tracks. That was good. The Otter descended and skimmed over the high-fenced perimeter. Three sets of thirty-foot reinforced and electrified fences, Ufuk told them. It would take an army to breach, he'd boasted.

"Where's our Predator friend?" Jess asked, glancing at the tablet. She hated talking to Ufuk, but her practical side overpowered her emotional. Now wasn't the time.

"It landed ten minutes ahead of us. No heat signatures anywhere. No transmissions."

Jess blinked and rubbed her eyes. Tiny black dots danced in her vision. She worried she was about to pass out before they grew in size. Tiny drones swarmed into the air from the base of the complex's tower.

"Our greeting party," Ufuk said. "I just activated the installation's networks."

"You weren't in contact before?"

"Sporadically, but not enough to maintain a secure connection. It was one of the things I was trying to do with Ain Salah. Build a communication network…but now we're here."

Jess retreated to a bench to strap in for landing. The Otter touched down roughly on the dirt track, waxy light seeping down through the high clouds. Peter taxied the aircraft toward the complex, bringing it to a standstill not far from the largest building. He relaxed visibly as it sighed to a halt, releasing his hands from the flight stick. They shook.

"That's good work, Peter," Jess said.

He returned her earnest smile, but glanced back at Massarra and his smile disappeared.

"The medical center is in there," Ufuk said, gesturing to the main building. "As with Sahl, the majority of the complex is underground. Let's get Raffa to the medical center."

He led Jess toward a smaller building, an innocuous gray block with a single door and barred windows. Ufuk approached the building, taking Jess with him, and located a fuse box connected to external cabling. Ain Salah followed on their heels, while the rest remained in the Otter, unloading.

"This is not the main entrance, of course. All my staff was evacuated. The only way to open it is from inside. What you might call a back door."

He slid a glittering key card—which Jess had never seen before—into a slot at the top of the fuse box. A soft hum issued from within and it hissed as vacuum escaped, then popped open to reveal a wiring junction box with a key pad. Ufuk entered a long code, and then took hold of the whole box and levered it away from the wall. It hinged to the right to reveal a dark pad with a light sheen. He placed his hand on it. Nothing appeared to happen, but Ufuk took it away after a moment, then leaned forward and held his face in front of the pad.

The pad illuminated, a soft glow that was enough to give Ufuk's face a pale blue luster. A hollow *thunk* reverberated. Ufuk took the door's handle and levered it open. Beyond it, the three of them entered a clean, white room, one wall filled with blank widescreen monitors. The walls began to vibrate softly, tremors filtering through the floor and into the muscles in her thighs. Then the whole thing began to descend.

"We'll be able to plug your robotic leg back in," Ufuk offered.

Jess wanted to tear it off and bludgeon him with it, but that wouldn't be practical. She took a step back from both of the men and raised her M4, pointed it at Ufuk. No tricks; she didn't have to explain.

"This is a small to mid-size launch vehicle facility," Erdogmus continued, pretending not to notice she pointed her weapon at him. "Based loosely on the Tanegashima Space Center in Japan—"

"Where are we going, Ufuk?" Jess interrupted.

"To get this place running."

The elevator—Jess realized that was what this whole room seemed to be a lift—thudded to a stop. The far wall slid open to reveal a long room with rows of terminals. Strip lighting flashed on the moment the elevator doors opened, but the screen remained dark and silent.

Ufuk approached one of the terminals and took out his tablet. He slid it into a dock and waited. At the far end the whole wall was taken up with large screens and, above them, were the words "Mars First Mission Control Center."

Jess walked the men into the room ahead of her. "Can we hurry this up?"

There was a soft hum in the background. The terminals flickered to life, lights dancing across polished screens.

"Good afternoon, Mr. Erdogmus," A deep, resonant voice boomed, one with a slight English accent. The voice felt immersive. "How nice to see you again."

Ufuk smiled a broad grin. "Hello, Simon," he replied.

6

Tanzania

"Easy, take it slow," Jess urged.

Raffa groaned in delirious pain as Ufuk and Giovanni eased him from the Otter and onto a stretcher they'd brought up from the medical center. Even the stretcher was like something from a science fiction movie. When Ufuk pulled it from a drawer, it looked like he'd taken out two rolling pins—but the hollow cylinders slid down to extend seven feet with a gossamer-thin-but-tough film between them.

Jess had kept Ufuk firmly in front of her as they'd jogged through the corridors, a forced march-run. The place reminded her of Sanctuary Europe. White walls glistening. That new-plastic smell. Everywhere they ran, the overhead lighting blinked on with wall-screens coming to life. She was hardly surprised to see an image of a woman that looked like Stephanie—Michel Durand's digital assistant in Sanctuary—flicker and appear on one of the walls, so she wasn't the least bit fazed when Ufuk spoke to "Simon," a digital artificial intelligence that he said ran the place.

Ain Salah had followed two steps behind, always watching, especially when Ufuk keyed things into the machines he brought to life. Jess was sure Ain Salah was fascinated with all this, and she would be too—if she hadn't already been in Sanctuary, and if she wasn't so worried about Raffa.

"I'm sure he'll be okay," she said to Ain Salah.

The man held Raffa's hand as they lowered him onto the stretcher. The small Egyptian's eyes teared up behind his thick-framed glasses. He turned to Jess. "I am not so sure." His hand trembled as he took off his glasses to wipe them. He held them in his hand at a distance and looked left and right, obviously overwhelmed.

Jess paused. She hadn't asked more about his family since they'd briefly talked in the tent, or said what the situation was, or how he'd hoped to reunite with them. He'd always been the steady voice on the radio, beckoning to them. A safe haven. He'd helped keep them secure, had saved their lives. Now she'd dragged him down here to the end of the world, maybe away from his wife and children. Another person she was responsible for, another family ruined, but she didn't have time to console him.

Overhead, Ufuk's tiny drone-sentinels buzzed back and forth.

Giovanni took the front of the stretcher, and Ufuk the back end. With Jess behind him, they took off at a run across the ankle-deep muck of ash to the open door of the main building. Peter slung a duffel bag of what medical supplies they had and picked up Hector, his small face streaked with dirt, his eyes bleary. Massarra came last. She'd grabbed the green rucksack with the secret metal box. Ufuk said something to her as they ran to the airplane, about taking it to the main facility, but Jess didn't care anymore.

Or rather, she would deal with it later.

They ran into the tunnel and wound their way down level after level. The blinking image of the female digital assistant followed them down, flickering across the wall screens. She, or *it*, was trying to help, Jess understood, but then she wasn't going to let Ufuk out of her sight. They reached the infirmary.

"On the bed," instructed a voice with a calm, mid-western twang.

An image of a doctor appeared on one wall of the infirmary. A panel slid open to expose a dozen drawers of medical supplies and bags of plasma.

"History?" the doctor queried.

"Gunshot through the upper left chest cavity," Peter Connor said as he rounded the corner and put Hector down. "Heavy blood loss, with systemic infection. Probably in shock."

Something was different about Peter. His voice had changed. His face was sterner. He didn't look like the goofy, wild-eyed

295

photojournalist Jess had met in Al-Jawf. Whatever the change was, Jess liked it.

Hector ran to Giovanni and nearly collapsed into his arms. His uncle propped him up onto the bed next to Raffa, and Peter said they'd take care of him as well. With the digital doctor making suggestions, Peter grabbed the medical supplies and got to work. In minutes an IV was hooked up, with strong antibiotics dripping into Raffa's veins.

"I've got this," Peter said, pushing Jess back to give him space.

"The boy will survive," Ufuk said from across the room. "I told you to trust me."

Jess just clenched her teeth and gripped her M4 automatic weapon. There wasn't anything she wanted to say to him.

Ufuk crossed the room toward her. "Please, you wanted answers. I can give you answers now."

"Stay back."

"I'm not armed." Erdogmus held his hands up. "But I do need to get to my control room. I've done everything you asked, and I can answer your questions now."

"Where's Massarra?" Jess growled. "Did she load that thing onto your rocket?"

"It's not a bomb. Please. Time is wasting. I need to secure the facility."

"Go ahead," Giovanni said quietly. "I'll stay with Hector and Raffa." He took a sideways glance at Ufuk. "And if anything happens to—"

"I know, I know." Erdogmus still had his hands up as he eased past Jess.

She relented and let him pass to follow him into the corridor, but she kept her M4 at the ready.

Ufuk led her up two levels, walking quickly. "Don't worry, we are in constant voice contact," he explained. "Just say the name of the person you wish to speak to."

"Giovanni?" Jess said hesitantly.

"Jessica?" echoed Giovanni's voice from inside the room Ufuk entered ahead of her. The Italian's face was displayed on a wall-screen inside. The room was thirty-by-thirty foot square, the sides lined with empty cubicles, each with a monitor, desk and chair. Only one entrance.

"Just checking," Jess replied to Giovanni with a tight smile. She saw Hector on the table beyond him in the image on the wall. The boy was wrapped in a blue blanket, and looked asleep. The image blinked off.

"Can I speak to Simon?" Ufuk asked as he stopped in the middle of the room.

Jess raised her M4 as if nodding it. "You go ahead."

"And would it be possible for you to point your weapon at the floor, perhaps? Despite appearances, you are making me a *little* nervous."

She lowered her weapon, but only a few inches.

"Simon," Ufuk said. "Did we successfully awaken the Mars First crew?"

"On Mission Day seventy-eight," Simon's soothing-but-all-encompassing voice answered immediately. "But not all—"

"I understand, Simon," Ufuk interrupted, and he smiled at Jess. "Did they process the information packets we included? And the other supply missions, are they within operational parameters? On rendezvous courses."

"Affirmative to all questions."

Ufuk's body relaxed at the answer. His smile widened. "Can you bring up a holographic display of the solar system, using the latest data from Mars First?"

The lights in the room flickered, and Jess took a half-step back. In the next instant, the room dimmed, but then filled with hovering bright dots. She thought tiny drone-insects, like the ones she saw in Ufuk's gardens in Sanctuary, had flown into the room— but there were also lines and circles arcing out in glowing traces that circled in the air within the room. A bright orb burned in the center.

Jess's jaw and M4 both dropped at the same time. She stepped to one side to inspect the floating display from another angle

"That's right, it's our solar system. Our *live* solar system, in real time."

Ufuk walked to the blue dot of Earth. He cupped it in the palm of his hand, then waved one hand in the air, gesturing a command. A fleck of dots burned bright just to his left. "You see that, Jessica?"

He pointed at the bright dots.

"Those are Jovian asteroids, ones that are on an intercept course with Earth. The data we have here is invaluable. Müller would give anything to get his hands on it. That's why he wanted— *needed*—to get access to my systems. Plus my launch facilities, my drones, networks…"

Jess was speechless for the first time in a long time.

"Simon, could you bring up your latest calculations for the Earth-Saturn intercept in seventeen months? We are still predicting that it will miss Earth?"

"Yes, it will still miss the Earth."

"Good."

"But there are complications."

The complacent smile slid from Ufuk's face. "Complications?"

The graphic surrounding Jess and Ufuk sped up and zoomed in toward Earth. From the distance, the giant orb of Saturn grew larger, its rings massive. The images flickered once and then twice…and then the room lights came back on in full brightness. The holographic images disappeared.

"Simon?" Ufuk frowned, and then louder said: "Simon!"

Clack, clack, clack. The sound of distant gunfire echoed through the walls, and then the reverberating rumble of an explosion. The wall screens glowed to life to show images of the Twin Otter outside on the landing strip. Ash and dust blasted away from it. Angular, military VTOL aircraft plunged from the sky.

The sound of clapping from the hallway. Someone was clapping. Jess turned and brought up her M4.

"Ah, ah, ah," said a voice from the hallway, one she would recognize anywhere.

On the wall screen in front of her, an image formed. It was Hector, with a gun to his head. Through the entrance to the room, six men in coal-black uniforms of the Sanctuary Europe military filtered in, each with respirators and helmets with full body armor, each with their own M4s raised.

Behind them came Dr. Müller, walking in almost casually. "Arrest them," he said.

Two more men entered, their weapons trained on Jess. She thought of shooting Müller, and almost pulled the trigger, but her eyes were locked on the image of Hector. The gun against his head. In a second it was too late; her weapon was taken from her. Her hands were zip-tied behind her back.

7

Tanzania

"Does anyone else here have a sense of *déjà vu?*" Müller asked.

There was no concern, no jubilation, simply a calm expression on Müller's face that conveyed he was taking no pleasure in this. His men took seats from the cubicles and sat Ufuk and Jess roughly into them. Four soldiers took up guard positions at each corner of the room, two at the entrance, and two flanking Dr. Müller as he paced in front of Jess.

"Seems we have been here before, Jessica. Me, with a gun in my hand"—he had a pistol in his hand now—"and you, tied up and surprised. Except this time, no cavalry is coming. No magical rescue." Müller stopped to address Ufuk: "And we even neutered your digital friend, Simon."

"Even if you kill me, you can't access my systems," Ufuk said.

"Security, it's all about security, isn't it?" Müller interrupted. "Something you are, something you know, and something you have. Something you are is easy: your fingerprint, an iris scan, or in this case, your living DNA…"

"Kill me and Simon will never respond to you."

"But you would never do that, would you?" Müller replied. "You are too high-minded to let everything end with your own death. Plan A, Plan B, Plan C…doesn't that sound familiar?"

At the room's entrance, Peter and Giovanni appeared with Hector shuffling in front of them, all of them at gunpoint. Ain Salah followed after them, his eyes down.

"It's time we stopped this reality game I've been playing with you," Müller said, indicating for his men to seat the rest of them in the middle of the room. He held out one hand to stop Ain Salah. "These miraculous escapes, one after the other. Meeting Bedouin in the desert, a smooth entry into Al-Jawf with a safe place to camp, food and water, and then—*behold*—a frantic escape under fire only to find an airplane fully loaded with just enough fuel to get to Tanzania.

Müller circled the room. "Miraculous?" he said as he help up one finger and pointed it at the ceiling. "Or helped along by Uncle Müller? I couldn't have made it too easy, or you might get suspicious. I needed to know everything you were hiding, all of your secrets, and to get access to this facility."

He pulled a small tablet from his pocket and stopped in front of them, held it out. A video played. A grainy image with audio of Jess and Ufuk in the tent at Al-Jawf, of someone speaking to them, talking about communications equipment.

"I am sorry." Ain Salah's head was bowed. "I had no choice. Dr. Müller appeared in Al-Jawf days before you did. He made deals with the Zuwayya, offered them weapons. He took my wife and son…"

Jess felt like she'd been punched in the gut, even beyond the numb shock. She'd trusted this man. Had never even suspected those soft brown eyes were deceiving them. The video had to be from the thick black glasses he always wore. The images on the tablet were right from Ain Salah's own eyes. Everything he'd seen, all the conversations they'd had, all recorded. How could he have betrayed them? Then again, if someone had taken Hector, what would Jess be willing to do? Who would she betray?

"I am no monster," Müller said to Ain Salah. "As agreed, you see?" he turned the tablet to Ain Salah, and a video of a woman and boy being set free played.

"You started a war," Ufuk said, his voice still calm. "Between the Toubou and the Zuwayya. How many more have you killed?"

"Replaced one warlord with another." Müller shrugged.

"You came all the way here from China?" Jess said to Müller. "How did you…"

"I *wanted* you to come here, to Tanzania. I was guiding you. The invisible hand. That attack on Al-Jawf was just a prodding to move things along. And the call from Abbie Barnes? It is true, for there needs to be truth in the great deceptions. Lucca is safe with her outside of Sanctuary China…"

Despite her shock, Jess felt the smallest bit of relief. At least one of them was safe.

"This was calculated to make Ufuk believe he was safe. To bring his guard down. And speaking of Abbie Barnes…"

Another video played on his tablet, this one of Abbie Barnes begging Jess to come with her, that her father General Marshall believed in her. It was during the destruction of Sanctuary, just before Ballie Booker and Michel Durand were killed. Jess winced at the memory. The video froze as Massarra took Jess's hand and led her away.

"You were arrested on suspicion of terrorism, and here you are stealing away with the Queen of Spades herself, Massarra Mizrahi. And this despite the daughter of General Marshall begging you to come to safety with her."

The mention of Massarra's name made Jess realize the Israeli hadn't been marched into the room. Where was she? Ufuk told her to go into the main installation. Had Müller not known she was here? Massarra had saved them more than once. Jess had to remain calm, wait for an opportunity. She had to play for time.

"But you destroyed Sanctuary," Jess said as she squirmed against the zip ties digging into her wrists.

"I did not," Müller replied, his voice emotionless. "It was you and your friends who destroyed it."

"That's a lie. I had nothing to do with it."

"Even if you did not participate," Müller said. "It was Ufuk and Massarra that set the charges that destroyed Sanctuary. Jessica, he has been lying to you. I am sorry for what I have done, I truly am, but Mr. Erdogmus is no better."

"More lies," Ufuk grunted. "Why would I? And you already admitted to bombing the Vatican before Nomad, and to destabilizing the region for Israel and Iran to attack each other."

"No, no, no," Müller tutted. "Those were fabricated videos, created by you. I never said any such thing. And you didn't even show up in court to defend yourself. You were gone from Sanctuary, all of a sudden, and then it was destroyed."

How to tell truth from lies? Jess knew one thing he said was a blatant lie—he did admit to bombing the Vatican—but Jess was the only person alive who saw him say it in person in that jail cell at Vivas, who'd seen him say the words. Everyone else had only heard a recording or watched a video.

And one more thing.

She realized he wasn't just talking to them right now. He was conducting his own trial, something others had to be watching, or would watch in the future.

Trial and probably execution.

Where was Massarra? On the wall screen at the far side of the room, the images of outside the facility still played. A bright flash. The Twin Otter's cockpit exploded, and a distant thud echoed down the hallway outside. A dozen more coal-black uniformed soldiers had exited the VTOL aircraft landed outside. Above them, Ufuk's tiny drones hovered and buzzed.

"Should have weaponized those drones, Ufuk," Müller said, seeing Jess's eyes watching the display. "Nice toys for surveillance, but not useful in a fight."

"This place was never designed for that," Ufuk replied.

"Something of an oversight, I'd say, and let's talk about that, shall we?" Müller couldn't help himself. The calm and serious expression had shifted to bemusement. "What this place was designed for? Your friends on Mars First won't be in much of a mood of talking with you. I mean, you killed Anders Larsson."

"He was your man, I had no choice," Ufuk replied after a pause.

"And yet he was *their* crewmate, and their friend. All the deceptions. Why would they trust *you* anymore?" Müller turned to Jess. "Even you must admit that our friend Ufuk seems to omit truth and lie, frustrating isn't it? To be lied to?"

Another video played on his tablet, this one of Jessica yelling at Ufuk on the airplane, just hours before. Of her pointing her weapon at Ufuk, marching him ahead of her.

"We have everything we need," Müller said. "Thanks to Ain Salah, I watched you enter your codes into the keypads. You've activated the facility—"

"It's not that simple," Ufuk growled, his voice low and angry now, the calm giving way to frustration.

Shouting erupted down the hallway.

"I know it's not that simple," Müller replied. "You are a clever man, but I will figure it out, whatever it is. I have enough information now. And"—he took a step forward and pulled Hector away from Jess—"I have the backup."

Ufuk's head dropped.

"Get your hands off him." Jess spat the words out and lurched forward, but one of the soldiers grabbed her and put her back into the seat. "And what does that mean?"

"Why don't you tell her?" Müller said quietly to Ufuk, obviously enjoying this.

Ufuk remained silent.

"What? What did you do?" Jess said, her voice rising.

"I programmed Hector as the second DNA key for unlocking Simon."

"A thing that you are, a thing that you know, and a thing that you have," Müller repeated in a singsong voice. "I have all your access cards, and dozens of hours of you tapping onto your tablet. If you won't cooperate, then we have Hector to help us if you come to a…well, if something happens to you."

"Like what?"

More shouting in the hallway.

Jess's heart came up into her throat, a numb tingling washed through her face.

Massarra was dragged into the room by two soldiers. She was bloodied and beaten. Through one half-open eye she looked at Jess and shook her head. Sorry, she mouthed silently. They dropped her on the floor in the middle of the room. Hector squealed and tried to run to her, but Müller held his arm tight.

And two more soldiers appeared.

These ones carrying the mysterious sleek metal container.

"God damn it!" Ufuk yelled and stamped the floor with one foot.

"I must admit, I am curious what's in this box," Müller said. "But Jessica is right. Perhaps it is a bomb. You do have one orbital-capable rocket sequestered in this facility"—one of the men who dragged Massarra in whispered in his ear—"but it seems this has been damaged badly in the fight to capture your woman. She doesn't give up easily. Killed six of my men."

On the floor, Massarra snorted and tried to get up on one elbow. "Seven," she sputtered. Blood oozed from her mouth.

"And something else I admit stumped me, Mr. Erdogmus," Müller said, relishing every word now. "Simon, if you could bring up an image of Mars First's trajectory?"

Nothing happened.

"Simon, comply," Ufuk said quietly.

The room lights blinked, and an instant later dimmed. The room filled with the glowing traces and dots of the solar system.

"I honestly couldn't understand why you sent your Mars First mission before Nomad, knowing that they would never reach Mars—but now I understand. Six other heavy missions, sent ahead in converging trajectories almost on the other side of the solar system from Earth when Nomad hit. The worst of the geomagnetic radiation missed them. So while even our most hardened military birds were damaged…"

The image centered on six lines converging in space, followed by the red line of the Mars First ship.

"It was brilliant," Müller admitted. "A hundred and forty tons of equipment, put into space on covert missions, hidden on the other side of the solar system from the worst of the radiation storms. And a manned mission to collect it all, and use Saturn to slingshot all of it back to Earth. Communications, global positioning…you would literally have any remaining governments in the palm of your hand. Except all of this is mine, now."

Ufuk gritted his teeth and didn't reply.

"One thing, though. One *complication*."

This was the same word that Simon used when Ufuk had asked about the Saturn intercept, Jess realized. The artificial intelligence had said that Earth would brush past Saturn, but there was a *complication*.

"Simon, play the Earth-Saturn intercept," said Müller. With one arm around Hector, he stooped to pick up the rucksack with Ufuk's sleek metal box in it. He was surprised at the weight and handed it to one of his men.

The holographic image zoomed back, and then zoomed in until Saturn filled a quarter of the room. Complete silence in the room. The distant orb of the sun burned bright from a distance, and then grew larger. The tiny blue dot of Earth appeared from the darkness, and in an instant, swept past the massive bulk of Saturn and its rings. Earth's trajectory wobbled.

"That's not possible. It's not what any of the data…" Ufuk's voice was low, his face open-mouthed with confusion. He muttered to himself for a few seconds before asking: "Sixty thousand kilometers still misses. Does it push Earth into an uninhabitable orbit?"

"It will change Earth's orbit, perhaps improve it, but *that* is not the problem."

From the look on Ufuk's face, he'd already guessed.

"Simon," Müller instructed. "Please replay the simulation, and slow down to real time, starting at a Saturn-to-Earth distance of seventy thousand kilometers."

The holographic image reset, and this time the wide rings of Saturn took up almost the whole width of the room. It took Jess a few seconds to understand what she was seeing. The Earth came edge-on toward Saturn, and as it passed, it etched a fine black line through the outer rings. It took her emotions a second to catch up to her intellect, and with this the terrible realization that the disaster of Nomad might not be over.

Earth was going to impact Saturn's rings.

"But they're mostly ice dust, aren't they? Like a fog a few meters thick?" Jess had considered the possibility when they did the first Saturn intercept paths on her father's laptop, but with the threat of an actual collision with Saturn a possibility, it hadn't been a priority.

"The rings vary up to a kilometer in thickness," Müller replied. "Most of it tiny clumps of ice a centimeter in diameter, but with chunks up to ten meters. And yes, usually objects like this impacting the atmosphere would burn up, maybe flash high in the sky, but the kinetic energy of a collision like this—"

"Forty kilometers a second," Ufuk whispered. "The intercept speed."

"That's right. Earth is going to cut a path a hundred thousand kilometers long through Saturn's rings in forty minutes. Tiny particles by themselves, but combined...it's unclear what the effects will be, as we don't have computing facilities to fully render the effects, and that's part of the reason—"

"It'll be a like a billion Hiroshima-sized atomic bombs going off," Ufuk interrupted quietly, his head sagging, staring at the ground. "All at the same time, in a knife-like arc that spans halfway around the world."

8

Tanzania

"You can have me," Jess said, her voice quiet but trembling. She struggled to control the anger and confusion boiling inside her.

"But I already have you." Müller tightened his grip on Hector's shoulder, the boy's eyes darting back and forth, searching for an escape. Müller nodded to the Sanctuary soldiers holding the green rucksack with the sleek metal box in it. The men turned and left the room at a jog. Ufuk grunted and bared his teeth in a silent snarl.

"I mean, I'll admit that you never said those things," Jess said slowly. "I'll testify that Ufuk falsified the video. That he destroyed Sanctuary."

This got Müller's attention. "I'm no fool—"

"I'm tired of running, tired of the lies. You saw us fighting on the airplane. That wasn't an act. The second we got here, I wanted to get away from this bastard"—she turned to Ufuk—"He lies, he cheats. And now this thing with Hector? He never told me."

Müller took hold of Hector's arm. "So you want to protect the boy?"

"I want to tell the truth." She squirmed against the zip ties. "And I want to protect what's left of my family. Giovanni. Hector. Raffa. If Lucca is in China, I want you to take us there. I want us to be safe and for this to be over."

"Transmission off," Müller said aloud. He handed the boy to one of the soldiers to check his tablet. Satisfied, he smiled at Jessica. "Interesting."

"Did you take Hector, in Al-Jawf? Was that you, because of what Ufuk did?"

"Jessica!" Ufuk yelled. "He's going to kill all of us. Stop."

308

"Not all of you." Müller began pacing in short circles. "And no, I didn't snatch Hector in Al-Jawf. Despite my preparations, that is still a very complicated place."

"Jessica, don't trust him," Ufuk urged.

Müller nodded at one of the guards.

"How can you trust him?" Ufuk yelled. "After what he's done to—"

The rifle butt of the M4 of the guard cracked into Ufuk's jaw, sending him and his chair crashing into the ground.

"A little late for talking about trust," Müller mused, resuming his tight pacing. "But Jessica, I sense there are conditions?"

"You can't kill anyone. Massarra, Ufuk, I want you to keep them alive. That's my condition."

"I wasn't *going* to kill them."

Jess sensed a sudden draft behind her. The room filled with a soft whirring. She craned her neck around. One of Ufuk's small drones, not more than two feet square, hovered in an opening in the wall that had just opened. The five remaining soldiers in the room all trained their M4s on it. The two outside the entrance pointed their weapons in each direction down the hallway.

"Still some tricks up your sleeve, eh, Ufuk?" Müller backed up a step toward the entrance just the same, and the soldier holding the boy did the same. "Like I said, you should have weaponized your little friends. We checked the schematics, there's—"

The drone tilted and accelerated forward, straight at Müller.

"Get down," Ufuk whispered and kicked Jess's chair hard.

She took the hint and swung her weight sideways.

The two guards closest to Müller opened fire, their silenced M4s stuttering and blazing. Rounds ricocheted and punctured the room's walls. The drone dinged sideways as it was hit, but still accelerated. Müller sidestepped easily and it darted past him.

It hit the wall and disintegrated into shards.

An instant later, a blast of heat hit Jess in the face as she fell sideways onto the floor, still bound in her chair. Müller was knocked from his feet by the explosion. More gunfire behind Jess, and then the blossoming heat of more explosions. More like ignitions. Screaming. One of the soldiers stumbled over Ufuk's chair. The man was on fire.

Müller scrambled back to his feet. Another drone sliced through the air to crash into the wall next to him. It exploded in a detonation of pink and red, lighting his coat in a burst of yellow flames. He screamed and pulled his jacket off and stumbled backward through the entrance, clawing at his face.

Jess strained to look around, her face pressed against the metal floor. Where was Hector? She caught a glimpse of his kicking feet as one of the men carried him over his shoulder into the hallway. More drones whirred over her head and exploded in the corridor. More screaming and staccato buzz of silenced automatic weapons.

"Hold still."

Jess's hands came free and someone pulled her upright. It was Peter Connor. Somehow he'd gotten free and had taken a knife from the soldier still writhing in flames on the floor. Peter cut Ufuk's and Giovanni's bindings, then grabbed the M4 from the floor and shot the soldier, hardly bothering to look at the man as he did.

"Is there a back way out of here?" Peter said to Ufuk.

"We need to get Hector!" Jess screamed. She wobbled to her feet to run into the hallway, but was pressed back by a blast of heat. The hallway was an inferno. More drones sped past them and exploded in the conflagration.

"This way." Ufuk pulled her arm. "It's the only way." He pointed to the opening in the back of the room. Two more drones whizzed through it and whirred past them into the corridor. "They're powered by liquid hydrogen, I told you."

The large wall screens were still active inside the room, despite punctures from bullets. The images were flickering, but still showed the scene outside. The tiny drones buzzed around the large military VTOL aircraft. Their automated Gatling guns targeted the drones, firing hundreds of rounds a second. The noise of it echoed through the blaze in the hallway. The drones circled and buzzed, an angry wasp nest, and dove Kamikaze-style into the military equipment and soldiers. Flames leapt into the air.

Müller appeared, the image grainy, but unmistakable—and still holding his face.

He ran into one of the VTOLs next to the entrance with Hector swung over the shoulder of the man following him. None of the drones dive-bombed anywhere near the path of Müller. In a blast of dust, the angular VTOL rose into the air.

Jess stared at the screen in mute disbelief. They had Hector.

"Come on," Ufuk urged. "We need to go. I'm closing down the facility."

Peter Connor had Massarra over his shoulder. She was streaked in blood. He and Giovanni eased her through the opening in the other side of the room. Jess watched the VTOL aircraft disappear into the distance, followed by a second that lifted off. The third one exploded in flames as it tried to get away, hammered by a barrage of dozens of killer drones. The aircraft tumbled to the ground in a blazing heap next to the destroyed remains of the Otter.

Ufuk had dragged Jess to the side of the room. "He'll be back, we have to hurry."

He jumped up into the opening, and Jess finally tore her eyes away from the screen and followed him. "We have to get Raffa," she whispered.

"Of course."

Lights flickered in the next room, and they exited into another hallway. This one was charred and still filled with smoke, but with no flames as the remains of extinguisher dust settled. Peter kept Massarra on his shoulder as they ran, and past each intersection, heavy doors sealed behind them. Rounding the corner to the infirmary, Jess took the lead, and ran straight into Raffa. He brandished a scalpel in one hand.

"Are you okay?"

The boy almost collapsed the second he saw it was them. Giovanni grabbed him and pulled him back to the bed, while Peter

311

rushed Massarra onto the one beside it. The digital doctor reappeared. Sirens wailed. Peter ripped open Massarra's shirt to reveal an oozing bullet wound. He swore and ran to the medical supply drawers.

Ufuk slid to the floor next to Massarra, his face in his hands. "All for nothing. It's all for nothing."

Jess knelt beside him. "You have to get me out of here. How do I follow Müller?"

"You can't. He's gone. We don't have anything that can match those aircraft, even if they're air-breathers."

"There must be a way."

Ufuk shook his heads, tears streaking his soot-stained face. "Müller's gone. No way we can catch him. He's won. And his men will be back. Soon. They'll bomb this place. He has everything."

Even through Jess's adrenaline and the confusion, she sensed the tears Ufuk cried weren't for Hector, and by "everything" he didn't mean the boy. She felt like smashing him in the face, dragging him into the hallway and beating the man to a pulp—but she still needed him.

Peter yelled instructions to Giovanni, who dug through the medical drawers. Peter had placed a device over Massarra's side, and an image of her internal organs displayed on the wall next to the digital doctor. The thump-thump of Massarra's heartbeat filled the room as they connected into her vitals that appeared on the other wall.

"Then we have to get out of here," Jess said to Ufuk, her voice calm. "How long do we have till they come back?"

"An hour?" Ufuk shrugged. "Maybe two, based on their incoming flight trajectories."

She wasn't going to be any use to Hector if she was dead, and the way Müller had looked at her when she volunteered to join him? He wanted *her*; he still needed something from her. There was value there, something she could negotiate.

"Not everything," coughed a weak voice.

It was Massarra. She tried to reach over the metal gurney-table with one blood-soaked hand to grab Ufuk's hair. "He doesn't have it," she gurgled.

Ufuk blinked once and then twice, then twisted around onto his knees, his face next to Massarra. "What do you mean?"

The Israeli lifted her head an inch and tried to smile. She could only open one eye a slit; the other was swollen to the size of a grapefruit. Three of her front teeth had been knocked out, the others streaked in blood. "Cryogenic room three, freezer two," she coughed. Her eye rolled back, her head slumped.

A high-pitched flat whine filled the air.

"We're losing her!" Peter yelled. He shoved Ufuk out of the way and scrambled for the defibrillation unit on the wall.

Ufuk was on his knees, his hands stained with Massarra's blood. He glanced at the Israeli on the table as Peter cleared her shirt, yelling instructions at Giovanni. Ufuk jumped to his feet and grabbed Jess by her collar, tried to pull her into the hallway.

"What are you doing?" Jess screamed at him, her eyes on Massarra's inert body.

"You want Hector?" Ufuk yelled back. "Then get that M4 and follow me." He stumbled out of the infirmary entrance without looking back.

Jess watched him go, glanced at Massarra. "Damn it," she cursed and grabbed the M4 from the floor and did her best to sprint after Ufuk.

Through one corridor and then the next, she hobbled on her prosthetic. Ufuk wasn't much faster. The guards had done a good job beating him. Sirens and alarms wailed as they passed from one area to the next, doors automatically opening before them and closing behind. They passed under a wide sign announcing: "Launch Installation."

"Where are we going?" Jess yelled.

They entered a cavernous room. The walls were charred in places, evidence of grenades. Explosions. In the middle of the cavern was the top-half of a missile. A rocket. The bottom half of it, just visible through grating, looked blasted by an explosion. Shards of metal. Two slumped bodies in coal-black uniforms on the floor, a third draped halfway in a doorway.

Must have been the location of Massarra's last stand.

"This way," Ufuk urged. He stood in a doorway marked, "Cryogenics Facility."

Jess followed him as quickly as she could, her patience rapidly draining. They had to get back to Raffa and Massarra.

Ufuk disappeared into a room just ahead of her.

She stumbled forward and opened the door, hung herself half inside. "What is wrong with you? We need to get back."

Ufuk stood in front of her with a dumb smile on his face. He'd put on two enormous yellow gloves that stretched up to his armpits. "Shall we find out?"

"I'm going to shoot you right now."

"Could you wait just one second before doing that?"

He held up one gloved hand to her, and with the other opened a huge stainless steel door marked "Freezer Two" in black-stenciled letters. He knelt behind the door, and then reappeared holding what looked like a massive metal roasting pan. Thick wisps of smoke oozed over the surface and spilled toward the floor.

"Liquid nitrogen," Ufuk explained as he placed the metal pan on to the table next to the freezer. The door swung shut by itself.

Jess entered the room fully, her M4 now slack by her side. "This better be good."

"It better be," Ufuk agreed. He dipped his right, gloved hand into the oozing steam. His face lit up as he found something. What looked like a white plastic container two feet long emerged from the evaporating liquid nitrogen before he lowered it back.

"Is that what was in your fancy metal container?" Jess asked. "From the airplane?"

Ufuk nodded emphatically. "What a clever, clever girl that Massarra is."

"Was."

"We don't know that. We should go back." He started to pick up the metal pan.

"Wait, what is this goddamn thing she died for?"

"It is the future of the human race."

Jess used the muzzle of her M4, clanked it against the metal pan to stop him from picking it up. "And what the hell does that mean?"

Ufuk relented and took a step back. "Actually, what I said is not quite correct. That is not the *future* of the human race…"

He took off one glove and pointed a naked finger at the boiling liquid nitrogen, a mad grin spreading across his face, and said: "That *is* the human race."

From the Author
A sincere *thank you* for reading, I hope you're enjoying the story so far. The series continues with the final book in the series!
Destiny
Now available from Amazon.

For free advance reading copies and more, join me
www.MatthewMather.com

AND PLEASE…
If you'd like more quality fiction at this low price, I'd really appreciate a review on Amazon. The number of reviews a book accumulates on a daily basis has a direct impact on how it sells, so just leaving a review, no matter how short, helps make it possible for me to continue to do what I do.

OTHER BOOKS BY MATTHEW MATHER

CyberStorm

Award-winning CyberStorm depicts, in realistic and sometimes terrifying detail, what a full scale cyberattack against present-day New York City might look like from the perspective of one family trying to survive it. Search for CyberStorm on Amazon.

Polar Vortex

A routine commercial flight disappears over the North Pole. Vanished into thin air. No distress calls. No wreckage. Weeks later, found on the ice, a chance discovery—the journal from passenger Mitch Matthews reveals the incredible truth... Search for *Polar Vortex* on Amazon.

Darknet

A prophetic and frighteningly realistic novel set in present day New York, Darknet is the story of one man's odyssey to overcome a global menace pushing the world toward oblivion, and his incredible gamble to risk everything to save his family. Search for Darknet on Amazon.

Atopia Chronicles (Series)

In the near future, to escape the crush and clutter of a packed and polluted Earth, the world's elite flock to Atopia, an enormous corporate-owned artificial island in the Pacific Ocean. It is there that Dr. Patricia Killiam rushes to perfect the ultimate in virtual reality: a program to save the ravaged Earth from mankind's insatiable appetite for natural resources. Search for Atopia on Amazon.

NEW RELEASE

The Dreaming Tree by Matthew Mather is now available!

Described by readers as *The Girl with the Dragon Tattoo* meets *Black Mirror*. A new breed of predator hunts on the streets of New York--chased by Delta Devlin, a detective whose gift and curse are eyes that see things only she can.
Search for *The Dreaming Tree* on Amazon.

Made in the USA
Middletown, DE
16 March 2022

62766163R00194